FINDING EDEN

A SWEET, OPPOSITES ATTRACT ROMANCE

TINA NEWCOMB

Finding Eden

Copyright © 2017 by Tina Newcomb

ISBN: 978-1-947786-04-2

Cover Design by Dar Albert of Wicked Smart Designs

All rights reserved.

This book is a work of fiction. Names, characters, places, business establishments, and incidents are either products of the author's imagination or are used fictitiously. Any resemblance to actual persons, living or dead, events, or locations is entirely coincidental.

DEDICATION

This novel, my first, is dedicated to my late parents.

Mildred West Hardy, instilled the love of reading when I was very young. She was my first reader.

Harold John Hardy, introduced me to non-fiction and continued feeding my interest after my mother passed away.

Though they are both gone from this world, I know they are watching over me and cheering from the best seats in the house.

Love you both!

CONTENTS

Colton McCreed peered down at the approaching ground as a shimmer of fear worked its way up his spine. The Cessna jolted and his stomach dropped. He'd landed at a lot of small airports, but never on such a tiny strip of asphalt. Would the pilot be able to stop before the plane plunged into the very cold looking lake on the far side?

He glanced at the burly bear of a man sitting in the pilot's seat who sported biceps the size of hams. The guy looked more like a wild mountain man than pilot.

"Your name is Beam?" Colton had asked at their introduction.

"Because I like my Jim."

"But…not before you fly. Right?"

A crazy gleam flashed in the man's eyes before he covered them with reflective lenses. Not the response Colton had hoped for.

"Are you sure you have enough room to land?"

"Pretty sure." Beam raised his sunglasses and squinted at the runway as if seeing it for the first time. "There's a life-jacket under your seat, just in case we slide into the drink.

You'll want to put it on quick before the temperature of the water sends you into hypothermia."

Great. "Shouldn't you be reassuring your—?" Colton lost his train of thought when the plane jolted, again.

Beam grinned and turned his ball cap backwards.

Colton's business manager suggested he fly, rather than drive into this small town. "You've never lived in rural U.S.A. If you want your story to be believable, you've got to integrate yourself into the community, live as the natives do. Attend town meetings and celebrations."

"Why can't I drive my own car?"

"You won't mix with the population driving around town in a Maserati."

"How rural is this place?"

"Eden Falls, Washington, has all the amenities you'll need. The crime rate is non-existent, so the residents will have an inherent sense of unity and trust, which is exactly the setting you wanted to portray in your next murder mystery." Jorge had held up his hands as if framing a movie screen. "Just imagine a serial killer moving unseen through a town idyllically named Eden Falls. Not a fictional place, but a real town. Mingle with the folks, visit the local tavern…"

For your sake, Jorge, there better be a tavern.

Colton held his breath as he zeroed in on the advancing patch of tarmac. One quick flash of a fire-blazing death shot through his mind, but he pushed the image aside—*too dramatic.* He used slow, calculated methods of demise in his novels.

Every muscle in his body tightened when the wheels of the single engine Cessna touched down. The pressure of the seatbelt strained across his chest as the pilot applied the brakes. Still braced, Colton's hand fumbled under the seat for the lifejacket and came up empty. He opened his mouth to yell at the pilot when the plane suddenly veered to the right. He exhaled a groan as his tight muscles dissolved.

Beam maneuvered close to the only building around, a white aluminum shed just big enough to hold the small plane. They jerked to an abrupt halt. "Didn't need that lifejacket after all, huh, city boy?"

He waved his enormous hand. "There's your welcome party."

Colton had been too preoccupied with his impending polar swim to notice a girl standing beside a rusted Jeep.

Beam popped his door open and climbed out before Colton could unbuckle his seatbelt. By the time he swung his own door wide, the bear of a man had engulfed the girl in a hug that took her feet off the ground. He frowned in their direction as he stumbled from the plane. Jorge told him Eden Falls was thrilled at the prospect of becoming the setting for Colton McCreed's next novel. He also said Mayor Alex Blackwood would be here to greet him. Instead, this pea-sized town had sent a girl.

As Beam unloaded Colton's bags and guitar case from the plane, she came forward and held out her hand. "Welcome to Eden Falls, Mr. McCreed. I'm—"

"Not Mayor Alex Blackwood."

A look of confusion passed over the girl's face and she retracted her hand.

"I was told he would be here to meet me."

The girl glanced at Beam who grinned as he swung Colton's bags into the back of the Jeep. Her eyebrows lifted over a pair of eerie green eyes. "Mayor Blackwood extends *his* apology. An unavoidable emergency came up."

Beam chuckled.

Colton glanced from the pilot to the girl. "He was supposed to show me around Eden Falls."

She flashed a smile that didn't quite make it to her eyes.

"I'll be happy to show you around town and answer any questions."

They were in the middle of nowhere with mountain peaks surrounding them. There was no way out unless he wanted to fly with the maniac, again. He should have known Jorge would distort the truth, lead him to believe there would be a welcome party awaiting a recognized author's arrival. He hadn't expected a parade, but at least the mayor could have shown up. He blew out a resigned huff. Jorge had accomplished his goal. He'd gotten Colton to this remote setting to write the story that had been tripping through his brain for several months—the story that wasn't coming together. For the first time in his career, he was experiencing writers block. That fact alone set him on edge.

Hands on hips, Colton turned to the girl. "I guess you'll have to do."

~

"*I guess you'll have to do.*" Who does this guy think he is?

Jorge Reis—*just call me Jorgie*—had been hounding Alex Blackwood for weeks to shower *New York Times* bestselling author Colton McCreed with all the warm fuzzies she could muster. Well, she didn't have time to coddle some guy who thought he deserved royal treatment. Sure, it would be good for tourism to have Eden Falls mentioned in one of his books. Look what *Twilight* had done for Forks. As mayor, she was open to the possibilities this opportunity might hold for their beautiful little town, but if she had to put up with Mr. McCreed's attitude, it would be a very long summer for both of them.

She dialed her patience to "Pamper" and smiled. "Climb in and we'll get started."

The author tugged on the Jeep's rusted door twice before it opened with a protest. Alex ignored his mutter of disgust and turned to Beam. "Thanks for making a special trip inland today."

He tipped his head toward her passenger who was scowling at them through the dirty windshield. "I might have scared the city boy a little."

Alex winked.

"How long's he staying?"

"All summer."

Beam took off his baseball cap and ruffled his hair, standing it on end. "Good luck."

"Thanks. I think I'm going to need it. Are you in town overnight?"

He plopped his cap back on his head. "Yep. Staying with Rowdy."

She thumbed over her shoulder. "Do you need a ride?"

"No, thanks. Someone's picking me up."

Curiosity nudged Alex like a prodding finger. "Someone?"

"Don't be nosy, cuz'." He pulled her screeching door open. "Tell Charlie I said hi. I'll see him on Memorial Day."

"He'll love that."

She slid behind the wheel and cranked the engine, which coughed and sputtered before grumbling to life. She really needed to break down and get a new mode of transportation. This rusty old bucket wouldn't last much longer, but it had been Peyton's and she wasn't willing to give it up. From the corner of her eye, she caught the author shaking his head. His self-imposed importance had her fighting a smile, but perhaps provoking him further wasn't a good idea. He'd learn his attitude wouldn't fly around here soon enough.

"How do you know him?"

His demanding tone filled the small confines of the Jeep,

crowding her and she didn't like to be crowded. She did like his cologne though. A subtle, masculine, scent surrounded her pleasantly. "Beam is my cousin. Our dads are brothers."

"His parents named him Beam on purpose?"

"His real name is Everett, but he acquired the nickname when he started playing linebacker in pee-wee football. The coach said he was like an I-beam, plowing down the opposition. The name Beam stuck."

"And he makes his living flying in and out of this place?"

This place didn't appear to be meeting Colton McCreed's expectations. Lucky for him, patience was one of her virtues. She smiled as she shifted into reverse and backed up with a jerk, hitting a nice-sized pothole in the process. "No. He lives in Seattle and makes his living flying tourists around in seaplanes, but he also flies into smaller Washington towns when someone needs a ride."

With a quick wave to Beam, she turned the Jeep around and headed down the rutted dirt road that led to the highway. Yes, *this place* really did have a highway. The bumpy ride would give Mr. McCreed a taste of Eden Falls right from the start. No sense in sugarcoating the town's shortcomings.

Colton braced a hand against the dashboard. "How long have you lived here?"

"All my life." She was born and raised here, and couldn't imagine living anywhere else. "Eden Falls has some of the prettiest views in the state. The drive in is gorgeous. Just about any outdoor activity you could wish for is available. We're situated between the two largest cities in Washington. Everything you need, if not within our own town limits, is close at hand. I think of *this place* as heaven on earth."

He turned a cynical eye her way. "You sound like a travel agent."

Her passenger grew quiet and Alex glanced at his profile. He had a nice face, not movie star handsome, but appealing.

He had that in-fashion, messed-up style going on with his sandy hair. His eyes were a blustery gray with heavy brows that hung low like threatening storm clouds to match what seemed to be a permanent frown. The feature that drew her attention was his nose. Alex had long ago dubbed herself a connoisseur of noses. If there were ever a contest, she'd be the first to volunteer as a judge. His was long and slender, but widened out right before the nostrils, with a definitive bump at the bridge. Yes, he had a very nice nose.

If he wasn't married, and if Misty Douglas didn't get to him first, he'd be a nice diversion for the single women of Eden Falls, as long as they didn't mind the perpetual scowl. She wondered if his frown was an L.A. thing, a brooding author thing, or just an unhappy with life thing.

～

*W*hen Beam pointed out Eden Falls from the sky, Colton had estimated about thirty streets with a river running along the north side. Nestled neatly within the surrounding mountain peaks, it was tiny compared to his hometown of Los Angeles.

Would there be a decent cup of coffee or pizza delivery available? Could he live in this place for three months without everything closing in on him? Was he renting month-to-month or had he paid for the summer in full? Jorge knew he didn't like to be tied down. Claustrophobia had a way of wrapping its tentacles around his roaming nature.

He pulled a notebook and pencil from his backpack as their surroundings turned more civilized. Even with smart-phones, laptops, and tablets available, he preferred a pencil and paper for taking notes.

The girl pointed to the left. "That's Eden Falls High School. The middle school is across the street."

He didn't care how many schools were in town. He didn't like kids, didn't want them, and had no plans to include them in his novels—or his life. "I assume, by the cars in the parking lot, school isn't out for the summer."

"Two more weeks."

"Are there enough kids to hold graduation?"

"We'd hold graduation for one senior or twenty, Mr. McCreed."

He smiled at the girl's snarky tone. He'd ruffled her feathers, but wasn't sure how. His questions seemed plausible. "I might be interested to see how a small town graduation differs from one in L.A. Would it be possible to attend?"

"I'm sure the student body and faculty would be thrilled to have you. The post office is on the right. My dad has been the postmaster since he graduated college."

He glanced up from his notepad. Jorge would be sending his mail there.

"Douglas Hardware and Lumber is on the left. The fire station is across the street."

Two firemen were in front of the red brick building washing a truck. The girl honked, and one of the men waved. The other flexed his bare chest muscles in a bodybuilding pose, and the girl broke into a smile. He cupped his hands and yelled something Colton didn't catch.

He studied her long enough to realize she wasn't as young as he'd first thought—college age rather than high school. Still, in her business suit and heels, she looked like she was playing dress-up—undoubtedly to impress him. "Friends of yours?"

"Friends of my brother. There's a gas station on either end of town and another one on Cascade Boulevard along with the IGA grocery store and a gym. If you like barbecue—"

"Is it members only?"

She turned a puzzled glance his way.

"The gym, is it members only?"

"Oh, yes, but you can get a month-to-month membership. My Aunt Glenda and Uncle Dawson—Beam's mom and dad —own it. I can talk to them for you, if you'd like."

Colton nodded. "Any good pizza around?"

"Renaldo's Italian Kitchen is on the square. They have great pizza and pasta dishes, and they deliver. We have Chinese and Mexican restaurants. Noelle's Café is great for home cooked meals. The café is also a popular breakfast destination. If you have a sweet tooth, Patsy's Pastries is a must."

He had an enormous sweet tooth, hence his interest in the gym.

They arrived in downtown Eden Falls. Town Square was a two-block park in the center with a one-way street that circled it. Shops around the perimeter wore welcoming exteriors. The streets and sidewalks were clean, and the park's grass was a vivid green. Purple and yellow flowers bordered the trees and huge pots of flowers hung from lampposts. A raised stage sat at one end with a banner advertising a Memorial Day concert.

He noted the Roasted Bean Coffee Shop, Renaldo's Italian Kitchen, One Scoop or Two ice cream shop, Eden Falls Emporium, Dahlia's Salon, and Pages Bookstore as just a few of the businesses they passed. The girl took a left, doing a three-sixty all the way around, pointing out places like Town Hall and the police station along the way.

"Do you fish?"

"As in sitting in a boat holding a pole?"

She flashed a you-are-a-moron glance. "Yes."

"Not so far, and if I can help it, I never will. Why?"

"I was going to point out The Fly Shop, but it doesn't sound like you'll need to visit. There's a drug store and two banks here on the square. The movie theatre is small, only one screen, but they play new releases."

As she took another left, he continued to take notes of the businesses along the way, impressed that there were only a couple of empty storefronts.

"Any bars in town?"

"The Cascade Club is across the street from the gym. Rowdy's Bar and Grill is down Main Street a block further."

The girl made a right turn into a residential area, left onto Cedar Drive, and pulled into a driveway halfway down the street. When she turned the key in the ignition, the Jeep's engine shuddered so violently, it rattled his brain. "Here you are. Home sweet home for the next three months."

Colton stared open mouthed. *No. No, no, no. This can't be right.* The whole house would fit inside his living room. He could already feel claustrophobia clawing at his throat. *I can't live here for three months.*

He shoved the passenger door open with a screeching protest and stared at the little green house with its white trim and black shutters. A concrete path from the sidewalk to the wooden porch steps cut the pristine lawn in half. Waist high bushes bordered with little red flowers flanked the front. He looked around at all the tiny houses of the neighborhood. Perfect, if he were a hobbit.

He pulled out his cell phone, ready to blast Jorge into the next century. The least his business manager could have done was ask for pictures of the place. He would have seen it was too small for Colton. He scrolled to Jorge's number and hit call. Of course, he got Jorge's voicemail. *Big surprise.*

The girl circled to the back of the Jeep to unload his bags, but he stopped her. "I want to see inside first."

"Sure."

She pulled a set of keys from a pocket as Colton followed her up the front steps. A metal glider and a couple of chairs with decent cushions made the porch look inviting, and afforded a spectacular view of the mountains. He followed her inside, cringing at the twang of the screen door spring. Prepared to hate the place, he was, instead, pleasantly surprised. It was small, but the high ceilings created a roomy feel. The living room had an overstuffed sofa and two easy chairs. A nice sized flat-screen hung on the wall.

She must have noticed his glance at the fireplace because she walked over to it and flipped a switch. "It's gas. You might like to use it since the nights are still cool."

He nodded without comment, still not ready to commit.

She led him into a small kitchen with a dinette set, but what grabbed his attention was the screened patio just beyond. The room was bright and spacious, and he knew it would become his writing area. He'd pull the kitchen table out there. This place just might work.

Beyond the window was an excess of green grass. "I don't do lawns."

A smile danced in her eyes, which were a spooky black-cat green. "I'll be here on Saturday mornings to mow, usually around eight or nine. I have to be at the baseball fields early, so I hope that won't be an inconvenience."

He was an early riser, so he shook his head, but curiosity got the better of him. "Why do you have to be at the baseball fields? Do you mow lawns there, too?"

She laughed for the first time since they'd met. She had a sexy, rusty laugh that didn't match her young face or petite form.

"No, I just watch the games."

His eyes wandered the room. The place was small, but not as bad as he'd first imagined. Maybe he could make do after all, although making do wasn't his habit. "How many bedrooms?"

"Two."

He followed her down the hall, his gaze dropped from the top of her head, where her blonde hair was tied into a crazy knot, to her waist, then dipped further south. She stopped abruptly at the first door, and turned. When she noticed him looking at her assets, she rolled her eyes.

"There's a full bath here and a half bath off the kitchen." Her words dripped with annoyance. "The washer and dryer are just inside the garage door."

He glanced in the bathroom. No Jacuzzi bathtub or multiple shower jets like his had, but he could make do. The next door opened to a bedroom, which held a bed, dresser, nightstand, and no room for anything else.

"The beds have clean sheets on them. There are extra sheets, blankets, and towels in this hall closet." She opened the door as if she needed to prove her words. "The kitchen is fully stocked with pots, pans, and dishes. Everything—"

"I don't cook. Or do laundry."

She lifted a shoulder, shrugging him off. "Well...everything is there if you change your mind."

He swiped a thumb across his lips. "I was told there would be a housekeeper."

"Felicia Kerns lives next door and cleans several houses in town. She said she could come in once a week."

Once a week? His housekeeper was at his L.A. home all day, everyday except Sundays and Mondays. She did the cooking, cleaning, and laundry. "Once a week won't be enough."

The girl's mouth twitched, but she kept her smile in check. "Felicia is pretty flexible. If you ask *nicely*, I'm sure she would be willing to work something out with you."

Colton frowned at her obvious dig. He thought he'd been more than nice, considering. He looked over the second bedroom, which wasn't much larger than the first, but he wouldn't be spending much time in here anyway. The place was small enough that he should be able to handle some of the mundane domestic duties himself.

After she helped him with his luggage, they ended up back in the kitchen. "Is the owner okay with me renting for three months with the option for longer if I need it?"

"She is."

"I was told I'd have the use of a car."

"There's a small Ford in the garage. It's an older model, but it will get you from point A to point B. The gas tank is full and the tires are new. The oil was just changed and all the fluids topped off." She pulled a set of keys from a kitchen drawer and handed them to him.

"Whom do I call if I have any problems?"

"Me. My home phone and cell numbers are here on the counter, along with some others that might be helpful. I printed out a map of Eden Falls and the surrounding—"

"I mean, *whom* do I call if the water heater goes out or the furnace blows up? Shouldn't I call the owner?"

She tipped her head, her green eyes locked on his. "I am the owner."

Colton couldn't have stopped his laugh if he'd tried. "You? Own this house?"

Any hint of the smile she'd shown earlier disappeared. His gaze dropped to her full lips and stayed longer than it should have. Too bad she wasn't a few years older.

"Do you need anything else?"

He raised his eyes to meet hers. "No. I think I'm set."

"Welcome to Eden Falls and happy writing," was said in an eat-dirt-and-die tone.

She walked out and climbed behind the wheel of the rusted jalopy. After she cranked the engine to life and drove away, he realized he hadn't asked her name.

CHAPTER 2

Alex pulled her cell phone out of her purse when she stopped for a red light and called Felicia Kerns. She explained the author staying next door might ask for a few more days of pampering a week. "He seems used to getting his way. Stand firm if you can't spare the time."

"I'm pretty booked, but I might be able to add a few more hours. I'll walk over and talk to him later today."

"Thanks, Felicia."

She pulled into the post office parking lot a few minutes later. Rita Reynolds, postal worker and town crier, stood behind the counter bending Aunt Glenda's ear with the latest gossip. Her dad was a few feet away straightening boxes, his usual grin in place.

Alex pecked her aunt on the cheek. "I just saw Beam."

"He said he was flying in today. I hoped he'd come to dinner, but he's not answering his phone."

"Someone's picking me up" and *"Don't be nosy, cuz"* ran through Alex's mind. She hadn't had time to speculate who picked Beam up from the airstrip. She couldn't mention the conversation to her aunt, because Rita would have it spread

around town before dark. Beam would tie her to the tail of his plane for involving Rita in his business.

Rita looked up—her eyes magnified to huge by her thick-lensed glasses—and squawked, a terrifyingly quirky habit of hers that caused most people to jump out of their skin the first fifty times they heard her. "Oh, Alexis! Denny said you picked up Colton McCreed."

Alex frowned at her dad for revealing details. She couldn't see his smirk from behind the large envelope he held up, but his twinkling, green Garrett eyes gave him away.

"What's he like? Is he as ominous as he appears on his book covers? He's a handsome man, but he never smiles in photos." Rita tipped her head at an odd angle, another quirky bird habit. "I'm not sure you should allow a man whose mind is so diabolical to stay in your rental. He might murder someone and bury the remains under the floorboards. You'd be smart to have your house inspected from top to bottom after he leaves town. Check for funny odors. That's a dead giveaway." She smiled a toothy grin. "*Dead* giveaway. Get it?"

"Ew, Rita," Aunt Glenda said, wrinkling her nose.

"We should be more worried about the way *your mind* works, Rita," Alex's dad said.

Rita whipped around, gaping at him as another squawk escaped. "Have you read his books, Denny? He writes about gruesome people committing heinous crimes." She riveted her huge eyes on Alex and shook her index finger. "Heed my warning, young lady. He would be just the type of person to bury someone under your house, and then direct the evidence toward you."

Denny walked up behind Rita and put a calming hand on her shoulder. "I'm sure Colton McCreed has researched the subject of hiding evidence extensively. He wouldn't bury the remains of someone he murdered under the house he's living in."

"I'll tell JT to keep an eye on him," Alex said to relieve Rita's look of skepticism. She rounded the counter. "Mr. Mc-Creed asked about a month-to-month at the gym, Aunt Glenda."

Her aunt waved a hand. "We're offering all kinds of summer deals right now. Tell him to come in and ask for me or Dawson."

"Will do. Dad, can I talk to you for a minute?" Alex dipped her head toward his office, indicating *in private*.

"Sure, puddin'." Arm around her shoulder, he led her to his office. He leaned against his desk after she closed the door. "What's up?"

"Have you heard of Evergreen Development?"

Her dad flexed his broad shoulders forward. "Can't say I have. Why?"

"They're interested in that huge strip of land along the river between here and Harrisville. Harrisville's mayor and their city planner are concerned."

Denny laughed. "That land has been nothing but a pool of contention since Melvin Murray put it up for sale. What's this Evergreen Development want to do with the land?"

Alex leaned against the door, imagining Rita's ear pressed to the other side. "They aren't saying. That's why Harrisville is concerned."

Her dad shook his head as he ran fingers through his hair. "I've never heard of them. I'll ask your Uncle Dawson."

"Thanks, Dad."

He grinned, his green eyes dancing with happy. "So, tell me about this author. I've read a couple of his books, and Rita's right, they're pretty gruesome. What did he think of Eden Falls?"

Alex shrugged, noncommittal. Her dad always looked on

the bright side of every situation and wore permanent smile lines at the corners of his eyes as proof. She usually did the same, but Colton McCreed had rubbed her the wrong way from the beginning. As mayor, she would play hostess. She wouldn't see him daily. She was busy and he was here to write a book, so she probably wouldn't even see him weekly. "He didn't say one way or the other."

"Your mother thinks we should invite him for dinner. What do you think?"

"I'm not sure he'd accept. He's not very friendly." Her cell phone vibrated. Caller I.D. showed Colton McCreed's business manager's number. "I need to take this. I'll see you at Charlie's game."

"Okay, puddin'. Have a good day."

She planted a kiss on her dad's cheek, waved goodbye to Rita and her aunt, and stepped outside before connecting the call. "Alex Blackwood."

"Alex. Jorge Reis here."

Alex sat on the retaining wall planter that ran along the front of the post office. Just last week, she'd turned the rich dirt and planted several rows of flowers that would spill over the bricks in the coming summer months. "Mr. Reis. How are you?"

"Please, just call me Jorgie."

Isn't going to happen.

"How's our boy?"

"He arrived safely. I showed him around town, and then dropped him off at the rental house. You should have the number."

"I have the number, but I'm not going to use it, yet. I hesitate to ask, was he nice?"

"Isn't he usually nice?" She was aware her tone sounded accusatory rather than curious.

"He can be bad-tempered at times."

She pressed a couple of fingers to her ear. The high school had just released its throngs. As kids streamed past, the noise level mounted. Rap music, blaring from the open windows of a passing truck, vibrated the ground beneath her feet. The kids along the sidewalk cheered.

"How did Colton like the house?"

Alex smiled, remembering Colton's expression when she pulled into the driveway. "I'm sure you'll hear all about it."

"I should have warned him it was small, but I knew if I did, he'd pitch a fit like a little girl." His words prompted a laugh from her. He laughed, too. "I'm sure the accommodations are fine. He's there to write. He's already left me several angry voicemails. I'll let him cool down a few days before I call him back. Listen, Alex, don't let him bully you."

She hopped off the wall. "So, he's bad-tempered and a bully?"

"He's just used to getting his way. Don't let him push you around."

She smiled. "I'm not easily pushed, Mr. Reis."

~

*C*olton spent his first morning in Eden Falls orienting himself with the town. He started out at Patsy's Pastries, where he had the best cream cheese—still warm, melt in your mouth—Danish he'd ever eaten. Unfortunately, he hadn't stopped at one. The coffee was excellent, too.

He browsed through the small library, satisfied they had plenty of his books in their inventory, and two on the shelf, which meant people were reading him. The place was old and smelled of polished wood, leather, and books, a combination he loved.

With parents too busy for parenting, he'd spent many hours in the library with friends named Tom and Huck. He became aware of racial inequality with *To Kill a Mocking Bird*, descended into savagery with *Lord of the Flies*, and immersed himself in the world built by J.R.R. Tolkien. His lights stayed on after reading anything by Stephen King. He'd become intrigued with words and how they could take him to a realm apart from the one in which he lived. Words and their endless combinations were the escape he built his future upon.

The little gray-haired librarian recognized him and introduced herself as Lily Johnson. He learned her husband owned The Fly Shop, and her son was a police officer. She filled him in on some of Eden Falls' history. He wouldn't use any of it, but the old girl was a talker and he didn't have any place he had to be, so he let her ramble.

His books were also on the shelves of Pages, the only bookstore in town. The owner, a short, feisty, redhead named Maude Stapleton, had to be the local comic relief. She was funny enough to charge admission into the place. They also had an extensive conversation, but she didn't fill him in on the local history as much as the local folklore. Before he left, he agreed to call his publicist to schedule a book signing.

Everyone he passed on the sidewalk either spoke or waved. Several people stopped to ask if he was Colton Mc-Creed. They didn't want anything from him. They just seemed curious to know if he liked their little town. A couple even offered assistance should he need anything.

Eden Falls was Norman Rockwell perfect. Clean, quaint, and beautiful. The citizens seemed like honest, friendly folk, which—he hated to admit Jorge was right, *ever*—was why he was here. He wanted to take that honesty, that sense of community, and twist it until it was unrecognizable.

He stopped at the IGA with no memory of the last time he'd been in a grocery store. He went up and down each aisle. Microwavable dinners, chips, peanut butter, and grape jelly, a loaf of fresh white bread all went into his cart. He'd flirted with the idea of flying his housekeeper up here for the summer, so he wouldn't have to deal with laundry, cleaning, or meals. Consuela would take care of everything, but the rental was *way* too small for the both of them. She'd have him out on his ear or he'd have her buried in the back garden before the first week was behind him. Nope, he'd have to fend for himself. Three months wasn't that long. He wheeled his cart back to the freezer aisle and grabbed two tubs of ice cream—another staple to what would become his extremely out-of-whack summer diet.

Back at the rental, he found a note stuck to the front door. He could talk to Dawson or Glenda Garrett about a month-to-month membership at the gym. The girl must have come by for a visit. He was actually sorry he'd missed her. He wanted to find out her name and thank her for showing him around the day before.

After stowing the groceries, he spent the afternoon driving around the surrounding area in the old Ford. His friends in L.A. wouldn't recognize him. The house and grocery shopping would stymy them. His transportation would have them laughing out loud. As basic as the car was, it got him from A to B just like the girl said it would. The house, like Eden Falls, had turned out to be charming. Oddly, the small space soothed the jittery urgency that had plagued him lately. The screened in patio was peaceful and opened his mind to inspiration, which had become almost non-existent the last few months.

While driving, Colton discovered Riverside Park, a beautiful spot where the spring runoff rushed by, raising the river high on its banks. The mountains beyond rose like majestic sentinels, filling him with an unexpected sense of peace. He stood on the grassy incline for a long time, taking in the town and the stunning scenery.

During the late afternoon, he pulled his notes together, and jotted down a very rough outline, which would no doubt change as the story developed and his characters came to life. He had the first of his microwave dinners, then grabbed a jacket, and headed for Rowdy's Bar and Grill. The walk would give him a chance to work off the cheese Danish, because he would be visiting Patsy's Pastries again tomorrow morning.

❧

*A*lex allowed the muscles in her shoulders to relax as she entered Rowdy's Bar and Grill. She loved the easy atmosphere her cousin had instilled when he bought and renovated the rundown property a few years earlier. A rich spicy scent permeated the air, bringing a delightful tickle to her nose. The hollowness in her stomach protested. Beside hamburgers, sandwiches, and a few appetizers, Rowdy offered one daily special, and today's was homemade chili—her aunt's blue-ribbon recipe.

Rowdy greeted her with a grin. He was almost as tall as his brother, but thinner like Aunt Glenda, where Beam was broad like Uncle Dawson. He wore his long, dark hair tied at the nape of his neck with a strip of leather. Two-day scruff grew along his square jaw, and his green eyes twinkled with their usual Garrett amusement.

"Hey, Low-rider." He and Beam had bestowed the nickname before she was old enough to remember. "Meeting the girls?"

"Yep." She bellied up to the bar. "Charlie is at the Blackwood's for the night."

"Want the usual?"

"Extra large nachos, loaded." She breathed deeply. "Add a cup of the chili, too. It smells fabulous."

"That's a lot of food."

Alex rested both elbows on the rich wood bar. She'd been on her feet most of the day, and it felt good to sit. "I missed lunch."

He grabbed a glass and the soda gun. "Jalapenos?"

"Of course."

He set a ginger ale in front of her. "Be right back."

"Why do you wear your hair like that? It makes you look like an old lady." Misty Douglas slid onto the stool on her right and pulled the clip from Alex's hair, allowing it to fall past her shoulder blades. She didn't stop there. "Did you get that blouse out of your mom's closet? I thought we were here to pick up guys, not chase them away."

Alex took the clip from Misty's fingers and slipped it into her purse. "Funny, I thought I was here to meet up with friends, not be criticized by them. And there's nothing wrong with what I'm wearing."

"The color washes out your complexion."

Alex glanced at Misty, who always looked like she'd just stepped off the pages of a fashion magazine. Not a shiny black hair out of place, her makeup was runway perfect. She worked on the square at Dahlia's Salon as a hair stylist, but spent more time in front of the mirrors than her clients did. "You were with me when I bought this top. You said the color brought out the pink in my complexion."

"I lied."

Imagine that.

Rowdy set a cup of chili in front of Alex. The heaping platter of nachos went between them, along with four small plates. She sent him a thumbs-up with her first spoon of chili.

"One day all the fat you eat is going to catch up with you," Misty said as she loaded a plate with nachos and all the fixings.

Alex watched Misty stuff a chip in her mouth. "I order the

same nachos every time we meet, and every time you say the same thing. Yet, you eat more of them than I do."

Normally, Rowdy would have come back with a one-liner in defense of his cousin. When he didn't, Alex glanced up. His attention was on the door. A moment later Stella Adams took the stool on Alex's left. Alex glanced back at Rowdy, who stood unmoving except for an almost unnoticeable tick in his jaw. *Interesting*. She turned to Stella. "Hello."

Stella grinned. "Hi."

"What are you smiling about?"

Stella leaned forward so she could see Misty. "School's almost out."

"What can I get you, Stella?" Rowdy asked.

"Mmm...I'll have a Diet Coke."

"Lime?"

She fluttered her eyelashes at him in her adorably flirty way. "Yes, please."

Misty leaned an elbow on the bar. "Hello? You haven't asked me what I want to drink. How come Stella gets special treatment?"

"I already know what you want, Misty. You've been ordering the same thing since I opened this place."

Misty flipped her hair over her shoulder. "Well, maybe I want something different tonight."

Rowdy raised a brow. "Do you?"

She scowled. "No, but as a bartender and the proprietor of this establishment, you should be bending over backwards for my patronage."

Alex bit her lip to keep from smiling, while Rowdy tipped back his head and laughed aloud.

"Look who's using her big girl words. Proprietor? Establishment? Patronage? Bravo, Misty."

"Shut up, Stella." Misty glanced at Rowdy. "I can take my business to the Cascade Club."

Alex knew the words "go ahead" were on the tip of her cousin's tongue. He'd never liked Misty. He thought she was a spoiled brat, which wasn't far from the truth. Luckily, Jillian Saunders arrival lightened the mood. She took the stool next to Stella. Once her and Misty's drinks arrived, the girls clinked their glasses together.

"Let the par-tay begin," Misty hollered.

Soon, Stella had them laughing over the adventures of one of her more challenging students, the one she was most excited to see move on to third grade. She'd spent nine months filling them in on this particular kid's antics. As the school year came to a close, Stella—a devoted second grade teacher—was ready to pass him off with a heartfelt good-bye and a slight push out the door. Before Alex could utter something comforting, Misty leaned close. "Whoa, ladies, who's that?"

They all looked at the man's reflection in the mirror behind the bar.

"He's cute," Stella said.

Misty swiveled on her stool. "Cute isn't the word I'd use at all. Not when yummy or delicious fit so much better."

Stella performed her signature eye-roll.

Alex watched Colton McCreed glance around Rowdy's, glad to see he wasn't wearing a look of distaste. "That's the author I told you about."

Misty turned wide eyes at Alex. "The guy Beam flew in yesterday? Why didn't you tell me he was so hot?"

Misty responded just as Alex had expected. She was so predictable when it came to men and her reactions to them. Alex glanced over her shoulder. "Is he?"

"Like you would notice," Misty said. "No one will ever measure up to Peyton in your eyes. He was just a guy, Alex, a regular guy who, despite what you believe, *did* look at other women. At some point in your life, you're going to have to de-throne him and move on."

"At some point in your life, you're going to have to stop sleeping with every guy you meet, because none of them can provide the answers you're seeking. And I don't have Peyton on a throne." *Maybe a short pedestal, but so what? He looks nice up there.*

"I'm not looking for answers, and I don't sleep with *every* guy I meet. But I would make an exception for this one. Is he rich?"

"He's a *New York Times* bestselling author, so he probably has money." Alex popped a chip in her mouth.

Stella pulled the plate of nachos in front of her and Jillian. "Shouldn't you ask if he's nice? Or married?"

"I have my priorities." Misty leaned back provocatively, jutting her chest out. "He's coming over—Introduce us."

Alex swiveled on her stool. The expression on Colton's face showed surprise when he spotted her, but his smile, when it appeared, seemed genuine, and didn't seem to hurt at all. In fact, it transformed him from dark and brooding to quite handsome. Peyton's face floated through her mind and melancholy surfaced. She reluctantly pushed him aside. Since she had the house to herself tonight, she could pull him back out at her leisure. "Are you unpacked, Mr. McCreed?"

His attention had settled on Misty, but slid back to her. "Yes. Thank you for showing me around town yesterday."

She lifted a shoulder. "Just part of my job."

His confused look told her he still didn't have a clue she was the mayor. "I also got your note about the gym. Thank you for checking."

"You're welcome." *See how easy a thank you is, Mr. New York Times?*

Colton's glance turned back to Misty, and Alex took that as her cue. "Colton McCreed, this is Misty Douglas, Stella Adams, and Jillian Saunders," she said, indicating each one at their introduction.

"It's very nice to meet you, Colton." Misty purred like a satisfied cat as she took his hand in hers.

Stella rolled her eyes again.

"The pleasure is mine." He pulled his hand free of Misty's, and reached behind Alex to shake hands with Stella and Jillian.

"Join us. There's a vacant seat right here." Misty patted the stool next to her.

As soon as he sat, Misty swung around to face him. Not unusual or unexpected. If a man paid attention, Misty's friends were forgotten, and she made sure men paid attention. She enjoyed the game, played with her victims, and that's what they were in the end. Victims. She set the rules, without a care for the feelings of others, and she made sure she won.

"Rowdy, this is Colton McCreed," Alex said, when her cousin sauntered over. "Colton, this is Rowdy Garrett. His brother is the pilot who flew you into town and his mom and dad own the gym were Jillian works."

~

*A*s soon as the girl referred to Beam, Colton could see the resemblance in both stature and looks. Rowdy wasn't as big as his brother, but not far from it. He had the same eerie green eyes as the girl, and the same smug grin as the pilot.

"Nice place you have here." It wasn't the contemporary glass and chrome bar Colton frequented in L.A. He felt as if he'd stepped through a time warp, straight into the Wild West. The long polished wood bar ran along the right wall with lines of bottles in front of the almost requisite mirror. The floor was wood. The walls were wood. The place even smelled of wood, in an oddly soothing way. Most of the tables and booths were occupied. Country music drifted through the air—not his favorite, but it definitely set the mood. The tantalizing smell of something spicy made him wish he hadn't filled up on a frozen dinner.

"Thanks." Rowdy extended his hand. "I hear you're spending the summer with us, writing a book about Eden Falls."

"Writing a book *based* in Eden Falls," Colton said, shaking Rowdy's hand.

"I've read a couple of your books, pretty grisly."

The kind of compliment Colton appreciated. "Thank you."

"What do you think of Eden Falls?"

He racked his brain for the questioner's name...possibly, Stella. His attention had been riveted on Misty while introduction were being made. From the door, the four women lined up had looked like a veritable smorgasbord of females. Though, he'd been surprised to find the blonde with a cascade of soft-looking curls was the girl who'd picked him up yesterday. "Quaint." He smiled at the girl. "Everyone has been very helpful."

Misty's hand wandered to his thigh.

"And friendly."

A man walked up behind the girl and placed his hands on her shoulders. She smiled up at him.

Misty half turned on her stool. "Well, if it isn't our illustrious chief of police."

"Misty," the man said, then turned from her without further comment or sliver of smile.

The tension between the two roused Colton's curiosity. There had to be as many secrets per capita in a small town as there were in a large city. In a place this size, those secrets would have more of an impact on the community as a whole.

The way that impact played out could make for some interesting story lines, with the end result destroying the concept
of trust. *Food for thought.*

"Hi, Stella, Jillian."

"Hey, JT," they said simultaneously.

"You keeping my sister occupied while Charlie's away?"

Again, the resemblance of this man to the girl was
obvious once mentioned. Pieces of an Eden Falls puzzle
began to fall into place. The girl, the bartender, the pilot, and
the chief of police were related. She was drinking with her
gal-pals, because her boyfriend, Charlie, was out somewhere.

"We're trying, but you know how she is when it comes to
Charlie." Misty signaled for a refill with one hand, and
moved her other high up Colton's thigh.

Colton twisted from her reach. He'd met hundreds of
women like Misty. Trouble with a capital T, but oh, so tempting. Still, until she understood his rules, he wouldn't be
participating in her game.

"JT, this is Colton McCreed," the sister said.

Colton stood for the introduction while JT leaned behind
Misty and held out his hand. "Nice to meet you, Colton.
You're the author staying in my sister's house."

Uh, oh. She really did own the house he was renting, and
he'd laughed. In her face. He glanced at the girl who was
watching him with her cat eyes. She looked so young, how
was it possible? Another piece of the Eden Falls puzzle he'd
have to fit into place later. He looked at JT. "And you're the
police chief."

JT smiled. "At your service."

"I've heard that one before," Misty mumbled.

Something had definitely transpired between JT and
Misty. "Would you mind if I picked your brain one afternoon? I have some questions about police work in a small
town."

JT nodded. "Come by Town Hall anytime. If I'm not in, someone will know where you can find me."

Before Colton could thank him, another man in full cowboy gear stopped behind their group. "Hey, Mayor, Patsy wants to know how many pounds of bacon you'll need for the pancake breakfast."

"I have the sheet on my desk, Manny. I'll check and give you a call in the morning," said the girl.

Colton stared at her as more pieces fell into place. Her meeting him at the airstrip, her showing him around town, her comment "Just part of my job" became clear. "You're Mayor Blackwood?"

The girl scooted off the stool and held out her hand. "Alexis Blackwood."

Alex, short for Alexis.

JT hooked an arm around his sister's neck. "I thought you picked Colton up at the airstrip yesterday. Didn't you introduce yourself?"

The smug grin that ran in the family appeared on her face. "I tried, but Mr. McCreed"—her grin grew—"was in a rush to get to the rental."

Colton wasn't a blushing man, but felt extremely hot under the collar of his shirt. Not only did the girl own the house he was renting, but she was Mayor Alex Blackwood.

He'd love to hit someone, namely Jorge, right now. How could he fail to mention Alex Blackwood was a female, and almost young enough to still be in high school? He'd been made to look like a fool in front of complete strangers, a feeling he didn't like. How many times had he offended her yesterday?

After all of his blunders, she'd just covered for him.

Misty swiveled her stool to face him. "Why would you be in a rush to get to Alex's rental?"

"Mr. McCreed's business manager showed him the

pictures I sent, and he was blown away by how cozy it looked. He was ready to get to work on his novel. Right, Mr. McCreed?"

What could he do but agree? "Right."

Stella scooted off her stool. "Well, I hate to break up this screaming fun party, but I'm going to call it a night."

"You okay to drive?" JT asked.

She performed a fake stumbling act. "I went crazy tonight and had lime with my Diet Coke."

"What would we do without our handy dandy police chief?" Misty mumbled as she tipped a beer bottle to her lips.

Colton took mental notes of Misty's verbal jabs for later examination. She was full of them, and the rest of the group largely ignored her.

Jillian also stood. "I need to go, too."

"I'll walk out with you," Alex said.

Colton touched Alex's arm to stop her. Apologizing was something he wasn't good at, so he made a point of never needing to. *Thanks Jorge.* "Alex, I just assumed—"

Alex laughed, the rusty, sexy sound traveling straight to his gut. "No harm done, Mr. McCreed. I'll tell Jorge how much you love the rental the next time I talk to him."

CHAPTER 3

C olton rolled to his stomach and pulled a pillow over his head, but it didn't diminish the irritating rat-a-tat-tatting. In fact, the sound grew louder. Who was up this early on a Saturday morning, and what were they doing to make such a racket? He lifted the pillow and glanced at the alarm clock on the nightstand—nine-fifteen. His second morning in Eden Falls, and he'd slept like the dead both nights, waking later than his incessant, as-long-as-he-could-remember, seven thirty internal alarm clock. He was now coherent enough to realize the irritating sound was a lawn mower. Mayor Blackwood was cutting the grass.

He threw back the covers, glad to be alone. If that dark haired, blue-eyed beauty had had her way, he wouldn't be. Last night, he'd run out of ways to tell Misty no without being rude. Before he did anything more than twisting tongues in the back parking lot of Rowdy's, she'd have to understand he didn't make promises. "Relationship" wasn't in his vocabulary, "commitments" not part of his future. He didn't plan on remembering first date anniversaries, or choosing "our song" with anyone. He was an "I'll try to call the next time I'm in town" kind of person. He very rarely made that call. He'd been labeled selfish, impermeable, and inconsiderate. He'd be the first to admit the shoe fit. The women he spent time with had to understand he was interested in a few hours or days of pleasure. If they happened to see each other again, great, if not...*c'est la vie*. He was always, *always* up front about his no-strings policy. Clear rules were better for everyone. He didn't have time for complications or misinterpretations. He never led a woman to believe anything more than he was willing to give.

Misty said she wasn't interested in relationships either, but she said it in the same way a woman says, "You don't have to buy me a Christmas present." No man, in his right mind, *ever* believed those lines. His mother was famous for saying things like that.

Colton stumbled to the kitchen, started a pot of coffee, and then climbed into the shower. Fifteen minutes later, with a strong jolt of wake-up juice in hand, he stepped onto the back patio. The sky was heavy with clouds, low over the mountain peaks, and the air held a chill he wasn't used to.

On the far side of the yard, Alex looked like a forest nymph pushing a large mower back and forth. She wore jeans and a heavy hoodie that swallowed her tiny frame, possibly the brother's, or the boyfriend's. After a last swipe, she cut the engine and looked up. He saluted her with his coffee cup.

The corners of her mouth lifted, impishly. "Sorry to wake you so early, but it's the only free time I have most weekends."

"You don't look sorry." Her shrug was so slight he almost missed it. Almost.

"I forgot to tell you garbage pickup is on Friday mornings, unless there's a holiday, then it's on Saturday." When he didn't respond, she put a fisted hand on her hip. "You're not going to make me come over and take the cans to the curb, are you?"

"Maybe I can talk Felicia Kerns into…" An incredulous look crossed her face, and he laughed. "I'm capable of getting the trash cans to the curb." *I think*. Taking the trash out was something he'd never done in his life.

She studied him a moment. "You know, you should do that more often."

"What?"

"Smile. It looks good on you."

He frowned. "I smile."

She ignored his protest. "I also forgot to mention last night that *just-call-me-Jorgie* called to make sure you got in okay."

Colton took a sip of coffee to hide the new smile her comment brought to his lips. Jorge said, "Just call me Jorgie," to everyone, but very few people complied.

"Funny, the son of a…gun won't return my calls."

She pulled the bag from the back of the mower and dumped the grass clippings into a black plastic bag. "He said something about letting you cool off first. Is there a reason for that?"

"We've been known to duke it out with words. He says I'm unreasonable."

"You?" She scoffed as she pushed the mower into a shed behind the garage.

He could have taken offense, but he was too busy looking around the backyard for the first time, enjoying the view. He stepped off the patio. The newly trimmed turf felt cool and ticklish on the soles of his feet. He scrunched his toes up. When was the last time he'd walked barefoot on grass? Come to think of it, when was the last time he'd stepped outside without shoes? When had life become so busy that he rarely took time for simple pleasures such as this? He inhaled—

vowing to change things this summer—and caught the sweet scent of freshly mown grass along with something else. Something fresh, and woodsy.

When he glanced up, Alex was watching him with a raised brow. He probably looked like an idiot out here scrunching his toes in the grass. "Want some coffee?"

"No, thanks." She thumbed over a shoulder. "I have to get down to the ball fields."

He followed her around the side of the house and watched her climb behind the wheel of the Jeep. After three attempts, she cranked the old engine to life.

"There ought to be a law against that thing," he shouted, knowing she couldn't hear him.

After she drove away, Colton refreshed his coffee, then wandered into the screened porch. The outline for his novel was on the table, summoning him with beckoning fingers, but the craving for some kind of apple pastry was stronger. He slipped on shoes, grabbed a jacket, and headed for Patsy's.

~

*A*lex was in her usual place, the top row of the bleachers, where she could see the entire field. Charlie, the man in her life, was on deck, swinging a bat, loosening up. He glanced up to make sure she was watching. *Such a male.* He turned to JT who stood next to the fence. She was too far away to make out what they were saying, but their laughter followed.

Charlie stepped up to home plate. Planting his feet, he raised the bat to his shoulder. He glanced at JT once more before turning his full attention to the game. He bent his knees, put weight on his back leg, and lifted the bat. A lump formed in Alex's throat at his batter's stance. At the perfect moment, he swung with all his might, smacking the ball straight to the large hole in right field.

Alex jumped to her feet. "Sweet hit!"

Charlie took off as fast as his little five-year-old legs could carry him. His right foot hit first base and JT yelled, "Keep going, Charlie. Keep going."

Alex was up on her seat when Charlie left first base, heading for second. The right fielder picked up the ball and launched it as hard as he could, almost making it to the infield. The first and second basemen ran for the ball as Charlie rounded for third. A fight between the two ensued, and Charlie pushed off third base.

"Come on home, Charlie," JT shouted.

Just before reaching home plate, Charlie dove. A cloud of dust billowed up, obscuring Alex's view for a second. When it cleared, she saw Charlie had come to a complete stop three feet short of home plate.

"Touch home," the crowd of parents yelled, almost in unison.

The first baseman won the tug of war and launched the ball toward home.

Charlie, scrambling on hands and knees, touched home plate just as the ball landed at the catcher's feet.

The teenaged umpire swung his arms through the air dramatically. "Safe!"

Charlie jumped up and high fived his coach, fireman Brandt Smith, then ran to the dugout to bump fists with JT. He waved to both sets of grandparents, who cheered from the bottom row of the bleachers, before he glanced at Alex, and pumped both little fists in the air.

Alex cupped her mouth. "Great hit, Charlie."

The love filling her soul at that moment was so over-whelming, tears burned her eyes, but those feelings quickly brought the crushing reality of a loss so intense it almost doubled her over. How could two such mixed emotions co-exist so companionably? Mysteriously, they'd shared mutual space for six long years.

Her son's baseball cap askew, his shirt covered in dirt, and his dark eyes shining—it was like looking at a miniature of his father. Her husband had loved the game. He would have been so proud of his son. If she could choose one moment for Peyton Charles Blackwood to witness, it would be this one.

She turned her back to the field and swiped under her eyes. If Charlie saw her crying, he'd say she was "being embarrassing", but his expressions and many of his manner-isms were just like his dads. She missed Peyton so much it physically hurt. Everyone told her it would get better with time, but that time was slow in coming. Maybe it never would arrive. Maybe she was destined to feel this hollow emptiness for the rest of her life.

She closed her eyes. The memory of Peyton so extreme at moments like this, she could smell his cologne, feel the strength of his arms around her, and his hands gentle but firm gliding over her skin. She could see the gleam of desire in his dark chocolate eyes. She let herself remember his warm breath on her neck and the low rumble of his voice whis-pering her name, sending goose bumps down her spine.

She bit her bottom lip and wiped her eyes again, before turning back to the field.

"Mind if I sit with you?"

Alex had been so involved in the game and her memories, she hadn't seen Colton climb the bleacher stairs. She was tempted to say, *Yes, I do mind*. Emotions were too near the surface. Instead, she swallowed the lump in her throat and sat, leaving room for him. She knew, from his hesitation, that he'd noticed the tears. Would he find the situation awkward enough to sit somewhere else? The answer was apparently no when he plopped down beside her.

~

*C*olton wasn't sure what he'd just interrupted, but hoped Alex wouldn't burst into tears, because he didn't do crying females. "This is quite a park," he said, hoping the comment was enough of a distraction.

She kept her eyes forward. "We take our sports seriously."

"I could hear the cheering all the way to Patsy's." He held up a white paper sack and a cup of coffee. "I'll share."

"Thanks, but I've already had breakfast."

"Mayor, I'm not offering you breakfast. I'm tempting you with pure, unadulterated, bliss." He shook the bag. She glanced his way and smiled. *Good. No tears.*

"Unadulterated bliss does sound tempting, but I have a hamburger date after the game."

Colton pulled an apple Danish from the bag and bit down, rolling his eyes and groaning for her enjoyment. He finished his mouthful and said, "I expected you to be at the big boy games watching your boyfriend. These are little fellows."

"My boyfriend?" Alex asked with a puzzled expression.

JT was down by the fence talking to a kid, as one of the teams ran onto the field. The kid looked up. Alex stuck her thumb and index finger between her lips and whistled like a guy at a boxing match. Colton laughed, shocked that such a loud noise could come from such a small package. He took another bite of heaven and pointed toward JT. "Is that your nephew?"

"Son."

Colton choked. "You're a mother?"

A tiny pucker appeared between her eyebrows. "Why are you so shocked?"

He dropped his Danish into the bag and used his index finger to turn her face toward him. Her skin was flawless, pearlescent, except for the light sprinkle of freckles dotting the bridge of her nose. Were those little freckles, along with her soft, full lips, the features that made her appear so young to him?

"I know I offended you the day we met, and I'll probably do so again when I say, you do *not* look old enough to have a kid." He lowered his finger from her face and pointed to the field. "Especially one that age."

He must have left a sticky print, because she scrubbed at the spot he'd touched. "I'm not sure if that's an insult or a compliment."

He raised an eyebrow. "Looking younger than you are isn't necessarily a bad thing."

"Unless you're a mayor trying to run a town. It's a little hard to get people, specifically men"—she glared in his direction—"to take you seriously, if they think you're still in high school."

Point taken. "You're right. I've made several wrong assumptions about you, and I'm sorry. I'm certain you run this town just fine, and I'll bet you're a great...mother."

She smiled, shaking her head. "It hurt to say that word, didn't it?"

"No. Well, yeah, I mean, it didn't hurt. It's just hard to imagine you as a..."

"Mother." She pronounced the word slowly as if he was of limited intelligence.

Time for another diversion. "So, which one is yours?"

"The shortstop."

The shortstop was the only kid who looked eager enough

to catch the ball, if the batter was lucky enough to hit it that far out. "He seems...enthusiastic."

Alex's countenance softened as she gazed at the boy. "He loves the game."

Colton pulled his Danish from the bag and took a bite. Where was the boy's dad? Alex wasn't wearing a wedding ring, but she did go by Blackwood rather than JT's last name of Garrett, so she must have been married at one time. Divorce was a touchy subject, and he'd offended her enough. He'd have to pick up more pieces of her puzzle from someone else.

The kid at home plate hit the ball, and Alex's son was the only one to run forward. He grabbed the ball and threw it to first. The first baseman dodged out of the way. Colton chuckled.

"Good try, Charlie. You did the right thing," JT yelled from behind the fence.

Colton glanced at Alex. "Your son's name is Charlie?"

She nodded.

"I thought Charlie was your boyfriend. Your brother mentioned him being away last night and I thought—"

"Jumping to conclusions again?" she asked, as the referee's whistle signaled the end of the game. "You seem to be very good at that."

"Guilty as charged, especially around you. Every time I think I've got you figured out, you throw something new at me."

"I haven't thrown anything." She narrowed her eyes. "Yet."

Touché. "I know it's not polite to ask a female her age, but, so I won't continue blundering..."

"I'm twenty-six."

He never would have guessed. "What made you run for mayor at the age of twenty-six?"

She smiled. She had a beautiful smile that put a sparkle in her eyes. "I was twenty-four when I ran for mayor."

"Of course you were." He looked back at her kid who took his after-game snack and stood off to the side. JT squatted down close and talked to him eye to eye. Soon, the kid's frown turned to a smile, and he high fived his uncle before racing to a group of grown-ups standing close to the dugout. He got hugs and high fives before charging up the bleacher steps. As he got closer, Colton realized the boy was part Native American. His black hair was barely visible beneath his hat, but his aquiline nose, almond shaped eyes, and bronzed skin gave away his heritage.

Alex pulled him close, hugging him despite the cloud of dust she created. "Great game, slugger. You hit a homer."

"I know! Did you see how far it went?"

She wiped at a smudge of dirt on the end of his nose. "I sure did. You were great." When Charlie's dark eyes landed on him, Alex turned. "Charlie, this is Mr. McCreed. He's visiting our town for a few months."

Colton stood and held out his hand. "That was a great game."

The boy looked at the outstretched hand a moment before placing his small one into it. "Did you see my homer?"

After a firm shake, Colton released the kid's hand. His first reaction was to wipe his palm down the thigh of his jeans to rid it of dirt, but he wouldn't offend the mayor again this morning. "I have to admit, I didn't get here in time to see it, but congratulations."

"Thanks. My Uncle JT is taking me fishing today with my mom and Uncle Rowdy."

"That sounds fun."

A light illuminated the boy's face. "You want to come with us?"

Alex's smug family-inherited grin appeared. "Mr. Mc-Creed isn't fond of fish."

Colton frowned at the little nymph. He knew she was referring to their fly-shop conversation. He had zero desire to sit in a boat, holding a pole all afternoon trying to catch something with scales that smelled. And once he caught it, then what? Gut it? No thanks. He'd go to a restaurant and have his fish served on a platter with a light lemon sauce or encrusted with almonds. "That's not entirely true. I like to *eat* fish."

"If you don't know how to catch 'em, my Uncle JT could teach you. He's really good at fishing. Huh, Mom?"

"Yes, Uncle JT is very good at catching fish, but Mr. Mc-Creed is busy. Maybe another time."

"Okay."

Charlie started to leave, but his mother caught his arm. "Charlie."

He turned back and held out his hand. "It was very nice to meet you."

Colton chuckled as he shook Charlie's grimy hand once again. "You, too, Charlie. I'm sure I'll see you around town this summer."

Charlie nodded and then glanced at Alex.

She winked. "You can go."

"Bye, Mr. McCreed." Charlie bounded down the stairs of the bleachers.

"Come meet the parents. I know Dad has read some of your books, and Mom is anxious to meet you."

Colton followed her and shook hands with Alice and Denny Garrett. The couple looked exactly as he would have pictured them, after meeting Alex and JT. Alex's blond hair and green eyes came from her dad. JT was built like his father but had his mother's dark hair. He also met Adam and Jeno

Blackwood, who were introduced to him by Alex as her in-laws.

As they visited, Colton caught a glimpse of what it must be like growing up in a small town, where everyone knew everyone else. Several people stopped by to meet him and to congratulate Charlie on his baseball game. He observed a camaraderie and trust that was probably life-long for most of the group, and he was going to twist and then reshape those characteristics to his advantage in his next bestseller.

When he left the ballpark, he looked back at Charlie sitting on JT's shoulders. Both sets of the kid's grandparents were here cheering Charlie on, along with his mother and uncle. But the dad was absent. A missing piece to the puzzle...

The direction of his thoughts made him want to laugh. He'd played soccer as a kid, and neither of his parents had ever made it to one of his games. He shook his head. He was here to write a book, not get caught up in local drama. He'd wasted enough time this morning. He should get back to the little rental and start work, right after a scoop of ice cream. First thing next week he'd look into that short-term gym membership.

Later that afternoon, Colton took a ride to the river. For some odd reason, Charlie's mention of fishing aroused his curiosity. He'd never actually watched anyone fish before. He surfed, and he liked to kick a soccer ball around, but that was the extent of his physical activities, other than working out at a gym. Not that he considered sitting in a boat, holding a fishing rod, physical activity.

He pulled off onto a dirt shoulder with a scenic view when he recognized Alex's rusted Jeep parked among other vehicles. The clouds, threatening rain earlier, had lifted. Rays of sunshine shone down in heavenly brilliance, glittering off the water's surface like thousands of diamonds. From his vantage point above the river, he recognized JT, Rowdy, Denny Garrett, and Alex. They weren't in a boat, but standing in water up to their thighs. Charlie must have grown tired of fishing, because he and Alice Garrett were arranging rocks further down the riverbank.

Colton saw Mayor Blackwood in another light, thigh deep in suspendered rubber pants, casting a line while keeping a sharp eye on her son. She fascinated him in an inexplicable way, pulled at his thoughts, made him wonder about her backstory.

He stood for a long time, mesmerized by the beauty of the majestic mountain peaks, the lush green of fern, and the richness of the earth beneath his feet. The scent of pine wafted through the air on the same breeze that whispered through the towering trees as the arc of fishing lines were cast back and forth. He'd never thought of fishing as art, but this, what was occurring before his eyes, was definitely a form of art.

CHAPTER 4

Waiting outside the high school doors for Alex, Colton recalled his own graduation. Families had surrounded his friends, congratulating them on their accomplishments, while he'd been the odd man out. Like so may other times in his life, his parents had failed to show. He should have been used to the disappointment, but missing his graduation had been like the ultimate slap. Their grand finale of "We don't care enough to rearrange our busy schedules for something that's important to you".

He'd celebrated by getting wasted, then arrested for breaking and entering and indecent exposure when found skinny-dipping with two strippers in the district attorney's pool. That got his parents' attention as well as the newspaper and tabloids'. The headlines read: Academy Award Winning Screenwriter and Actress Bail Eighteen-Year-Old Son Out of Jail. When he left for Columbia University shortly after, he vowed two things: He wouldn't allow himself to be disappointed by his parents again, and he wouldn't become a poster bad boy to gain his parents attention or, worse, their affection. By the time college graduation arrived, he'd settled into his new role as "Impenetrable McCreed". He was incapable of giving or receiving love, which suited his busy, overindulgent, lifestyle.

He didn't enjoy walking down memory lane, and was glad when he spotted Alex striding toward him. She greeted him, and gave him a brief history of the school as they walked inside. Before he realized what was happening, she'd turned him over to Stella and the Adams family. They consisted of a Mr., a Mrs., and four of five sisters—the fifth being the graduate—who Stella affectionately called Oops. He didn't mind the hand off or being surrounded by pretty females, but he did wonder why the mayor disappeared. When he opened the program, his question was answered. Mayor Alexis Blackwood was giving the commencement address.

He followed the Adams family to their seats, five rows from the front of the auditorium and dead center. Most graduations were sleeper events, but Colton wouldn't be able to close his eyes where he sat, and hoped the ceremony was as brief as the town.

"Pomp and Circumstance" began to play over the P.A. system as the curtains on the stage opened. Alex sat on the far left of five people next to the podium. Everyone stood as the seniors filed down both aisles, caps on their heads, blue gowns flowing. One graduate walked up the stairs to the stage and hugged Alex before sitting in the remaining chair. After the audience sat, a preacher gave the invocation. Then Principal Stephens, a tall thin man sporting an extreme comb over, got up to welcome the graduates and guests. He announced they had a celebrity in the house and asked Colton to stand. He did so with mixed feelings. As much as he liked the limelight in promotion of his books, this was the graduates' night, and he wasn't comfortable stealing any part of their thunder.

Principal Stephens gave a five-minute, yawn-inducing speech before introducing Valedictorian Adelaide Adams, part of the Adams family. Her humorous speech ended in a standing ovation. A musical number performed by a small a cappella choir followed. Then Mayor Blackwood approached the podium. Within thirty seconds, she had the audience laughing and cheering enthusiastically. She flashed her contagious smile, and Colton, along with everyone else in the auditorium, smiled right back. He still struggled with speaking in public and envied her comfortable ease in front of an audience.

He expected a sugarcoated speech about the things the graduates could accomplish if they concentrated on the hard work ahead. Instead, Alex focused on the moment, the here and now of their accomplishments, and encouraged the audience to do the same. Fifteen minutes later, she sat down to fervent applause.

Awards were given out. The Honor Society was acknowledged and applauded. Then each graduate walked across the stage to receive their diploma and a handshake, which turned into more hugs than handshakes, from Mayor Blackwood and Principal Stephens. The ceremony was painless and over in less than an hour.

When Colton stood, people immediately surrounded him asking for autographs. Alex took pity and rescued him a short time later.

As they walked toward her demolition derby wannabe, he said, "Nice speech, Mayor. You struck my funny bone."

Her eyes narrowed. "You thought my speech would be dry?"

"I didn't say…" She had an uncanny knack for catching him and calling him out. "To be perfectly honest, yes. Most graduation speeches are dry. But you have a delightful sense of humor, and a unique ability to charm an audience."

"Delightful sense of humor. Unique ability to charm. I think I just received a compliment."

"It was a compliment." Her mock wide-eyed surprise made him laugh, which made her laugh. He enjoyed the rusty sound. "You and Miss Valedictorian were both extremely entertaining. I enjoyed the evening."

"Thank you."

They reached her rust-bucket Jeep and he turned to her. "How about a slice of pizza to celebrate?"

"That's a tempting offer, but I already have a date."

He held up his hands in surrender. "Don't misunderstand me. I wasn't implying a date."

~

*T*he reason Alex found this guy so egotistically, pompously, irritating raised its arrogant head. Like she'd ever consider going out with him. The idiot. Time to give back a little of what he kept dishing out. "The word date was a figure of speech, Mr. McCreed. As a rule, I don't date men over forty."

She basked in her moment of triumph when every muscle in his body tensed rigidly.

"I'm not forty."

"I said *over forty*." She laughed when the mouth in his big head dropped open. *Checkmate. At least for tonight, Mr. Mc-Creed*. She pulled the screeching door of her Jeep open, but a nagging conscience stopped her. Misty had mentioned she and Colton were seeing each other later this week. Even though Misty was a friend, she was a user and held little regard for other people's feelings. Not to warn Colton would be unfair. She turned. "I should tell you about Misty. She—"

"I'm a big boy, Mayor."

"But—"

He held up his hand. "Save your sermon. I've been with women like Misty before, and I know their type."

She shrugged. *Can't say I didn't try.* "Enjoy your pizza, Mr. McCreed."

~

*C*olton finally reached the front of the long line at the griddles. In all his travels, he'd never been to a Memorial Day pancake breakfast. The mayor, wearing a cowboy hat to block the early morning sun, wielded a spatula as efficiently as she gave a speech.

"Morning, Mayor."

She glanced up and smiled. "Morning, Mr. McCreed. You just getting here?"

"Yep. Missed the flag raising. How'd it go?"

"Just like it was supposed to." She raised both fists in the air like a little kid and sing-songed, "Yay!"

Colton chuckled. Oddly, he'd been doing that a whole lot more since he'd met her. She had a snarky tongue, but could make him laugh quicker than anyone had in a long time.

She stacked four monster pancakes on his plate. "Syrup is at the end of the line. Enjoy."

"Is this the famous Colton McCreed I've been hearing so much about?" A curvaceous, platinum blonde stepped up next to Alex and held out a hand. "Patsy Yarberry of Patsy's Pastries."

"There really is a Patsy?" Colton shook the woman's hand. She was dressed in skinny jeans and a skin-tight tee that said *Blonde With Brains* across the chest.

"There really is a Patsy. I hear you've become my best customer. Is it the pastries or the pretty girls I have working behind the counter that has you coming in so often?"

Colton grinned, instantly liking the woman. "I won't lie. I

enjoy the sweet pleasures I get from those girls each morning."

"Oh, brother," Alex murmured.

Patsy threw back her head and laughed at his innuendo. "I like you, Colton McCreed. I look forward to seeing you around town this summer."

Before he reached the syrup, Alex's son blocked the path. He sported a milk mustache along with a mile-wide smile. "Hi, Mr. McCreed."

"Hey, kid. Looks like you enjoyed breakfast."

"I love pancakes." Charlie's smile disappeared. "You didn't come to my baseball game."

The seriousness of the kid's expression made Colton feel he needed a valid alibi, but didn't have anyone to vouch for his whereabouts. "I...was working."

Charlie eyed him a second before pointing to a group of people at a picnic table. "You can sit by us. We have lots of room."

After liberally dousing his pancakes in butter and syrup, he joined JT and the rest of the Garrett family. He'd traveled the world in his thirty-four years, first with his jet setting parents, and later on his own. He'd grown up on movie sets with his actress mother and his screenwriter father, and had been exposed to every situation imaginable. Yet in all those travels, he'd never spent a holiday in a small town—he didn't imagine Christmas in Aspen counted. The sight of brothers and sisters, uncles and aunts, grandparents and grandkids, coming together in celebration warmed his crusty, card-carrying cynical heart.

The Garrett family made room for him. Denny's brother, Dawson, and his wife, Glenda, joined them. Soon followed by Rowdy and Beam, who gave Colton a resounding slap on the back. "Hey there, city dweller. Good to see you're surviving in our isolated part of the world."

The group included him in the conversation, gathered him in as if he were a long lost relative. Their kindness tugged him from the comfort zone he wore like a second skin, exposing his underbelly to anticipation, and the sense of belonging he'd yearned for since early childhood. He'd learned to squash those yearnings because they usually ended in rejection and disappointment. He'd masked his vulnerability with a façade of indifference and callousness. Over the years, many tried to knock a brick from his wall of protection —until now, no one had succeeded. That these strangers were able to accomplish such a feat in so short a time was irksome.

*N*ext on the list of Memorial Day traditions for Eden Falls, the Annual Police Department and Firefighters Baseball Game, a.k.a. Gunslingers vs. Smoke Eaters. The ballpark was already crowded when Colton arrived, the smell of hotdogs and popcorn hung heavy in the air. He was, again, welcomed into the middle of the Garrett family—at least the ones who weren't playing on one of the teams. Denny Garrett explained there was no prize or trophy. The winning team just earned the distinction of strutting through town for a year, knowing they'd bested the other guys.

A rule made by founder of the game, Dawson Garrett, each team must have at least three females appearing on their roster, and one of those females had to play in every inning. The fire department wore red jerseys. The police were in blue.

By now, Colton recognized about half of the players. Charlie's coach was pitching, Rowdy was on first base, and Beam on second for the fire department. For the Gunslingers, JT was pitching, Stella was second baseman, and the mayor was in centerfield.

In the top of the third inning, Charlie, who was sitting in front of Colton, turned. "Look, Mr. McCreed. My mom is up to bat!"

"I see that."

The kid had been bouncing all over the place, a boundless bundle of energy. With his syrup-covered shirt hiked up and the band of his Teenage Mutant Ninja Turtles underwear showing, he climbed over the bleachers like a little monkey. He smelled like dirt, bruised bananas, and something Colton couldn't quite identify, but if he could smell it, the kid was too close.

The gunslingers had two runners on base when Alex took a batters stance and faced off against Charlie's baseball coach. He wound up and let the ball fly. She flinched, but didn't swing.

"Strike!"

She turned on the umpire, her voice loud enough for the crowd. "You've got to be kidding me, Jerry. That was *so* not a strike."

"Alex…" the ump warned.

She slung the bat over her shoulder. "It was high and wide, and you know it."

The bleachers around Colton erupted in laughter when the umpire backed up a step.

"Come on, Alex," the pitcher yelled. "That pitch was a perfect strike."

Alex spun with a hand on her hip. "Maybe you need to see Doc Ryan for an eye exam, Brandt."

Brandt took off his baseball cap and winked. "My eyesight is perfect, darlin'."

Catcalls and wolf whistles sounded from the bleachers.

Alex stepped up to home plate, took her time planting her feet and raising the bat. The pitcher wound up, and let the ball go with a speed that surprised Colton. The little pixie smacked it with all her might. The crowd followed the ball with their eyes—foul.

Charlie stood and cupped his mouth. "Come on, Mom. Bring 'em home."

Another round of laughter rippled through the crowd.

~

*A*lex searched until she spotted her little man, and gave him a thumbs up. *This one's for you, Peyton. I wish you were here to cheer me on, along with our son. Except, you'd be right behind me, bringing me home if you were here, wouldn't you, sweetheart?*

She settled her feet and set the tip of the bat on the corner of home plate before raising it behind her head.

"Come on, Alex, you can do this," JT yelled. "Don't let that big lug intimidate you."

Alex slid a quick glance at the occupied bases. JT was on second, Stella on third. Her eyes met Brandt's just as he wound up. The bat and ball connected with a force that jolted her whole body. She pushed off home plate before the ball cleared the pitcher's reach, headed straight for their weak left fielder. She made it to first and rounded for second, but stopped when the ball was thrown infield. A quick glance toward home plate confirmed both Stella and JT were safe. She returned to first with a satisfied smile, her ears tuned to one little voice.

"Way to go, Mom."

She looked at Charlie who stood on the seat of the bleacher, pumping his fists in the air.

"Good hit, Low-rider," Rowdy said.

"Hey, Rowdy. No fraternizing with the enemy," Brandt called from home plate.

Rowdy frowned down at her. "No fraternizing? He's the one dating you."

"We're not dating," Alex said. "We've only been out a couple of times."

"Last I heard, that's called dating."

Instead of answering, she turned the tables on her teasing cousin. "Speaking of dating, what's going on between you and Stella?"

"Stella?" He rolled his shoulders as if loosening up. "Nothing. Why would you think there was?"

"Because you haven't taken your eyes off her since the game started."

He pulled the brim of her baseball cap down to hide her eyes. "You don't know what you're talking about."

She pushed her hat back into place and raised her eyebrows. "Really?"

"Really." Rowdy looked away—toward Stella. "Last I heard she was dating some fifth grade teacher she met at a teacher's conference."

Alex found it very interesting that her confirmed bachelor cousin was keeping tabs. Instead of pursuing the subject, she put her thumb and finger between her lips and belted out a whistle. "Watch out, Russ. Their pitcher has poor eyesight." She turned back to Rowdy. "So, when are you and Beam going to cross over to the right team?"

Rowdy's grin was so much like his father's, which was so like her father's, it made her grin right back. "My dad was a smoke-eater before JT became a gunslinger. You two are the ones playing for the wrong team."

Keeping a foot against first base, she prepared to run. "We'll see who's playing for the wrong team at the end of the game."

"As mayor, shouldn't you be impartial?"

Russ' bat connected with the ball and Alex took off,

yelling over her shoulder. "I was a gunslinger's sister before I became a mayor."

*F*rom her periphery, Alex saw Brandt Smith approaching after the game. She knew he was going to ask her out. Going to a movie with someone, besides her five-year-old son was great, but there was no spark for her, and she didn't believe there was for him, either. He was fairly new in town and she'd become his safety net.

Her friends and family pushed her to date, but she wasn't in a hurry. Life was busy enough managing a town and running a business. As it was, Charlie saw too little of her. She counted herself lucky to have so much family support. Her parents were great to take Charlie, and if JT wasn't working, he was there for her. The Blackwood's loved spending time with their grandson. Peyton's two older brothers and their wives often included him on their outings. Family surrounded Charlie, but it didn't make up for a missing father.

"You were ruthless out there today," she said when Brandt sat down next to her.

"You wouldn't have accepted anything less."

"You're right. You played a great game."

"You can say that because your team won."

Alex stuffed her mitt into her gym bag. "I can say that because it's a fact. The fire department played an awesome game."

"Your hit won the game."

She blew a breath on her fingernails and polished them on her shoulder. "All in a day's work."

Brandt laughed. He was handsome, tall, and broad with a great smile that he flashed often. "A bunch of us are headed to Harrisville for some drinks and pizza." He dipped his head and looked under the bill of her baseball cap. "Want to join us?"

"I can't. My parents have this annual family thing they do on Memorial Day."

"Maybe next time."

She pulled off her hat and met his gaze. "No. I don't think so."

He nodded. "We've run our course."

"Sadly, I don't think we ever had a course."

"Yeah. I think you're right." He laughed and wrapped his arm around her shoulder. "I hope that doesn't mean we can't be friends."

"We'll always be good friends." She grabbed her bag and stood, then leaned forward and planted a kiss on his cheek. "Have a nice afternoon, Brandt."

He smiled. "You, too, Alex."

~

From his earliest recollections, Colton had been in multitudes of situations where strangers surrounded him, but never had he felt as comfortable as he did sitting on the deck in the Garrett's backyard. Their guests, milling about with plates of food, laughing and relaxing, had a way of making him feel at ease. He was used to people expecting something from him. Manuscripts had to be read, multiple edits had to be completed, deadlines had to be met. There were meetings and phone calls with agents, publicists, editors, and publishers. These people expected nothing. They weren't out for money or to further their careers. They were here to relax, and enjoy a nice afternoon with friends and family.

The weather couldn't have been more perfect if ordered specifically for the day. A slight breeze rustled the leaves of the trees lining the yard. The sun dipped behind an occasional cloud, dappling the yard in brief shadows. Music played from speakers. Coolers were filled with drinks. Kids played tag on the outskirts of the yard, and adults gathered in circles as jokes were told and stories repeated. Alex and Alice bustled about making sure everyone was fed. Denny and JT checked on everyone's drinks and manned the grills, where hamburgers and hotdogs were lined up like little soldiers.

A rapport permeated the air, a bond Colton had never experienced, and it brought on a bout of envy. Envy that people lived with this assurance of love. Envy that he'd never shared a laugh with his dad standing at a grill, or dropped a casual arm around his mother's shoulder. For the first time in his life, he wondered what it might feel like to have a wife and children. That thought fled when Misty Douglas appeared, and took a possessive hold on his arm.

*A*fter dinner, Colton strolled inside the Garrett's home. He stopped at the door to the living room, which wore a tidy, yet lived-in feel. The room invited him in, and wrapped itself around his soul—a lot like Alex's rental had done. The perfect amount of pictures graced the walls and mantel, beckoning him to step in for a closer look. Alex and JT had grown up here. The photos revealed the story of a happy family through the many stages of their lives.

He picked up a picture of Beam, Rowdy, JT, and a tiny Alex holding up their catches after a day of fishing on the river.

"That was the first fish I ever caught."

Colton turned. Alex stood just inside the doorway. "It's almost as big as you."

A wrinkle appeared between her brows. "Not true."

He held the picture so she could see. "Almost. I bet your

brother and cousins were mad you caught the biggest fish that day, and on your first attempt."

"I didn't say it was my first attempt."

He set the picture back on the mantel and pointed to another in which Alex wore her hair in pigtails. She stepped closer, and he caught the sweet smell of her perfume. Subtle. Pleasant. Unlike Misty's overpowering scent. "How old where you here?"

"First grade. The photographer tried to get me to smile, but I'd just lost a front tooth. Misty made fun of me all the way to school that morning, so I wasn't about to smile."

He glanced her way. "You have a beautiful smile."

"Thank you. You have a nice smile, too. When you use it."

"I smile."

~

*A*s Colton walked from his house to the Town Square and back each morning, the ideas that had been swimming around in his mind began dropping from his fingers to his computer screen. The level of support and community he witnessed was amazing. People watched out for their neighbors and trusted strangers. He knew, when this book was released, he'd owe Jorge Reis *big time* for getting him up here. Jorge would be sure to collect, because this book would climb to number one faster than any other Colton had written. He could feel it.

His literary agent had called twice to see how things were going, and expressed enthusiasm when Colton voiced his ideas. She'd been with him from the start, before there was even a finished first novel. She'd encouraged, bolstered, pushed, and, when he got it right, was the first to celebrate his victory. And hers.

His only diversions were his gym workout each morning where he, on occasion, ran into Rowdy and JT, and his stop at Patsy's Pastries. He looked forward to a grueling workout, which he rewarded daily with sweet indulgences. The moment he walked through the door, he was surrounded by the scent of sugar, cinnamon, and yeast, with hints of citrus, berries, apples...the list went on and on, and so did the selections. He could taste the sticky sweetness in the air and carried it out with him when he left. The vast array beckoned with tempting flakiness or drizzles of translucent glaze.

Not a creature of habit, he was eager to try a different enticing treat on each visit, savoring the tantalizing flavors and countless textures. He was in his own little Colton-fabricated heaven while at Patsy's. It was true love at first bite, and that love grew every day.

He usually sat at one of the six tables out front, and enjoyed his sinful pleasure while he watched the town come awake for the day. Shop owners unlocked their doors and flipped their signs to OPEN. Birds filled the early summer air with cheerful melodies, waiting for unnoticed leftovers from Patsy's clientele. Hanging flower baskets adorned each old fashioned lamppost around the square. Marilyn Willis, in her green Eden Falls Park shirt, usually stopped to chat while she supplied the blooms with their morning drink. Colton sat back, appreciating the clean air and the sun on his face. Early mornings were for indulgence.

On his walk back to the rental house, he'd made it a habit to pop into one of the shops along the way. Twice now, he'd stopped by the river to watch men and women fly fishing, their lines dancing gracefully in the sun. Out of curiosity, he stepped into The Fly Shop one morning. A man with a white fringe of hair around his head greeted him with one of the firmest handshakes he'd ever experienced.

"Everyone on the square said you've been stopping by

their shops after your trip to Patsy's, and I was beginning to feel left out. You met my wife your second day in town. Lily Johnson? She's been the librarian since the doors opened. My son, Mac, said JT introduced you at the Garrett's Memorial Day picnic. He's been with the police department for a few years now. I'm Rance Johnson." Colton opened his mouth, but Rance held up his free hand. "Oh, you don't have to introduce yourself. I know who you are Colton McCreed. I've read every one of your books. Don't ask me which one I like best though, 'cause I couldn't tell you. I liked them all. I'm impressed with your work. Come see if you're impressed with mine."

Colton, who still hadn't gotten a word out, was ushered past an ancient cash register to a table in a back room. "Here, have a seat, young man, and take a look at this."

Colton had no idea what he was supposed to look at. The table was covered with hooks, feathers, some kind of string, and small tools. Rance pulled a chair from under the table and motioned for him to sit. He received a personalized lesson on how to tie a fly. When he left an hour later, he'd not only created the ugliest fly ever tied, but he'd signed up for fly-fishing lessons. Jorge would laugh him out of L.A., after telling him he'd lost his mind. Maybe he had. This place was different from any he'd ever visited. Already, he felt as if he could leave here with a handful of life-long contacts, and he'd only been here a couple of weeks.

After writing for a several hours, he decided he'd delayed going to the Post Office for as long as possible. Jorge had forwarded some mail, and Colton was sure there was a pile by now. When he entered, a tiny gray haired lady with glass lenses so thick they doubled the size of her eyes, squawked like a bird, startling him and causing the three people in front of him to turn and stare. JT had warned him about the comical creature who worked behind the counter. He said she was acknowledged as the town's gossip, and known to be quite proud of the label.

She motioned him to the front of the line, ignoring her other customers, who didn't seem to mind.

"I thought you'd never come to get your mail. It's been stacking up for over a week. You have a couple of bills that need attention. I'm Rita Reynolds." She thrust her weathered hand over the counter.

"Hi, Rita. I'm—"

She flapped a hand. "Oh, everyone already knows who you are. I just told you I had your mail stacking up. I have a question. Why don't you smile on your book covers? You have a nice smile, and straight, white teeth. Did you wear braces as a kid?"

Colton couldn't help but chuckle at the little bird behind the counter, flapping her hands as though she might take flight at any moment. She spoke every sentence with an energy that would tire him if he had to listen very long. "I'll work on smiling more." *Since this is the third time I've been called out on it.*

She tipped her head at an odd, pigeon-like angle. "You don't have to work on it. You've already got it. Just use it."

He nodded in agreement as the door opened and the line grew by two more people. Rita was finally quiet, her hands folded on the counter. He waited, but she didn't move.

"So...can I get my mail?"

"Squawk!" She turned and almost disappeared. He leaned over the counter and saw she'd been standing on a stool. The woman couldn't be more than four foot ten. She went around a cabinet and came back carrying a U.S. mailbox that was almost as big as she was. She climbed on the stool and pushed the box across the counter. "I'll expect the box back tomorrow."

There was no way he'd be returning that soon. He reached in and began to gather his mail.

"I know you frequent Patsy's Pastries every morning, and it's not for the company. I'll bake you a batch of my famous fudge brownies with walnuts and coconut. Everyone around here will tell you they're the best in the state." She pointed to the people behind him who were all nodding, even the mayor, who hid a smile behind the envelope in her hand. He could see the twinkle of merriment in her green eyes. "You can pick the brownies up tomorrow, when you bring the box back, or not at all. *Squawk!*"

He dropped his mail back into the box. "I'll see you tomorrow."

Denny Garrett stuck his head out of an office. "You'd better be careful, Colton. Rita has snagged two husbands with her famous fudge brownies."

Colton glanced at the tiny woman who was grinning like the Cheshire Cat.

CHAPTER 5

Colton sat on the porch strumming his guitar. A sequence of events in his manuscript weren't falling into place, and he wasn't sure what he wanted to alter to make it work. For some peculiar reason, plucking the strings of his guitar helped clear his mind and allowed him to reorganize.

Several people walked past the house and waved, or called out a hello. He lifted a hand in acknowledgment or returned the greeting aloud—so unlike him. All this unrestrained friendliness was not his cup of tea. Yet, after saying "nice afternoon" a few times, the greeting became automatic.

"Hi, Mr. McCreed."

Colton leaned forward so he could see the sidewalk where a dark headed boy stood. "Charlie? Is that you?"

The boy's timid "yes" surprised him. The few times he'd been around Charlie, the kid was anything but shy.

"Come on up." Colton, who usually avoided kids, wasn't sure why he extended the offer, but Charlie ran up the walk, not giving him time to rescind the invitation.

Charlie hesitated at the bottom step.

"Come on. I don't bite."

He climbed the stairs and stood with his back to the railing.

Colton set his guitar aside, picked up the white paper bag sitting next to him, and held it out. "Would you like a chocolate chip cookie? They're from Patsy's."

Charlie glanced at the bag longingly, but shook his head. "No. Thank you."

Right. No cookies from strangers. Colton set the bag next to his guitar.

Charlie looked at the front door. "My mama and daddy lived here before I was born."

Colton's eyebrows rose when he realized the opportunity. There was something ethically wrong about interrogating a child without an adult present, but he wasn't the law, and his curiosity got the better of him. "Where is your dad?"

"He died."

Whoa. Not the answer he'd expected. The boy's words were so straightforward they caused Colton's chest to tighten. "How did he die, Charlie?"

"He was a marn...mar..."

"A Marine?"

Charlie nodded.

"Was he killed in Iraq?"

Charlie toed a nail sticking up from the porch floorboards and nodded again.

Oh, boy. "I'm sorry. I bet you miss him."

"He died before I was born." Charlie stood on one foot holding his arms out for balance and then hopped to his other foot. "My mom says he watches me from heaven."

Moms will say anything to appease their kids. "You're five?"

"Yep, but my birthday is in July. That's next month. Do you want to come to my party?"

So, Alex was pregnant with Charlie when her husband was killed in Iraq. She wasn't divorced but widowed.

"Mr. McCreed?"

The boy calling his name brought him back to the present. "Sorry. What did you say?"

"Can you come to my birthday party?"

Not on your life. "Sure…we'll see. If I'm in town, maybe I can make it."

"Is that yours?"

Colton glanced in the direction Charlie pointed. His guitar. "Yes."

"Can you play any songs I know?"

Colton picked up the guitar and patted the chair next to the glider he was sitting on. Charlie sat on the edge. "What songs do you know?"

Charlie looked up at the porch ceiling as if he'd find the answer written there. He turned to Colton, his dark eyes twinkling. "My mom sings "You Are My Sunshine" to me before bed sometimes. Do you know how that one goes?"

Colton strummed a few cords thinking it was an appropriate song for Alex to sing. He began and Charlie joined in with his five-year-old, off-tune voice. As the kid sang, he moved from the chair to the edge of the glider.

"Hey, that's just like my mom sings!" Charlie said as Colton strummed the last cord.

Colton laughed at the kid's excitement. "What other songs do you know?"

Charlie climbed up next to Colton, which was a little too close. When Colton moved away, Charlie scooted right along with him. Before they'd finished "Row, Row, Row Your Boat", Charlie had pressed up against him, his hand on Colton's thigh. Next, they sang "Farmer in the Dell". Without thinking it through, Colton set the guitar on Charlie's lap and wrapped his arm around the kid to help him reach a few simple cords.

About ten minutes into their lesson, Charlie smiled up at him. "This was fun, but I have to go home."

Colton stood and set the guitar inside the house. He wanted to make sure Charlie got home safely, and he was curious to see where Alex lived. Charlie talked non-stop while they walked the three blocks. The kid was as happy go lucky as his mother seemed to be, a permanent grin etched on his bronzed face. His coloring was a sharp contrast to his mother's, but he carried some of her features — a nose that was a little too big for his face, and that crazy sunshine smile.

Charlie ran up the steps and through the front door of a Craftsman-style home. The welcoming porch had pots of pink flowers and a swing on one end, a wicker loveseat and two chairs on the other. The screen door spring stretched with a twang as he followed Charlie inside. When the screen slammed behind him, Alex called, "Charlie is that you? You were supposed to be home thirty minutes ago. Where have you been?"

Colton trailed Charlie into the kitchen just as Alex pulled the kid into her hip. "I'm afraid it's my fault."

She let out an audible gasp with a hand to her chest, then relaxed when she realized it was him. "It's your fault my son is so late?"

"Guess what Mom? Mr. McCreed has a guitar, and he teached me to play."

Alex met Charlie's wide-eyed enthusiasm with excitement of her own. "Really? He *taught* you to play?"

"We were singing and lost track of time. Sorry he's late."

"Mom, can Mr. McCreed eat with us?"

"Uh…" She looked like a bunny caught in the crosshairs of a gun sight. He hoped his eyes sent the message, *Sorry, Mayor, but I'm not declining the invitation to partake of a home-cooked meal*, because whatever was cooking smelled delicious. After an awkward silence and some lip-biting on her part, she smiled. "Sure. Would you like to stay for dinner, Mr. McCreed?"

The anticipation made his stomach growl in answer. "That would be great, if you have enough."

"My mom always makes lots of food, huh, Mom?"

Alex ruffled her son's hair. "Go wash your hands and set another place at the table, please."

"Come on, Mr. McCreed, we have to wash our hands in the bathroom. My mom says germs can make us sick." He bent at the waist and added a retching sound, which made Colton laugh as he followed Charlie down the hall.

He glanced into the first room they passed, obviously Charlie's with its vibrant solar system comforter. Stars and planets hung from the ceiling in a colorful array, and a poster of Spiderman was framed above the dresser. The next room held a bed and a desk with no room for anything else. Framed pictures lined the wall opposite the bathroom. The one that caught Colton's eye was a close-up shot of Alex in a wedding dress and a Native American man in a tux. Alex looked over the top happy and so did the groom, both almost nose-to-nose, caught in a laugh as they gazed into each other's eyes. The photographer had done an excellent job of capturing the perfect moment in time, freezing it forever.

"Here's the bathroom, Mr. McCreed."

He and the kid washed their hands side by side, a new experience for Colton, and not too painful, despite the splashing and flinging of water. Did the kid ever pause long enough to take a breath? Not that Charlie rattled on about anything uninteresting. He just never stopped talking.

Dinner was grilled salmon with a delicious sauce, sautéed Brussels sprouts, and the best mashed potatoes Colton had ever tasted, which was lucky, because he hated—Nope, hate wasn't a strong enough word for how much he detested Brussels sprouts.

Charlie glanced at Colton's plate and pushed the bowl of vegetables forward. "My mom makes you try everything on the table. She doesn't make you eat it if you don't like it, but she says you have to try."

"I've *tried* Brussels sprouts, and I *know* I don't like them."

"But these have bacon and almonds." Charlie nudged the bowl closer.

"I'm pretty sure, even with bacon and almonds, I still won't like them."

"But you have to try them. Huh, Mom?"

The pleasure in Alex's eye was so full of payback, it spilled over to the corners of her mouth. "Sorry, Mr. McCreed, but it is the rule. What kind of example would you set if you broke the rules in front of an innocent child?"

He frowned at her and then glanced at Charlie. The kid's expression was expectant. He peered into the bowl and shuddered before searching out the smallest piece of revolting green he could find. He jabbed his fork in, well aware both the *innocent child* and the sadist were watching. The piece was too big to swallow. He held his breath and chewed and chewed and then chewed some more. It wasn't the slimy disgusting thing he remembered as a kid. These were cooked al dente with a hearty flavor of bacon. The slivers of almonds added an unexpected roasted crunch.

Charlie laughed. "Look, Mom. He likes it."

Little Miss Sunshine with her beaming smile and dancing eyes turned the serving spoon in his direction. "Would you like more?"

~

*A*lex wasn't sure how she felt about the exchange taking place between her son and the author as they finished their dinner. This was the first time a male, other than family, had eaten with them. She'd been taken by surprise when Charlie issued the invitation, but wasn't sure why. Charlie was just as friendly and outgoing as his father had been, and Peyton wouldn't have thought twice about extending the invitation.

She stood. "Are you both finished?"

Colton sat back and rubbed his stomach. "Those were the best mashed potatoes I've ever eaten."

"What about the Brussels sprouts?" Charlie asked.

"I enjoyed the whole dinner, including the Brussels sprouts. The salmon was delicious, and the sauce." He groaned and rolled his eyes dramatically, sparking a laugh from Charlie. "Thanks for letting me stay. It's been a long time since I've had a home cooked meal. Even the cold glass of milk was good."

An unexpected pleasure bloomed in the middle of Alex's chest. It had been a long time since she'd cooked for a man—not that she'd cooked for Colton, but it was nice to hear someone besides her son express appreciation for the fruits of her labor. "I'm glad you liked it. Charlie, are you finished?"

Charlie answered a quick yes before going into a full-blown explanation of the differences between each of the Teenage Mutant Ninja Turtles.

When her son stopped long enough to take a breath, Alex said, "Charlie, you need to take a shower before dessert."

"Aw, Mom." He grumbled with an air of persecution only a five-year-old could produce.

She leaned over and kissed the top of his head. "Don't 'aw, Mom' me, little man. You're the one who came home late."

"But I don't need a—"

"Shower," they both finished at the same time. "And yes you do. You smell like a wet puppy dog instead of my son."

Charlie laughed his little boy belly laugh. "She always says that."

"Go on, handsome. And Charlie," she added, when her son pushed back from the table, "don't forget to wash *all* your body parts, not just the ones that show."

The kid frowned. "But I don't have to brush my teeth yet."

"No, sweetie, not yet."

"Sorry for just showing up," Colton said, after Charlie left the kitchen. "I could tell Charlie's invitation caught you off guard."

"It did, but it's okay. We just don't have many visitors for dinner." She wiped the already clean counter, unsure why she felt so fidgety. "I hope Charlie wasn't a bother earlier."

Colton laced his fingers and rested them on top of his head. "No. He's a great kid."

Alex turned to look at him. His posture was that of a confident man. She knew so little about him, and he didn't seem in a hurry to leave, so she asked the first question that popped into her head. "Do you have children?"

"No, and I don't intend to."

His immediate answer surprised her. "You don't want children some day?"

"Nope. Not my thing."

She leaned back against the counter. "Not your *thing*?"

He moved his hands from the top of his head to his stomach. "Look, some people are meant to have kids and some aren't. I'm in the *aren't* category. I don't want kids, haven't got a built in daddy gene. I don't think babies are adorable and, contrary to what people say, they don't smell delicious. I can go anywhere I want, whenever I want, and I don't have to worry about dragging a diaper bag around, or finding a babysitter. I can jet off to Spain tomorrow if I want, and I like it that way. I enjoy my freedom and don't plan on making any changes."

She picked up a dishtowel and hung it over the oven handle. *Jet off to Spain tomorrow.* What must that kind of freedom be like? Lonely, she decided. She'd had Charlie at twenty-one. He was her life. "What if your wife wants children?"

"There won't be a wife."

Alex walked to the table and pushed Charlie's chair in. "No wife, no children, no commitments..." *Lonely and sad.*

"I told you, I like my freedom. If I had a wife, I couldn't jet off when I want to." He grinned. "A wife would crimp my style."

A pajama-clad Charlie charged into the kitchen, his smooth skin, free of dirt streaks. His appearance saved her from saying what was on the tip of her tongue.

"Did you have dessert yet?"

Alex pulled her son close and stuck her nose in his wet hair, grateful for every black strand on his head. "Ah, there's my little man. I knew he was in there under all that dirt and sweat and puppy dog smell."

"Mom..."

She smoothed his rumple towel-dried hair. "Do you like berry cobbler, Mr. McCreed?"

"I like any kind of cobbler."

"With vanilla ice cream," Charlie added, pumping a fist in the air.

Colton laughed. "I like cobbler with ice cream even better."

∾

*O*ver dessert, Charlie dominated the conversation once again, with tales of a tree climbing expedition. Colton laughed like he hadn't in years, and it felt good. The happy talk brought back recollections of the tree-climbing-kid-days of his youth. He'd allowed his feelings of unimportance and neglect to dominate for so long, he'd forgotten the happy times he'd enjoyed in childhood.

After dessert, Alex asked if Colton would excuse them. It was Charlie's bedtime.

"Mind if I use the bathroom before I leave?"

He followed them down the hall and said good night to Charlie at his bedroom door. Alex pushed the door closed, but for a slight crack. Colton continued down the hall to the bathroom. When he came back into the hall, he heard Charlie saying, "And bless Mr. McCreed." The words stopped him in his tracks. His chest tightened for a second time since Charlie had stepped onto his porch.

After his "Amen," Alex said, "Climb into bed now, sweetheart. It's late."

"Sing to me."

Colton leaned against the wall and listened to Alex sing "Dream A Little Dream Of Me". He stared at the wedding picture that emanated pure happiness, while listening to her lovely voice. With his full belly and pleasant surroundings, he was feeling quite content, and also slightly amazed that he'd enjoyed his time with mom and son. Even though all this domestic ambiance wasn't his usual scene, it was easy to be around Alex and Charlie.

Just as he pushed away from the wall, afraid he might fall asleep himself, he heard Charlie say, "Mom, I like Mr. McCreed."

"I'm glad, sweetheart, but he won't be in Eden Falls long."

"Why?"

"He's an author. That's someone who writes books. He's here to do research for his next book."

"What's re…search?"

"Research is when you study something. Mr. McCreed lives in a big city and he wants to write about a small town, so he's here to see what that feels like."

"And when he gets done he'll go back to his city?"

"That's right."

"But maybe he'll like it here and want to stay, because we're nice to him."

"Maybe, but I don't think that will happen, honey."

Colton could hear the smile in Alex's voice. He took a half step and peered into the room. Alex was sitting on the edge of her son's bed, stroking his black hair back from his forehead.

"But maybe he will," Charlie said.

"Maybe, but I don't want you to get your hopes up. He already has a home, and a family, and friends somewhere else." She paused a moment. "Charlie, I want you to remember Mr. McCreed is a very busy man, so you can't go over to the rental house and bother him, okay?"

"I didn't bother him. He said I could come up on the porch. He said I could have some of Patsy's chocolate chip cookies and I said no, thank you."

Alex smiled as she pulled the sheet up closer to her son's chin. "Thank you for using nice manners."

"Mom?"

"Hmm?"

"I told him my dad is dead."

Alex ran an index finger down her son's nose, causing his eyes to flutter closed. "That's okay, sweetheart."

Colton left his spot when Alex leaned down and kissed her

son's forehead. He wasn't ready to leave yet, so he sat on the sofa and looked around the living room for the first time. The house was small, like the one he was renting. It was uncluttered and modest, but comfortable and homey. Alex would have made it that way for her son. Was the one he was renting decorated for the husband who hadn't returned home to her?

"Can I get you anything?"

Her words startled him. He hadn't realized she'd come down the hall. "No, thanks." He watched as she sat on the other end of the sofa. "I hope you don't mind that Charlie told me about his father."

Her shoulders seemed to wilt slightly. "It's not a secret."

"Can I ask what happened?"

"He was killed by an IED."

He turned toward her, lifting a knee to the sofa. "How about a condensed version of you and him."

She studied him a moment. "Not for your book."

"No. Just to satisfy my own curiosity."

She tucked her feet up under herself and pulled a pillow into her arms like a protective shield. "Peyton Blackwood was one of my brother's best friends and, like JT, six years older. When I turned sixteen, he asked me out." Her gaze met his. "My parent's had a fit. Even though they'd known Peyton and his family forever, they thought he was too old for their little girl." She was quiet a moment, a sweet smile on her face. "He could have gone to college on a baseball scholarship, but with all that was going on in the world, he felt joining the Marines was the right thing to do. On his fourth tour of duty, a roadside bomb killed him the same day I discovered I was pregnant. Peyton never knew."

He raised his arm to the back of the sofa. Because of the wedding picture in the hallway, they'd obviously gotten married. Had her parents consented or had Alex and Peyton eloped? There were so many questions he wanted to ask but, all he could manage was, "I'm sorry, Alex."

One of her shoulders lifted in a slight shrug. "It was a long time ago and, as you can see, Charlie and I are doing okay."

She turned away, but he caught her misty eyes. Her false bravado was better than a crying female any day. "You both seem to be doing very well, under the circumstances."

There was a lull in their conversation, but it wasn't uncomfortable. He could hear the soft whir of the dishwasher at work, and the ticking of the clock on the mantel. The quiet was nice but didn't last long, because his curiosity got the better of him—again. "Do you date?"

He could tell by the flash in her eyes dating wasn't a subject she cared to discuss with him, but she'd asked her wife-and-children questions earlier. Now it was his turn.

"Not much. Most men don't want a ready made family, and I don't want Charlie getting attached to someone who isn't interested in him."

"Misty mentioned you and the fireman coaching Charlie's baseball team are an item."

"Brandt and I have dated a few times, but we're just friends."

He regarded the irritation that had settled between her brows and decided to turn the conversation a bit. "I don't think you having a child would detour me from asking you out."

Her frown deepened. "You're contradicting yourself. You said earlier that you don't want children."

"I don't, but kids don't have to be involved in the dating process."

"*Dating process?* Boy, you are a sweet talker."

He shook his head. *Women and their romantic expectations.* "Dating doesn't mean marrying. Dating is a process."

She stared at him a moment before the corners of her mouth lifted. "I think most daters would disagree. Dating isn't the process. Eliminating after the dating is the process."

"Eliminating is definitely a process, but only if you're looking for commitment. If not, dating is going out, having a good time, and enjoying the moment. I've dated women whose children I've never seen."

Her expression changed again. "I'm not interested in dating a man who wants nothing to do with my child. What would be the point?"

"The point would be two people hooking up, having a great time without sticky little fingers messing up their clothes, or whiny voices interrupting."

"*You* are exactly the kind of guy I wouldn't want parading through my house."

"We wouldn't be parading through your house." He flashed the smile that worked so well for him in bars and raised an eyebrow. "We'd be meeting for a nice dinner, followed by drinks at a club and then—"

She held up a hand to stop him. "I don't need to hear anymore. Let's just agree to *completely* disagree."

❧

*A*lex's first impression of Colton hadn't improved a whole lot. He seemed so detached and callous, void of warmth. His opinions were precise. Have a great time with no attachments. Leave your heart at home. What had caused those sentiments, and how could a person live that way for very long without their heart withering completely? Had some woman hurt him beyond repair? "Can I ask a question?"

"Sure."

"What if you'd fallen in love with the woman—the one with kids—and wanted to get married?"

"Wouldn't happen. I told you that earlier."

"Right, no wife, no commitments, but what if you had fallen in love?"

"I don't believe in love." He raised an ankle to the opposite knee. "I believe people can be overcome with passion, desire, lust, whatever word you want to give that emotion. We believe its love, so—because we're all selfish by nature—we make false promises in order to get what we want. We promise lifetimes, exclusivity, etcetera, but once the passion fades, the promises we made become lies."

Alex had never heard such a crock of crap in her life, had never met anyone as cynical as Colton McCreed. She couldn't even think of a response to his little speech. She knew she led a sheltered life in this sleepy town, and had never met anyone with Colton's worldly, self-centered point of view...except maybe Misty. He, like Misty, didn't seem to think of anyone else's feelings. They would either get along well or clash fiercely. She didn't want to be around for the latter.

He laughed. "You're speechless."

"I am."

"It's getting late." He stood. "I'll leave you to ponder my words."

I have better things to do with my time.

He turned at the door. "Thanks, again, for dinner, Mayor. I appreciate being included, even if you were forced by a five-year-old."

"You're welcome." She stopped just short of adding, "Anytime."

She watched Colton until he reached the sidewalk, and then shut the door. To her amazement, she did ponder his words. How was it possible to go through life and not believe in love? How would he describe his feelings toward his parents, his family, and friends, without the word love? You couldn't have a child and not believe the overpowering sensation that engulfed you was love.

She curled up on the sofa and her thoughts of love turned to Peyton. What she'd told Colton was true. Her parents had not been happy with her decision to marry right out of high school. The Garrett's knew Peyton, knew the man he'd become, and loved him as JT's friend. They also knew he'd seen much of the world and were afraid his knowledge, as well as the age difference, would be too much for their baby girl. They worried Peyton's absence would be a hardship on her, and wanted her to wait until Peyton got out of the Marines, or, better yet, until she graduated college. She had a close relationship with her parents and understood their concern, but she loved Peyton so completely, she couldn't imagine living life without him, which—in the end—was how things had ended.

She and Charlie now lived life without Peyton.

CHAPTER 6

Colton rarely attended weddings, especially when he didn't know the bride or groom, and wished he'd turned Misty's invitation down. With any luck, it would be as brief as the high school graduation. He checked the knot of his tie one last time and then glanced at his watch. Time to go.

Misty opened her apartment door and turned for him to admire. She was stunning with her jet-black hair and big blue eyes. He appreciated a woman with shapely legs, and typically, he didn't mind her showing them off, but Misty's sapphire blue, rhinestone studded mini dress seemed over the top for a small town wedding.

She ran her fingers down the lapels of his suit and batted her had-to-be-fake eyelashes. "We'll be the best looking couple there."

"Except for the bride and groom." He didn't like her easy use of the word couple. They would never be a couple.

She waved a dismissive hand. "We'll be show stoppers compared to them. Jolie is horse-faced with mousey colored hair, and Nate is nothing but a country bumpkin."

Great. Can't wait to witness two unattractive people tie the knot. "And we're going because?"

"I have to go. Jolie is a friend—sort of—and everyone in town will be there." She got a malicious grin. "I can't wait to stand her up. We'll be the couple everyone is watching."

There was that "couple" word, again. "Misty, we're not a couple. And why would you want to outdo a bride on her big day, especially if she's your friend?"

"We're not *close* friends," she said, ignoring his couple remark.

*O*nce inside the church, Colton recognized quite a few Eden Falls residents as they were shown to their seats. He nodded at Alice and Denny Garrett, and Rita Reynolds sent him a grin. Rance and Lily Johnson waved. He acknowledged the couple who lived next door to the house he rented. He'd been able to finagle another two days a week, plus laundry, out of Felicia Kerns.

Not long after they were seated, the organist began "Pachelbel – Canon in D". A single violin soon joined in, followed by another, and then a harp. The music was so simple, yet so moving, it raised the hair on Colton's arms.

The same preacher from the high school graduation walked through a side door at the front of the church and took his place. Colton's imagination was pretty vivid, but the tall slim man who walked out next did not meet his idea of a country bumpkin. He did, however, look as if he might throw-up all over his black tuxedo.

The first couple to walk down the aisle was Alex and Charlie's baseball coach. Alex's petite frame emphasized the fireman's build. He was over a foot taller than she was and had shoulders as broad as a barn. Alex looked pretty in her purple dress, her blond hair in a knot on the back of her head with a purple flower attached.

"Brandt has the I.Q. of a fruit fly. He's a fireman, because he doesn't have the brains to do anything else."

Colton glanced at Misty. "JT said he's the town's only paramedic."

"And Alex thinks she's so important because she was elected mayor," Misty continued as if he hadn't spoken. "She said she ran because she cared about the town, but I haven't seen her do anything very remarkable." Misty looked up at him. "Perhaps it's a Napoleon complex because she's so small."

A crazy defensiveness rose in Colton. He leaned close. "I believe your criticism of Alex is off-base. She won the office of mayor because the voters respect her."

Misty's eyes narrowed. "Why are you defending her?"

That's a very good question. "I've seen how much she cares for Eden Falls, and I've also seen the reaction she creates. She seems sincere, and most people admire that quality in a political leader."

"Leader?" She laughed loud enough to turn heads their way.

Misty kept up a running commentary of each couple as they entered and every fault they possessed—"Stella's makeup is too light." "Jillian needs an update on her hair color." "Jolie went overboard with so many bridesmaids, and the dresses she picked are hideous." "JT is convinced he's the sexiest man in town. When they passed out humility, he was too busy looking in a mirror."

Colton finally realized her remarks stemmed from jealousy. All her friends were in the wedding party, and she was watching from the sidelines. He was witnessing the reason.

The wedding was, by far, the smallest Colton had ever attended, but the setting was tranquil, and the ceremony short and sweet. Once the vows were repeated, and the groom's skin tone returned to normal, he walked his radiant bride down the aisle.

The congregation, clapping as the happy the bride and groom exited the church, would be disappointed when the couple's dream ended. Colton was sure they thought they were in love and that their union would last forever, but there was no such thing as happily ever after. One morning in the near future, one of them would wake up and realize it was all an illusion. Their fantasy would be replaced with real life, and real life sucked.

~

*A*lex knew Jolie had paired her with Brandt on purpose. They'd walked down the aisle together. Now, they were seated next to each other for dinner. Sometimes it seemed everyone in town was trying to match her with someone, when she wasn't ready to be matched. She believed, when the right man came along she'd know it, just as she'd known it with Peyton. She wasn't close-minded to the idea of loving again; she just wouldn't settle for anything less than the true love she'd shared with Peyton.

Alex looked around at the tables filled with well-wishers. Events at The Dew Drop Inn were bittersweet for her. Eight years earlier, she and Peyton had held their reception here. She'd sat in the same place as tonight, looking into the eyes of the man she thought she'd spend forever with. Every time she stepped inside the Inn, haunting memories filled her. Unfortunately, it was the only place in town with a room big enough to hold a reception of any size, except the high school gym. No amount of flowers, tulle, or lattice could transform a school gymnasium into an enchanted evening for a bride.

After dinner and toasts, the dancing began. Alex excused

herself from the table before Brandt felt obligated to ask. She made her way around the room, stopping to speak to the bride's parents and then the groom's. She'd known both families her whole life. She posed for a couple of photos and then, literally ran into Colton McCreed. His hair was still a mess, and he had three-day-old whiskers on a face that was more angles than curves, but he looked quite handsome in his expensive suit. Then again, who wouldn't look attractive with the beautiful Misty on their arm?

"Mr. McCreed, you clean up nicely."

"So do you, Mayor."

"That's a pretty dress, Misty."

Misty's eyes traveled Alex's length. "No offense, Alex, but that dress does nothing for your…"

Alex stopped listening after *"no offense"*, because she knew Misty's insult wasn't far behind. Did people suppose the words no offense excused them from the hurtful remark that always followed?

Luckily, Jolie's mother interrupted the conversation. "Alex, everyone's remarking on the gorgeous flowers. I've already handed out all the Pretty Posies business cards you gave me."

"I'm glad you—"

"Wait." Colton turned from Jolie's mom to her. "You work at Pretty Posies?"

"She doesn't work there, she owns Pretty Posies." Jolie's mom hugged her. "I just wanted to say thank you. The arrangements turned out more beautiful than Jolie or I imagined."

"You're welcome."

Jolie's mother turned as a guest called her name.

"*You* own Pretty Posies?"

Misty frowned up at Colton. "It's no big deal."

"Why is everything I do so shocking to you, Mr. Mc-

Creed? You were insulted when I picked you up from the airstrip, and laughed when I told you I owned the house you're renting. You were stunned to find out I'm a mayor, spit out your breakfast when you discovered I have a son, and now you're astonished that I own a flower shop."

Colton lifted his eyebrows. "I see Little Miss Sunshine has a temper."

"You should see her when—"

"There must be medication for whatever it is you have," Alex said, interrupting Misty. She spun on her heel and walked away.

Do I really have to put up with his idiocy all summer?

She spotted Jillian sitting at a table rubbing the arch of her bare foot, and sat in the vacant chair next to her.

Jillian grimaced. "These shoes are killing me."

Jillian worked as a personal trainer at the gym Alex's aunt and uncle owned, and lived in athletic shoes, so Alex could sympathize. "How's work?"

"Busy. Now that school is out, I've started teaching swim lessons at the city pool three mornings a week."

"I bet that's fun."

"For who?" Jillian asked with a smile. "Most kids are terrified of the water. I spend half my time coaxing and bribing. I had to chase a kid down yesterday."

Alex smiled back. She could imagine it would take the patience of Job, but Jillian possessed that special characteristic, as did Stella. They were both wonderful with kids.

Jillian kicked off her other shoe and went to work massaging her instep while watching the dance floor. Alex turned to see who had caught her friend's attention. Brandt was dancing with one of Jolie's cousins.

A light bulb flashed on—Brandt and Jillian. Both were tall, athletic, and outdoorsy. Jillian was a personal trainer who swam, hiked, biked, and ran. Brandt wasn't just a firefighter, but a paramedic, who spent as much time outdoors as possible. She glanced back out at the dance floor, and then at Jillian who was still watching. She might have to make a subtle suggestion to Brandt, because Jillian was much too shy to take matters into her own hands.

"It didn't take Misty long to latch on to the author."

Alex noticed Misty walking toward the restroom. Colton stood next to the bar staring at her and Jillian. She turned her back on him. "It never does."

"Have you read any of his books?"

Alex shook her head. "Not yet."

"I helped Lily Johnson unload a new shipment of library books. Several were his."

"My dad and Rowdy have both read his books and said they're good."

Jillian nodded her head to the right. "He's coming over."

"Evening, ladies." Colton slid into the chair next to Alex.

Fabulous.

She ignored his and Jillian's conversation as she glanced around the room. Stella and Rowdy were laughing together. JT was talking to the cousin Brandt had been dancing with earlier. Jolie's parents were dancing next to the bride and groom.

Colton stood. "Mayor, can I have this dance?"

She glared up at him. "I don't feel like dancing."

He pulled her up by the elbow. "Excuse us, Jillian. I have some groveling to do."

Colton led her to the dance floor, and twirled her into his arms. Okay, so he had some nice moves and nice manners—when he thought to pull them out—and he smelled incredible. But she wasn't letting him off the hook just because he'd worn a spectacular scent.

"Start groveling."

"You kind of hurt my feelings with your medication remark."

She pulled back. "I hurt *your* feelings?"

"Kind of. It's not my fault *you* keep surprising me with these revelations."

She released a half laugh. "You just turned the blame on me."

Colton gave her a sexy grin that in all probability never failed him in these situations. It did nothing for her. Well, maybe a little something, down deep in the pit of her stomach.

"You weren't supposed to notice that," he said.

She used one of Stella's signature eye-rolls. "Obviously."

"Look, I'm sorry, Alex."

She studied him a moment. He looked serious…and contrite.

"No more mistakes." To her surprise, he dipped her and whispered near her ear. "I know all your secrets."

She stared into his stormy eyes. "I don't have any secrets, Mr. McCreed."

He lifted her upright and tucked her close. "Not now that I've discovered them."

"I never had secrets to begin with."

He relaxed his hold. "Okay, can you give me a break here? Please? I am sorry that I've been jumping to so many conclusions about you. I've been unfair. You are a very capable mayor, and a great mom." He stopped dancing and waved his hand around. "And these are just about the best flowers I've ever seen."

She laughed. "You are so full of it. You don't know anything about my mothering or my mayoring, and you probably don't know a daisy from a dahlia."

∼

*C*olton laughed along with Alex. She made it easy. Smiling and laughing seemed as simple as breathing for her. "You're wrong. I've seen the mayor in action, and she was riveting. I've also seen the mother. She's very patient and sweet, yet parental with her son. You're obviously good as a businesswoman, or you wouldn't be asked to do"—he waved his hand around again—"whatever it is you do for a wedding. And I do know what a daisy is. As for the other flower you mentioned…not a clue."

"Wow, there were several more compliments in that little speech."

"Oh, and I think you look amazing in that dress." Her reaction to his glance traveling down her body did just as he'd intended. The blush that stained her cheeks was innocent, yet, surprisingly sexy at the same time. Her eyes flashed with heat. What would show in those mossy green depths when she was in the throes of passion?

He squashed the thought as soon as it popped into his head, unsure where it had come from.

The music stopped and she stepped away. "Thanks for the apology, the compliments, and the dance, Mr. McCreed."

He winked and her blush deepened. "You have a nice evening, Mayor."

CHAPTER 7

Alex pulled her Jeep to a stop in the rental house driveway. Crazy as it sounded, she enjoyed mowing. Neither of her yards were big, and the physical labor wasn't major, but it felt good. Each gave her fifty minutes to do something as mundane as walking back and forth, clearing her mind, and relaxing.

She and Eden Falls' town manager, a pompous know-it-all, were at odds over purchasing books and supplies for the library. He planned to order what he thought they needed rather than consulting with Lily Johnson, who'd been Eden Falls' librarian since the library had opened it's doors. Alex had torn up the order and told him to talk to Lily first. That they were at odds was nothing new. He seemed to thrive on arguing over every tidbit of business that arose between them. He was a big man who used his size to intimidate. After eighteen months of working with her, he'd finally realized she didn't intimidate easily, so he created conflict for the mayor's office every chance he got. The whole situation was beyond frustrating.

She pulled the mower from the shed and pushed it around

to the front yard. That would allow Colton a few more minutes of sleep, though she wasn't sure why she was accommodating him. So far, he'd proven himself to be a self-absorbed, arrogant pig, who, despite all his reckless assumptions, made her laugh.

~

*C*olton opened an eye at the familiar noise and smiled. Saturday morning—the mayor was mowing. A groan reminded him that he wasn't alone, causing *him* to want to groan.

"What is that racket?" Misty mumbled.

He swung his legs over the side of the bed and stood. "Alex is mowing the lawn."

She squinted up at him with her amazing blue eyes. "Can't she mow some other time?"

He pulled a T-shirt from a hanger; grateful Felicia Kerns had agreed to do his laundry. "Charlie must have a game this morning."

"Can't she mow after the game?"

He didn't answer as he pulled on a pair of jeans.

A frown line creased her brows. "Where are you going?"

"To get a cup of coffee. I have to work today."

"Mmm…breakfast in bed? You're so sweet."

He ruffled a hand through his hair as he looked back over his shoulder. "I'm not sure how you got 'breakfast in bed' from 'I'm going to get a cup of coffee'. I don't cook."

She got up on an elbow. "You could take me out for breakfast."

"I just told you, I have to work."

"You also have to eat."

She's going to push this. "Misty, last night was great, but, as I explained before you spent the night, I don't do relation-ships or commitments."

She sat up letting the sheet slip to her waist and batted her mascara matted lashes, her black hair falling in a waterfall of messy curls. "What happens if you fall in love?"

He planted both hands on either side of the doorframe. "I've been told I'm incapable of that emotion."

She pursed her lips into a pout. "But it's possible."

"Not for me. I like my life the way it is and have no inten-tion of making any changes."

"I don't see how you can say you'll never fall in love. You can't—"

"Misty, this is non-negotiable." He pushed away from the door. "I'm not interested in more than what we just had. I've been up front with you from the beginning, and you agreed. You won't change my mind if countless other women haven't been able to."

"Countless?" Misty narrowed her eyes. "You're a little full of yourself, don't you think?"

Maybe countless was an exaggeration, but he'd stopped keeping track years ago. He'd also stopped sleeping with women who showed any inclination to want to change him. "Get dressed, and I'll take you home. I have a lot of work to do."

He stopped at the front window on his way to the kitchen. Alex was still working there. He started a pot of coffee, then took a quick shower. Fifteen minutes later, he stepped onto the back patio. Alex had just rounded the corner of the house. She stopped, pulled the bag from the back of the mower, and dumped the grass clippings in a nearby container. She was so deep in thought she didn't see him until he shut the mower off.

"Morning, Mayor."

She pulled an earbud from her right ear. "Morning, McCreed."

Good. At least she'd dropped the mister. The title made him feel old. "You still mad at me?"

"No." She reattached the mower bag. "You're lucky I don't hold grudges. I might turn into a character from one of your novels."

He raised his eyebrows. "You've read my books?"

"No, but Rowdy tells me they're pretty gruesome." She looked toward the mountain peaks. "There are a lot of places a body could go missing out here."

Colton laughed at her implication. Little Miss Sunshine probably released spiders, rather than squashing them. "I'll keep that in mind. Does Charlie have a game this morning?"

"At eleven."

"How about a cup of coffee?"

"No thanks." She reached for the starter, but he moved his hand to stop her.

"You left the reception kind of early last night."

"Yes, I did."

"You left with the firefighter who walked you down the aisle."

She shifted her weight to one hip as she studied him. "I didn't know anyone was keeping tabs."

"Just me. Your secret's safe."

She released her rusty laugh. "Sorry to disappoint you, McCreed, but, as I told you last night, I have no secrets. I'm a public figure, so my life is an open book. We had a similar conversation about Brandt Smith a few nights ago, and I told you then he and I are just friends. He just walked me to my car."

Misty, enveloped provocatively in a sheet, chose that moment to step out of the house. The sheet was wrapped tight, and draped low in all the right places. She must have taken some time in front of a mirror to get not only the sheet, but also her hair, just right.

"I thought you were coming back to bed." Misty glanced past him. "Oh, hi, Alex."

"Morning, Misty. You need to pull that sheet up in the back a little before Felicia Kerns calls JT to complain."

Misty batted her lashes innocently. "You think she'll be upset to find her husband peeking out the window?"

"I think she'll be upset to find her fourteen-year-old son peeking out the window."

"Oh, that's right." Misty turned toward the Kern's home. "Cute little Erick is probably home..."

"Go put your clothes on, Misty," Colton said.

Alex lowered a lever, pulled a cord, and pushed away from them.

"Aren't you coming back to bed?"

Colton turned his attention from Alex to Misty. "I told you I have to work. Get dressed and I'll take you home."

Misty stormed inside and he followed, already regretting their night together.

Thirty minutes later, Colton dropped an angry Misty off at her apartment and headed for the ballpark after a quick stop at Patsy's Pastries. It was a perfect, sunshiny, summer day, and games were underway on every field. The aroma of grilled hotdogs and fresh popcorn, greeted him as soon as he stepped from the car. He spotted Alex and climbed the bleachers just as Charlie's game started. "Mind if I join you?"

She looked past him. "You're Misty-less."

He scooted her over with his knee and sat. "I told her I had to work."

"And yet you're here."

He shrugged. "Research."

Alex looked toward the dugout and whistled when Charlie's team took the field. Her son ran out and took his place at shortstop, smacking a fist into his mitt and bending forward in anticipation.

Colton stayed the whole game, cheering for Charlie and the rest of his team, along with Alex and all the other parents. Surreal, a place he never would have imagined himself to be on a Saturday morning, cheering a bunch of five-year-olds to victory. Unexpectedly, it felt...right.

Brandt Smith shot a couple of glances their way. Colton wanted to reassure the guy there was no reason to worry. Whether they were just friends, as Alex said, or not, he had no intention of moving in on Mr. Universe's territory.

When the game was over, Charlie hugged both sets of grandparents before charging up the bleachers to get his hug from mom and a high five from Colton.

"Great game, Hotrod."

"Did you see my hits?"

"Yep, I also saw that catch you made. Great job!" Colton exaggerated his enthusiasm for the kid's sake. The enormous smile on Charlie's face loosened the lock on his big empty heart just a smidgeon.

"Thanks. Uncle JT is taking us for pizza and then we're going fishing. Wanna come?"

JT had followed Charlie up the bleachers and plopped down next to Alex. "You're welcome to join us," he said to Colton.

"It's going to have to be the three of you for pizza," Alex said. "I got a late order for a birthday bouquet. I'll have to meet you at the river later this afternoon."

"Do you ever get a day off?" Colton asked.

"Mmm...Not very often."

"I'll keep Charlie," JT said. He pulled his nephew

between his knees. "We'll grab some pizza and then bring a couple of slices to the shop before we hit the river."

"I don't want to mess up your plans."

"You're not messing them up. We're just changing them a bit. Right, Charlie?"

"Yeah, Mom. Change of plans."

"Well, I'd love a couple of slices. Thanks." She patted her brother's knee.

Taking care of Charlie wasn't just on Alex's shoulders. Raising the kid was a family affair. The only child of absent parents, Colton had grown up ignored and lonely. When he was young, he'd wanted a brother or a sister, maybe one of each. His nanny said, "Be careful what you wish for." He should have listened, because he'd gotten those siblings as a teenager—several steps and halfs from both his mom and dad's remarriages. He wasn't close to any of them, primarily by his own choice. He found most of them greedy and self-serving like his parents. And himself. But hey, the apple didn't fall far...

With only a couple fly-fishing lessons under his belt, he decided writing the afternoon away was a better option than going to the river. He wanted to be able to hold his own, before showing up in waders to make a fool of himself, but he joined JT and Charlie for pizza.

He spent most of their lunchtime fascinated by the loving banter uncle and nephew shared. Interaction of that kind was alien to him. JT and Charlie's relationship left him with a yearning that he'd repeatedly experienced since stepping into this strange, new world that was Eden Falls. The yearning had been imbedded deep in his soul as a small child and grew stronger as he observed parents with their children in what he considered a normal way of life.

One particular event came to mind unbidden. Henry, the family chauffeur, dropped him off at the library. After picking out a few books, he found a comfortable chair near the children's section. He planned to read until it was time for Henry to pick him up, but a mother reading to her children on the other side of a dividing wall interrupted his plans. The longing to be included was overpowering, the spell only broken when Henry reappeared to take him home.

~

*A*lex always spent Monday's in the mayor's office. After the weekend, Pretty Posies was usually slow. Tatum Ellis, Alex's right hand at the flower shop, along with Stella, who helped out during summer break, kept things running smoothly so Alex could take care of Eden Falls' business. She spent the first two hours of her morning with the Fourth of July committee reviewing plans for the holiday parade and ensuring everything was on schedule. Two late entries for floats had come in, and the 4-H club was still waiting for the State Health Department to okay a hotdog stand in the park. Then the lineup for "The Summer Concert in the Park" series had to be tweaked because the lead singer of the Jewel Tones, the first band on the schedule, was having his tonsils removed. Lucky for them, Maude Stapleton's son had a garage band that was thrilled to fill the spot.

Alex struggled to keep her mind on business, as the picture of Misty wrapped in a sheet traipsed through her thoughts. At the time, she'd been annoyed. She knew Misty would be all over Colton from the day she'd picked him up at the airstrip. Why did it bother her that he'd succumbed? No man, it seemed, was immune to Misty's wiles—except Brandt. Misty had propositioned him soon after he'd moved to town and he'd turned her down. Misty had considered him her sworn enemy ever since.

Alex turned her attention back to the budget for the kids summer recreational program.

Her part-time assistant, Camille, leaned through her open door. "Alex, this is—"

Before Alex could stand to greet the man standing next to Camille, he doubled over with laughter.

"Oh, man! I see why Colton was spitting mad at me. You look way too young to be running a town." He stepped inside her office and held out his hand. "Jorge Reis, but you can call me—"

"Jorgie," Alex said as she shook the man's hand. It was a name she wouldn't be able to use, especially after putting a face to the name. In her mind, a Jorgie should be short, robust, and red-cheeked. This guy was tall, lean, and movie star handsome. Dressed in creased khakis and a cobalt blue dress shirt, he could have walked off the pages of *GQ*.

He aimed startling blue eyes that were filled with amusement at her, then turned and winked at Camille. "Thanks, sweetheart."

Camille lifted an eyebrow at Alex before closing the door.

"Have a seat, Mr. R...Jorge." She indicated one of the chairs in front of her desk. "Mr. McCreed didn't mention you were coming to town."

"Mr. McCreed?" Jorge laughed, again. "Mr. McCreed doesn't know I'm here. I thought I'd surprise him. I had some business in Seattle and decided to rent a car and drive over at the last minute."

She leaned back in her chair. "Welcome to Eden Falls."

"Thank you. I can see why tourists flock here. The town is very quiet and quaint. I'll bet our boy is going stir crazy by now."

The image of Misty wrapped in a sheet flitted through Alex's mind again, like the scene from a horror movie burned into her brain. She pushed the image aside. What Colton Mc-

Creed did with his spare time was none of her business. "Actually, Colton seems to be enjoying himself."

Jorge crossed an ankle over the opposite knee. "Is he getting any work done?"

Did *just call me Jorgie* expect she was babysitting *our boy*? "I have no idea. If going to ball games, weddings, graduations, and visiting the local bar and pastry shop is his equivalent of research, then I'd say he's getting a lot of work done."

Her answer brought on another burst of laughter. "Oh, man, Colton has his hands full with you. The house he's renting is close by, right? Let's drive over and see if he's even started on that book."

The man must think I have nothing better to do than chauffer him around town. Sadly, she didn't. Other than finishing the budget, she didn't have anything else on her plate until two, when she was speaking at the Eden Falls Senior Center. "Sure, I can drive you over."

"How about I drive? Colton e-mailed me about that rusty old Jeep of yours. I saw it in the parking lot and had to take a picture—a vehicle from *Deliverance*."

"Okay, you drive," Alex said, amused at his reference. Her rental was only a few blocks from the square. She'd walk back.

"This *is* a small town," Jorge said, when they pulled to a stop at the curb minutes later.

Jorge stood to her side when Alex knocked. Colton opened the front door. Shirtless. She diverted her eyes as her cheeks heated.

He pushed the screen open. "Hey, Sunshine. To what do I owe—?" His smile disappeared when he spotted Jorge. "What are you doing here?"

"Hello to you, too." Jorge chuckled. "I came to make sure everything was going okay."

"If you were so concerned, you wouldn't have ignored my calls for almost two weeks."

"I returned your calls when I knew you'd calmed down." Jorge stepped around Alex and entered the house. "Everything worked out just fine, didn't it?"

Alex tried to look anywhere but at Colton's bare chest. *How does a guy who sits behind a computer all day have a chest that looks like that?* "Okay, well, it was nice to meet you, Jorge."

She turned to leave, but Colton snagged her arm. "Where are you going?"

"I'm sure you two have some catching up to do." Her traitorous eyes slid down his chest to his abs.

He noticed her gaze and grinned. "You have to stay, Alex. We need a referee to make sure there's no bloodshed. Jorge is lucky I've gotten over the worst of my mad, but he still has some making up to do. He's going to take us both out for a nice lunch."

She stepped inside and noticed right away that Colton had moved the kitchen table into the screened porch, a perfect place to write. Other than that, everything looked as it had the last time she'd said good-bye to her husband.

Peyton had been so proud of this house and the fact that he could buy it for her. While deployed, she'd worked hard, along with her father, JT, and all the Blackwood men, to get the fixer-upper into shape. She'd filled it with hand-me-down furniture and homemade drapes, finishing just in time for another homecoming. Peyton had walked around the outside and then from room to room, paying attention to every detail with open appreciation.

For the short time they'd had together, they'd made this house their home. She still loved the house, but couldn't bring herself to sleep here without him. She also wasn't able to sell it until she found someone who would love it as much as she and Peyton had. She glanced at the big throw rug under her feet remembering the day they'd brought it home, rolled it out, and...

"You okay, Alex?" Colton walked into the room, sliding his arms into a T-shirt.

"Yes." She watched the muscles bunch and bulge under his skin as he pulled the shirt over his head. "I...I'm fine."

"This place is great," Jorge yelled from the backyard.

*J*orge took them to Renaldo's Italian Kitchen. Alex tried to decline the offer of lunch, but both Jorge and Colton ignored her argument. "I'm taking you to lunch, Alex. It's the least I can do to repay you for putting up with this guy."

"He's right," Colton said. "It is the *least* he can do. Jorge is all about the least he can do."

"What are you talking about? I'm the one that made all of this possible. Look at this place, Colton." Jorge waved his arm around. "You're in the Garden of Eden—get it, Eden Falls, Garden of Eden—for the whole summer." He slipped an arm around Alex's shoulder and pulled her close. "And the mayor here is Eve herself."

"Okay. Down boy," Colton said, putting himself between Jorge and Alex as they walked inside. "Alex doesn't date men over forty, so that takes you out of the running."

"Only by a year. You'd make an exception wouldn't you, sweetheart?" She didn't have time to respond before he said, "Oh, Colton, I forgot to tell you your mom called. She said she stopped by your house and your wicked housekeeper wouldn't say where you were."

"She got in touch with me."

"Does your mother live close to you?" Alex asked.

"Too close." Colton steered her to a booth with a hand on

her back, and then slid in next to her. Jorge took the other side.

That was all the answer she got. His lowered brows and the turbulence brewing in the gray depths of his eyes warned her not to pursue the subject.

Lunch was wonderfully entertaining. Colton and Jorge bantered back and forth, showing no mercy in their quest to belittle each other. She witnessed a side of Colton she'd never seen. Once the ominous exterior lifted, he was charming and funny and...moderately likeable.

Halfway through their pizza, a real storm brewed. Misty walked in, took one look at the booth where she and Colton were sitting next to each other, and stalked over. Without a word, she slid in next to Jorge.

He turned to her with raised eyebrows. "Hello."

She flipped her hair over her shoulder and blinked big, blue eyes. "Mind if I join you?"

Jorge glanced at Colton first and then Alex. "Friend of yours?"

"Misty Douglas, this is Jorge Reis, my business manager. We're having a meeting."

A warning flashed across her face. "The three of you were laughing way too hard to be having a meeting"—she nodded at Alex—"and how does she have anything to do with your business?"

"She's our fair and completely impartial mediator, though I think she's leaning toward me," Jorge said.

Misty leaned toward Jorge. "I can be fair and impartial. What is she mediating?"

Jorge pointed between himself and Colton. "Anything to do with the two of us needs mediating. Eve here—"

"Eve?" Misty turned lethal eyes on Alex. "Did you tell him your name is Eve?"

"Eve is a nickname I gave her." Jorge winked at Colton

and Alex with the eye Misty couldn't see. "Anyway, gorgeous, we have to get back to business; so, if you'll excuse us."

Jorge's dismissal wouldn't sit well with Misty. She glanced from one of them to the other. Alex watched the wheels in her head turning, summing up the situation, trying to figure out how she could come out ahead. Jorge was a handsome man, impressively dressed for casual Eden Falls. Would she try to use him to make Colton jealous, or just use him? Sad that Misty was so transparent, but also beneficial. Her beacon flashed like a lighthouse on a rocky shore, warning of impending danger. Too bad not everyone knew the signs, or heeded the warning.

Misty stood, still calculating her options, before choosing indifference. "I can't stay anyway. I'll see you later, Colton."

Colton didn't nod or make a verbal commitment. Had the sun already stopped shining on Misty's fairytale island?

❧

*A*fter lunch, the three of them stood on the sidewalk facing Town Square. Colton put a hand to his belly, full and satisfied. He'd grown comfortable with his surroundings. As crazy as it sounded, he felt more at home here than in L.A. The manuscript he'd struggled with for months was coming together. He was pretty pleased with his circumstances, with Eden Falls, with the rental. Jorge was awed by the mountain view and the pretty park before him.

"This is where I leave you gentlemen."

Alex's words brought him back to the moment.

"What? Why? I don't want to spend the rest of the afternoon alone with Colton."

Alex turned to Jorge, but placed a hand on Colton's arm. An unusual warmth spread from the spot she touched. "I have a prior commitment, but Colton knows the town well enough. He can show you around and introduce you to some of Patsy's *sweet pleasures* for dessert."

Jorge cocked an eyebrow at her words.

Alex laughed and the rusty sound hit Colton in the chest. He rubbed the heel of his hand against his breastbone at the unusual feeling.

She held out her hand. "It was nice to meet you, Jorge."

Jorge pulled her in for a quick hug. "Believe me, the pleasure was all mine."

Colton stood in the shade of a tree with Jorge, and watched Alex cross the street. She had on a skirt just tight enough that Colton could see her fanny twitching from side to side.

"She might look young, but she knows her stuff."

Colton nodded. "Yes, she does. Did you know she owns the flower shop across the square?" Colton pointed out Pretty Posies. "And she has a five-year-old son."

"No way is she old enough to have a—"

"Believe me, I've gotten myself into all kinds of trouble making assumptions, and most of my blunders could have been avoided if you'd done a little more research on the mayor."

Jorge glanced over at him with an odd expression.

Colton frowned. "Why are you looking at me like that?"

"You're different. I can't pinpoint a specific thing, but this town is changing you."

"No."

Jorge nodded his head. "I mean it. You look—I gasp at the thought—happy."

Colton snorted. "I'm the same guy I've always been. Nothing's changed."

"You laughed more during lunch than I've ever heard you

laugh before. You're actually happy." Jorge smiled. "It looks good on you. "

"Shut up," Colton grumbled.

Jorge looked across the street in the direction Alex had gone. "Maybe you could try some of that happy on our little Eve."

"First of all, she isn't *our* little Eve. Second, don't try that psycho mumbo jumbo on me." He looked off across the square. Patsy's Pastries beckoned him with sugar-laced fingers. "I have no interest in the mayor. You know I don't do kids and she's got one, so don't go there."

"What about the woman who interrupted our lunch?"

Colton shook his head. "Don't go there, either. I did and regret it." He lifted his chin. "Hey, Rance."

Rance stopped to pat Colton on a shoulder. "Hey, Colton. Ready for your next lesson?"

"Tomorrow at ten."

"Lesson?" Jorge asked.

Rance glanced at Jorge. "Fly fishing."

Jorge released a booming laugh. "This town isn't changing you. It already has."

~

*A*lex pushed back from the dinner table to answer the knock she'd been expecting. Misty didn't wait for an invitation, just stormed into the living room as soon as Alex opened the door.

"What are you trying to do, get Colton for yourself?"

"Keep your voice down, Misty. Charlie's in the kitchen."

"He is *so* not your type, and I saw him first," Misty said, ignoring her as usual.

Alex held up her hand. "Technically, I saw Colton first, but there is nothing going on between us. His business manager came to my office and asked me to show him where Colton was staying. They invited me to lunch."

Misty crossed her arms. "I thought it was a business meeting."

"Jorge told you that to be nice. You were going to cause a scene, and he was trying to stop you. It was an innocent lunch."

Misty glared at Alex. She looked like a spoiled child not getting her way. Alex nodded toward the kitchen. "Would you like to join us for dinner?"

Misty stalked into the kitchen and helped herself to the extra pork chop and potatoes Alex made, in expectation of this visit. "How come I wasn't invited to have lunch? Why you?"

Misty was like a dog with a favorite chew toy. She wouldn't let go without baring her teeth and growling a few times. "Misty, it meant nothing."

"If it meant nothing, why did you and Colton look so cozy?"

Alex glanced at her son who looked up wide-eyed at the mention of Colton's name. "Mr. McCreed is my friend."

CHAPTER 8

Colton couldn't remember a more beautiful morning. He was walking and he was enjoying nature, which was completely out of character for him. He didn't walk anywhere in L.A. Never stopped to enjoy the rustle of leaves in the trees or notice the green of the grass. In fact, he couldn't remember ever feeling so at peace with his life. The agitation and gloom that ran through him like blood through veins was slowly leaking away. He stopped to watch a cloud float by.

"Hi, Mr. McCreed!"

Charlie, wearing his usual happy face, stood outside Patsy's Pastries with JT.

"Uncle JT said I could get a donut. Want to come?"

"Absolutely."

They reached the pastry case just as Patsy came through the kitchen door.

"A gorgeous morning, and three good looking men in my shop. This must be my lucky day." She leaned forward. "I hear you're learning to fish, Colton."

That little tidbit was something he wanted to keep to himself a bit longer.

"Why didn't you come to the river with us on Saturday?" JT asked.

"Until I can create the art form you do, my feeble attempts are best unobserved by anyone but Rance."

JT grinned. "Everyone has to learn. We wouldn't take too many pictures, and *I* wouldn't post anything on social media. Can't speak for the rest of the county."

Yeah, that's what I need, a video of me flinging my line up into the treetops all over social media. Colton turned to Patsy. "Thanks for sharing."

"Anytime, sweetheart. What can I get you?"

"I'm trying to wean myself from this madness. I came in a whole hour later than yesterday. At this rate, I'll weigh three-hundred pounds by the time I go back to L.A."

"You'll be the handsomest three-hundred pounder around," Patsy said with a wink.

After they made their choices, JT invited Colton to join them at a table under the green awnings out front. "Charlie, you need to eat fast, or you'll be late."

"I'll eat on the way." He stuffed a hunk of chocolate glazed donut into his mouth and took off at a jog down the sidewalk.

"Don't forget to chew," JT called out.

Charlie waved without looking back.

JT ran fingers through his hair. "I'm going to catch it for letting Charlie have donuts for breakfast again."

"Did you have him overnight?"

"No, Alex had an early morning meeting." He leaned back in his chair as Charlie disappeared through Pretty Posies door. "Man, I love that kid. I remember the day I found out about Peyton—worst day of my life—my best friend gone at such a young age, leaving my little sister a widow. Then the day Charlie was born, he had all this black hair sticking up in every direction and these chubby little cheeks. My heart melted into a puddle."

Colton wasn't sure how to respond. Sharing feelings wasn't his forte, so he sat quiet.

JT rubbed a hand along his jaw. "I've tried to fill the empty spot of father for Charlie, but sometimes I feel it's not enough. Alex is such a great mom, and Charlie is lucky to have two sets of grandparents close by to help, but I still feel he's getting shortchanged. He deserves more. So does Alex."

"Charlie is a nice kid. Your family has done a great job of raising him. I'm sure, if Peyton could, he'd say the same thing."

"You're right. He would." JT shook his head. "Even after all this time, I still miss him, you know?"

Colton didn't know. He'd never had a friend mean that much to him. Another wave of envy settled over him. This time he could only blame himself. He'd spent his childhood and teen years trying to get his parents attention, trying to be noticed by them. His adulthood was spent moving in the opposite direction, pushing not only them, but also everyone else away. He was a closed off, hardhearted person by choice. He had plenty of acquaintances, but no true friends. He kept people at arms length by choice. He probably should have gotten psychological counseling when he was younger, but he deemed himself too far-gone to care about such things at this late date.

"Sorry to dump on you. It just gets to me every once in a while."

Colton leaned back in his chair and tried to act as if listening to people's problems was an every day occurrence. "Not a problem."

JT watched morning traffic circle the square. "Tell me about life in the big city."

"You've never lived in a big city?"

"No. Well, I went to college in Montana." JT waved to a passerby. "Billings is more populated than here, but it's not Los Angeles."

"Well, imagine the complete opposite of here. Noise. Smog. Crime."

"Lots of parties?"

"Some." Colton shrugged. "Same people, different venue. It gets old."

Colton looked out at the lazy little town coming to life for the day. "When I first arrived in Eden Falls, I was afraid I'd get claustrophobic, but so far, it hasn't happened. I don't miss the constant ring of the phone or the doorbell—not that I answer it much. My housekeeper takes care of that." *Usually by pretending not to speak English.* "I'm enjoying the quiet."

"I bet the nights in Eden Falls are boring for you."

The nights hadn't been boring—not at all. "Different. Relaxing. Do you know the only person to come to my door since I've been here, besides Misty, has been Charlie?"

"Uh, oh." JT glanced his way. "Has he been a problem?"

"Any other time I would say yes. Kids—not my thing. Don't like them. Don't want them. But Charlie is..." He chuckled. "Charlie. He's different. He makes me laugh. He can be a little touchy, feely at times. He likes to hold hands, but I guess all kids are like that. Especially if they have an affectionate mother."

They sat in companionable silence for several minutes. The sun was shining, the birds were singing, and Colton felt a part of his surroundings. Rack up a first—not only was he feeling this way, but he was acknowledging the fact.

"I know you workout at the gym, but if you're ever interested, I run the trail along the river up to the falls most mornings—weather permitting. It's an easy—"

"Yeah, running a trail sounds a little too close to nature for me. I think I'll stick to the treadmill," Colton said.

A car horn honked and they both glanced toward the street. Misty held up her hand to stop another car before she stepped onto the sidewalk.

"Uh, oh," JT said for the second time since they'd sat down. "A quick word of warning—Misty will go to just about any lengths to get what she wants, and what she wants, this week, is you."

Misty stopped in front of them, hands on hips, staring at Colton. "Why haven't you called me?"

You are going to be the biggest mistake I've made in a very long time. "I've been busy."

"You're too busy to call me, but you're not too busy to sit here eating donuts with JT."

He lifted a shoulder. "I'm conducting research."

She leaned forward, until her nose was just inches from his. "You think I'm stupid enough to believe that?"

"I think you're having trouble understanding that I came to Eden Falls to write."

"I didn't have any trouble understanding you on Friday night, did I?"

JT pushed back his chair and stood. "This is where I say have a nice day and disappear."

She turned to him with a smirk. "Jealous?"

JT's gaze raked Misty from her over-made-up eyes to her red-painted toes. "Not in the least."

Misty's lips thinned into an angry line. The tension that beat between them was almost visible.

"I'll catch you later, Colton."

"See ya, JT."

~

*A*lex moved around her small flower shop with a delighted familiarity. She knew every inch of this place, every nook, and cranny. She'd spent almost as much time here as she had at home or in school. She'd grown up here, working side by side with Grandma Garrett. Not only had her grandmother taught her the name of each flower, she'd also shown her how to arrange those flowers into bouquets to show them off to their best advantage. Watching Grandma Garrett put together an arrangement had been like watching someone perform a magic trick. A flip of the wrist, a sleight of hand—Presto! Grandma Garrett had also guided her through the business side of owning a flower shop. She'd taught Alex the importance of meticulous record keeping, working with snarky brides, or grieving spouses. It was all part of owning a flower shop, and she loved every second of her time here.

Her shop was the one spot in town where Peyton didn't overrun her thoughts—her safe spot. By the time they started dating, he was already a Marine. When home on leave, Pretty Posies wasn't a shop he frequented. Any other shop in Eden Falls held memories, but here, her thoughts settled on Grandma Garrett.

After an early morning meeting with the city planner, she needed to lose herself in the beauty of creation. The intolerable man had tried to bully her into eliminating the Tiny Twirlers in the Fourth of July Parade, but she'd laughed at his tirade. Miss Martha's girls were the darlings of the parade, and as much a part of Eden Falls tradition as The Fly Shop's fish float.

She swept the backroom and moved a couple of plants around. She readjusted the window display, propped the front door open and pulled buckets of flowers into the sunshine. She was dusting shelves when Charlie charged through the door. Her smile disappeared when she saw he was covered in chocolate glaze. Again.

"Let me guess, you had a morning treat at Patsy's with Uncle JT."

"How'd you know?"

~

*a*fter Misty stalked off, Colton had every intention of walking back to the rental to write. Instead, his feet took him to the flower shop. When he entered, he flipped the little bell over the door, sending a happy jingle echoing through the shop. The announcement of his arrival was unnecessary. Alex was behind the counter at a small sink washing chocolate off her son's face. Charlie turned his head and giggled. "Hi, again, Mr. McCreed."

"It looks like you're wearing your breakfast, Charlie."

"He had a healthy breakfast at home. This is Uncle JT's doing."

"Gotta love those uncles."

Alex shot him a look of disapproval and he grinned. Her mad was about as threatening as a butterfly beating something with its wings.

Charlie pulled away. "Mom, you're scrubbing too hard."

"Oh, sorry, honey." She bent and planted a kiss on his cheek.

Charlie groaned and raised his arm, but Alex grabbed his hand and planted a kiss on the other cheek. "Don't you dare wipe that kiss off, young man. It has to last all day. Now get going before you're late, and no donuts for a week."

"Where are you off to?" Colton asked, as Charlie ran around the counter.

"Rec."

"Bye, sweetie. Have fun."

"Bye, Mom. Bye, Mr. McCreed." Charlie bolted through the open door.

Colton raised a brow. "Rec?"

"Summer Recreation." Alex went to the door to watch her son disappear around the corner. "It's a school sponsored summer program to keep kids busy and off the streets. It's four hours, four days a week, and just five dollars a day. High school kids run the program for college credit. A couple of teachers are there to supervise."

"What does Charlie do there?"

"Today they're painting the birdhouses they've been building."

"What about after rec is over?"

Alex turned a narrowed eye on Colton. "He goes to my parent's house or to my in-laws. Sometimes Stella or JT take him for the afternoon. He goes swim—"

"I didn't mean any offense, Alex." Colton held up a hand of surrender at her mother grizzly's growl. "I was just curious. I know you're a good mom. I'm sure it's hard raising a son on your own."

She wilted in front of him. "If I were raising him alone, I wouldn't be washing chocolate frosting off his face after he's already had his breakfast." She walked over to a table and adjusted a bucket of orange flowers.

Colton glanced around. "Rance mentioned this used to be your grandmother's shop."

A slight smile curved her pretty lips. "It was. The building was an old S&H Green Stamp store. Coming from an affluent background, you probably have no idea what that was. Anyway, when the building became vacant in 1968, my grandmother bought it and opened Pretty Posies. Back then, she grew most of the flowers in a green house my grandpa built for her. She loved flowers and putting them together in unique—out of the ordinary—ways. I would come here every night after school to help and..." She stopped, a crease appearing between her brows. "Sorry. I'm rambling."

"Don't be sorry. It's a nice place." She moved to the counter and he followed. "I imagine you do a great business being the only flower shop in town."

"I'll never be rich, but I do okay."

He leaned forward, his elbows resting on the counter. "Doing okay's important, but having money is nice, too."

She shrugged. "Since I've never had much money, I guess I'll never know what I'm missing."

Money was nice. He couldn't imagine life without it, but he'd always had it. He'd never had to do without. Did she ever fret she might not have enough to pay the mortgage? He was sure her family would help if she ever ran into trouble, but would she ask? She didn't seem the type. Colton didn't know what to make of this little pixie who seemed so content in her skin, so confident in her world.

He was a little unsettled that his mind wandered to her face, her lips, several times a day. He found himself wondering where she was or what she was doing.

"Rance also said your grandmother believed that flowers speak some secret language, and she taught you that language. Since that sounds a little disturbing, perhaps you could elaborate."

She laughed, and he enjoyed the sound as well as the merriment in her eyes. "It's not a secret language, and the flowers don't actually speak."

"Care to explain?"

"During the Victorian era, flower symbolism became a popular way of communicating." She pulled a pink blossom from a bucket at the end of the counter. "This pretty peony was a symbol of anger."

Colton nodded to a flower sitting in a white pot. "What about that thing?"

"That *thing* is a purple hyacinth, and it represents forgiveness. A blue hyacinth is constancy, and a white one is beauty."

"And roses?"

"Each color has a different meaning."

He found the subject intriguing, and Alex fascinating. "Do you have any orders to fulfill at the moment?"

"A birthday bouquet."

"Can you put it together using the language of flowers?"

She motioned for him to follow her into the backroom, pulling three colorful flowers from a bucket as she went. "Gerbera daisies—cheerfulness."

She moved to a large worktable and picked through a bucket of pink roses. "Grace."

His eyes followed her as she moved around the room adding flowers and greenery to the growing bouquet. When she held out the finished product, he blinked in amazement. "You have a rare gift for creating delicate beauty."

The simple blush that touched her cheeks was lovely. "Not rare. There are people all over the world creating beauty. You just have to pay attention. Some people can arrange flowers, some paint, some sew, or quilt, or make pottery." She nodded at him. "Some write."

"I wouldn't consider what I do a rare gift."

"Most people don't consider their gifts rare or even gifts. But what you do is unique. You put words together and create a story that people want to read." She paused a moment as if considering whether to continue, then smiled. "I finished one of your books last night."

He only held a handful of people whose opinions mattered, and he wasn't sure why Alex was one of them. Maybe because he knew she'd be brutally honest. His books got great reviews, every one of them a *New York Times* Bestseller. What could she say that would hurt his feelings? Still, he hesitated a moment before he asked, "What did you think?"

She blew out a breath. "I liked the story line."

He leaned a hip against her worktable. "I can hear you screaming but."

She went to a sink and filled a vase with water. "But... some of the scenes were extremely graphic."

"And?"

She turned to look at him. "And what?"

"I've been writing long enough to know when there's a *but*. An *and* usually follows. What's your and?"

She set the vase on the table between them. "*And* the language was very strong."

"I don't write children's books."

"Phew." She pantomimed wiping sweat from her brow. "Thank heavens for that."

He chuckled. "So why did you read it?"

"If you're going to mention our town in a book you're writing, I, as mayor, should read a book you've written."

Given his childhood, receiving rejection wasn't his strong suit. "So...you didn't like it."

She started doing something with the stems of the flowers she'd picked out. "I told you I liked the storyline. The plot had plenty of intrigue. I liked how the killer had a point of view"—her eyes met his—"though I'm a little afraid of how you got into a killer's head so intimately."

Now he knew which book she'd read, and it wasn't the one he would have picked for her.

She smiled. "Maybe Rita was right about you."

Colton moved around the table to stand next to her. "What did Rita say about me?"

"That I should have the house checked for bodies after you move out."

He laughed and then grew serious. "You don't believe her, do you?"

She shook her head as her eyes danced with amusement. His gaze fell to her mouth. She must have noticed, because she pressed her lips together tightly.

He looked back into her oddly colored eyes, a mossy green that seemed to change with the light. "The killer's point of view was a new angle for me. I've never written a book from that perspective."

"The suspense and twists kept me enthralled," she said in a shivery voice.

"You're making fun."

Her eyes grew wide. "No. Not at all. I'm saying, obviously not too well, that for a murder mystery—not a genre I usually read—I liked it."

He took a step back, fighting the urge to touch her hair, which looked silky soft and tempting. "What genre do you read?"

"I like happily ever afters or, at least, the potential for one."

"Sappy."

She laughed. "Happy, not sappy."

"Same thing."

A frown line formed between her brows. "You don't believe in happy endings?"

"Why would I believe in something I've never seen?"

"Do you believe in God or a higher power?" At his nod she added, "but you've never seen that higher power."

"I've never seen God, but I've seen his hand in things like nature or...in your relationship with your son."

She blinked quickly several times as if fighting tears. "That is the sweetest thing I've ever heard you say."

He held up both hands. "Well, don't get used to sweet from me."

"Never." She swiped some stem clippings into the trash with the side of her hand. "Martin Luther King, Junior, said, 'Faith is taking the first step even when you don't see the whole staircase.' Sometimes you just have to believe it will all turn out in the end."

"Call me unfaithful then, because I like to see the staircase."

She stopped what she was doing with the flowers and turned to face him. "What about your parents?"

"Bitter divorce years ago."

"Hmm." She walked into the front of the shop and he followed. "You don't have any friends who are happily married?"

Still tempted to run his fingers through her hair, he stuffed his hands in his pockets. "I have friends who pretend they're happily married."

She raised her eyebrows. "Wow. You're quite possibly the most cynical person I've ever met."

"I'm a realist."

"My parents have been happily married for thirty-five years."

"They say they're happily married for your and JT's benefit."

She released an exaggerated sigh, her shoulders slumping. "You forgot to take your medication this morning. Didn't you?"

He laughed and headed for the door. Before going out he turned to her. "You know, Sunshine, I'm glad there are people in the world with your glowing outlook."

"It would be a pretty bleak place if everyone thought like you."

"Most people do think like me. They just hide it from people like you."

~

*A*lex walked to the front window and watched Colton cross the street. He stopped to talk to Maude Stapleton as he passed Pages Bookstore. He was much more likable than the person she'd met a few weeks earlier. Even though Eden Falls seemed to have relaxed his irritability, he still had a very negative outlook on life. She wondered what had caused pessimism to take such a firm hold on him. Was it the bitter divorce of his parents, or was there something deeper? Had his heart been broken by a past love?

She'd noticed his gaze drop to her mouth. For a split second, she'd thought he might try to kiss her. She would have stopped him.

Wouldn't she?

Yes, she would have stopped him. Her husband had been the last man to kiss her.

Outside, Colton turned from Maude and glanced at Pretty Posies.

Alex touched her top lip with the tip of her tongue. What silly thoughts. She shook herself and returned to the bouquet she'd started.

CHAPTER 9

Colton raised his hands over his head, stretching back muscles that had been hunched over his makeshift desk all afternoon. He'd put a lot of words on the computer screen and felt good about his progress.

A light tapping turned him toward the front door. Charlie stood on the other side of the screen with a huge grin.

"Hi, Mr. McCreed."

"Hey, kid. What's up?"

"I came over 'cause we're friends, huh?"

Colton pushed the screen door open. "Yeah, we're friends. Come in."

Charlie looked into the interior of the house and shook his head. "My mom says no."

"Did your mom send you over?"

"No." He averted his gaze. "She said don't bother you."

Colton chuckled as he stepped onto the porch. "Want to sit out here for awhile?"

"Could you bring your guitar?"

"Sure. I could use a break. Have a seat and I'll go get it."

Colton slid his bare feet into loafers and grabbed his

guitar. Once outside, He sat on the glider and Charlie sidled up against him, which Colton overlooked when he saw the wonderment in the kid's expression. He wore his feelings out in the open like his mom, but most kids probably didn't learn how to hide hurt and disappointment until they were older.

Charlie looked up with his big dark eyes. "My mom said you write on your computer all day."

"It's my job." He could tell by Charlie's scrunched eyebrows he didn't understand. "Your mom's job is working at the flower shop each day. Mine is writing."

Charlie set a hand on Colton's thigh. "Did you write today?"

Colton glanced down at the grimy little fingers and realized he didn't mind so much—at least not with Charlie. "Yes."

Two dirty sneakers started swinging back and forth. "What did you write about?"

"Eden Falls. I was trying to set the background."

The swinging stopped and the scrunched eyebrows returned. "Set the ground?"

Colton realized he'd gotten ahead of the five-year-old's understanding, again. "I was trying to paint a picture of this town with words instead of colors."

Charlie's features relaxed and he laughed. "You can't paint a picture with words, you silly goose."

Colton laughed along with the boy. He'd been called a lot of things in his lifetime, but never silly goose.

"Is your picture almost done?"

"No. I have a long way to go." Colton strummed the guitar and Charlie wiggled even closer. "Want to sing a song?"

Charlie nodded eagerly.

"What other songs do you know?"

Charlie's expression brightened even further, if that was

possible. "We sang "John Jacob Jinglehimer Schmidt" today at Rec."

"What else did you do at Rec?"

"We painted bird houses and made necklaces and had snacks."

"You made a necklace?"

Charlie's little fingers pulled a cereal necklace from beneath the neck of his shirt. He took a bite and four pieces of what looked like Froot Loops disappeared in a couple of crunches. A little boy doing the things little boys did. Those tiny luxuries were never part of Colton's childhood.

"Sing the song for me. I'm not sure I remember it."

Charlie took a deep breath and sang, keeping time with his swinging legs. At the end he said, "Your 'pose to get quieter for the song part and louder for the na-na-na-na-na-na-na's."

"I haven't heard that song since I was a kid," Colton said strumming the tune.

They both sang the song through a couple of times, the words getting softer and the Na-na-na-na-na-na-na's growing louder, just as Charlie had instructed. Next they sang "Bingo" and then they laughed through the two verses of "On Top Of Spaghetti" Colton could remember.

Finally, Charlie slid off the glider. "I better go."

"Hold on. I'll walk you home." Colton put the guitar inside hoping there might be another invitation to dinner. He was tired of eating the few things he knew how to cook or at a restaurant. When they got to the sidewalk, Charlie slid his hand into Colton's, as though that was where it belonged. Colton's knee-jerk reaction was to pull away, but he didn't want to hurt the kid's feelings, so he let Charlie hang on. As they strolled along, Charlie told him about the dog his Grandpa Blackwood had and how much he wanted one.

"We builded a doghouse and then my grandpa let me help

paint it. It's green and we put sh..." Charlie looked up at the porch ceiling in thought. "I don't remember the word, but they were scratchy and we put them on the roof to keep the rain off Buster. That's his name and he's brown with white around his eyes."

"Is shingles the word you're trying to remember?"

"Yeah. And we hammered them down. Grandpa let me help and even gave me a hammer for just my size!"

"It sounds like you're a good helper."

Charlie let go of Colton's hand and walked backwards. "My mom said maybe when I get older I can have a dog, but her maybe's mean no."

Colton had laughed more in the last forty-five minutes than he had all week. Maybe Jorge was right about this place changing him...just a little. He followed Charlie up the front porch steps and into the house, which smelled like Italian tonight.

"Charlie, you're late," Alex called from the kitchen.

"Sorry, Mom."

"Where have you been?"

Colton followed Charlie into the kitchen. "Sorry, Mom. My fault, again. We were singing and lost track of time."

Alex turned a stern look on Charlie. "What did I tell you about going to Mr. McCreed's house?"

"But I thought it was our house."

Alex took her son's face between the palms of her hands. "It is, honey, but Mr. McCreed is using it for the summer and you can't keep bothering him."

Colton stuffed his hands into the pockets of his jeans and rocked back on his heels. "I had just finished when Charlie knocked. He gave me a much needed break."

"Can Mr. McCreed eat with us?"

Alex's gaze moved from her son to him. "I guess so."

Charlie grinned at Colton. "That's her teasing voice. She

makes it sound like she doesn't want you to, but she really does."

Colton couldn't tell by her furrowed brow and lip chewing if that was true or not, but he wasn't going to argue.

Alex turned to the oven. "Wash up you two. It's ready."

After much slinging of water, Colton helped Charlie set another place at the table while Alex dished up lasagna. She passed the salad bowl around and then a warm loaf of bread drizzled with garlic butter. Colton couldn't stop his mouth from watering. He'd worked through lunch with only a gigantic mug of coffee and one—okay two—blueberry crumbles and a bear claw for breakfast.

He watched Alex and Charlie interact through dinner, Mom asking son about his day and him filling her in on every important-to-a-five-year-old detail. She looked content and so did Charlie. The most amazing part was he felt content sitting here at their table with them.

Alex asked him about his writing and he explained, as he had to Charlie, that he'd spent the day setting the background of his novel. She asked questions as if what he'd written mattered to her and Charlie. The whole scene was out of the ordinary for him and caused another memory perforation of days long past—him at the round kitchen table with his nanny, the family cook busy at the stove, while he finished his homework. Both of them asked about his day and then listened with real interest as he filled them in. It had been a long time since anyone, besides Jorge or his agent, acted like they cared, and both of them were concerned because it was their business.

After dinner, as Alex rinsed the dishes and Charlie loaded the dishwasher, Colton helped by clearing the table and wiping everything down. He'd formulated a plan and wanted to prove he could be useful before asking.

When the kitchen was clean, he and Alex settled on the

front porch to watch Charlie and his friend Tyson kick a soccer ball around the yard. At a lull in their conversation, Colton said, "This might be a little presumptuous of me, but if I were to buy groceries and bring them over once a week, could I beg a home-cooked meal from you?"

Alex's back seemed to stiffen and her gaze skittered off in another direction.

"I can cook a few basics, but in L.A. my housekeeper does all the cooking. Eating out is getting old. You come up with a menu and I'll buy everything you need, or I'll give you the money and you can buy the groceries—whichever is easiest for you. I'm not a picky eater."

She pursed her lips. If only she realized how beguiling... "Have I shocked you beyond words? Come on, Mayor—just once a week. And I promise to bring my best behavior." He held up three fingers like a boy scout. "I swear to *try* whatever green-thing you serve."

She shook her head. "It's not—I mean... I..." She glanced out at her son, took a deep breath, and released it slowly, relaxing her body. "I guess once a week would be alright. Wednesday nights are best. Will that work for you?"

Colton couldn't stop the grin. "Any day you say. I'll pick up whatever you need. What does Charlie like?"

She smiled. "I'm lucky. Charlie likes just about any *green thing* I put on the table. Why don't you pick up a couple of steaks for next week? Nothing fancy. I'll provide the rest."

"We could do a trial run tomorrow night if you're not busy."

She laughed. "Okay. Steaks tomorrow night."

～

*a*lex came out of the walk in cooler and slid the door closed when her mom stepped into Pretty Posies.

"Hi, sweetie," Alice said.

"Hi, Mom. Is everything okay?"

Alice set her purse on the counter. "Everything's fine. I just slathered Charlie and Tyson in sunscreen and dropped them off at the pool. Adam Blackwood is there with his kids and said he'd watch them, so I thought I'd come by and say hi."

"I'm glad you did," Alex said kissing her mom's cheek.

"I've got a roast in the oven for dinner. Can you and Charlie come over?"

"We'd love—Oh, wait. No, we can't make it."

Her mom picked up a picture frame. "Plans?"

"Sort of. Colton McCreed offered to buy groceries one night a week if I'd cook. He's bringing steaks tonight."

Her mom set the frame back in place and turned with raised brows.

Alex shook her head. "Don't get any ideas, Mom. It's nothing like that. Colton and Misty are seeing each other, and you know she doesn't cook."

"What does Brandt think of this arrangement?" Alice asked as she pulled a stool from underneath the counter.

Alex sat next to her. "It doesn't matter what Brandt thinks."

"Oh?" her mom asked with raised brows.

"Sorry. I didn't mean to sound insensitive, but Brandt and I are just friends."

Her mom leaned forward and took one of her hands. "What happened?"

"Nothing. Brandt is a nice man, but there isn't any spark between us."

"Peyton has been gone a long time, honey," Alice said, rubbing her thumb over Alex's knuckles.

"This isn't about Peyton. Well, it is, but not the way you think. I'm not afraid to move on. I just...I want what Peyton and I had, and I don't feel that with Brandt. He doesn't feel that with me either." She shrugged. "Who knows if I'll ever love that strongly again?

Alice placed a hand against Alex's cheek. "I can't believe my optimistic baby girl is talking like this. Of course you'll love that strongly again."

Alex smiled at her mother's words, especially since Alice was the pessimist of the family. "I hope you're right, but it won't be with Brandt. Or Colton McCreed."

"I should have invited Colton over for dinner before now. The poor man is probably starving to death if he's dating Misty. Come tonight and bring him."

Alex tipped her head back and forth as if she was weighing her answer. Her hesitation toward Colton joining them once a week had nothing to do with cooking for an extra person. It was the bond Charlie was forming with a man who would be leaving town at the end of summer. Going to her mom and dad's for dinner tonight would add a distraction for Charlie. "Colton has already dropped the steaks off."

"Save them for next week." Alice stood. "If Colton loves home cooking, he'll love my roast."

"You have enough?"

Alice fluttered a hand. "I made plenty. JT is bringing a new girl."

Another new girl? At least it isn't Misty. The short time Misty and JT dated had baffled Alex. JT had known Misty since childhood, knew the kind of person she was, and still he'd gone out with her, when she asked. To the family's relief, it hadn't lasted long, and JT hadn't been very broken up when the relationship dissolved. Still, the three-month *Misty Incident*, as Alex called it, had been a puzzle.

Alex walked Alice to the door. "I'll call Colton. I'm sure he won't mind where he eats, as long as it's not in a restaurant."

"Your dad will be happy. He was complaining last night that the only time he sees you is at the baseball field or in church."

"I'll make him doubly happy and bring dessert."

~

Saturday night Alex pulled into Rowdy's parking lot, her windshield wipers slapping furiously at the sheet of rain coming down. The dark clouds overhead made it seem much later than it was.

She didn't go out often, but tried to meet up with her friends at least once a month. Tonight, they were here to celebrate Jolie—just back from her Hawaiian honeymoon.

Her car door opened before she could turn the engine off. Colton pushed back the hood of his jacket just enough for her to see his face.

She blew out a breath. "You scared me to death. What are you doing?"

"Getting soaked. Do you have an umbrella with you?"

She grabbed a small one from the passenger seat and popped it open. They huddled close and made a mad dash for the door, which he pushed open as she lowered the umbrella and shook it out.

"You know that jalopy of yours is a road hazard."

Alex pulled off her dripping jacket. "It's not a jalopy"—she wrinkled her nose—"okay maybe it is, but it isn't a road hazard. Everything is in working order. It has the required seatbelts and is perfectly reliable transportation."

Colton shook the water from his hair like a dog, sending sprinkles everywhere.

She frowned and wiped the drops from her face. "*Just call me Jorgie* took a picture of my Jeep to show his friends back in L.A. Too bad he didn't get that picture while you were in the passenger seat. That'd give his friends, and yours, something interesting to talk about." She widened her eyes in exaggeration. "Hey! My Jeep is going to be famous in L.A. Maybe I can get a movie deal out of it."

"Sure, if it's a demolition derby movie. I wouldn't put much stock in the picture being shown around. Jorge doesn't have many friends." Colton laughed at his own joke, amusement softening his gray eyes. He was much easier going than the man she'd picked up from the airstrip. Was this the real Colton McCreed? The one his friends back home knew?

"That's not a very nice thing to say, especially since Jorge isn't here to defend himself."

Colton leaned close and wiped a drop of rain from her nose. His touch sent an odd quiver through her stomach and she stepped back.

"You don't realize the impression you made on Jorge. He asks about you every time he calls. He insists I've found Eden, and you're Eve."

"It's a good thing your name isn't Adam. He'd be pairing us up."

The amusement drained from his face.

"Relax, McCreed. I was just kidding."

"I'll catch you later, Mayor." He took two giant steps and was swallowed in the crowd.

Alex turned and met the steely blue fury emanating from Misty's eyes. She looked over her shoulder in the direction Colton had disappeared. *Chicken*.

Before she could greet her friends, Misty attacked. "You

said there was nothing going on between you and Colton, but every time I turn around you're with him."

Luckily, it was tourist season, and, because it was pouring buckets, Rowdy's was packed. With the noise level at nuclear, only a few people turned to look at red-faced Misty. "We got out of our cars at the same time and walked in together."

Misty crossed her arms over her chest. "What were you talking about?"

"He was making fun of my Jeep."

Done with the conversation, Alex turned her attention to the beaming Jolie as she filled them in on the details of her honeymoon. The newlywed was tanned and brimming with delight. She told them about the beaches, flipped through pictures on her cell phone, reminding Alex of her own honeymoon. She and Peyton spent two blissful weeks in St. Lucia, where they swam, sailed, hiked, and loved.

She pasted on a happy face and asked Jolie for details every chance she got.

Misty brooded and criticized everything from the conversation to the appetizers they shared. She was short-tempered, mad at the world, and they all did their best to ignore her. Of course, she didn't notice because her attention was on Colton, who was also doing his best to ignore her.

Stella spent the night watching the door for her boyfriend, who cancelled more dates than he kept. They were supposed to go to a movie after girls' night, but he ended up a no-show.

Alex noticed Beam was in town. He sat at the end of the bar with Colton, both flirting with every female who walked past. She expected that from Beam, but the sight of Colton actively involved caused a strange tightness in her chest, which didn't make sense. What difference did it make to her if Colton flirted? None. Yet, her gaze kept straying in that direction.

Brandt stopped by their table to say hi. Jillian sat up a little taller, but Brandt's gaze skimmed past. Alex wasn't a matchmaker, but she might have to intervene here. The two of them together made sense.

An hour later, Alex got up and said her goodbyes. Feeling edgy, she'd had enough of the noise and chaos on a rainy Saturday night at Rowdy's Bar and Grill.

~

*W*hen Alex called the town council meeting to order, the number of Eden Falls' residents in attendance surprised Colton. She'd stopped at the rental to tell him they'd have to cancel their Wednesday night dinner due to the council meeting changing nights. He talked her into swapping to Thursday this week instead. He wasn't about to give up his home-cooked meal or his night with Alex and Charlie, because one of the council members had a dog show to attend tomorrow.

Jorge suggested he go to a council meeting, so Colton sat six rows back and observed Alex—who'd gained his growing respect and admiration—in yet another of her roles. She wasn't a mother sitting at a baseball game, or a business owner arranging flowers for the Senior Centers' monthly luncheon. Tonight she was a mayor. She wore a long, gauzy white dress with a brown belt and sandals. Her blond hair cascaded down her back in a perfect disarray of waves, giving her a tousled in bed look. He fought to keep his mind on the meeting rather than that image.

Amid the joking and laughing, she ran a smooth meeting. She showed professionalism even when a white haired, eighty-something-year-old man made a motion to change the law regarding the harassment of Sasquatch.

"Mr. Polanski, you bring this up at every meeting. There

is nothing I can do about a Washington State Law. If Sasquatch is eating your chickens, you should report it to the police. JT may be able to catch the perpetrator."

"I don't want JT catching nothin'. If there's a reward for capturin' Bigfoot, then he would get it. That ain't gonna happin' on my property."

Colton laughed along with the rest of the audience.

"If there is a reward, JT, as a public servant, wouldn't be able to accept it," Alex said, her tone firm but patient. "Please, talk to JT the next time one of your chickens comes up missing."

Colton made notes of the characters sitting at the long table with Alex. On the far left was Maude Stapleton, the red headed Betty White who owned Pages Bookstore. She had him and most everyone else in the room laughing at her comic humor.

Next was the high school science teacher, Benny Mayfield. He made as many scathing remarks as Maude made comic. His expression remained sour, even when everyone else was sharing a laugh. Bet he was a load of fun for the kids.

Manual Hernandez sat next to Alex, and was just as happy. He had thick black hair and dark twinkling eyes. If he weren't already married, Colton would suggest the two of them give it a go. Imagine their cheerful home.

On Alex's right was Marty Graw. Really? Was that just a cruel joke or were his parents announcing when he'd been conceived? He was a short, pudgy man, who owned several fast food franchises, and would forever be haunted by his name.

The last two council members were Noelle Treloar, who owned Noelle's Café, and, completely unexpected, Rowdy Garrett.

At the end of the table sat the town manager, a big guy

named Han Jorgensen, who enjoyed throwing his weight around. He nit-picked almost everything the council agreed on, and disagreed with Alex every chance he got.

The personalities were a crazy combination, but they seemed to work for this town.

Halfway through the meeting, Misty slid into the chair next to him. She made it obvious she didn't appreciate his attention elsewhere. She disrupted the people around them with her stage whisper, until the mayor asked if she had something to share. "If not, be quiet or step out."

Colton stood and pulled Misty up by the arm.

Once outside, Misty yanked from his grasp. "What are you doing?"

"Escorting you out. You interrupted the entire meeting."

"Well, I wouldn't have to if you'd call me." She linked their fingers. "Why is it I have to be the pursuer in this relationship?"

With some effort, Colton pulled his hand free. "Misty, I want you to listen to me. There is no relationship between us. I came to Eden Falls to study small town life and to write."

She stepped in front of him and ran her hands down his chest. "I can tell you everything you want to know about this dismal little town. I can tell you who is seeing who behind his wife's back."

"It's whom."

"What?"

He shook his head.

"I can tell you who hasn't come out of the closet yet. I can tell you who's pregnant and hasn't told her husband, because he doesn't want any more kids. I can tell you which couples are happily married and which couples ought to throw in the towel. I can tell you how—"

"What can you tell me about Misty Douglas?"

She took a step back. "I can tell you she hates Eden Falls

and wants out. She's the best hair technician within two-hundred miles and bored silly with this—"

"Why do you hate Eden Falls?"

"You're kidding right?" She gestured with both hands. "Look at this place. It's a dead end."

"You just said you're the best hair technician within two-hundred miles, which is something you can do anywhere. Why don't you leave if you're so unhappy?"

She shifted her weight to one hip and folded her arms across her chest. "It takes money to move."

"Have you asked your dad for help? It wouldn't take a fortune to get settled in Seattle or Spokane or Tacoma."

"I'd rather go to Los Angeles with you. I could become a hair stylist to the stars."

He felt his jaw tighten as frustration rushed through him. Reminding her, yet again, that he wasn't interested was useless. *And women say men have selective hearing.* "What can you tell me about Alex?"

Misty's blue eyes flashed, then narrowed to angry slits. "Why are you interested in Alex?"

He shook his head. "I'm not interested in the manner you're implying."

"Good, because she's been romantically defective since she first met Peyton."

"Why do you say things like that? In fact, why do you make so many derogatory remarks about the women you call friends?"

"I don't make derogatory remarks about anyone—unless they're true."

Impossible. "Rather than defend Alex because she is your friend, or show sympathy because she lost her husband, you say she's romantically defective. Why?"

"Brandt's been after her for months, and she won't give him the time of day. She's frigid."

"That's exactly what I'm talking about," Colton said pointing a finger at her. "Why would you say that?"

"Because we live in a small town and word gets around. It's how we entertain ourselves in this podunk place. What do you care?"

"Alex is a nice person. She comes from a nice family. She works hard and very rarely takes a day off. She worked a full day in her shop, and then came here to conduct a two-hour meeting for the betterment of the town you live in. Shouldn't you support her as a friend, rather than knock her down?"

Her face turned mottled red, and she stomped her foot like a spoiled child. Then, in the blink of an eye, a smile curled her mouth. She moved close and ran her fingers down his chest again. "Come to my place, and I'll fill you in on anyone in town. You tell me their name and I'll tell you anything you want to know. My job at the salon is like a bartender's. People talk."

He opened his car door. "I have to work."

She stepped back and pursed her lips. Not as tempting a look as when Alex did it. "I'll see you tomorrow then."

Not if I can help it.

CHAPTER 10

C olton put in a full day of writing, exhilarated with the direction his manuscript had taken. He was up before dawn with a subplot epiphany and immediately started on the changes. As he closed his laptop for the day, he heard a knock on the front door and assumed a dark eyed boy was waiting on the other side. His assumption was correct. Charlie waved through the screen. "Hi, Mr. McCreed!"

"Hi, buddy. How about you call me Colton instead of Mr. McCreed?"

"Because we're friends?"

"Yep, because we're friends." Colton felt his mood lift further at the smile that lit Charlie's face. Anticipation of dinner at the mayor's lifted his spirits even higher.

"I came to get you."

Colton pushed the screen open. "Come in while I get my shoes."

Charlie backed up a step. "My mom says I can't."

Alex probably meant don't even knock. "It's okay. I'm all finished for the day. And we're friends."

Charlie's hesitation fled as quickly as his grin appeared.

He stepped inside. "My mom is making spaghetti and meatballs, and they're the best. Even my grandpa says so."

"They're the best, huh?"

Charlie's eyes grew wide. "Yep, my grandpa likes them so much he ate five once. All by hisself."

"Well, I'm pretty hungry, so I may eat even more than five."

"Me too." Charlie's belly laugh amused Colton.

As they walked along the sidewalk, Charlie slipped his hand easily into Colton's. Instead of annoyance, a perplexing sense of connection—another new sensation—came over him. His experiences in Eden Falls seemed to be a never-ending lineup of firsts.

Charlie jabbered the whole way about nonsensical things that were significant to a five-year-old. They had to stop for a procession of ants, and were waylaid again to watch a bee gather pollen. Charlie noticed things Colton normally overlooked. He asked questions that caused Colton to pause and think. Twice, he told Charlie they'd look the answers up together.

At Alex's house, Charlie bolted up the porch stairs and through the front door. Colton knocked before following him inside. "Hello?"

Charlie's excited voice came from the kitchen. "But Mom I didn't bother him. He said come in because he was done."

Colton stepped to the kitchen door. "Hello?" he repeated.

Alex looked up. "I'm sorry Charlie keeps coming—"

"It's all good, Mayor." Colton wrapped a hand around the back of the kid's neck. "I was finished for the day."

"I told him you make the best meatballs. Even Grandpa says so."

Alex smiled down at her son. "Thank you, sweetie. Dinner's ready, so go wash up."

This time Colton held out his hand, and Charlie took it

with a grin. If holding hands on the way to the bathroom made the kid happy, why fight it?

Once back in the kitchen, Alex said, "Charlie, can you get Mr. McCreed a glass?"

"Mom," Charlie replied in exaggerated annoyance. "His name is Colton."

Alex raised her eyebrow and opened her mouth to correct her son, but Colton held up a hand. "I told him it was okay to call me Colton."

"Because we're friends," Charlie inserted.

Alex released a breath. "Sorry. Can you get Colton a glass, please?"

At the table, Colton could feel Charlie's undivided attention on him as he took his first bite of meatball. He chewed, making a big deal of it before turning the kid's way.

Charlie pointed a finger at him. "I told you she makes the best meatballs in the whole wide world."

Alex clasped her hands to her chest. "This compliment comes from a five-year-old who hasn't been further in the world than Spokane on the East and Seattle on the West, and all his meatball experiences have been local."

Colton swallowed his mouthful and smiled at the happy little face across the table from him. "I, on the other hand, have traveled all over the world, and I have to agree with Charlie. This is the best meatball I've ever eaten."

Charlie laughed and looked at his mom. "Colton should eat here every night!"

❧

*A*lex almost choked on her mouthful of spaghetti. She was really going to have to talk to Charlie about his impromptu invitations and suggestions. She felt her face heat and set down her fork. "Charlie, Mr. McCreed—*Colton*—is here to write a book. Every time he comes over here or you go over there, he has to stop writing. He's only going to be here for a short—"

"He said I could go in," Charlie said, his dark eyes pleading his case.

"Charlie, as much as I love your mom's cooking, and as much as I enjoy your company, your mom is right. I'm not going to be in town for very long, and I have to finish the book I'm writing, so we should keep our dinners to once a week." He raised his eyes to capture hers. "At least for now."

Suddenly, Alex wished Peyton was here. A veil of melancholy settled over her like a familiar blanket. He should be sharing dinner with them. They would have had another child by now, maybe a little girl with Peyton's black hair and beautiful bronzed skin. Pink would have looked startling on her. Alex swallowed hard to fight the sting of tears as she pushed the sadness away.

Colton was studying her as if reading her thoughts, while Charlie happily chattered away about his day at recreation. She imagined, as a writer, he spent time observing people and their different emotions. The way those emotions splayed across someone's face. Was her moment of pain so obvious to the naked eye? What did he see when looking at her?

Alex turned her attention back to Charlie. She hadn't liked the idea of these once a week dinners from the start, concerned her son would develop too strong an attachment to Colton. He was completely captivated with his new friend. She knew he'd be sad when Colton went back to L.A. Like any mother, Alex wanted to protect her child from hurt for as long as possible.

～

*C*olton had looked forward to JT's barbecue since he'd received the invitation two weeks earlier. JT said what started as a small get together for Father's Day had grown into a huge cookout in just a few years. The only thing that postponed the annual event was bad weather.

Following JT's directions, he took a left off the highway and followed a dirt road angling toward the mountains. The trees grew thicker and the homes more sparse and setback, their driveway entrances dotted with mailboxes. He finally spotted Alex's jalopy and pulled to a stop behind it.

He studied the house from a distance. Its contemporary lines and walls of windows would look out of place in town, but it fit in perfectly with the surrounding majestic pines. The tall windows would provide stunning view of sunsets.

The number of cars parked down the wide drive and along the road led Colton to believe quite a crowd had already arrived. He followed the laughter and music along a path that ran next to a wide stream—very picturesque. He continued through a stand of pines that parted into an open space behind the house.

There were about sixty people milling around with drinks in their hands. He was greeted by many on his way to the food tables, which were set up under a tent. He spotted Misty off to one side with Beam, her blue eyes firing darts at the guy. *Sorry buddy*, was his first thought. His second was a hope she'd turned her interests in another direction. It was amazing how quickly he'd fallen out of *like* with her. In fact, she'd proven to be a hard person to like.

Colton set the box of brownies he'd bought at Patsy's on what looked like a dessert table. He'd finally learned you didn't go to gatherings in Eden Falls without an unofficially expected offering.

Pages Bookstore owner, Maude Stapleton, caught him as he was leaving the tent.

"When are we going to set a date for a book signing?"

Oops. He'd forgotten all about that. He pulled out his cell phone and set a reminder. "I'll call my publicist first thing Monday morning. If you haven't heard from her by Tuesday afternoon, call me."

He turned when he felt a tug on the back of his shirt.

Charlie grinned up at him. "I've been waiting and waiting for you."

"Hi, hotrod." He ruffled Charlie's black hair before the kid took his hand and led him through the crowd to where JT, Alex, and Rowdy stood.

"Hey, Colton, glad you could make it," JT said.

"Thanks for the invite." He glanced back at the house. "This is quite a place you have here."

"I'll give you the grand tour later."

Colton really didn't care much about the inside of houses unless he was staying there, but would go along if JT wanted to show him. "Sure."

Beam joined them, clapping Colton on the shoulder. "You up for another plane ride?"

Colton blew out a breath. "After the last one, I'm not sure."

"You're leaving?" Rowdy asked.

"Only for a couple of days," Colton said. "I have several meetings in L.A."

"I'll swing by Alex's rental and pick you up on my way to the airstrip," Beam said. "Tuesday at nine?"

"Nine is good. Thanks."

JT thumbed over his shoulder where a volleyball net was set up. "We're headed over to play a game. How's your spike?"

Colton hated to admit it, but he couldn't remember the

last time he'd played volleyball...possibly spring break in college? "Rusty."

"We'll spot you," Rowdy said, pushing him in the direction of the game.

Colton had the best afternoon he'd had in a long time. A backyard barbecue in Eden Falls was different from the parties he attended in L.A. He played that game of volleyball and did okay. He kicked a soccer ball back and forth with Beam, who was quite a character with an interesting sense of humor. The food, which everyone contributed to, was great. Again, he felt like he was part of a community. Included and involved. Life in Eden Falls was filled with family, friends, and simple indulgences. A day didn't go by where he didn't feel as if he didn't belong. He'd integrated himself in with the natives just as Jorge suggested.

He had such a good time, he didn't think of the book he was working on once.

As the afternoon wore on, he lost count of how many times Charlie's hand found his. They sat side by side during lunch and he leaned over to wipe mustard from the kid's mouth a couple of times. He laughed when Charlie executed an adult worthy burp, and then tried to look stern when Alex turned a mother's eye on them. He knew he failed when Charlie flashed his irresistible smile and uttered, "'Scuse me."

*A*fter lunch, Colton wandered through the house with JT, Charlie tagging close behind. The floor plan was open, and the floor to ceiling windows created a tree house effect on the top floor. The master bedroom jutted over the stream out back. He could hear the water through the open windows.

"Very Frank Lloyd Wright. Where did you come up with the design?"

"This was my Grandma and Grandpa Garrett's house. I inherited it when they were killed in a car accident."

"Alex acquired Pretty Posies from the same grandparents?"

JT nodded as he walked to a window overlooking the party. "Both Beam and Rowdy received money. Beam invested in a plane, and Rowdy bought a dilapidated piece of real estate on Main and turned it into the bar and grill."

Colton joined JT at the window. "Have you ever been sorry you got a house instead of money?"

"No. Are you kidding? They knew I loved this house. We used to have the best family parties here."

"The upstairs looks newer. Did you add on?"

"No. I've been renovating room by room. I started upstairs because it was easier. The main floor will take longer, especially the kitchen."

Colton was impressed. "Do you do most of the work yourself?"

JT chuckled. "Yeah, when time and money permit."

He envied a man who could do that kind of work with his hands, something he'd never learned. "Those were all size-able inheritances. Where did your grandparents come into money, if you don't mind me asking?"

JT pointed out the window at the surrounding pines. "Lumber. My grandfather owned one of the largest lumber mills in the area. He sold it for millions."

Yet, all the Garrett descendants lived modestly.

"Charlie?" JT said to his nephew who was sitting in one of two chairs near the huge stone fireplace. "Will you go outside and make sure everyone's having a great time. I need to talk to Colton for a minute."

"What should I do if they're not havin' fun?"

"Offer them some chips."

"Okay!" Charlie grinned and bounded out of the room.

JT smiled after the kid. "He's my hero."

"I think it's the other way around."

"No, Charlie's the greatest." JT turned to face him. "I wanted to talk to you about Misty."

Colton shoved his hands in his pockets and turned back to the window. "There goes my great afternoon."

JT chuckled, but didn't apologize.

"Believe me, Misty was the biggest mistake I've made in a very long time. I've told her over and over there is no "us", but she's just not getting it."

"She's getting it." JT sat in the leather chair Charlie had vacated. "She just doesn't care. When Misty wants something, she'll do whatever she can to get it. Your feelings aren't a factor in the equation. She is a taker. Always has been."

He walked over and took the chair opposite JT, "You sound like you're speaking from experience."

"I dated Misty for a few months." JT looked up at the ceiling and shook his head. "I have no idea why. We ran into each other at a party, and she asked me out. I knew what she was like and still I went."

JT glanced at him. "She also tried to get ahold of Peyton before he and Alex were married. Peyton told me about her cornering him with her shirt unbuttoned. She told him Alex would never find out. He said nothing happened between them, and I believed him. Misty told Alex it was the other way around. That she was the one fighting Peyton off. Misty doesn't play fair." He glanced toward the window. "She's outside right now making accusations about Alex."

"Why?"

"She's telling people Alex is trying to steal you away from her."

"The girl's crazy," Colton said, crossing an ankle over the opposite knee.

They were silent a moment, and then JT leaned forward and rested his elbows on his knees. "Mind if I ask about these dinner arrangements with Alex?"

The real reason for showing me the house, big brother is concerned. "That's exactly what the dinners are, an arrangement. Charlie invited me to dinner one night. Alex couldn't refuse without seeming rude, and I didn't let her off the hook." He held out his hands in question. "What man in his right mind, living alone on take-out, is going to refuse a home cooked meal? After two of Charlie's surprise invitations, I offered to buy groceries once a week if your sister would cook for me."

"So there's nothing going on between you and Alex?"

Colton grinned and shook his head. "Absolutely nothing. She's not interested, that I know of, and I'm not looking. We have a nice dinner and enjoy each other's company with Charlie as our chaperone."

JT pressed the pad of his thumb to his lips. Colton recognized an anxious expression when he saw it. "Relax, big brother. You have nothing to worry about where Alex and I are concerned."

~

harlie followed JT and Colton inside. When he came running back out, asking everyone if they were having a good time, Alex knew JT was talking to Colton about Misty. She'd asked her brother to talk to him, after JT had warned *her* about Colton. Yes—someone in this small town had seen Colton coming from her house after dark and gone to JT.

"He's only in town for the summer, Alex," he'd said.

The same warning she'd given Charlie. "You're listening to gossip?"

JT had taken her shoulders in his hands and leaned down so they were eye to eye. "I worry about you."

"There's nothing to worry about. You're welcome to join us for dinner any Wednesday."

There wasn't anything to worry about, because there was nothing going on between her and Colton—except for the tingling sensation in her stomach calling her a liar whenever Colton was near.

Stella plopped into a lawn chair next to her. Once again, her boyfriend was a no-show. Alex glanced around for Rowdy. He was near the grills with a scantily clad woman, but his gaze was on Stella. When he spotted Alex watching, he looped his arm around the woman's neck and nodded as if he was actually paying attention to what she was saying.

"That was fun," Stella said, fanning her face. "I haven't played volleyball since JT's barbecue last year."

"That *was* fun." Jillian took the lawn chair on the other side of Alex. "What's going on between Misty and Beam? They look like they're arguing."

Alex looked around until she spotted Beam and Misty. They did look like they were arguing, which seemed strange. Her easygoing cousin never argued with anyone.

"That's the second time I've seen them arguing today," Stella said.

Alex watched Misty turn on her heel and leave Beam with a puzzled look on his face. "He probably said something that offended her."

"Speaking of the devil," Stella said as Misty stalked toward them.

Misty sat in the last vacant lawn chair with a weighty sigh, hoping someone would ask her what was wrong, but Alex already knew. Colton wasn't playing *her* game by *her* rules.

"I need your help with—"

"Count me out."

Misty's head snapped in Alex's direction. "What do you mean, count you out? You don't even know what I was going to say."

Alex crossed one leg over the other. "Actually, I do, and I'm not going to help you devise a plan to trap Colton."

"Because you want him for yourself!"

"You don't have a problem with the word trapped?" Stella asked incredulously.

"I don't plan to trap him, just...nudge him in the right direction."

"There is nothing going on between me and Colton," Alex said for the second time that day. "Colton doesn't want children. Do you really think I'd put Charlie in that type of situation?"

Misty shrugged. "Obviously you would, because you and Colton are together all the time."

"No one is after Colton but you, and you're after him for the wrong reasons."

"I agree with Alex," Stella said. "You don't really care about him. You just want out of this town, and you think he can provide you with a one-way ticket. Count us all out of your scheming plans."

Misty pushed out of her chair. "You guys call yourselves friends? You can all rot in this place, but I won't." She stomped off in her four-inch-high wedge sandals.

～

*C*olton met the local preacher, Josh Brenner, at JT's party, and after some friendly badgering, accepted his invitation to attend services the following morning. He had no religious background and never attended church, other than occasional weddings or funerals. He'd seen Josh at

Patsy's Pastries and thigh-deep in the river. Who couldn't like a guy who fished and ate pastries? Besides, a writer never knew what experience might inspire a sentence, a scene, or a whole novel.

Colton entered the church and scanned the seating options. Misty looked surprised when she saw him. She motioned him over. *Nope.* Rita Reynolds flapped her arms and patted the empty seat next to her. *Another not happening.* Every time he went in to get his mail, she squawked loud enough to make him jump, and then proceeded to discuss ways to murder people—in depth. He'd come to the conclusion that the tiny woman was as crazy as Misty. Charlie's grin settled his seating dilemma. The Garrett family had just enough room at the end of their pew. He scooted into place.

He was impressed by how well behaved Charlie was for the hour long service, sitting quietly, playing tic-tac-toe with JT—a game his uncle let him win almost every time.

The sermon itself wasn't earth shattering. Angels didn't descend from Heaven, but, luckily, neither did a bolt of lightning. He did pay attention. He even glanced up a couple of times, expecting the preacher to be looking directly at him when he expounded on a certain principle. He wasn't.

After the service, he was invited to lunch at Denny and Alice Garrett's house. He sat back and observed the solidarity between the family members. Alex and her dad teased, JT and his mom teased, they all teased with Charlie. They were the epitome of a happy family. He was included and still wasn't sure if he enjoyed or resented the camaraderie.

By the end of the afternoon, he found the thought of going back to the empty rental house depressing. Charlie saved his evening with an invitation to help him and the mayor put a jigsaw puzzle together at their house. He could tell by Alex's forced smile she wasn't overjoyed by her son's spontaneous invitation. He accepted before she could say her usual, "Charlie, Mr. McCreed is a very busy man".

An hour later, he sat on one side of Alex's kitchen table. She was across from him, and Charlie was all over the place as they pieced together Noah's Ark. He and Alex worked on the edges while Charlie put animals together. When he looked up to hand Charlie a piece to a giraffe's head, he noticed a bush move outside the kitchen window. He dipped his spoon into the root beer float Alex had made each of them. He knew she kept the ice cream in the garage refrigerator and there was a side door he could take to get outside. "Alex? Would you mind if I get more ice cream?"

"I want more ice cream, too," Charlie said.

Alex started to move her chair back, but Colton stood. "I'll get it."

He went through the door, making sure it was closed before going into the yard. He expected to find a kid lurking behind the hedge, window peeping. Instead, it was an adult arm he reached out and grabbed. Misty let out a small squeak before he covered her mouth. "What are you doing sneaking around, peering in windows like some psycho?"

She pulled free of his grasp. "I'm the one who should be asking the questions. What are you doing here all cuddled up with Alex?"

He felt the cold fingers of dread curling around the base of his neck. He'd met his match with Misty. She wasn't going to let go of the one night they'd spent together.

"As you can *see*," he said gesturing toward the window, "we're helping Charlie put together a jigsaw puzzle. Now, get out of the bushes."

"Why are you in the bushes, Misty?" Charlie's voice came from behind them.

"She…thought she lost her sunglasses and was looking

for them." Colton backed out of the hedge, pulling Misty with him.

"She could help us finish the puzzle."

Great. Now he knew how Alex felt about the kid's impulsive invitations.

"I'd love to help." Misty clapped her hands like a child.

He followed Charlie and Misty inside and met Alex's puzzled gaze. "Look who we ran into."

Charlie laughed. "She was in the bushes looking for her sunglasses."

Alex's eyes narrowed as she looked at Misty. "Did you find them?"

"I remember now," Misty said, thumping her palm against her forehead. "They're in my car."

"Silly goose," Charlie said.

Colton lifted a leaf from Misty's hair and twirled it between thumb and forefinger. Alex stared at the leaf for a moment, then turned to look out the window. He watched a plethora of emotions move over her face. Lifted-eyebrow realization changed to puzzlement, which turned to flared-nostril fury. She stood from her chair. "Puzzle night is over."

"Aww, Mom."

~

*O*n a whim, after putting in a full day on the computer, Colton walked to Alex's house. He could hear laughter coming from the backyard and pushed through the gate to find Charlie and JT throwing a baseball.

"Hi, Colton!" Charlie waved.

"Hey, buddy."

"You're just in time to take my place." JT opened Alex's kitchen door. "Alex, I gotta go," he yelled inside.

"Night shift?"

JT nodded.

Alex appeared holding out a uniform shirt. "All done."

"Thanks." He took it from her and slipped it over his tee. "Have I ever told you you're the best sister in the whole world?"

"Occasionally, when you have holes that need mending. Next time, don't wait until the last minute to bring it over."

"Sorry. I let laundry back up." He pulled the end of her braid. Then, he ruffled Charlie's hair. "See ya."

"Bye, Uncle JT."

Alex glanced at Colton with lifted brow after JT slipped through the gate. "Did you forget what night it is?"

"Would you feed me if I had?"

"After last night—"

"I'm not here for dinner," he said, interrupting what she was about to say, worried she'd make an excuse to discontinue their dinners after the Misty-in-the-bush fiasco. "There's a kid's movie playing at the theatre. I wondered if you and Charlie would like a night out. My treat. We can stop and grab a hamburger on the way home."

She blinked.

He liked that he'd surprised her.

She glanced at Charlie, who was bouncing on the balls of his feet in anticipation, and laughed. "I think you have your answer."

"Yippee!"

Colton looked at his watch. "The next show starts in thirty minutes. Think we can make that?"

"We can try. Charlie, go change into a clean shirt and wash your hands."

The kid bounded through the kitchen door.

"A kid's movie?" Alex asked with a slight smirk.

He shrugged. "I like animation."

She beckoned him with a finger. It was a simple gesture

but very beguiling. "Come in while I scrub this lily poop off my arms."

"What?" Colton followed her to the kitchen sink. She held up her hands and he bent to see yellowish-orange smears on both arms. "Please, tell me that really isn't poop."

She smiled, and he experienced a jolt of desire. Her lips were quite possibly the most tempting he'd ever seen.

"I was arranging some lilies before JT showed up for repair work on his uniform." She pulled a white lily from a vase and sniffed its heady fragrance. She held it out to him. When he inhaled, she touched the flower to the end of his nose and then laughed. "Now you have lily poop on your nose."

He frowned and scrubbed at the tip of his nose with his palm.

"Anatomy of a lily." Alex pointed to the blossom's center. "This is the stamen, and this pod on the end is the anther. It produces the pollen. You have pollen on your nose."

She dampened a paper towel and touched it to a bar of soap. With his chin in her hand, she dabbed at the spot.

Her fingers felt warm against his skin. "What are you smiling about?"

She turned his face slightly. "I've never told you what a great nose you have."

"Pardon?"

She was close enough that they were breathing the same air as she studied where the pollen had been. His senses sharpened as his gaze roved her face, ending again, on her lips. Her scent, floral and soft—not as strong as the lily's— danced near the edge of his awareness, along with her touch.

"I have a thing for noses. I noticed yours the day I picked you up at the airstrip. Of course, I couldn't tell you then, because I didn't think you were a very nice man, but I can tell you now."

Her words brought his gaze up to meet hers. "Because, now I'm a nice man?"

She nodded slowly as if she'd just made up her mind about something. "You are a nice man with a very nice nose."

"Thanks. I think."

∾

*A*lex wasn't sure where the movie invitation had come from. With all the kids in the theatre, she wondered if Colton was wondering the same thing. She knew he wasn't fond of children, though he seemed to enjoy Charlie's company. Still, this was like trying to mix oil and water.

With her crazy schedule and money not growing on trees, a movie was rare. To enjoy popcorn and a soft drink on top of that—Charlie was in heaven. He sat between them, enthralled at what was taking place on the screen. The colors were vivid and the music lively. She enjoyed his wide-eyed wonder, and was grateful that Colton had offered to bring them.

Her eyes traveled from her son to Colton, who seemed just as engrossed in the story as her son. She had a hard time believing this was the same ornery man who'd climbed out of Beam's plane. The same man who'd blustered about not liking kids. He seemed to have softened since arriving in Eden Falls. His jaw wasn't quite as ridged and his scowl seemed a thing of the past.

She glanced back at the screen as she reached for the bucket of popcorn sitting on Charlie's lap. Her hand collided with Colton's. Her instinct was to jerk back, but he captured her fingers until she glanced his way. He stroked his forefinger along her palm before releasing his hold. She pulled her hand away, stunned by her body's reaction to his touch. She let Colton and Charlie finish the popcorn.

CHAPTER 11

Colton got out of the Lincoln Town Car in front of his house. His flight from Seattle had been uneventful. He wished he could say the same about the plane ride from Eden Falls to Seattle. Beam had scared the ever-living daylights out of him more than once. Colton had been queasy for an hour afterwards.

Hollywood wanted to turn one of his books into a movie, so he was in L.A. to begin negotiations. He had a meeting later with Jorge and his attorney to look over the contract. Tomorrow he'd meet with a producer and several screenwriters. Since he was in town for a few days, his publicist had scheduled a speaking engagement Thursday night. He'd be back in Eden Falls on Friday.

Consuela greeted him at the door with a pat to his cheek, a bottle of water, and her broken English. "You are skeeny."

"You need your eyes checked, Consuela. I've been eating the best pastry in the state of Washington every morning. You should come back with me and take some baking lessons."

She swatted at him. "You no 'preciate my cook-eng, I go cook for Meester Jorge. He pro'ly pay better than you, too."

"That cheap buzzard wouldn't give you half what I pay." He wheeled his suitcase in. "I brought you some dirty clothes."

She planted her hands on her ample hips. "Tha's what you bring Consuela? Dirty clothes? You can' find someone who wash for you?"

"Lucky for you, I did find someone to come in three times a week. She cleans and does laundry."

"How tha' lucky for me?"

"I'd be shipping my clothes home once a week."

His housekeeper's eyebrows rose almost to her hairline. "Maybe is time you learn to use a wash-eng machine."

"Then I wouldn't need you." He laughed when she stuck out her tongue.

Consuela was the one constant in his life. She had an apartment over the garage, and was there every day to cook and clean except, Sundays and Mondays when she visited her sister. She'd been with him since he turned twenty-two, received his sizable trust fund, and bought this house fresh out of college. She occupied the space a grandmotherly figure would have filled, if there had been a grandmother. Despite her having the tongue of a viper, he'd grown to love her.

The earth trembled beneath his feet at the realization. There was someone in this world he loved—though not romantically. The insight almost brought a tear to his eye. Almost.

He strode over to the credenza and flipped through the mail that wasn't important enough for Jorge to ship. Mostly junk. He moved to the wall of sliding glass doors, pushed one open, and walked to the railing. The air hanging over L.A. was heavy with smog—not a sight he'd missed, and certainly not the fresh air he'd become used to in Eden Falls.

"You have call from tha' hussy."

"Which one?" Colton asked without turning around. He

imagined Consuela framed in the open doorway, her hands fisted on her hips. She wasn't fond of Maci or Talia. She put up with Victoria.

"Maci. She call all the time. She no' believe me, you are no' home. I hang up o' her.

He'd get an earful from Maci, who didn't like Consuela any more than Consuela liked her. Maci knew he'd be out of touch most of the summer. He hadn't told her where he was going, afraid she'd show up. She was a little like Misty that way.

"Your mama, she call, too. She no' nice woman."

No secret there. He turned to look at his housekeeper. "I have a meeting with Jorge later. Can I bring him home for a late dinner?"

"You bring Mr. Jorge anytime, bu' leave the hussy home. She no eat wha' I cook. *Too fat-neng*," she mimicked perfectly, except for the broken English. "She whine too much."

Colton laughed. Heavens above he'd missed this woman.

"Wha' time you be back?"

"I'll call. I'm sure Jorge has missed your cooking as much as I have." He leaned against the railing, crossing one ankle over the other. "But, I have to warn you, I did find a girl in Washington who can cook almost as good as you."

"A girl?"

"Figure of speech. She's a woman, a mayor, and a mother. She has a five-year-old son."

Consuela's brown eyes softened. "He good boy?"

Just the thought of Charlie made Colton smile. "Yes, he's a very good boy. His mother, her name is Alex—"

"Alex. Tha' boy's name," Consuela interrupted, wrinkling her nose.

"Her name is Alexis, but everyone calls her Alex. She's done a good job raising her son alone."

Consuela took the end of her apron and swiped at a dirty spot on the glass door. "Alexis. Now, tha' pretty name. Is she pretty?"

He pictured Alex in his mind. "She is pretty, very sweet. Well liked."

She stopped polishing long enough to shoot a glance his way. "Why she rais-eng the boy alone?"

"His father was a Marine. He was killed in Iraq."

Consuela tsked and then cocked an eyebrow. "You li' thees girl?"

"Yes—Well…I like her as a friend."

She rolled her eyes dramatically. "You li' all women as frien's."

"No, this is different." Or was it? He was definitely feeling something for Alex. Her eerie green eyes had haunted his dreams last night. "She's…just a friend."

"Thees Alexis, if she smart, she won' put up wi' your nonsense." She turned and disappeared back into the house.

"You're right, Consuela," he mumbled to the empty doorway. "Alex would not put up with me."

~

*A*lex jolted awake when the phone rang. She sat up and grabbed for the receiver before it could wake Charlie. No one she knew would call this late unless it was an emergency. "Hello?"

"Hey, Sunshine. Did I wake you?"

She felt a smile tug at the corners of her mouth. "No one I know calls this late unless it's an emergency. Who is this?"

His familiar chuckle sounded in her ear. "You know who it is. I'm sorry to call so late. Jorge just left. He talked about you all through dinner, even invited my housekeeper to sit, so he could tell her about your Jeep."

She laughed. "I told you my Jeep would become famous. Tell Jorge we're ready to go to work for the right price."

"I'll do that."

She could hear the smile in his voice and was glad she'd put it there.

"Anyway, Jorge got me thinking about…"

Alex waited through a lengthy pause. "Are you still there?"

He cleared his throat. "Yeah. How's Charlie doing?"

She fell back onto her pillow. "He's fine."

"Did he have fun at Rec today?"

Colton McCreed is calling at eleven twenty-three to ask about Rec? "He said he did."

"What did they do?"

She closed her eyes trying to recall. "They made macaroni pictures to display in the library."

"Sounds like fun."

Alex held the phone away and looked at it. The voice belonged to Colton McCreed, but this had to be an imposter. She put the receiver back to her ear in time to hear him say, "Did you fall asleep, Mayor?"

"No. I'm here." The purple crescents she'd wear under her eyes tomorrow from too little sleep would look attractive.

"I have a surprise for him."

"For Charlie?"

"I scored a poster signed by all four Ninja Turtles today."

Colton McCreed took the time to get a present for Charlie? And not just any present, but something that would mean the world to him. "He'll love you forever."

"You'll have to contain him, Mayor. Remember, I don't do the *L* word."

She smiled. *Maybe you do the L word, you just don't realize it, yet.*

~

*C*olton slipped behind the wheel of his Maserati convertible. The leather seats—nothing like the cloth of that old Ford he'd been driving—fit the contours of his body perfectly. *Man, I've missed this baby.*

He zipped down the hill from his house a little faster than he should, top down, wind whipping through his hair. He'd have to take Maci for a ride along the coast tomorrow if she was free. Talia was headed to Italy for a modeling job in the morning, so they were having dinner tonight. Victoria was out of town and wouldn't be back until next week. He thought he'd miss these ladies over the summer, but calling them had felt mechanical. He shook his head at the thought. The feeling of routine would disappear once he was amid the nightlife familiar to him.

His thoughts turned to Alex and their conversation last night. He wasn't sure why he'd called her other than she'd been in his thoughts. Once on the phone, he'd had a hard time letting her go. Her sexy, sleepy voice had conjured images better left unimagined.

Half an hour later, he pulled into the parking lot of an office building and stopped next to a valet parking sign. He tossed his keys to the pimple-faced attendant. "Not a scratch."

Jorge greeted him just inside the lobby. "Today is all about you, Colton. Today we change the course of your career."

~

*A*lex was at the stove when Charlie ran into the kitchen. "Mom, I'm going to pick Colton up for dinner."

"He's not home, sweetie. He had to go to California for

the week." Her son's chin dropped to his chest and his shoulder's slumped. *Not good*. Her son was becoming too used to Colton at their house, and involved in their everyday lives. "But Jillian and Stella are coming over, and you can invite Tyson. We can eat on the patio."

Her words produced the smile so much like Peyton's.

She turned back to what she was doing, remembering Peyton's playfulness when she was cooking. She was always slapping his hands for lifting lids and sampling. He'd wrap his arms around her waist and nuzzle her neck until they were on the floor wrapped up in each other, dinner forgotten. That playful part of him lived on in Charlie's bright smile and twinkling brown eyes. She could see Peyton just under the surface when Charlie laughed. Her memories turned into the lingering ache she was so acquainted with.

When the phone rang later that night, long after the house was quiet, she suspected who the caller was before answering, and felt an unexpected stir of anticipation.

"Hey, Sunshine. You miss me?"

She leaned back into the cushions of the sofa. Her mind had turned to this man several times in the last twenty-four hours. She didn't like it, but hadn't done a lot to stop it either. "Charlie does, but we filled your seat tonight with Tyson. Stella and Jillian were here, too."

"No Misty?"

"Nope."

"Did you check the bushes?"

She laughed. "No, I didn't think of that."

"So you and Charlie have already replaced me with a towheaded kid sporting freckles?"

"He's cuter." She tucked her feet under her.

"Hey, I'm cute."

She pulled on a loose string at a hole just starting in the knee of her jeans. "According to whom?"

"Come on, mayor, admit it. You think I'm cute."

She swallowed, nervous about the direction the conversation had turned. "You're okay looking, for a city dweller."

"Wait, Stella was there? I thought she was going to a concert in Seattle."

"That fell through, hence the invitation for dinner."

"What happened?"

"Her boyfriend had something come up." *He called with some unbelievably stupid excuse, and Stella believed him. Again.*

"Is this the same guy that didn't show up for JT's barbecue?"

"Yes." She didn't trust Stella's boyfriend. Len cancelled, always at the last minute, with excuses that sounded too farfetched to be true. She was afraid Stella was going to get hurt.

"Was she disappointed?"

"She makes excuses for him, which is so unlike Stella. I don't understand. She's gorgeous, could have any guy, in fact..." She stopped short of mentioning Rowdy. She just assumed he watched Stella out of interest, which didn't mean anything. She sure wasn't going to start a rumor.

"In fact what?"

"Mmm...nothing."

"Really? You're one of those people?"

"What people?"

"The people who throw tidbits out there and then don't fill in the blanks?"

She pulled a throw off the back of the sofa and flung it over her legs so she wouldn't continue worrying the threads on her knee. "You should love those people. You're one of them. Authors leave readers hanging for the next revelation, the next clue. Isn't that called a cliffhanger?"

"In real life it's called annoying."

He had a knack for making her laugh, which was amazing considering the man she'd first met. Not in a million years would she have imagined herself curled up on the sofa talking to Colton McCreed like they were—dare she go so far as to say—friends.

"You didn't tell Charlie about my surprise, did you?"

"Of course not."

"Good. I'll be back in time for his Saturday morning game."

Another little shiver of anticipation wiggled its way through her, which was irrational. Even if he weren't with Misty, he was leaving at the end of summer, so, anything between them, other than friendship, was impossible. "He doesn't have a game due to the Fourth of July parade."

"Will I see you both there?"

"Actually, we're both in it."

"Really? Well…I'll be standing on the sidelines watching for you." He was quiet for a moment. "I'd better let you go. I'm meeting a friend for dinner."

She glanced at the clock on the mantle. Nine-thirty—kind of late for dinner. They'd never talked about his personal life, and she wondered if the friend was male or female. *None of my business.* "Have fun."

"Always do. 'Night, Sunshine."

"Goodnight, McCreed." After she disconnected she leaned forward and put her face in her hands. *This might become a problem.*

~

*C*olton sat back on the sofa chastising himself for calling Alex for the second night in a row. His only excuse, she'd been on his mind all day. Actually, she hadn't been far from his thoughts since he'd arrived in L.A. For some crazy reason, he valued the friendship they seemed to be building. He'd told Consuela they were just friends, and he'd never been *just friends* with a woman before. Another first. But he enjoyed Alex's company. Both she and Charlie made him notice, and then appreciate, the simple joys of life. She had a positive, calming affect over him that he'd never felt around another person before, and he appreciated that gift from her.

But, he didn't want her to think there was more to the calls than simple friendship. And women did tend to jump to conclusions. Yet, Alex wasn't like most of the women he'd met. She was beguiling, but in a neighbor next door way. There wouldn't be any ulterior motives to her friendship, or expectations.

He shifted positions, never realizing how uncomfortable his sofa was until this moment. He glanced around his professionally decorated living room devoid of color and personality. Why had he ever agreed to the tasteless art on the walls or the uncomfortable furniture? The room was sterile and uninviting. No wonder he felt so agitated all the time. This place didn't have the relaxing atmosphere he'd become used to in Eden Falls.

Maybe it was time for a change.

~

*C*olton felt a boyhood eagerness the moment Beam touched the Cessna down in Eden Falls. He stopped at the rental long enough to drop his bags inside the front door, and then headed for the mayor's house. He kept telling himself he was in a rush because he wanted to see the delight on Charlie's face when he opened his gift. Deep down he denied there was more to his eagerness.

When Charlie, who was playing in the front yard, spotted

him, he ran as fast as his little legs could carry him, and launched himself. Colton had no choice but to catch the kid in mid-air. He wrapped his arms around Colton's neck and squeezed. Other than the perfunctory hugs at parties or the touch of a woman in his bed, Colton didn't hug. In fact, he couldn't remember the last time he'd been hugged like this.

"I missed you."

Charlie's simple words caused a lump in Colton's throat to form. It felt good to be missed even if it was by a five-year-old. His eyes locked on Alex. She was sitting on the porch steps next to Charlie's little tow-headed friend, Tyson. He patted Charlie's back and set him down. "Hey, guess what? I brought you a present."

Charlie eyed the cardboard tube Colton had dropped onto the grass, his eyes lighting with uninhibited joy. "What is it?"

"Let's go up onto the porch and see."

Charlie ran ahead and plopped down next to his mother. Without thinking, Colton bent and kissed Alex's cheek. Her eyes grew wide, and her mouth dropped open. He shouldn't have done that. "Hi, honey, I'm home," he said, trying to make light of his action.

"Uh...I see that. What do you have there?"

"A surprise for Charlie." He handed the tube to the boy. "Let your mom help you, while I get something to drink."

～

*A*lex wasn't sure how she felt about Colton going inside and making himself so at home. *What was he thinking to kiss me like that? In front of Charlie, no less. We barely know each other.* Luckily, Charlie was too engrossed in his gift to notice.

She wiggled the end off the tube. Charlie tipped it upside down and shook. When nothing came out, Alex slid her fingers inside and pulled the poster free. Colton came out and squatted down behind them as Alex unrolled the poster.

"Awesome! Look, Tyson. It's the Ninja Turtles, and they signed it!" Charlie ran a finger over one of the signatures in wonderment. Then he jumped up and caught Colton around the neck for another hug. "Thanks, Colton. This is the best present ever!"

Colton laughed. "You're welcome, buddy."

"Can I hang it up in my room, Mom?"

Alex stood. "Let me get some tape and we'll hang it temporarily. Tomorrow, we'll buy a frame to keep it safe."

As Charlie and Tyson barreled inside, Colton held out his hand, and Alex pulled him to his feet. He tugged a small package wrapped in brown paper from his back pocket. "I have something for you, too."

She looked at him in surprise. "You didn't have to—"

"It's no big deal, just a little something I picked up."

He took the poster from her so she could unwrap a book, an antique, titled "The Language of Flowers". She ran fingers over the embossed letters and the image of a rose on the front, then lifted the delicate cover and examined the pages yellowed with age. Blinking back tears, she glanced up at Colton. "I don't know what to say. This is beautiful, Colton. I...I love it."

"Don't get all sentimental on me, Mayor. It's just a small token of appreciation for all you've done. I'm not real good with thank yous."

She looked from him to the book with its tarnished leather cover. "You're wrong. You're very good with thank yous. This is...so perfect." She ran a finger under a watery eye. "I've never received such a thoughtful gift."

He shrugged as if the gesture meant nothing, but she knew a book like this took some thought. And time to locate.

"I'm glad you like it."

~

*C*olton didn't have any trouble finding a good spot for the Fourth of July parade, since half the town seemed to be participating. It began on the west end of Main Street, circled the square, and ended in the middle school parking lot. The high school band started the procession with an out of tune rendition of the "Battle Hymn", followed by a mounted posse with JT in the lead. Next was a car decorated as a fish, advertising The Fly Shop. Rance waved from the driver's seat. A fire truck passed with firemen atop throwing candy. Then came a passel of kids dressed as cowboys and Indians, riding bikes they'd done their best to decorate as horses. A boy with a painted face and a huge headdress rode straight for him. He had a grin the size of the state of Washington. "Hi Colton!"

"Who is that?" Colton teased.

"It's me! Charlie."

"Wow. You look fierce."

"I know," Charlie replied with all the confidence of his age.

After a wobbly kickoff, he rode away. Colton couldn't help the chuckle that bubbled up from deep inside. The kid just did that to him. Made him happy.

He watched for an hour as floats and bands and kids marched along the parade route. The last entry to roll past was a convertible with Mayor Alexis Blackwood sitting on the back. She wore a flowery dress, her sunshine smile, and looked as bright as the summer day. As she passed, she executed a perfect beauty queen wave for him.

He turned to follow the convertible, but Misty grabbed his arm. "I've been looking everywhere for you."

He looked down at her possessive hand. "I've been right here."

"I need to talk to you." Her tone turned from flirtatious to stony.

He took a deep breath and blew it out. "Okay, talk."

She glanced around at the crowd. "Not here. Can we go for a drive?"

"No."

Her blue eyes blazed. "It's important. I promise you're going to want to hear what I have to say."

He was certain nothing Misty had to say could be *that* important. He turned and pointed to one of the evergreens shading the front lawn of Eden Falls' Town Hall. "We can talk over there."

Misty pulled him to the backside of the tree. He wasn't sure what to expect, but he had a feeling some kind of proposition was coming. Then there would be some pre-Fourth of July fireworks when he turned her down. He wished there were fewer people around, afraid of what Misty would display, but he'd had all the private with her that he was going to have. They might as well get this—whatever this was—over with, rather than draw it out and ruin the whole day.

He stood with arms folded over his chest. "What's so important?"

"I'm pregnant."

His mouth dropped open like one of the fish mounted on The Fly Shop's walls. A scary tingling started at the base of his skull and moved along his shoulders, then down both arms. He closed his jaw to make sure he still could before it dropped open again. "You're what?"

She looked down at her feet. "You heard me, Colton."

He collapsed onto the grass. His chest felt as if an elephant had decided to sit there, crushing the air out of him. When his arms began to itch and his lips went numb, he was sure he was having a heart attack. He sucked in a breath. "I must have heard you wrong, because that's not possible."

She glared at him. "What do you mean it's not possible?"

He squinted up through the sunlight that contorted her features. With her hair lit from behind, she resembled Medusa. "I mean it's not possible. We were only together one night, and I was careful. I'm always *very* careful."

She sank to the ground. Her smirk made him want to strangle her. "Obviously, you weren't careful enough."

"No." Colton lowered his shaking head to his hands. "No, no, no, no, *no*!"

"Do you think saying that repeatedly will make the baby magically disappear?"

"This *can't* be happening." He looked over at her.

"Well, it did." She smiled, and he was tempted to strangle her for a second time. Instead, he ripped up a handful of grass and threw it, and then another, acting like a child himself.

She leaned back on the palms of her hands. "It doesn't have to be so awful, does it?"

"It couldn't be any more awful. I don't want kids."

"For not wanting a kid, you sure are chummy with Charlie."

"Charlie's not *my* kid. I like my life the way it is. I don't have time for kids or relationships. I told you that from the begin—"

"Stop yelling at me. Do you think I planned this?"

A sick suspicion flooded through him. Both Alex and JT had told him she'd do anything to get what she wanted. JT had warned him more than once. He narrowed his eyes. "Did you?"

Her hand swung through the air, but with his foggy brain, he couldn't move out of the way fast enough. Her palm connected with his cheek, the stinging force snapping his head sideways. Before he could react, she jumped to her feet and stomped off.

He fell back onto the grass, holding the side of his face, sick to his stomach. This couldn't be happening. Misty had to be mistaken. He was not father material. After the childhood he'd experienced, he didn't want to bring a kid into the world. He didn't want to be responsible for the mayhem that would indelibly follow. He had no reference to follow, no guidebook.

He also had no one to blame but himself. He pushed the heels of his hands into his eye sockets until he saw red. What now? His life had just been turned upside down and inside out in a split second. Two little words and everything, *everything*, instantly changed.

He wasn't sure how long he lay there, but didn't move when Misty came back and sat next to him. She was humming a tune that irritated him to the core. He took a breath and blew it out hard. "What now?"

"Now, we plan a wedding."

"Not in this lifetime." He stood and walked away.

CHAPTER 12

Colton spent the rest of the afternoon by the river, watching the water rush past—along with his sanity. *This can't be happening, this can't be happening*, kept running through his mind. He was having a nightmare. Any moment he would wake up, gasp a sigh of relief, and never, ever, go near another woman again.

Okay, that was extreme. But still.

As dusk fell, he made his way back to the town square for the fireworks display, his eyes searching out the person who was quickly becoming his security blanket. He spotted Alex, and plopped down next to her. Stella and Jillian were next to her. Charlie and Tyson ran circles around the small group, waving lit sparklers.

Stella leaned around Alex. "Congratulations, Daddy."

Alex raised her brows. "Misty was just here."

Colton fell back on the blanket and put his forearm over his eyes. "This can't be happening, this can't be happening—"

"Hi, Colton!"

Colton peeked around his arm at Charlie. "Hey, buddy."

"Are you sick?"

"Very." He'd been sick to his stomach all afternoon.

"Mama?"

"He's not really sick, baby." Alex pulled Charlie to her other side so Stella could hand him another lit sparkler. "He's just got a lot on his mind."

Charlie glanced at him with worry. "You can have my sparkler, Colton."

"No thanks, Charlie. I'm okay. You and Tyson have a good time."

Charlie stepped back, still looking anxious, so Colton sent him a smile.

Stella propped herself up by her elbows. "So, it looks like you'll be taking more than just a novel home with you."

He ignored her.

"Misty said there's going to be a wedding, and the whole town is invited."

Colton turned to look at Stella, temped to ask where her boyfriend was. The Fourth of July and Len was absent, again. That would be cruel—him lashing out to hurt someone because he was so angry with himself.

This town is turning me into a namby-pamby.

"So what's the scoop?"

"We're not getting married, Stella. I'm not going to compound this..." He almost said mistake, but he'd never utter that word. His birth had been a mistake, and he'd always known it. He would never let this child...*his child*...feel his or her birth was a mistake. "I'm not going to compound the situation with marriage. It would be different if we loved each other, but we don't."

"What are you going to do?" Jillian asked, her expression laced with concern.

He looked at the darkening sky. He'd been running different scenarios through his brain ever since Misty had poleaxed him hours earlier. "I'll"—he forced the next words out of his mouth—"move Misty to L.A., if that's what she wants. I'll get her a townhouse or condo and provide her with whatever she and the baby need."

"You're going to keep her as your mistress?"

"No, Stella." She was the next person he wanted to strangle. "Misty and I won't be together. She'll be free to see whomever she wants."

"She'll consider that moving from one prison to another," Alex said, her voice almost a whisper

Colton jumped to his feet. "We're not getting married. That would only cause a whole new set of problems. We made a baby. I'll shoulder my responsibility. I'll provide for Misty and the"—it was still so hard to wrap his head around the fact that he was going to be a father—"and my child."

He glanced down at Alex, took a moment to hate himself for the disappointment he'd put on her face, before he turned and walked away.

❦

"*Y*ou shouldn't have been so hard on him, Stella." Jillian said.

"Maybe he needs someone to be hard on him. He seems to be one of those guys who moves through life with a ticket on the E A S Y train. Well, guess what? It's time to face reality." Stella smiled. "And reality with Misty will be terrifying."

Alex watched Colton shoulder his way through the crowd. Her heart went out to him, but she and JT had tried to warn him. Actions had consequences, and those consequences weren't always pleasant. She couldn't stand the thought of an innocent baby paying the price for those actions.

Alex stood and looked around until she spotted Misty. She was talking with the girls from Dahlia's Salon. Pregnancy would explain Misty's lousy moods lately, but was she actually pregnant or making it up to win the game? JT had to talk to Colton, tell him he should attend a doctor's appointment with Misty to make sure she was telling the truth. Alex hated to believe Misty was capable of a lie on that scale, but she wouldn't put it past her. Colton should cover all his bases before buying a condo and moving Misty anywhere.

~

*W*hen the fireworks started, Alex lay back on the blanket and pulled Charlie close. As the bright colors exploded overhead, they were unaware Colton stood back scrutinizing their interaction. Charlie pointed at the sky, and Alex oohed and ahhed at the appropriate times.

Could he do that? Could he hold his child close while watching fireworks overhead? He could, because he'd planned to do that tonight with Charlie.

He was going to be a father, whether he was prepared for it or not. What kind of father he would be was his choice. Now was the time to decide.

His own father hadn't been too bad when Colton was very young. They'd never watched fireworks together, but when his dad was around, he'd spent small moments with Colton. Once his parent's divorce was underway, Colton became the bargaining chip. Mom used him to squeeze more money from dad. Dad used him to strip any remaining dignity from his mom. His mother started using drugs and alcohol to deaden the pain and humiliation of her husband going through women, each one younger than the previous.

Colton had been caught in the middle, between two selfish parents who'd cared nothing about the pain the fallout had caused him.

He'd need to read parenting books and take classes, gather advice on what to do. He already knew first hand what not to do.

~

A week before his trip to L.A., Colton had started running the trail along the river with JT each morning. After JT coaxed and prodded incessantly, Colton tried the trail just to shut him up, and became hooked. He climbed out of his car the morning after the fireworks and scanned the towering pines that lined the river. A mist hung over the tree-tops. The eagle's nest JT had pointed out the last time they were here was visible, but he couldn't see the eagle.

He turned when he heard JT's tires crunch over the gravel when he entered the parking lot and pulled to a stop. After their greeting, they performed a quick warm up before they began their jog in silence.

The mist had sealed in the scent of pine and damp earth. Both had become very familiar to his seemingly heightened senses. The river gurgled over rocks and splashed against the bank, lending a calm to his soul. The only other sound was the soles of their shoes meeting the dirt underfoot. He found it hard not to be awed by the overwhelming beauty of this place.

"Congratulations."

Colton glanced over at the grin JT wore. "I figured you'd heard."

"Secrets don't stay secret for very long in a small town. Are you sure Misty's pregnant?"

Colton stumbled, but caught himself before hitting the

ground. What an idiot. The thought had never occurred to him.

"Alex called me last night and said you should check before making plans," JT said as if reading his mind.

Alex doubted her friend. "I never thought Misty might lie. I did ask if she'd planned it."

"Bet that went over well."

"She slapped me so hard I saw stars." He raised fingertips to his still tender cheekbone.

"Maybe you should make sure she's pregnant, and then make sure it's yours."

Colton stumbled again. *Double idiot.* "Has she been seeing someone else?"

"Not that I know of."

Colton glanced over at JT. "Do you think Alex would know?"

"If Alex knew, she would have told you."

As they ran, Colton tried to concentrate on his breathing, but his mind was racing in too many directions

"Misty told Alex you're getting married."

Unbelievable. "She seems to be telling everyone that, but I have no intention of ever getting married. Especially to someone I don't love."

"You should have thought of that before you slept with her."

Colton snorted. "That's something I would expect the mayor to say. Do you two telepathically send messages back and forth?"

JT grinned. "Great minds think alike."

The sun broke through the mist momentarily, casting beams of light through the boughs onto the trail. "I guess I should demand a paternity test."

"Yes you should." JT glanced his way. "And if the baby is yours?"

"If the baby is mine, I'll move Misty to L.A., get her settled in a condo. I'll pay all the medical bills and give her money for anything the baby needs."

"A kept woman."

They'd reached the spot where Colton usually turned around while JT continued on to complete his ten-mile run.

He stopped, heaving for air. "I'm not a rotten piece of scum who knocks up a woman and then leaves. I also don't plan on keeping a woman. I have no intention of ever being with Misty again. She'll be free to see whomever she wants, whenever she wants, as long as she takes our child into consideration. I'll do the same." He bent and rested his hands on his knees. "I'll write her a big fat check once a month so she and our baby can live comfortably. I won't be an absent father. I'll be there for him or her. I'm a selfish S.O.B. who never wanted kids, but because of one stupid night, I'm now going to be a dad. I'll do the best I can, but I'm not getting married and compounding my stupidity."

JT, who'd been jogging in place, stopped and set a hand on Colton's shoulder. "Can you take a day off from writing, Mr. Big Shot from L.A.?"

Colton straightened, hands on hips, chest still heaving, but not from jogging. "If I sat down at my computer today, I'd probably kill off all my characters for stupidity."

"I have the day off. Maybe we can talk Alex and Charlie into a picnic and some tubing."

Colton squinted through the rays of sun breaking through the pines. "I hesitate to ask, but what is tubing?"

⁓

The river moved slowly as Alex rounded a bend. She glanced back to make sure Charlie was close. He and Rowdy were scanning the trees that lined the banks for birds. At the same time, Rowdy was keeping a stealthy eye on Stella, who was close behind with Colton.

Her gaze moved further up river to JT and the woman he'd brought with him. Bridget. Talk about ditzy bombshell. Between Misty and Bridget, she was beginning to think her brother had lost his mind.

Alex leaned back in her tube, enjoying the slow pace as she rounded another curve. The hot temperatures, the fluffy clouds passing overhead, and the unreal blue of the sky made for a perfect day. She closed her eyes.

She'd been tubing this river with friends and family since she was little. Once July hit and the water warmed a little, they'd come here with a group and tube down to Hunter's Campground, where they would have already dropped coolers for lunch. They'd laze the rest of the afternoon away in the sun or load a truck back up with tubes and make another run.

The cold hand that wrapped around her ankle opened her eyes.

Colton grinned. "Now that my butt is numb from the frigid water, this is more relaxing than a trip to the spa."

"Really?" She asked with mock, wide-eyed excitement. "We've had this secret all this time and didn't even know it? We'll have to start charging admission."

He clung onto her ankle with one hand and raised his sunglasses with the other, his gaze intense.

"What?"

"Has your opinion of me changed drastically, now that I've gotten one of your friends pregnant and refused to marry her?"

Alex glanced around for Charlie. He'd taken ahold of a low branch, waiting for JT and Bridget. Stella had caught up to Rowdy, and they were laughing about something. Alex turned back to Colton, who was still watching her. His gray eyes didn't appear so stormy anymore. In fact, they were very attractive eyes that seemed to be looking into her soul at the moment. "I'm not sure what my opinion is, Mr. McCreed."

He settled his sunglasses into place. "Digressing to Mr. McCreed says a lot."

"I know Misty well enough to realize she might have done something to enhance her chances of getting pregnant, but I never thought she'd use a baby as a means of escaping Eden Falls." She moved a hand along the cool surface of the water. She didn't understand Misty's way of thinking. She never had. The way she used people and exploited facts for her benefit was beyond Alex's comprehension. She glanced up and met Colton's gaze. "She's not a very nice person."

"What's her story?"

For the second time since she'd met him, she said, "Not for manuscript purposes."

"Just between us."

"On Misty's sixth birthday, her mother, Arleen Douglas, sat her on the porch steps, got in the family car and drove away. Forever. Mr. Douglas had just purchased the hardware and lumber store. He was so busy trying to make a go of the new business he'd invested everything into, he didn't have time to give a little girl, whose mother had just abandoned her, the attention she needed. My mom, Stella's mom, and Jolie's mom all took turns having Misty over, became surrogate mothers. We all understood something terrible had happened and tried to be there for her, but nothing anyone did was ever enough for Misty. She always wanted more."

"That explains a lot."

"She has always believed two things. First, her mother left because Eden Falls is so small and boring. Second, if her mother had stayed, her life would be a magical fairy tale instead of what it actually is. She looks at Eden Falls as her bane. Living here weighs her down, holds her back from being *someone*. You can take her away from it all. You can offer her something new and exciting—a whole new life.

"This is just my theory, but it seems, because of the abandonment, Misty has always been afraid of being hurt by others, so she does the hurting first. She leaves others before they can leave her. She broke up with boys, and now men, before they can break up with her. She's always used her mom's leaving as an excuse for her bad behavior. She justifies every wrong with that defense. She looks for how a person or situation can benefit her, never the other way around."

She allowed a small laugh to escape. "I can't believe I just told you all of that. I wouldn't, except I believe this baby, if there is a baby, is going to need a sweet, loving, *grounded*, father, because I'm not sure what kind of a mother Misty will be. She hates that her mother left, which, in her eyes at least, is her father's fault or Eden Fall's fault, but I wouldn't be shocked if Misty did the same thing."

Colton's Adam's apple bobbed in a nervous swallow.

"I'm not telling you this to scare you, but to warn you. I'm not sure you can count on Misty to stay in L.A. and take care of the baby, if that was your intention."

❧

*A*lex wasn't the bearer of good news. Not only was he going to be a father, but he also might end up the sole parent once this child was born. He couldn't do this alone. He, who had no experience to fall back on, might have to be the guiding force for his son or daughter. He couldn't travel to book signings and appearances with a child, so he'd have to hire a nanny. He'd have to conduct interviews and make sure he had someone he could trust. Consuela might agree to help. He hadn't even thought of how she might react to a child in the house.

He leaned his head back and closed his eyes against the bright sunlight. "I guess you wouldn't be willing to move to L.A. and—"

"No."

He smiled. "You didn't let me finish."

She released a quick laugh that held no humor. "I didn't need to."

Taking off his sunglasses with one hand, he scrubbed the fingers of his other hand through his hair. "I have every intention of being a father to this baby, Alex. I don't have to marry Misty to do that. If she chooses to stay and be a mother, she won't have to work another day in her life. If she wants to work, I'll make certain the baby has the best childcare available."

"Money is nice, Mr. McCreed, but what about your baby being born out of wedlock? Will you give him or her your name? And what about love? Can you give this baby the love it will need?"

He pounded a fist on the tube creating a hollow, non-threatening sound that defeated his purpose of pounding his fist in the first place. Fortunately, Alex didn't laugh. "My name is Colton. I hate it when you call me *Mr. McCreed*. I feel like we've become better friends than that, Alex."

"Okay...*Colton*, can you give this baby the love it will need?

He locked an arm over Alex's tube and pulled it around so they were eye to eye. "I don't know. I think I can, thanks to you and Charlie. My dinners with you seem to have softened my perspective a little. I've seen what a family can be, what having a relationship with a child should be. I respect and admire the way you've raised your son, and I'd want to have that kind of relationship with my child. You were dealt a raw deal when you lost your husband, Sunshine. I believe you, Peyton, and Charlie would have been the ultimate happy family." He leaned forward and wiped the tear that left a trail down her cheek. "If anyone deserves a happily ever after, it's you and Charlie."

She gave him a feeble smile. "Thank you."

"It's pretty staggering when you think how the direction of your life can change in an instant or with a word—or two. Everything that happens after that moment is dependent upon your reaction."

Of course, he was thinking of yesterday afternoon when Misty told him she was pregnant. Alex, on the other hand, was probably thinking of the moment she was informed of her husband's death, which made him wince at his poor choice of words. He glanced over, afraid of what he might see, but she was smiling. "What?"

"The direction of my life changed the moment Charlie was conceived. I can't imagine my life without him. I'm not sure I could have moved forward after Peyton's death without knowing I was carrying a part of him with me."

She amazed him. He was always thinking the negative of a situation and she was just the opposite. They were lost in their own thoughts as the river carried them along. Finally he said, "Now, it's my turn to lecture."

She released her rusty laugh. "You lecturing me…this should be interesting."

"For you to have a happily ever after, you have to date. I don't mean to sound cruel, but your husband's been gone a long time. Don't you think you should move on with your life?"

Her eyebrows drew together in a frown. "I don't need to be reminded. And I date."

"When? I haven't see you out with anyone since I've been here."

"I went to the movie with you and Charlie a week ago."

"That's not the same as dating and you know it." He gave

her a moment for rebuttal and when she didn't, he added, "Come on, Sunshine. Spill it. Something's on your mind."

"I just wish everyone would quit worrying about me not dating. I'll meet someone when the time is right. It's not like I sit at home and whine about my circumstances. I'm happy. I live a full, busy life."

His smile turned into a laugh.

"What?"

"You're a very passionate person when you want to be."

She studied him a moment. "Aren't you? Passionate about certain things?"

Other than writing, he couldn't remember the last time he'd felt passionate about anything. Even writing had taken a leave of absence from passion. Luckily, it was coming back. "You're trying to change the subject."

"No...maybe. Yes."

"You need to date, and please, look for someone better suited to you than Hercules."

"Hercules?" she asked with raised eyebrows.

"If the shoe fits."

She smiled. "I thought writers frowned on clichés."

"They do, and you're still trying to change the subject."

She ran her fingers through the water again, keeping her gaze averted. "I'll date when the time is right. I'm not in any hurry."

He knew he wasn't going to get more out of her on the subject. He wasn't sure he wanted to. "Are we good, or do you think me a scoundrel who pillages women and villages?"

She laughed. "Oh, I definitely think you're a scoundrel, but I don't think you've done much pillaging of women or villages. Could you keep that down to a minimum—for my sake? I'm not sure how to handle a pillager."

He was relieved Alex didn't despise him. For some unexplainable reason, her opinion meant a lot, and her friendship had grown important to him. In fact, several friendships he'd made in this little town were important. He released her tube and splashed water at her. She splashed him back. Within seconds they were both off their tubes, having a full-fledged water fight.

That night Colton lay on the sofa blaming his change of heart on Alex. The more he thought about it, the more he didn't want his son or daughter to be born out of wedlock. As much as he hated the decision, marrying Misty was the right thing to do. Misty would want an elaborate wedding, but she'd have to settle for a quiet elopement.

His thoughts turned to Alex. He'd been wrong about her on so many levels. As mayor, she was sensitive, yet capable. She was sure of herself without conceit. She was ambitious, but with the town's interest in mind rather than her own. There was no pretense or guile about her. She was honest, hardworking, and loyal to the community. She seemed to have business and motherhood balanced about as well as any working mother could. Even though she worked long hours as a mayor and a business owner, she made time for her son, and Charlie was a well-rounded, fine mannered, happy child.

He appreciated her honesty. She was thoughtful and sweet. And surprisingly sensual.

There was something very sexy about a woman who knew who she was and what she wanted. Her wholesome, girl next-door appearance fooled him at first. Had he ever been around anyone as authentic as Alex seemed to be? The answer was yes. The people in this town were made of the same stuff. What you saw was what you got, no bones about it. Honest and true to heart. It was comforting to be around people who were so down to earth. Living here for the summer was an experience he'd never forget. He was sure he'd pull the memories out often. Alex and Charlie would be at the heart of those memories.

He smiled at the thought of his first day in town. He had definitely been wrong about her from the very beginning.

CHAPTER 13

After tucking a sleeping Charlie into bed, Alex walked into the living room and fell back on the sofa next to Stella. The front door burst open, bouncing off the wall behind it. Alex jumped up and faced Misty, who stood glaring at her.

"You can't just bust into my house anytime you want, Misty."

"You scared us to death," Stella said, hand still to her chest. "Don't you know how to knock?"

Alex shut the front door and ran fingers over the fresh gouge in her wall.

"Why are you trying to sabotage my relationship with Colton?"

"How is Alex sabotaging something that doesn't exist?" Stella asked with a laugh.

Alex stepped into the hall to see if Misty's ruckus had roused Charlie. He'd been so exhausted after their day of fun and sun on the river, he'd fallen asleep on the car ride home. No sound came from his room. She returned to the living room where Misty and Stella were exchanging volleys.

"You don't know anything, Stella, so stay out of this." Misty pointed a finger at Alex. "You and Colton went on a picnic today."

"No, I went on a picnic with Charlie. Colton was there, because JT invited him."

Misty fisted her hands on her hips. "Why wasn't I invited?"

Alex laughed, because Misty was so crazy-person preposterous. She'd cheated on JT, yet expected him to invite her to the river with them. "You're kidding, right?"

"Why would JT invite you?" Stella asked.

"Stay out of this, Stella." Misty turned to Alex. "Why didn't *you* invite me?"

"It was JT's party. He called and asked if Charlie and I wanted to go to the river. Tatum said she'd watch the shop, so I said yes."

Misty plopped down in a chair. "Why don't I believe you?"

"Maybe because you lie so often, you think everyone else does," Stella said.

"I don't lie…unless I have to." Misty leaned back and put her feet up on an ottoman. "You both have to help me. Colton says he won't marry me."

Alex exchanged a glance with Stella before she sat on the other end of the sofa. "We're sorry about your situation, and we're sorry things aren't working out the way you'd planned, but there is nothing we can do to help."

"You can talk to Colton. For some weird reason, he listens to you. Tell him it would be best for the baby if we got married."

The audacity Misty possessed never failed to floor Alex. She shook her head. "I've already told you, I'm not getting involved. This is your mess. You'll have to find your own way out."

Misty shot Alex a murderous look before turning to Stella. "You talk to him then. Reason with him. You're good at convincing people to do things they don't want to do."

Stella rolled her eyes. "What are you talking about?"

"How do you get the brats you teach to do their home-work? Use your teacher voice. Talk to him."

Stella leaned forward. "My students are not brats."

"If you were my friends—"

Alex held up her hand. "Stop right there. You're not going to play the friendship card on this one. You slept with someone you barely knew, and now you're pregnant. There is nothing we can do. You're going to have to deal with the situation yourself."

Misty jumped up and stormed out the same way she'd entered, slamming the front door against the wall, again.

⁓

*A*lex delivered flowers for a small wedding early Saturday morning, and then was off to Charlie's game with Tatum and Stella manning the shop until noon. When she arrived, Colton and Rowdy sat in her usual top bleacher spot. She hugged her parents and the Blackwood's, gave Charlie a few encouraging words before mounting the steps. "What are you two doing here?"

"I haven't been to any of Charlie's games this year," Rowdy said.

Alex grinned. "He got to you yesterday on the river, didn't he. Made you feel guilty."

Rowdy nodded. "He's good. Reminds me of his mom."

"And I came to check on my landscape artist. She didn't show this morning." Colton patted the bench beside him.

She sat. "Wedding flowers had to be delivered for a noon wedding. I'll have to mow after work tonight."

"Why don't you, Charlie, and I get some dinner after-wards. My treat."

"Charlie has a birthday sleepover at four."

"Then it will just be the two of us."

"I don't think so." She pronounced each word deliberately. "I had an angry Misty in my living room last night. I'm not getting into the middle of whatever's going on between the two of you."

"There's nothing going on between us."

Rowdy's loud bark of laughter echoed over the bleachers.

Alex raised a brow. "Well, Misty thinks there is. She was mad she didn't get invited to the river yesterday, and assumed we—you and I—were together."

"We were together."

"But not the way she means."

Alex turned her attention from their conversation to the game. Her son approached home plate, swinging the bat back and forth, stretching out his muscles. He glanced up at her with his happy eyes, so much like his father. She missed her husband the most at moments like this and wished he could be here to cheer his son on.

~

*C*olton stood over the intimidating lawn mower. He'd never pushed one in his life, but it couldn't be that difficult.

He glanced over the levers then squatted next to the handle he'd seen Alex pull to start the thing. The handle was attached to a cord, but did he have to push a button or flip the bar on the handle first? He'd looked through the kitchen drawer where he'd noticed manufacturers warranties for the fridge, stove, washer, and dryer, but saw nothing for this contraption.

If that tiny mayoral nymph could do it…

~

*a*lex pulled to a stop in front of her rental wondering why the neighbor's son was mowing the front lawn. Colton came down the porch steps and took her arm. "He's already been paid, so we can go."

She glanced over her shoulder as Colton turned her around. "You paid the neighbor to mow the lawn?"

"I'm contributing to his college fund."

"Where are we going?"

He stopped. "To dinner. Remember? You. Me. Going to dinner."

She pulled from his grasp. "Ohhh…riiight. Nope. Still not a good idea."

"Why?" He took her hand and led her to the old Ford, parked at the curb. "It wasn't our place to invite Misty, therefore it's not our problem. I'll drive, because that jalopy of yours scares me."

Once they pulled away from the curb, she said, "It was Peyton's."

He glanced at her. "What was Peyton's?"

"The Jeep." She had very few of his possessions left. Charlie kept one of his father's baseball hats and a glove. Peyton's metals were in a box in her nightstand drawer. JT had made a display box for the flag she'd been given at Peyton's funeral, which sat on Charlie's dresser. The Jeep was all she had left. "It was Peyton's Jeep, before…"

"Sorry. I shouldn't be making fun of it."

Alex smiled. "Don't be sorry. It is a jalopy, I just can't give it up, yet."

They drove to South Fork about forty miles away, had a nice dinner, and didn't bring Misty into the conversation once. This was the first time Alex had ever been alone with Colton for any length of time since the first day they'd met. They talked and laughed comfortably, until she started probing about his childhood. He evaded her questions until she pinned him down.

He fell back against his chair. "Why do you want to know?"

Good question. "Because I don't know anything about you. Not really."

He studied her for a long minute. "You didn't do an internet search on me when Jorge called?"

"No."

"Why?"

If she read his books, she probably would have done a search. Since she didn't, the idea never occurred to her. "Jorge answered any questions I asked, so I didn't feel the need."

He planted his elbows on the arms of his chair and rested his chin on his fingers. "Why are you so curious now?"

"I'm just making conversation. You know all there is to know about me, but I don't know anything about you. You grew up in Los Angeles. Do you have a big family, cousins, lots of friends? As a kid, what did you do in your spare time? Do you have any pets?"

Colton picked up his water glass. He looked into the bottom before taking a swallow and setting back down. *He's contemplating how much to tell me, but why?*

"Despite your opinion, I'm still seven years from forty. I grew up in L.A., attended private schools, and went to college at Columbia. I wanted to be a writer for most of my life." He set his glass down. "Both my father and mother were only children, so no aunts or uncles, no cousins, no family dinners, no pets. Yes, I had friends in school, got into trouble a little more than I should have."

He ran fingers through his hair. When he first arrived in town, his hair, sticking up in every direction, drove her crazy. She wanted to comb it, tame it into some sort of order. Now, she couldn't imagine it any other way.

"My father was, still is a screenwriter. He traveled all the time, was on location all over the world. When he was home he kept crazy hours, worked day and night. He was a ladies man. Whenever we were in public, he flirted openly with women, whether my mother was present or not, and they ate it up. I remember the looks my mother gave him."

He twisted his water glass back and forth in a nervous fashion. "Even at a very young age, I knew what he was doing was wrong. I knew he was hurting my mom"—he glanced at her—"but I worshiped him anyway, the way a child adores his father. I basked in the attention he gave me, when he had the time, which wasn't often. He was a lousy husband, but he wasn't a bad dad, just busy. He was always on the phone or in meetings. He had this huge at-home office that was off limits. I'd sneak in every chance I got, just to be near him. He'd pull me up on his lap and let me sit there while he conducted business, until my nanny came to drag me away."

She could tell him talking about his childhood was hard. Sometimes dredging up memories was like that. "You grew up privileged."

He looked down at the table with a huff of laughter, minus the amusement. "Yes, privileged. We had a cook, a housekeeper, a gardener, and a driver. We lived in a Beverly Hills mansion with a pool even my rich friends envied. My parents sent me to boarding school. I caused so much trouble, they were forced to find another. And another. I did everything I could to get their attention. It didn't matter to me which one noticed, I just wanted one of them to show they cared. Growing up privileged isn't always a plus."

The pain in his voice twisted her heart. It sounded like he'd lived a very lonely childhood and needed to vent. She should stop asking personal questions. But then again, venting could be good for the soul. And she was curious. "What did your mother do that she was so busy?"

He looked at her as if she should know the answer. "She's an actress."

"Really? What's her...?" Alex's mouth fell open. "Your mother is Corinna McCreed. I can't believe I never put that together before. Wow. An actress for a mother and a screenwriter for a father—"

"Yeah, wow," Colton said, his voice flat.

She reached across the table and put her hand on his. "I'm sorry."

~

*C*olton had started his story. He might as well finish. He wasn't certain why he felt compelled to fill in the blanks for Alex. Perhaps because she was a sympathetic listener, perhaps because he knew she genuinely cared. She wasn't out to gain anything by it other than personal knowledge, and she would never use it against him. He also liked the cool of her hand on his.

"My mom's career started to dry up in her early thirties, and my dad took the flirting farther than just public displays. He was caught in several affairs by the media, and my mother handled the betrayal with alcohol and pills. She filed for divorce, and I was the pawn in their game of *Let's See Who Can Inflict The Most Damage*. Neither wanted me, but to wound the other..."

"I'm sorry, Colton," Alex said, again. "I shouldn't have pried."

"Now, maybe you'll understand." He linked their fingers

together. "Because of my delightful childhood, I never wanted to get married or have kids."

"Not everyone has an idyllic childhood. That doesn't mean they won't be wonderful parents. Just because you were raised—"

"Don't go there, Alex. I'm sure my parents didn't wake up one morning and decide to be crappy parents. I'm busy. I travel a lot. I can cut that down some, but I'll still be gone. You said yourself, you're not sure what kind of mother Misty will be. What kind of life does that leave for our kid?"

"All anyone can do is try their best. No one is perfect." She leaned closer, trying to make her point. "I've seen you with Charlie and know you have fantastic potential. Your son or daughter will be very lucky to have you as a father."

"You can't know that."

Her smile lit her face making her green eyes twinkle. "You are a gloomy cynic, but anyone can make changes if they're serious about it."

"I told you before, I'm a realist."

"You're a cynic about relationships and marriage and children. You assume because your parents were unhappy together that everyone is or will be." She pulled her hand free of his grip and waved it around. "You think because your parents' divorced you're destined to the same fate. As a writer and being in the world as much as you are, you should know that's not the case. You've seen my parents, Adam and Jeno Blackwood, and my aunt and uncle. All three couples have had long, happy marriages. Look at Rance and Lily Johnson. They've been married forever. I'm sure there have been bumps along the way. No one has a perfect life, but we should grow from those bumps and become stronger."

"You're like that little dandelion that somehow escapes destruction and finds a home between the crack in the sidewalk."

She sat back, her eyebrows drawing together. "You're comparing me to a weed?"

"No, not a weed, a survivor"—he lifted his fisted hand—"a fighter for happiness."

She laughed at his theatrics, which made him smile.

"I've never met anyone as optimistic as you. I don't know how you do it, but you make even me—*a gloomy cynic*—believe that anything is possible."

She put her palms together in prayer fashion and bowed. "Then my work here is done, Grasshopper."

He threw back his head and laughed.

~

*A*lex lay in bed that night thinking of her conversation with Colton. After he'd told her about his childhood, she could see why he might have trepidations about being a father. Her childhood, compared to his, had been wonderful. Idyllic. But she also believed what she'd said about him having fantastic potential. He was great with her son, and Charlie responded well to him. Once Colton got his daddy feet under him, she knew he'd do just fine.

Her thoughts moved a little deeper, to a more worrisome notion. Colton had traveled the world over. Besides her honeymoon, and she'd been no further than a three state radius on the east and south. He was a famous author, and she was a small town mayor. He knew more people than she'd ever meet in her lifetime. They couldn't be more different—optimist, pessimist—yet, as they'd talked, as he'd held her fingers, rubbing his thumb over her knuckles, as his gaze repeatedly dropped to her lips, Alex felt a stirring she hadn't felt since her husband left her for the last time.

That stirring had her stomach quivering more in fright than anticipation.

～

*G*oing to church on Sunday mornings, like so many other things in this quirky little town, was becoming a habit. Aside from entertaining Charlie with a couple of games of tic-tac-toe, he'd grown to enjoy the sermons and the priest. Joshua Brenner had become a friend and fishing buddy, another first—friends with a priest.

Colton's mind drifted today during the hour-long discourse, though. He kept thinking about his dinner with Alex. She'd created a belief that, just maybe, he could be a good father. She and Charlie seemed to bring out the best in him. A feat no one else was able to accomplish.

Colton approached Josh after the service, as usual, and they shook hands. "I'm glad you're here today, Colton. Could you stick around for a few minutes? I'd like to chat."

"Sure." Colton wondered what they had to chat about, other than fishing and pastries. Whatever it was couldn't take long, because he'd planned to hit the river for a couple of hours before Sunday dinner at the Garrett's.

Once Josh was finished shaking hands and waving good-bye, he led Colton down into the bowels of the old stone church. They entered a tiny space that held a desk, a couple of folding chairs, and a small bookcase. It smelled dank and dusty.

Colton glanced around the dark space. "You need a new office. This is one of the most depressing places I've ever seen."

Josh looked around as if noticing for the first time. "I guess you're right. It's not a very pleasant place to meet with people."

"Isn't there an empty room upstairs you could convert? I'd be happy to help you move."

"That's nice of you to offer, Colton," Josh replied with a

smile. "I'll keep that in mind." He gestured to one of the folding chairs in front of the small, badly scarred desk. "Please, have a seat."

Colton sat, and Josh took the chair next to him.

"I'm sure it's no surprise why I want to talk to you."

The seriousness in Josh's voice raised a red flag. Instantly, Colton knew why he was here. He attempted humor with, "I thought you might want to discuss the virtues of lemon bars."

Josh was gracious enough to flash a smile before he laced his fingers together and looked Colton in the eye. "Misty came to see me. She said she's pregnant, and you won't marry her."

"Did she ask you to talk to me?"

Josh nodded. "But I would have wanted to anyway."

"I've changed my mind about marriage, but Misty doesn't know that yet. I would appreciate it if you'd keep the news to yourself, until she and I visit the doctor together."

Josh nodded. "Of course. May I ask, why the change of heart?"

"Alex."

Josh smiled. "Alex can be quite persuasive."

"She didn't try to talk me into marriage, she just…gave me a boost of encouragement." Colton leaned forward, elbows on knees, and stared at the wooden floor. For some reason he couldn't explain, he wanted Josh's approval. His next statement would most likely destroy any chance. "Misty and I were together one night, Josh. I don't love her, and she doesn't love me." Colton turned his gaze on the priest. "Marriage isn't going to make us grow fonder of each other. In fact, I doubt a marriage between us will last past the baby's birth."

"If the marriage dissolves, the child will grow up—"

"With two parents living apart." Colton straightened. "It's

been done before. I know it's not ideal, and I'm sure you disagree, but staying in a marriage without love would be miserable, and that wouldn't be a happy environment for the baby." He held up his hand when Josh opened his mouth. "I speak from experience, so I am taking the baby into consideration when I say these things. I never wanted to be a father, but I've come to terms with Misty's pregnancy, and…I might not be the best, but I *will* be a better parent than my mom or dad were."

"That's all any of us can do, strive to be better. I am sorry you had a bad experience."

Colton waved Josh's concern away. "Water under the bridge."

Josh took a deep breath and let it out slowly, while tapping the tips of his fingers together. "Misty wants to plan a large wedding and has asked me to officiate."

"Yeah, well, Misty lives in a little make-believe world all her own. I'd be honored if you'd perform the ceremony, but we'll have a small wedding in my living room with a couple of witnesses."

The silence that filled the room was deafening. Colton wondered what was going through Josh's mind. Was he praying for Colton's soul? *Sorry, Josh, it's too late*.

Josh reached over and rested a hand on Colton's shoulder. "Would you like me to talk to Misty?"

"Can't think of anything I'd like more, but it's my responsibility. I'll take care of it."

*A*n hour later, Colton was up to his thighs in the river, watching the sun sparkle off the water. A slight breeze ruffled the evergreens and rattled the leaves on the surrounding trees, as if applauding the beauty. Fishing lines arcing through the late afternoon air mingled with dragonflies hovering over the river's glittering surface. The sight captivated him.

The tranquility of this place silenced his screaming soul, anchored his wandering spirit. He felt truly at peace with himself, his decisions, and his surroundings, for the first time in his life.

~

*S*aturday arrived bright and beautiful, perfect for a sixth-birthday celebration. Still, Alex was concerned Misty would cause trouble. There were forty people in her backyard, and she didn't want a scene to spoil Charlie's special day. Charlie would be upset if Colton wasn't invited. And Misty wouldn't tolerate being left out—even if it was the last place she wanted to be.

Alex went inside to mix a second container of lemonade. Colton stormed in behind her. He held a card between his finger and thumb, as if he was carrying hazardous waste.

"She's delusional. Look at what she's handing out."

Alex set the pitcher on the counter and took the card from him. The words "Save the Date" were printed in bold black cross the top. She smiled.

His eyebrows lowered, and his gray eyes clouded even darker. "Oh, well, I'm glad you're so entertained. Misty is passing those cards to everyone here, and you think it's funny."

She slipped the card into his shirt pocket and patted a hand over his heart. "Everyone in this town knows Misty. They also know that you're not getting married. These cards aren't going to change that fact."

Colton leaned against the fridge and closed his eyes. "I haven't told you yet. I've decided to marry her."

"Oh?" Alex tried to mask her surprise. "What made you change your mind?"

"You." He opened his eyes and pinned her with a look. "Your little lecture on the river. I don't want my child to be born out of wedlock."

Alex didn't want to take the time to examine her feelings. They didn't matter. This was about Colton and Misty. It always had been. "Does Misty know?"

"No, and until I'm certain she's pregnant, I'm not telling her."

"Smart decision." Alex looked away, picked up a measuring cup. "I wouldn't let Misty get to you. She's desperate. Since she doesn't know your decision, she'll try anything to get you to cave."

He lifted her chin with his index finger and turned her face to his. She tensed, fighting the sensations he triggered whenever he touched her. "No one on earth can be as sunshiny as you. Do you ever have a down day or get mad?" When she narrowed her eyes, he added, "At anyone besides me?"

"Yes." Turning her head from his touch, she scooped sugar from a canister and poured it into the pitcher.

"When? Because I haven't seen it."

"I discovered I was pregnant the same day two soldiers came to my door to inform me my husband had been killed by an IED. That was a down day."

Colton hung his head, his chin resting on his chest. "I'm sorry. That was tactless of me, Alex."

She turned to him. "Just remember, things could be worse."

∾

*F*eeling like a jerk for bringing his petty problems to Alex, Colton went outside to find Charlie. He walked the perimeter of Alex's backyard, keeping as much distance between him and Misty as possible.

There were more kids here than he was comfortable around, but he might as well get used to the feeling. He tried to imagine himself in a backyard with his own child, and found he could, though the picture that came to mind wasn't in L.A., but here, in Eden Falls.

"Are you going to be a no show?" Stella approached, waving a Save the Date card in front of him.

"I'm going to pass out cards that say, *Don't buy a gift you can't return*."

"I thought I might get you a blender."

"I already have one. I think."

"Hi Colton!" His legs were hugged by a now six-year-old.

He turned around and picked Charlie up for a hug. "Hey, my man. Happy birthday."

"Thanks. Mom said I couldn't ask people if they brought a present."

Colton and Stella laughed. Alex would cringe if she knew Charlie was going around saying that to the guests.

"I brought you a gift, and you're going to love it," Stella said, smoothing Charlie's midnight black hair off his forehead.

His big eyes lit up. "I am? What is it?"

Stella ruffled the smoothed hair. "You'll have to wait until present opening time."

He turned dark eyes on Colton.

"The present I brought is over on the table with all the other presents."

"Will I like it?"

"You'll love it better than Stella's."

Stella punched him in the shoulder.

Minutes later, Charlie was blindfolded and standing in front of a piñata that hung from a tree. Colton stood back from the line of fire with his arms folded across his chest, encouraging the first swing.

Misty appeared at his side and slipped her hand around his waist. "You're invited to dinner at my dad's place, Wednesday at seven-thirty. He wants to meet you. After dinner, we can make some definite plans."

Colton had already planned to visit Mr. Douglas, but he wouldn't be attending Wednesday night dinner to do so. He'd go to the Douglas' house tomorrow after church. "With all the Save the Date cards you've passed out, it looks like you've already made plans."

"We can't wait until the last minute, Colton."

"We aren't discussing anything until I visit with the doctor at your next appointment."

Her blue eyes flashed dangerously. "You doubt I'm pregnant?"

"Until I have proof, you can forget about making any more plans." He unhooked her hand from his waist and walked away.

~

The neighborhood Misty's dad lived in was just inside the town's limits. The houses were set further apart on what appeared to be an acre of land. Colton found the address, pulled around the circular drive, and parked. He hated meeting what may turn out to be his child's grandfather, under these circumstances, but knew visiting was the right thing to do.

When the front door opened, Colton saw the look of recognition on Mr. Douglas' face. Without a word, he opened the door wide so Colton could enter, and gestured him to a chair near the front window.

They sat opposite each other in a comfortable living room. Misty might not have grown up with a mother, but she hadn't gone without the necessities of a comfortable life. Colton knew first hand those necessities alone weren't enough. Had she grown up wondering if her father loved her? Had Mr. Douglas been too busy to show his daughter that she wasn't a mistake?

"First I'd like to apologize, Mr. Douglas. I should have introduced myself sooner."

"I wish you had, Mr. McCreed."

"Colton, please."

"Alright, Colton. You can call me Mason."

Colton sat forward in his chair, elbows on knees, and laced his fingers together. "I'm sure Misty has told you to plan a large wedding, but…"

Colton spent the next hour talking with Misty's dad. He assured Mason he'd take care of all of Misty's medical expenses. He didn't explain that he expected proof before he followed through with any plans to get married. He wouldn't offend Mason by voicing his uncertainty. When he left, he and Mason weren't chummy, but they parted with a firm handshake and what Colton felt was a solid understanding.

CHAPTER 14

Alex sat on the floor with her laptop perched on the coffee table, assembling a slideshow of bridal arrangements from her hundreds of pictures. A loud knock on the front door startled her. She jumped to her feet, and hurried to the door before another knock could wake Charlie.

Misty stalked in. "Where is he?"

"Where is who?"

"Colton."

Alex fought her rising irritation as Misty stomped past and plopped into a chair without invitation. "I haven't seen him since church this morning."

"We were supposed to have dinner at my dad's Wednesday night, but Colton went there today after church. Dad said they talked, but he's being very vague with the details."

Misty scratched her stomach, and Alex glanced at the baby bump under her shirt—a very defined baby bump. Colton told JT he and Misty had only been together that one night which would make Misty about six weeks along. Her bump was more defined than it should be for six weeks. Alex stared at Misty's stomach as realization caused her brain to buzz with white noise. *Misty's pregnant, but the baby can't be Colton's. She's carrying someone else's baby. Someone who can't provide her with all the things she wants. Someone local?*

Alex sank onto the ottoman in front of Misty. "Whose baby are you carrying?"

For a split second, shock registered in Misty's expression, then her features relaxed. "What are you talking about? It's Colton's."

Alex's glance dropped to Misty's stomach, again, to confirm her suspicion. Misty tried to cover the evidence, but the truth was glaringly obvious.

"You're lying." She met Misty's eyes. "Whose baby are you carrying?"

Misty groaned theatrically as if she were the victim in her own charade. "That stupid cousin of yours."

The white noise grew louder. "Rowdy?"

"No, not Rowdy. Beam."

Beam? "But when...? How long...?" Alex let the questions trail away when she remembered Beam telling her he already had a ride the day she picked Colton up at the airstrip. How had she not known?

"You were going to pass Beam's child off as Colton's, and never..." Alex couldn't finish the sentence. The thought was incomprehensible, despicable. "I can't believe you would do such a thing."

Alex stood and walked to the window. The full dark outside made Misty's reflection visible on the glass. She showed no remorse or embarrassment. Instead, her features were hard. Defiant.

"How long have you been seeing Beam?"

"Long enough to get pregnant."

Alex turned. "The guy you cheated on JT with was Beam?"

"I didn't cheat on JT."

Irritation flared. "I'm not sure what it's called in Misty World, but when you're dating one guy and go home with another—"

"It wasn't Beam. Do you really think your honorable cousin would do that? He actually called JT and asked *permission* to date me."

"JT never mentioned you and Beam were seeing each other."

Misty pushed out of her chair and walked to the opposite side of the room, her arms crossed under her breasts. "Maybe because it's none of your business."

"Does Beam know you're carrying his child?"

"If he knew, he'd be down on one knee." Misty kicked at the rug with the toe of her sandal. "He's already asked me to marry him."

Alex knew her mouth dropped open. Felt the movement, but couldn't stop it. Beam—the confirmed bachelor who flew sightseeing tourists around, the Beam she'd go to if she was ever in trouble and JT or Rowdy weren't around. Her sweet hulk of a teddy bear cousin *wanted* to marry Misty? "I can't believe you and Beam have been dating all this time and I didn't know."

"We don't date. We sleep together." Misty chewed the inside of her cheek. "He wants more, but I don't want everyone in town thinking I'm dating Beam."

Alex quickly closed the distance between them. "You've finally offended me to the point where I want to punch you in the face. In fact, if you weren't pregnant..." She had to stop and suck in a shaky breath to calm herself. "You couldn't ask for better men than Beam, Rowdy, or JT, and you know I'm not saying that because they're family. You stepped all over

JT, and now you're trying your best to do the same thing to Beam. How dare you, Misty? How. Dare. You!"

Misty backed up a step at Alex's outburst. "Sorry I can't live up to your high and mighty standards."

"You don't have standards. You've never had any. I know what you did to Peyton back in high school. I was there. You ambushed him, unbuttoned your blouse. You kissed him."

"Oh, for cripes sake, I kissed him, and he just stood there like a mannequin."

"You were my friend." Alex splayed her arms at her sides. "Do you have any idea what that word means? You unbuttoned your blouse, and you kissed my boyfriend. Why would you do that?"

"Because you had everything," Misty snarled as she leaned forward, placing them nose-to-nose. "You had the cute little body, the friends, the perfect big brother, the good grades, and the dreamy boyfriend. You had it all. You've always had it all."

The hatred in Misty's voice, the anger in her eyes, shocked Alex. "You could have had those things and more, but you were too busy trying to take from others. I would never have done anything to hurt you the way you hurt me that day."

"You had a mother."

Alex held up a hand. "Do not go there. A lot of people grow up without a mother. At some point in your life, you've got to stop blaming your actions and failings on your mother walking out."

When Misty turned her back, Alex knew her words fell on deaf ears; but somewhere inside this shell of a person there had to be a shred of decency. For some crazy reason she couldn't explain, she wanted Misty to come to the right decision on her own. She wanted Misty to realize and admit she was wrong. "You'd prevent Beam from knowing his child, and deceive Colton into believing the baby was his, for your own selfish desires? You have to understand how twisted that is. What you're planning is…It's beyond belief."

Misty turned back, her eyes filled with tears. Not the kind squeezed out in an emergency, but real tears. "Beam is bad-boy fun, but he isn't someone you marry. He's just someone you pass the time with until the real thing comes along."

Alex couldn't believe how insult after insult came from Misty's mouth, without a blink of her eye. "Bad-boy fun Beam would take the shirt off his back and give it to anyone in need."

"He doesn't have any money."

Alex released a huff of breath. "Finally, we get to the crux of it. Money. You'd tie yourself to a man who doesn't love you, and possibly never will, for money. You'd throw away a chance at real happiness with someone who wants to make a life with you—who'd give you and the baby *you made together*, a home—for the money Colton could provide." Alex looked heavenward and closed her eyes. "Misty, you have to know—please, *please*, tell me you know—what you're doing is wrong."

Misty walked around her and sat on the sofa. "If I marry Beam, we'll be poor."

"What do you think Beam used to buy his airplane? How do you think he bought a house in Seattle? He may never be as rich as Colton, but he's far from poor."

Alex pushed her laptop aside and sat on the coffee table facing Misty. "What do you think is out in that big world that you'd be missing with Beam, but getting with Colton? Would a life in L.A. make you happy? Will fancy clothes and shiny cars make you happy? Money does not buy happiness. Happiness is something you have to find within yourself." She put her hands on Misty's knees. "You're pregnant now, soon to be responsible for a little being who'll depend on you for love and support. Can't you give him or her that without piles of money? And what about Beam? Is he supposed to go through life never knowing his son or daughter? Would you truly be that selfish?"

Misty examined her cuticles.

Alex was using a logical argument on a selfish, material-istic shell. Time to pull out the big guns. "I've tried to reason with you. Now I'm going to tell you, I won't let you do this to Colton or Beam. Colton shouldn't be held responsible for a child you and Beam created, and Beam should be able to know and raise his son or daughter. If you don't tell them the truth, I will."

Misty pushed up from the sofa so fast she knocked Alex sideways. "I should have expected this dribble from Little Miss Sunshine, with your perfect life."

Alex stood slowly, her pent up energy leaking out like the air from a hole in a balloon. "If my life was perfect, I'd have Peyton here helping me raise Charlie. Nobody's life is without flaws. You lost your mom. I lost my husband. Life goes on. You made a choice to sleep with Beam, now you deal with the consequences. Are you going to tell them or am I?"

"I'll tell them." Misty spat the words before stomping out of Alex's house, slamming the door behind her.

~

Colton sat at the bar in Rowdy's. Beam sat next to him. Since it was a slow night, Rowdy leaned against the bar while Colton dumped his problems into the open. Rowdy, not a Misty fan, was sympathetic to his predicament, throwing out a suggestion here and there. Beam, not so much. He popped peanuts into his mouth from the bowl in front of him, and listened without comment. Colton finally turned to him. "No words of advice?"

Rowdy focused on something behind Colton. "Maybe later. The she-devil just walked in."

Colton caught Misty's reflection in the mirror behind the bar. She stopped behind him, her lips pressed together in a thin line. Beam slapped the bar with his plate-sized palms and pushed up from his seat. The lightening quick action startled Colton, and he glanced up at the man who wore a dark expression. He stepped aside, and Misty slid onto the stool he'd vacated without making eye contact with any of them.

Colton glanced at her, not sure what to expect. Mason must have told her they'd had a chat by now.

"I have something to tell you."

She paid a great deal of attention to Beam's glass, until he grabbed it and turned to leave. "Beam, you need to hear this, too."

Rowdy must have assumed that included him because he stayed where he was. Beam drained the last of the liquid from his glass. Rowdy motioned for a refill, but Beam shook his head.

Misty picked up a napkin and tore off a strip, and then another.

A sense of dread descended over Colton like an icy cloak. He'd never seen her act this apprehensive. He turned to face her, his elbow on the bar. "What is it, Misty?"

She tore another strip off the napkin. "I'm pregnant, but it's not your baby."

Colton felt a pinch between his eyebrows as her words ricocheted around in his head, searching for a logical spot to land. "What did you say?"

Misty sucked in a shaky breath. "The baby isn't yours. It's Beam's."

Beam tipped his head as if he hadn't heard right. Surprise

registered, and then his expression softened into something close to serene. "Does this mean you're ready to settle down?" he asked in a tone Colton had never heard from the bear of a man.

"What did she say?" Rowdy asked.

Colton's glance bounced from Beam to Misty. In a split second of time, something very important had transpired. Something that would have a huge impact on his life—but he wasn't sure he'd heard right, either. "You're telling me, the baby you said was mine never was?"

"You catch on quick." Her voice was flat, her eyes trained on the napkin she was shredding into tiny pieces.

Colton's mind began to spin in confusion, his emotions in chaos. Relief or loss? Happiness or grief? He drew in a strangled breath. "I'm not going to be a father?"

"Misty," Beam said.

Colton held up a hand. "Did you know all along it was Beam's baby?"

She turned to him, her blue eyes as hard as stone. "It doesn't matter. You didn't want a baby. You're off the hook. Now you can go play house with Alex."

"What do you mean, it doesn't matter? It matters to me. You told me I was going to be a father. I've come to terms with the fact, accepted the responsibility, and now you tell me I never was the father. You yank the rug out from under me, again? What's wrong with you, woman?"

"Misty, I'm only going to ask this question one more time. Will you marry me?"

"Wait! One more time?" Colton stumbled to his feet. "You knew this baby was yours all along? You let me go on and on tonight, knowing the baby was yours?"

"I didn't know, until now"—Beam took his eyes off Misty for a moment—"but I did wonder."

Colton shook his head, trying to find his way through the

thick fog that had descended. He wanted to reach out and grasp something solid, preferably Misty's neck. He glanced at Rowdy. Nope, he looked just as dumbfounded. Colton turned to Beam. "Let me get this straight. She was trying to pass your baby off as mine, and you want to marry her?"

Misty bit the inside of her cheek as apprehension crossed her face. She glanced from him to Beam. "Yes. I'll marry you."

Colton shook his head in disbelief. What had just happened? For two weeks, he'd believed he was going to be a father. He'd found his footing, started to look forward to his child, plan for the future. And just like that—poof—the baby Misty was carrying wasn't his. Had never been his. She used the baby as a bargaining tool, just as his parents had used him.

To put a cherry on top of the hot-fudge covered nightmare, Beam, the man he'd just bellyached his dilemma to, wanted to marry the psychopath.

Colton fished some bills from his wallet, slapped them on the bar in front of a speechless Rowdy. "Keep the change."

He pointed at Beam. "Good luck to you. You're going to need it."

～

The next morning, Colton was so tired and irritable, he felt as if the only thing that would help was an intravenous drip of strong coffee straight into his system. He knew he looked like death, but didn't care. He was here to run. Hard.

He parked next to JT and climbed out of his car, frustration churning through him like an angry sea.

JT regarded him with a quick grin. "Howdy."

"Howdy?" Colton shook his head. "I'm going to church,

fishing with a preacher, tubing down a freezing river, and listening to country music, but I refuse to greet anyone with *howdy*."

JT laughed. "Somehow, I thought you'd be in a better mood after discovering you're not going to be a daddy."

"You heard?"

"Yep, Alex called last night. Apparently, Misty went to her house looking for you. Somehow, Alex guessed the baby wasn't yours, and read Misty the riot act. She said when Misty left her house, she'd promised to tell you the truth."

Colton released a huff in disgust as they started jogging at an easy pace. "So it wasn't Misty's guilty conscience that made her confess."

JT sent him a sidelong glance. "You thought Misty had a conscience?"

"Idiotic on my part. Did you hear your cousin is the father?"

JT raised his eyebrows. "So, she confessed everything to you?"

"Yeah, Beam and I were at Rowdy's. Misty waltzes in and blurts out the baby isn't mine but Beam's. I'm laying into her for trying to dupe us both, and he's asking her to marry him." Colton shook his head. "They're both crazy."

"Put all this drama in your book. It'll be a best seller."

"No one's been murdered, *yet*."

He wasn't as forgiving as Beam, where Misty was concerned. She'd tried to turn his life upside down without batting an eye. If it hadn't been for Alex, she might have succeeded. "You didn't have any idea that Beam and Misty were seeing each other?"

"Beam asked me months ago if I'd have a problem with them dating. He didn't want to cause bad feelings between us, because Misty and I had dated. I told him good luck."

Colton raised an eyebrow. "That's the same thing I told him last night."

"I haven't seen them around town together, so I assumed Misty shot him down."

Colton stopped running, too tired and out of sorts to continue. "She is a piece of work."

"Agreed. Hey, meet me at Noelle's in an hour. We'll have a celebratory breakfast," JT called over his shoulder before he picked up his pace.

Colton grunted out a confirmation. He'd spent half the night wondering why Misty had come clean with the truth. Now, he knew. Alex caught her in the lie. As he headed back to his car, he glanced at his watch. The flower shop didn't open until ten and it was only eight. He'd shower, have breakfast with JT, and then pay Alex a visit.

~

*A*lex knew Colton had entered Pretty Posies. She'd propped the door open, and he was the only one in town who flipped the bell rather than just calling her name. Her stomach muscles quivered as she climbed off the stool next to her worktable. She glanced in the small mirror her grandmother had hung on the wall just inside the door. Finger combing the few strands of hair that had escaped her ponytail was like a blinking neon sign announcing her growing attraction to the egotistical maniac. *Not good.*

Colton had his back to her, peering through the walk-in cooler's glass. "What can I do for you this morning?"

"I need to buy some flowers. Which of these say thank you?" he asked, waving a finger back and forth.

Alex stepped past him and pulled a dark pink rose from a bucket of water.

"I'll take two dozen of those. I'll need a card, too." He

moved to the cash register. "Add what you need to make this a spectacular bouquet."

She felt his eyes on her as she stepped behind the counter. She pulled a small card from the display and held it out to him.

"I was hoping for something nicer."

She just happened to keep a file of cards under the counter. Thumbing through them, she selected one that was blank inside. "This one is pretty and generic."

Colton took the card from her, picked up a pen, narrowed his eyes in thought, and then started to write. She got busy filling out the order. When he was finished, he slid the card into the envelope, sealed it, and passed her a credit card. Their gazes caught, held for a long moment before his dipped to her mouth. She pressed her lips together self-consciously as she ran his credit card.

He smiled. "When can you have the flowers ready?"

"An hour."

"I'll be back."

When he turned for the door, she said, "You don't want them delivered?"

"No, I want to deliver these myself."

Alex knew Colton was back an hour later when the bell jangled. She sent Tatum, who'd arrived for her shift, out to deal with their customer. She heard them greet each other, and carry on a brief conversation, but she couldn't make out what was being said. They both laughed a couple of times before Tatum appeared at the door of the backroom. "Colton wants to see you."

Alex set her jaw and stood. *Quit acting so silly!* She glanced in the mirror, and then mentally slapped herself. When she entered the front of the shop, Colton handed her the bouquet she'd just arranged and left through the open front door.

Stunned, Alex set the vase down and pulled the card free of the envelope.

I know you won't believe it, but I knew it from the start.
There is no other mayor, with a bigger heart.
These flowers are to say thank you for discovering the truth
I'll add to your achievements, a great detective, or queen
sleuth.

Alex's laughter bubbled to the surface despite trying to hold it back. Colton might be a wiz at writing novels, but his poetry needed serious help. She stepped out onto the sidewalk just as he opened the door of her old Ford. "Thank you for what?" she called out.

"For talking to Misty. By the way, Charlie invited me to dinner tonight, and I accepted."

"It's Monday."

"Don't worry, I'll come on Wednesday, too." He climbed behind the wheel, flashed that infuriatingly attractive grin he'd been so stingy with when he first came to town, and drove away.

~

olton sat on Alex's sofa while showing Charlie where to place his fingers on the guitar strings. He'd been working with the kid for a couple of weeks. Even though Charlie's little fingers could only stretch so far, he was a fast learner and a patient pupil. He could already pick out a couple of simple songs, which filled Colton with a ridiculous sense of pride.

While helping Charlie, his eyes strayed to the door leading into the kitchen. Alex moved in and out of sight with her confident ease. She wore a pair of slim jeans and a simple

T-shirt. Her blonde hair, usually clipped up, hung wavy down her back in an inviting cascade of softness. She glanced into the living room, and their gazes collided and held for a long, fascinating moment. His heart gave a couple of hard thumps.

She broke their connection by glancing at Charlie. "Come and get dessert."

"Just a minute, Mom. This is a really 'portant part."

"Important," Colton said, emphasizing each syllable.

Charlie watched his mouth form the word. "Important," Charlie repeated.

Alex rested a shoulder against the doorjamb. "Since when is anything more important than dessert to either of you?"

Charlie looked up with a determination that made him appear years older than his actual age. "I'm learning a really hard part."

"Your ice cream is melting," Alex said.

Colton watched with interest as her tongue slid along the serving spoon she was holding. "Our ice cream's melting buddy. We'll do this later."

After they'd scraped their bowls clean, Alex told Charlie it was time to get ready for bed.

"Ah, Mom."

"No arguments, sweetheart. I let you stay up later than usual tonight so you could work on your 'portant part."

"Important." Charlie glanced at Colton for confirmation and then smiled when Colton nodded. "Can Colton read me a story?"

Alex looked at Colton, her mossy green eyes shining with amusement.

"Sure, I'll read a story. Go get ready for bed and brush your teeth. I'll be there in a minute."

"You sound like Tyson's dad," Charlie said with a laugh as he scampered down the hall.

The comment sent an unexpected skittering of disappointment down his back. Misty's announcement had left him with such mixed emotions. He should be grateful, and he was. To know he wouldn't be tied to Misty for life was a sheer blessing from heaven. Still, a small part of him felt unsettled by the news.

He was amazed at how quickly his heart had been turned from one set of ideals to another.

~

*A*lex rinsed the dishes and Colton loaded the dishwasher, as had become their habit. When she passed a bowl, their hands touched and an unwelcome warmth spread through her, quickening her heartbeat. She pulled back, then hoped her reaction went undetected, but Colton stopped what he was doing, and turned to her.

"Colton, I'm ready!" Charlie called, saving her from an even more uncomfortable moment.

She watched him walk down the hall, a little in awe of the changes he'd made since coming to Eden Falls. He'd been so adamant about never wanting kids, yet he'd accepted his responsibility for Misty and their baby before learning the truth. He was wonderful with Charlie, teaching him to play the guitar, cheering at his baseball games, now reading him bedtime stories, and reminding him to brush his teeth. They were best pals in her son's eyes. As she'd feared, Charlie had become attached and would be crushed when Colton left town.

She didn't like that she was also becoming attached to the author. She found she was just as anxious as Charlie when Colton arrived for their dinners. She knew, once he went back to L.A., Wednesday nights would become like any other night of the week, a little bit lonely.

Colton's voice carried down the hall as he read to Charlie.

She would have guessed he'd read a children's story outright, in monotone. Instead, he embellished by using a different tone for each character. Charlie's little belly laugh was priceless. Listening to them made her heart ache for what her son had already lost—it ached even more for what was still to come. The one man, besides family, her son connected with, would be leaving town soon, and had no reason to return.

She leaned back against the counter and eavesdropped on the two of them talking and laughing until Colton called from Charlie's bedroom door, "Your turn, Mom."

She walked down the hall as Colton crossed to the bathroom. She tucked the sheet around her sleepy son and smoothed his hair back from his forehead, before sitting on the edge of the bed.

"Colton's my best friend, Mom."

Her chest tightened. "Your best friend?"

"Well, except for Uncle JT and Tyson. And I like Uncle Rowdy and Uncle Beam. Can I have that many best friends?"

She smiled. "There are no rules. You can have as many best friends as you want."

"Like you and Stella and Misty and Jillian and Jolie."

"Yep, just like that."

Charlie stifled a yawn. "I don't want him to move away."

"I know, sweetheart, but he has to go back to Los Angeles."

He scrunched up his black brows. "Why?"

She ran a finger down his nose, which caused his eyelids to droop. "Because that's where

his house is."

"But he could get a house here."

She ran her finger down his nose again. "All of his friends live in Los Angeles."

Charlie's eyes slid shut before he blinked them open. "Aren't we his friends?"

"Yes, baby, but if he doesn't go back, all of his other friends will be sad."

"Will he come to visit us?"

"I'm not sure, sweetie. Now close your eyes and go to sleep." She planted a kiss on his sweet, bronzed, cheek. A little bit sad mingled with happy that he looked so much like his father.

"Sing," he whispered.

She did.

CHAPTER 15

Colton listened to the soft voices coming from the other side of the door. Charlie's words touched him more than he wanted to admit. When had this little kid, so unexpectedly, crawled into his heart? He'd been thinking of both Alex and Charlie more than he cared to. When he finished a chapter or saw a rainbow, his first thought was to call Alex. When a frog jumped near the riverbank or he spotted a deer, he wished Charlie was near.

He was glad today was Monday, which still gave him their Wednesday night dinner to look forward to. He liked glancing up and finding a pair of green eyes watching him from across the table. The same green eyes that were keeping him awake nights.

He went into the kitchen and pulled one of Charlie's apple juice boxes from the fridge. He'd become addicted to the things—along with milk—another first.

When Alex came into the kitchen, he was standing with his back to the sink, waiting.

"Can I get you some water or…" Her words trailed away

when she spotted the juice box sitting on the counter next to him.

"Tell me about Peyton."

"Peyton?" Several emotions crossed her face at once. "Why?"

I have no idea. Because he was important to you. Because he was Charlie's father. Because he lived in the house I now live in. Take your pick. "Curiosity. Unless it's too painful."

She picked up a towel and wiped an imaginary spot on the countertop. "What do you want to know?"

"What was he like?"

Her glance drifted to the window behind him, as if contemplating what she might say. "Peyton was…smart, funny, sweet,"—she raise and lowered her eyebrows a couple of times, guy fashion—"a hunk."

"A hunk?" He chuckled. "Didn't that word lose its popularity sometime before you were born?"

"Possibly, but it works when describing my hus —Peyton."

"What did he do in his spare time?"

Her smile turned sad, as if haunted by memories, and sweet at the same time. "He didn't have a lot of spare time, but when he did he liked being outdoors. He loved to fish. Loved to hike. Loved spending time with his family. He was very personable and had a lot of friends. He and his brothers were close." She met his gaze. "Everyone liked Peyton."

"Everyone still does. Whenever his name is mentioned, it's always in a positive light."

"He was a positive person, but he also had a temper. I mean…he wasn't perfect. We all have our faults, and Peyton had his. He liked things to run smoothly. If they didn't, he could get impatient, and a little ornery."

Her eyes shone as she talked about her husband. She really

was a beautiful person—inside and out. Her countenance changed as often as the Washington weather. One minute she was as innocent as a child, teasing over a glass of milk. The next she was as enthusiastic as a game show contestant. She captured his attention wearing jeans and a T-shirt while mowing, or in a summer dress waving to the crowd on a parade route.

The word adorable popped into his head. Tonight, she looked adorable with her soft mass of curls and her nearly naked-of-makeup face. The blush that pinked her cheeks was always just right. He'd never been attracted to adorable before. Adorable was another first.

"He was fiercely loyal to friends and family, extremely respectful of his parents. He enjoyed spending time with them. Even though they don't mention him much anymore, I know they miss him so much. He was the baby, the youngest of three boys, who were all very intelligent, very athletic. With two older brothers, he felt he had to prove himself, but the Blackwood's never applied that pressure. It was self imposed."

Melancholy wove its way into her expression. "He would have been a great father. He wanted a house full of children, and he would have been good with them."

"I didn't mean to make you sad, Alex."

"You didn't. I'm not sad. I just miss him." She pulled the dishtowel through her hand, and then hung it on the handle of the refrigerator.

"How old were you when you got married?"

"Eighteen. He was deployed shortly afterwards."

"So you didn't have much married time together."

She shook her head.

"This is a huge change of subject, but I have to know. How did you convince Misty to tell me the baby isn't mine?"

She smiled, looked down at the floor. "Misty showed up last night. I noticed her baby bump is more prominent than it should be at six weeks." She nodded to the bouquet sitting on the kitchen table. "Thank you, by the way. The flowers are beautiful, even if I arranged them myself."

"I owe you much more than flowers, Alex. This is the biggest thank you of my life. I was prepared to be a father. What you saved me from was a life with Misty."

"You're welcome, but it would have come out eventually. A pregnancy and due dates are hard to hide."

"It wouldn't have been hard to hide from me. I know nothing about baby bumps."

"Your first trip to the doctor with her would have revealed the truth."

He lifted a shoulder. "Maybe, but I'm still grateful you brought her to her senses before I went through with a wedding."

She smiled and his gaze dropped to her mouth. He'd wanted to nip her bottom lip since the first day he'd met her. "Thanks for dinner. It was delicious, as always."

"You're welcome."

"I'll see you Wednesday."

"About that." She wrinkled her nose in the cutest way. "It might be better if we didn't have these dinners every week. Maybe twice a month instead."

"Wait a minute," Colton said, pushing away from the sink. "What brought this on?"

"Charlie is becoming too attached. It's going to be hard for him to say goodbye, and impossible, for a while, for him to understand you won't be coming back."

Colton crossed the space that separated them. *These dinners are the one thing I look forward to each week. You and Charlie have become my lifeline in this place.* His thoughts surprised him, but he didn't have time to consider what they meant. "Come on, Alex. I've explained to the kid I'm leaving."

She backed up a step. "He knows you're leaving. He just doesn't understand that you're not coming back. He's never lost anyone before."

"What about his father?"

"He never knew his father."

He took another step closer, and she looked up at him with those mossy green eyes. Without thinking, he reached out and wrapped his hand around the back of her neck, lowering his mouth to hers. She tensed, the muscles under his hand going taut. Her mouth tasted sweet, like vanilla ice cream and apples with the tang of cinnamon. Like the pie ala mode she'd served for dessert.

Until that moment, he'd never taken the time to consider how intimate the act of his lips touching another's could be. A kiss had always been just a kiss, a first step that led to so many other pleasures. This kiss was different, touching a deep uncharted chasm of emotions he'd never taken the time to explore, hadn't even known existed. His chest expanded with sensations that filled him unexpectedly, sensations he'd never experienced. He teased her lips open, and she complied. His heart went from pumping hard to skipping a beat. Or two.

He pulled back slightly, afraid to look into her eyes, yet anxious to see if whatever had just occurred between them was visible to the naked eye.

~

*W*hen Colton leaned back, Alex searched his face. Confused by the emotions reverberating through her, and by what she saw in Colton's face. The softness around his eyes, the slight look of dismay had to match her own. His gentle lips were a surprise, the intensity of the kiss rocked her with feelings she hadn't experienced in a long time. A quivering started in her belly, flowed to her thighs, and then down to her knees, making her body quake. After a moment's hesitation on both their parts, he pulled her into his arms and kissed her again.

And she let him.

Alex couldn't believe this was happening, but she didn't seem to possess the power to make it stop. Why end something that consumed her with pleasure? Starbursts of decadence exploded through her system, leaving her fighting for breath, while a heady recklessness blended into a sweet ache that had her clinging to him. It had been such a long time since she'd been in a man's arms. A man's lips had not touched hers since... Peyton's face, suddenly vivid in her mind, caused her to break their kiss, to push Colton back a step. "I...I can't do this." She was embarrassed by her breathless protest.

Colton didn't release her. His fingers held on to her bare arms, his thumbs moving back and forth, causing goose bumps to pepper her skin against her will. "Because of Charlie?"

"Because of a lot of things. Charlie doesn't understand why you can't stay. If he saw us like this, it would confuse him even more." She looked at the floor. "How could I expect him to understand something I don't?"

He tipped his head to the side and lowered his voice. "What is it you don't understand? That you're attracted to me?"

"I don't do casual flings, Mr. McCreed. I'm not Misty — who, until yesterday, you thought was carrying your child." When he frowned, she could see her words had hurt, and regretted them.

"We're back to Mr. McCreed?"

That's the part that offended you? She took a step back, forcing him to release his hold. "That's where we need to keep it. We can't have these Wednesday night dinners anymore. It's going to be too hard on Charlie when you leave."

"What about you, Alex? Is my leaving going to be hard on you?"

"We're not talking about me," she said looking away. "We're talking about a little boy who isn't—"

"Let's talk about you." He lifted her chin until her eyes met his. "Was that your first kiss since Peyton left for Iraq, almost seven years ago?"

"That's none of your business." She turned her back to him, trying to contain the quivering that had morphed from need to anger. She just wasn't certain whom she was mad at, Colton for kissing her, or herself for allowing it to happen. "I think you should leave."

"Why, because you're having a hard time accepting you're attracted to someone other than Peyton?"

She turned. "Leave Peyton out of this. This is between you and me."

"Exactly. This is between you and me and the connection we felt during that kiss."

You felt it too. "There was no connection. There wouldn't have even been a kiss if you'd learn a little restraint."

"You're lying to yourself, Sunshine. You felt the connection, too. I saw it in your eyes. Maybe if you'd let go of your inhibitions and relaxed a little, it wouldn't have been seven years between kisses." He raised an eyebrow. "I'll be happy to show you what you've been missing."

She pointed in the direction of the front door. "Get out."

It was his turn to cross his arms. "Misty was right when she said deep down a part of you died right along with your husband."

Alex saw red at his statement. *How dare Misty discuss me with Colton!* "Get out."

~

*C*olton watched her cheeks flush enticingly. The pulse point at the base of her neck beat wildly, like the wings of a hummingbird in flight. He lifted his gaze to hers. Maybe he'd gone too far with that comment. He'd hit below the belt, but she had to realize she was young and vibrant, and she'd been alone for too long.

"First, answer my question. Was that your first kiss since your husband left for Iraq?" The answer was written on her delicate cheekbones as her blush deepened, and in the flash of her green eyes, confirming what she wouldn't admit aloud.

She started for the living room, but he caught her arm in his hand. "Now, for the million dollar question. Why me?" He pulled her a step closer, and then another, pleased that she didn't put up a fight. "Am I the reason you want to discontinue our Wednesday night dinners? Have I awakened desires long dormant, and you're afraid to act on them? Afraid to admit you might be human?"

"How dare you incinerate…"

Her mouth dropped open at her blunder, and he took full advantage by kissing her again. An unusual stirring filled his chest, and words of promise zinged through his mind, words he'd never spoken aloud to any woman. He pushed them aside.

She trembled under his hands, and he pulled her closer. His lips moved to the tender flesh on her neck, nipping until her head dropped back allowing him access. "I believe the word you're looking for is insinuate and I obviously dare."

"You…need to leave," she whispered.

"Let me stay with you tonight. I can show you the part of life you've been missing."

"I will be in love with the man who shows me that."

"You don't have to love every man you go to bed with."

Two hands, planted on his chest, pushed hard enough that he stumbled back a step. "I do."

"I could relieve some of the sexual tension you've allowed to—"

"Are you listening to yourself? You sound like a late night television commercial trying to sell yourself and your sexual favors."

"What's a sexsal favor?" came a sleepy voice from the hallway.

Alex dodged around Colton and scooped up her son who was rubbing one eye with a fist. "What are you doing out of bed, sweetheart?"

"I heard fighting," he answered laying his head on her shoulder.

"We're not fighting," Alex said.

"Sorry, we were being so loud, buddy," Colton said at the same time.

"Say goodnight to Colton, baby." She glared at him over her shoulder. "He's leaving."

Charlie raised a hand from his mom's shoulder. "'Night, Colton."

"'Night, Charlie. Sleep tight."

"Don't let the bedbugs bite," Charlie mumbled back.

As Alex disappeared down the hall, Colton grabbed his jacket from the back of a chair and did his own disappearing. The evening was beautiful, hanging on to the moments between dusk and full on dark. Crickets were tuning up for their nightly serenade, stars dotted the sky, and his mind was on the move. *What am I doing kissing Alex? Have I lost my mind? Absolutely. Kissing her was a huge mistake. Yet... it didn't feel like a mistake at the time. In fact, kissing her felt more right than anyone I've ever kissed.* He almost stumbled at the thought. Admitting something like that should have him running as fast as possible in the opposite direction, not wanting to bite into that plump bottom lip of hers.

Jorge was right. This place had changed him. He liked greeting people on the street, waving from the front porch. Here, he was Colton McCreed neighbor, not Colton McCreed author. Sure, everyone knew about his books, but he was a person first. Eden Falls had changed him, but so had Alex and Charlie. Because of them, he would be leaving this place a much richer man than when he'd arrived.

With his thoughts running rampant, he turned the first corner he came to, and didn't stop until he hit the entrance of Rowdy's Bar and Grill.

~

*A*fter she tucked Charlie in for the second time, Alex wandered into her bedroom. She was still vibrating with anger, and wrapped her arms around herself as she sank onto the bed. Her first kiss after her husband's death was with an arrogant, egotistical, self-indulgent, city dweller who decided it was his duty to remind her what it felt like to be a woman.

What an idiot she was to allow it to happen. And to kiss him back.

She prided herself on her common sense. Where had it been tonight—on vacation?

Well, he could just eat his dinners at Renaldo's from now on, or maybe Misty could heat him a can of SpaghettiOs— though that was questionable.

She pressed her lips together. They felt swollen— undoubtedly from inactivity. The anger that boiled just under the surface flitted away on wings of wonder as she remembered the sensations that had coursed through her as Colton held her in his arms. Sensations she hadn't felt in years, which left her trembling, weak-kneed, and wanting more. That wonder was just as quickly replaced by embarrassment at her reaction to those sensations. How would she face Colton after tonight?

Tossing and turning hours later, Alex glanced at the alarm clock on her nightstand. Two-thirty-seven. Colton's kiss had awakened her sleeping senses and sent her mind reeling in various directions. Was he sleeping soundly, knowing he wasn't going to be a father after all? And what of poor Beam? She hadn't talked to him since he'd discovered the truth. What was going through his mind?

Misty and Beam. The most unlikely combination she could imagine.

She rolled over and fluffed her pillow. She'd spent many sleepless nights after she'd received the news about Peyton, followed by days of walking through a foggy haze. She forced herself to eat for the baby she was carrying. After Charlie was born, she was too exhausted not to sleep, but it was never dreamless. She'd never been allowed that luxury. Disappointments, what-ifs, and memories were never far away. Her heart ached for Peyton. She wanted him to be with them, to be a part of this wonder that was Charles Peyton Blackwood.

She didn't try to stop the tears that leaked from the corners of her eyes and wet her pillow, but this time the tears weren't for Peyton. They were caused by that empty hole in her heart that was turning traitor on her. That hole had begun to fill in, against her will. Fill with feelings for a man who would be leaving town for good in just a few short weeks.

CHAPTER 16

Alex looked out over Mason Douglas' backyard. Misty had pulled out all the stops for her quickie wedding and reception. An arbor had been draped with hundreds of flowers—a symbolic slap across Alex's face—bought from her biggest competitor in the area. Misty was still too angry with her to be pleased with anything she might have assembled. She'd rather have Misty bad mouthing the florist in Harrisville than Pretty Posies.

A dance floor was constructed, and a band, flown in from Tacoma. Nothing local was good enough for Misty. The food, catered from Seattle, was served buffet style with so many choices it bordered on ridiculous.

After pictures were taken and the dancing started, Alex found Beam on the deck, overlooking the party. She slipped her arm through his. "What are you doing up here by yourself?"

"Taking a breath." He glanced at her. "Sorry about the flowers, Low-rider."

"No need to be sorry. If Misty is happy, that's all that matters."

He didn't reply.

Alex studied the big man next to her. All that was left of his scraggly beard was a neatly trimmed goatee and mustache. She hadn't seen his hair this short or shaped since she was in elementary school. His tux fit his broad shoulders impeccably, but Misty wouldn't have settled for anything less. She was puzzled that Beam knew Misty so well, and still wanted to be with her.

"I guess you can't help who you fall in love with," he said as if reading her mind.

She gave his arm a squeeze. "I think you'll be a wonderful husband and father."

He chuckled, a sound as familiar and comfortable as her brother's. "You're full of crap, but thanks anyway. And thanks for guiding Misty's conscience."

She shook her head. "No thanks necessary. I'm happy it all worked out in the end."

Beam lowered his elbows to the deck railing, and Alex leaned back next to him. "I told Misty, if she can prove to me she's ready to settle down, I'll set her up in her own salon after the baby's born."

"You're generous." She glanced over her shoulder at the crowd. "Does it bother you that Misty's been with almost every *single* guy in this town?"

She was surprised when he laughed. "There is no *almost* to it. And no, the past is the past. I haven't exactly been a saint myself."

"Are you leaving a trail of broken hearts behind?"

"I don't think I broke any hearts, but I got around." Beam blew out a breath. "The only detail bothering me now is her thing for the author."

Alex leaned her elbows on the deck railing to match her cousin's stance. "She doesn't have a thing for Colton. She just spotted an opportunity to escape this town and grabbed for it. She was more interested in his money, than she was in him. Wow. That sounds shallow. Sorry."

Beam waved her apology off. "I know money is important to her, but I think the reason it's so important is the stability it offers. Her mom left, and her dad was busy. She didn't have what we considered a traditional home life. I think she just craves the constancy of a stable environment. And love. I can give her both. I'll never be rich, but thanks to the inheritance from Grandma and Grandpa Garrett, I have enough, and I make a nice living."

Alex didn't believe stability was what Misty craved. She hated playing the devil's advocate, but felt she should warn Beam just as she'd warned Colton. Misty might disappear the same way her mother had. "What if love and stability aren't enough?"

Beam straightened to his full height. "I guess we'll cross that bridge when we come to it. I'll raise this baby alone, if I have to."

Her handsome cousin could have his pick of women, but had chosen Misty, who would not only be unbearable to live with, but impossible to please. He'd have his hands full with her and a newborn. "I'll be rooting from the sidelines. If you need help, all you have to do is call."

"I know I can count on family. If I need help, Mom will take the baby in a heartbeat. She's so excited. I think she and Dad had given up hope of ever becoming grandparents."

Minutes later, Beam was pulled away by friends, and Alex's attention drifted to Misty. She looked exquisite in her strapless wedding dress with its embroidered bodice and huge ball gown skirt that covered her baby bump. Her midnight black hair swept into a messy updo, and the sweetheart neckline of her dress made Misty appear, oddly enough, innocent.

The truth about the baby's father would have come out, but Alex felt certain Misty wouldn't have been the one to reveal that truth. Beam was a big man to forgive such an infraction.

Over the evening, Alex was careful to keep her distance from Colton, stunned he'd even attend after what Misty had done. Chicken that she was, she'd sent him a text saying she couldn't cook Wednesday night. Instead, she and Charlie had gone to a petting zoo in Harrisville, then to dinner.

Colton had asked her and Charlie to come with him tonight, but she'd declined. For her hearts sake, her best course of action was to steer clear. His time in town was running short. Once he was back in L.A., he'd have no reason to return. She already regretted how often he invaded her thoughts. Charlie talking about him nonstop didn't help.

Brandt approached with an invitation to dance. Once on the floor, she glanced around until she spotted Charlie. He was sitting with Grandpa Garrett. By the way her father moved his arm, baseball was their topic of conversation. She smiled at her son's animated expressions as he talked. His black eyebrows rose as he listened.

Brandt turned her, and she caught sight of Colton. He stood on the deck talking to Misty's dad. Good. She hoped there would be no hard feelings between the two of them. Misty's lies had stirred enough trouble in town.

She spotted Rowdy watching the dance floor. She followed his gaze to where Stella danced with Len. Her boyfriend had finally shown up for a date. When she looked back in Rowdy's direction, he was gone.

*A*n hour later, Alex pulled into her driveway, careful not to jostle a sleeping Charlie. Before she could get out, a car pulled in behind her. Colton climbed out. Without a word, he scooped Charlie into his arms and carried him down the hall. Her heart melted at the sight of her son's little face turned into Colton's neck.

I'm not going to come out of this unscathed.

She was aware of Colton's heated gaze as she undressed Charlie and tucked him into bed. Warmth moved down her spine, making her nerve endings tingle and her skin heat. She forgot for several heartbeats that she was a mayor, a shop owner, and a mother. For those few thumps of her pulse, she was a woman in a floral summer sheath, and a man wanted her.

Only for the night. The thought brought her back to an empty reality. He didn't want *her*. He just wanted a woman — no strings, because he was leaving — and she was convenient.

They backed into the hall, and she closed Charlie's door. "Why are you here?"

He pulled her into his arms and kissed her, and she let him. She'd told herself to stay away, but those words flew from her mind as soon as his mouth found hers. She couldn't think clearly when his musky cologne mingled with the summer-evening, out-of-doors scent of his skin. She felt her body's betrayal, as she pressed closer. When he started backing her toward her bedroom, she came to her senses. She turned her head to break the kiss. "I don't do one night stands, Colton."

"This won't be a one night stand. I'm here for at least four more weeks."

She looked up into his eyes. "Why?"

"Why? You know I'm here for the summer."

"But why? You said last week, your research is finished and the book is writing itself. Why stay?"

He lifted a brow. "Are you trying to get rid of me?"

"Maybe."

"I've already paid rent."

She shook her head. "I haven't received August's rent. If I do, I'll send it back to you."

He took her chin between thumb and forefinger. "Why are you trying to get rid of me? What are you so afraid of?"

His finger traced under her chin, down her neck, to her collarbone. She knew he'd feel the goose bumps that popped up under his touch. *I'm not scared. I'm terrified that I'm falling in love with the wrong man.*

"I'm not sleeping with you." She moved out of his arms. "It's late. You have to go."

He changed direction. Instead of leaving, he led her to the sofa. She found herself on his lap, being kissed breathless. For once, she let herself go. She acted selfishly, taking as much pleasure as she could stand from his kisses. For the first time in seven years, Peyton wasn't on the fringes of her awareness.

~

The next afternoon Stella showed up at Alex's door. Charlie was at JT's, so they had the house to themselves. Alex pulled two chaise lounge chairs into the shade of a backyard tree, while Stella grabbed two cold drinks from the fridge.

"So, what did you think of the wedding?"

Alex handed Stella a glass full of ice. "I thought it was nice. I can't believe Misty pulled it together so quickly."

"Did she talk to you?"

"No." Alex watched Stella pour a Diet Coke over the ice. "She's still angry with me for discovering her secret."

"She couldn't have hidden it forever. What was she thinking?"

"She found herself in a desperate situation. I don't think she knew she was pregnant when Colton came to town. When she discovered she was, Colton became her ticket out. I just hope she doesn't break Beam's heart."

"Personally, I think Beam's lost his mind."

Alex looked up into the tree. The leaves were still in the afternoon heat. "I guess you can't help who you fall in love with," she said, repeating Beam's words of last night.

Stella glanced over. "So, you really think he's in love with her?"

"Yes." She thought of her conversation with her cousin at the wedding. *Heaven help him.* "Yes, I do."

Stella sat back and took a sip of her drink. "So, what's going on between you and Colton?"

Most of the time, Alex appreciated, possibly envied, Stella's ability for bluntly stating what was on her mind. Today, not so much. She lifted a shoulder, attempting nonchalance. "Nothing."

Stella smirked. "Last night, it looked like something."

A guilty blush crept up Alex's cheeks. The front curtains had been closed, but Colton's car had been parked behind her Jeep until after midnight. "What are you talking about?"

"He watched you and Brandt dancing. The scowl he wore looked a lot like jealousy to me."

Relief floated over her. For a moment, she thought Stella was talking about her late night with Colton. She was also amused that her friend confused jealousy with lust or loneliness or whatever it was Colton felt for her. "Colton's not jealous. He's just stuck in this little town, and the woman who was supposed to keep him entertained ended up pregnant with someone else's baby. Jealousy isn't in Colton's realm of emotions."

"He's been hanging around here an awful lot."

"He likes the food, and he's comfortable around Charlie. He can relax here."

Stella took another sip from her drink, but Alex could

almost see the wheels turning. She finally glanced over. "Who knows? Maybe he wants—"

"Sex, Stella. He wants sex."

"That's a start."

"It's not a start for me, and you know it."

Stella set her drink down and turned sideways, pulling her knees up. "The love you and Peyton shared was enviable. I don't mean to sound unsympathetic, but Peyton is gone, and has been for a long time. He would never want you, the love of his life, to live out the rest of your days alone and loveless. He'd be the first to tell you to find a man who made you laugh, who could light up your world, and who would be a good and loving father to Charlie. Brandt isn't that guy."

Alex swiped at the tears Stella's words evoked.

"Oh, Alex, I didn't mean to make you cry."

"No, it's fine. You're right about Brandt. He isn't the guy. He and I both agree on that. Our dance together was just one friend asking another. You're also right about Peyton. He would be the first to tell me to move on, but a one-night stand or, in this case, a month long affair, isn't me. Even if it was, I have Charlie to think about."

"Colton cares about Charlie. I've—"

"Colton isn't that guy either. He doesn't want to get involved in a relationship. He wants a short term, no strings attached, affair."

It was getting harder and harder to turn Colton's advances down, but she prided herself on being a responsible parent, and she would continue to be one. Charlie was her life, and at the heart of almost every decision she made on a daily basis.

"People change, Alex. Colton could decide to stay."

"He won't. He has a life in Los Angeles, and he'll be going back to it in a few weeks."

"You care about him. I can see it in your eyes." Stella raised a brow. "And in your blush."

"Enough about Colton," Alex said, unable to stop her clipped words. "Tell me about you and Len. Things looked like they were going well last night."

Stella got all googly eyed and, to Alex's relief, the subject of Colton was forgotten.

*A*fter Stella left, Alex got in her Jeep and drove to the cemetery. She hadn't been here since May. She and Charlie always met the Blackwood family on Memorial Day to celebrate the memory of Peyton. Today, she needed to visit alone.

She parked and reached into the backseat for the flowers she'd picked up at Pretty Posies. Gathering clouds covered the blue sky of earlier, and the scent of rain wafted past her nose on a growing breeze.

As she walked along the path, she glanced down at the headstones that had become familiar over the last seven years, reading the names as she went.

Peyton was buried under a willow tree, next to his Grandma and Grandpa Blackwood. With the river in the foreground and the mountains as a backdrop, it was the perfect spot.

She swept a hand across the marble bearing Peyton's name. It had taken her a long time to get used to seeing it there. Clearing grass clipping away, she unscrewed the vase attached to the headstone and set it upright. She filled it with water from a bottle she carried, and arranged the flowers carefully. Then she sat, leaning back, her weight on the palms of her hands, and smiled.

Hi, sweetheart. Sorry it's been so long since my last visit. Life is crazy.

Charlie celebrated his sixth birthday a couple of weeks ago. We had a party in the backyard, and he had so much fun.

Your family came. They are so wonderful with him. He spent a lot of time with your dad this spring building a doghouse. Your dad let him help, even gave him a small hammer to use. She touched the marble with her fingertips. *His mannerisms remind me of you so often. He's a happy boy, smart and funny and full of love. You would be so proud.*

A lump grew in her throat and she sucked in a shaky breath.

He's made a new friend. Colton McCreed—an author—in Eden Falls for the summer, researching small town life for his next novel. He and Charlie have really connected. Colton comes to dinner once a week. He buys the food and I cook. I'm not sure why I feel the need to tell you. It all started so innocently, and now…it's not. The whole situation has become complicated.

She smiled as a tear tickled her cheek. *Remember how we used to think it was so funny when people used "it's complicated" as an explanation? Or an excuse?*

Well, it's not so funny anymore.

She swiped at the tear.

Colton is teaching Charlie to play the guitar.

He and JT have become friends.

And…I like him, too.

You were the love of my life, Peyton. I brought pink carnations today. They mean I'll never forget you. Ever. And I won't. But it's time for me to move forward with my life. Oh, not with Colton. He's not looking for love or a relationship, but I do hope to find someone who is as good with Charlie. Maybe you could steer someone my way.

She smiled, pulled a few sprigs of rosemary from the flowers in the vase, and placed them just below Peyton's name.

Rosemary is for remembrance. I'll always remember how much you loved me. I'll always remember our time together.

Stella said our love was enviable. And it was, wasn't it? It was wonderful, bigger than life, perfect. Stella also said you would never want me to live out the rest of my days alone and loveless. I know that's true. I've been telling myself that I'm not opposed to love if it finds me again, but I've been lying. It wasn't until recently that I started believing what I've been telling myself—does that make sense? Not that I'm in love, again, but...I think I've been too afraid to even think about it.

She wiped away the tear that dripped onto his headstone with her fingertip.

I miss you, sweetheart. I miss you more than any words can express. I miss your beautiful eyes. I miss your touch, simple things like you holding my hand, or your arms around me, making me feel safe. I miss your smile, and your laughter. And your big heart.

Thank you for giving me such a beautiful gift in our son, and thank you for loving me so well. I'll never forget our life together.

I'll never forget you, Peyton Charles Blackwood.

She stood and slowly walked to the old rusted Jeep that used to be her husbands. Maybe it was time to look for a new car.

❧

*C*olton showed up again that night. After Charlie was tucked in tight, he pulled her close and kissed her until the electric awareness crackled between them. He was definitely right about one thing. His kisses awakened sensations she hadn't felt in a long time. She wanted to be angry that he was the one bringing her back. Instead, she lowered her guard and allowed the sensations admittance. They swirled around her in whisper soft touches as he teased, tormented, and tried to entice her back to her bedroom.

"I don't do one night—"

"I told you last night, it won't be a one-night stand. We'll have an every night event until I leave. I want to make love to you, Alex, then wake up in the morning with you curled against me, and do it all over again."

She bit the inside of her lip at his words *make love*; because he also said *until I leave*. There was no question he would be leaving, and that was what she had to remember. "In your own words, *I don't do the L word*."

"Making love isn't being in love. I've told you I don't believe in love, but I can love what I plan to do to you. You don't have to be in *love* to make love to someone."

I do. "What would I tell Charlie if he woke up and found you here?"

"We'll go into the kitchen and make breakfast together." When she didn't respond, he added, "Look, Charlie knows I'm leaving. I've explained it to him. You've explained it to him. He'll be fine. Kids are resilient."

"You know this from all your experience with children?"

"I know it because I was one of them. My parents put me through emotional turmoil, and I turned out just fine."

According to whom?

Maybe Charlie would be fine after some time had passed, but she wouldn't. She'd lied to Peyton earlier. Love had snuck up on her unexpectedly and surprised her with its intensity. Just her luck to fall for a guy who lived over a thousand miles away, didn't want a wife or children, just a casual fling while he was in town. She on the other hand, after seven lonely years, had discovered she wasn't immune to the feelings a man could invoke. But she wanted more than Colton could give. She wasn't willing to admit her love only to watch him walk away.

Since when did falling in love hurt? Tumbling into love hadn't been painful with Peyton. The transition from him being her brother's best friend to the man she loved had been smooth and easy, the emotions, new and exciting. This time around, her nerve endings felt like they were coming back to life after being numb, pins and needles screaming for a relief that would never come.

Beam was right. Life didn't always let you choose who you fell in love with, but she wouldn't risk her heart to the hurt of losing another man forever.

Colton pulled her down next to him on the sofa. "Haven't you ever wanted to have sex with someone you don't love, don't even care about? No rules. No regrets. Just two people in the dark."

His words—*with someone you don't love, don't even care about*—smashed any hope her heart might have contemplated. He and Misty were more of a fit for each other than he thought.

～

*C*olton took Alex and Charlie to dinner in Glenwood the next weekend, a homey Mexican restaurant that Alex had been coming to since she was little. The owners, Carlos and Rosita Gutierrez visited Eden Falls every Thursday to pick up flowers for their tables.

The minute they entered, Rosita rushed forward with clasped hands. "Ah, Alex, what a handsome man you have found."

Alex hugged the woman, trying not to laugh at the panic etched on Colton's face. "Rosita, this is Colton McCreed. He's visiting Eden Falls for the summer. We're just friends."

"Colton's my best friend," Charlie said.

Rosita cupped Charlie's face. "That's just the way it should be between father and son. Even if it isn't blood that binds them." She gave Colton a wink. "The love that shines from the eyes is evident for the world to see, if one is paying attention."

Alex felt sorry for Colton. He was physically uncomfortable under Rosita's close scrutiny. Not even when he'd thought he was going to be a father had he looked so miserable. She tried, for his sake, to laugh the whole incident off, but he didn't relax until they were back in Eden Falls.

~

*C*olton watched Alex smooth the hair from Charlie's forehead and kiss his cheek. The sight warmed his heart. When had these two started to mean so much to him? How had he allowed it happen? He was leaving for L.A. soon with no intention of returning. When he left this place, he'd make a clean break—no looking back.

There's no love shining from my eyes, Rosita.

Alex and Charlie had begun to mean too much to him. He would not let himself get caught up in the illusion of domestic bliss, because that was exactly what it was…an illusion. He had a full schedule once he got back to L.A. It would be Christmas before he had any time to himself. Victoria had asked him to join her in Mexico for the holidays, and Talia had invited him to Aspen. He had a world of options open, and none of them included Eden Falls.

That didn't mean he couldn't enjoy the time he had left.

He stepped into the hall as Alex backed away from Charlie's bed. Once she was through the door, he closed it and pulled her into his arms. His mouth was on hers instantly. She smelled soft and powdery, and the scent was intoxicating. Her lips were warm and responsive, as was her body, as she wrapped her arms around his neck allowing him to draw her even closer.

What was it about her that had him so crazy? She wasn't

exotic, but girl-next-door beautiful. She wasn't sophisticated, but down home comfortable. The way she parented Charlie was sweet. With all she'd been through, all she did on a daily basis, she still found time to take care of those around her. Her nature was to worry about others rather than herself. He respected her. He admired her for her strength, her enthusiasm, her spunk. She had so many brilliant qualities. Put them together and they made Alex unique, unlike any woman he'd ever met.

He slipped his hands up her sides and she stepped back, breaking the kiss.

"No," she said too loudly then whispered, "I'm not sleeping with you."

He pulled her to him again. "I don't want to sleep with you either. I want to keep you up all night. We need to make the most of the time we have left."

Colton backed her a step toward her bedroom.

"Wrong direction, Mr. McCreed."

He let himself be led to the living room. "Why do we always digress to Mr. McCreed?"

She raised her eyebrows. "Maybe you ought to ask yourself that question. The answer is pretty obvious to me."

He drew her down onto his lap, into his arms, and nibbled her neck, appreciating the shiver that moved through her small frame.

"Are you seeing anyone in L.A.?"

Her question stopped him for a moment. "I see a lot of people in L.A." He moved her hair back to get to the sensitive spot just below her ear, buying time, formulating his answer. He knew what she was asking, and his response would make an enormous difference to her and the way she felt about him.

"You know what I mean." She turned her head, denying access to her lips. "It's not a hard question."

He nipped her earlobe. "I see women if that's what you're getting at, but none of them are what you'd call a *girlfriend*."

She pushed back from him. "Would you call them ladies of the evening?"

"No, Alex. They're women friends that I...go to parties with—"

"Sleep with?"

He knew where this conversation was headed, and the outcome wouldn't be good. "Occasionally."

A tiny pucker appeared between her brows as she scooted off his lap. He was tempted to run a finger down her nose, but decided that would be risking a digit. Or a limb.

"How many women friends do you go to *parties* with?"

He closed his eyes. "Let's not do this. We only have a short time left and—"

"And you want to include me in your collection of women *friends* before you leave?"

He released a frustrated breath. "It's not like that."

"Really?" She scooted further away. "What's it like?"

"It's different with you."

Her eyebrows rose. "How is it different?"

"They don't mean any..." He let the words trail away. He wasn't romantically involved with Talia or Maci or Victoria. They were just women friends with benefits, but somehow saying it aloud would make him sound incredibly superficial. "I admire you."

He could tell by the set of her jaw he'd said the wrong thing.

"You know I'm too busy for a permanent relationship. Why do women always want more than a man can give? I've been honest with you from the beginning. I don't want marriage or kids."—He held up a hand—"Don't take that the wrong way. I think the world of Charlie. The kid will always have a special place in my heart."

Her green eyes darkened.

"And you, too, Alex. I've enjoyed this summer. Getting to know you and Charlie has been the best part."

She crossed her arms around herself, closing him out. "How many?"

"How many what?"

"How many women *friends* are you occasionally sleeping with on a regular basis?"

"I don't sleep with any of them on a regular—"

"How many?"

He looked away. For some absurd reason he didn't want to see her expression when he answered. Why did he care what Alex thought about his life style? He was happy, and his women friends didn't complain. He refused to feel guilty about the way he lived. He wouldn't let this girl from a small town in the middle of nowhere, guilt him into believing he was doing anything wrong. He ran his fingers through his hair in frustration. Still, she'd been the one to bring Misty to her senses. If she hadn't...

Looking away was cowardly, so he turned back to face her. "Three."

~

*W*hy did Colton saying "three" aloud make her feel sicker than she already felt? How could she have been so stupid? How had she let herself fall in love with someone so night-to-day different? He was rough seas, she was smooth sailing. He scoffed at her optimism. He had three women on standby. Standby—the word made her nauseous. She was nothing but a small town girl to him. Someone he admired, because she shouldered a lot of responsibility. She was naïve and inexperienced. What was she doing with such a worldly man, so out of her element?

She stood, picked up a sweater from the back of the sofa, and wrapped it around herself, suddenly chilled. "You need to leave."

"Alex—"

She turned her back on him. "Please, Colton, I need you to go."

Colton stood and picked up his jacket as Alex walked to the front door and opened it. He stopped in front of her and reached out, but she flinched away.

He dropped his hand to his side. "So, I'll see you and Charlie at church in the morning?"

"Church?" She almost laughed, considering the conversation they'd just had.

He stepped onto the porch, and she shut the door.

CHAPTER 17

Colton slid into the pew next to JT. He leaned forward and acknowledged Alice and Denny Garrett. "Alex and Charlie aren't here yet?"

JT looked back towards the door. "I haven't seen them."

A few minutes later, Josh entered from a side door and walked to the podium. Both JT and Colton glanced over their shoulders.

Where is she?

Alice turned to JT. "Did you talk to you sister this morning?"

JT shook his head and glanced at Colton. "You haven't talked to her this morning?"

"No."

JT pulled out his cell and sent a quick text. They all waited, watching the screen. There was no response.

Colton paid no attention to the sermon as his frustration with Alex grew. Had she deliberately keep Charlie home because of their conversation last night—her idea of punishing him for his lifestyle? Frustration turned to anger over the long hour.

After church, Colton called her cell, but still got no response. The Garrett's sent JT over to Alex's house to check, and Colton followed. Her Jeep was sitting in the driveway, but she didn't answer the door, so JT used his spare key to open the door. The house was empty. JT pulled out his phone and tried Alex's cell again. This time she picked up. JT pushed the speaker button on his phone. "Where are you?"

"Good morning to you, too, big brother."

JT leaned back against the table. "You had us worried, Alex. Where are you?"

"Charlie and I decided to take a bike ride this morning."

"Why didn't you call?"

"I didn't know I had to check in with you. Charlie forgot it was Sunday, suggested a bike ride, and I thought, why not?"

"Where are you?" JT asked for a third time.

"The falls."

"You and Charlie rode all the way to Eden Falls?"

Her laughter almost pushed Colton's anger over the edge. She sounded as if she didn't have a care in the world. "We've ridden up here tons of times, and you know it. We're fine."

"Why didn't you answer my calls?"

"You know service on this road is spotty."

"I'm coming to get you."

"What's up with you? We'll be home after our picnic."

"Call me when you start down, so I have an idea when you'll be home. Then call me when you get home, so I know you made it safely."

After JT disconnected the call, Colton held out his hand. "Let me borrow your truck. I'll go pick them up."

"What's going on between the two of you?" JT held up his hand. "And don't insult me by saying nothing."

Colton lifted a shoulder. "We had a misunderstanding."

"I guess, since she's the one who missed church, it was you who was misunderstood."

"It was nothing."

JT sat in one of Alex's kitchen chairs. "You're leaving in a few weeks. Don't start something you can't finish." He looked up, worry etched around his eyes. "She's a lifer, Colton. She's only been in love once, and she lost him. When word came that Peyton was killed, it almost destroyed her, and maybe it would have if she hadn't been carrying his child."

"When I leave here, I don't plan on coming back. Alex knows where I stand. I've been straight up with her from the beginning."

"Straight up about what? Alex is not like Misty. You should know that by now. She's lived a fairly sheltered life, considering. She's...inexperienced." He stood and ran fingers through his hair. "She'd kill me if she heard me saying this. If you care about her..."

Colton held out his hand, again, tired of the lecture. He felt he was pretty suave where women were concerned—at least until he'd stepped foot into this crazy town. "Let me borrow your truck, JT."

"Don't make me regret this" JT pulled his keys from his pocket. "Because, friends or not, I'll have no qualms about shooting you."

~

*A*lex explored around the edge of the pool at the bottom of the falls with Charlie. The August day was sunshiny gorgeous. The fine mist of the waterfall that settled over their exposed skin felt refreshing after the hot bike ride. Charlie's happy chatter and little boy laughter filled the summer air and her heart. The last time they'd been here, it was spring and still too cold to splash around in the water.

Peyton had been a nature lover. The two of them had spent many hours hiking, biking, and wandering the trails around Eden Falls. She took a moment to tell Charlie that now. She enjoyed telling her son about Peyton. He always had a million questions, which she was happy to answer. She wanted Charlie to know everything about his dad.

"Look, Mom!"

She shaded her eyes against the sun and looked in the direction Charlie pointed, expecting her worrywart brother, then frowned at the man walking toward them.

"Hi, Colton," Charlie shouted, waving wildly.

Charlie's devotion-filled voice tugged at her heart.

"Hey, buddy." Colton sat on the grass and pulled off his shoes and socks. "Is the water still cold, Mayor?"

"A little." She scanned the parking lot. "How'd you get JT's truck? He's pretty particular about who drives it."

"I asked."

She stepped out of the water and sat on the grassy bank. Leaning back on her palms, she closed her eyes and tried to relax the sudden tension in her shoulders. Her outstretched legs warmed by the sun.

"Did you eat lunch?" Colton asked as he stepped into the water.

"We had tuna salad on crackers and string cheese and grapes and apples and juice boxes," Charlie said.

Colton chuckled. "That sounds like quite a spread. Did you leave any for me?"

"We have a whole bunch left. He can have some, huh, Mom?"

"Of course. Why don't you show Colton where the basket is, sweetie?"

"First I want to show him those shiny rocks."

Alex listened to their voices, her son's excited one and Colton's encouraging one. They had the connection she'd wished for her son. Listening brought a burn of tears to her eyes that she quickly blinked away.

"We're going to eat, Mom."

Colton and Charlie climbed up the slight bank of grass. Colton held his hand out to her. "Want to come with us?"

She glanced at him, resentful that he'd invaded their quiet little world—and not just today. She and Charlie didn't get time away very often, and here he was butting in on the little bit of peace she'd felt since last night. "No, I think I'll stay here and enjoy the sun."

Her son and Colton's laughter in the distance brought a smile to her lips. She was a firm believer that life is what you make of it. She'd been given so much that she felt ungrateful to think it wasn't fair the way things turned out sometimes. She'd known the type of man Colton was from the beginning. He'd never misled her. Or Charlie. Her son would be disappointed, but Colton was right. Charlie knew Colton was leaving at the end of summer. She was the one who should grow up and accept the situation.

When the laughter stopped, Alex got up and wandered toward the blanket she and Charlie had spread out earlier in the shade of a tree. She wasn't prepared for the sight that met her. Her son was asleep on his side, Colton behind him with an arm curled around Charlie's middle. Seeing them like that squeezed her heart uncomfortably. This would be a moment she'd pull from her memory often.

"Have a seat, Mayor. I'll keep my hands to myself," Colton said without opening his eyes.

She sat.

He got up on an elbow and looked at her with his stormy eyes. "Why didn't you come to church this morning?"

"It was a beautiful day, and Charlie wanted to go for a

bike ride." She lay down on her side facing Colton, Charlie between them. She moved a lock of hair from her son's forehead, then ran her index finger along the outer rim of his ear. "We don't get to do things like this, spur of the moment, very often.

"So it had nothing to do with our conversation last night?"

It had everything to do with our conversation last night. "Why would it?" The words sounded childish. Of course, he knew she was lying.

He touched her wrist, and she pulled her hand back. A flicker of hurt crossed his face at her reaction, but she wouldn't apologize. "I want to call occasionally…to talk to Charlie. Believe it or not, I'm going to miss him."

"I believe you." Her gaze dropped to Charlie. She wanted to stay mad, and was afraid if she looked into his gray eyes for very long—she wouldn't. As much as Colton squawked about not wanting to be around kids, he and Charlie had a unique relationship. He'd gone from irritated by a touch, to initiating the contact. Charlie had wiggled his happy self into Colton's inner sanctum, crumbling his stronghold, as only Charlie could.

"You look sleepy," he said.

"I am a little."

"Didn't sleep well?"

~

*A*lex's gaze lifted to his and then fluttered back to Charlie. In that brief moment, Colton read many words, and was grateful she didn't utter any of them aloud.

"Close your eyes. I'll stay awake."

Alex tucked an arm under her head, took one of Charlie's little hands in hers, and closed her eyes.

Colton waited until he saw her rhythmic breathing, then reached across Charlie and moved a strand of hair from her forehead, just as he'd seen her do countless times with her son. He loved touching her silky soft hair. He smoothed a finger over the arch of her brow. When had he stopped thinking her nose was too big for her face? It was perfect. She was perfect. Her lashes fluttered when he ran the backs of his fingers over her cheek. He hesitated, but she slept on.

A moment later, he couldn't help himself, and reached out again to trace the pad of his thumb over her full bottom lip. She turned her head a fraction, and he withdrew his hand a second time.

Is this what normal families did on weekends? Ride their bikes, have picnics, and take naps together? Did husbands watch over their wives and children while listening to the distant sound of a waterfall? Did dads feel as protective over their families as he felt at this moment?

Why was his mind wandering in this direction? He needed to get out of this town and back to L.A. This place had messed majorly with his whole psyche. When he got away, this world would all become a distant memory. As that last thought swirled through his mind, he got up on an elbow, leaned over Charlie, and pressed his mouth to hers.

She made a soft sound in her throat. "What are you doing?" she whispered against his lips.

"Do you want me to stop?"

"No."

He continued kissing her until he felt Charlie stir between them. He drew back, and she opened her eyes and looked at him as if she were examining his soul. Then she smiled and his hard heart fractured slightly, allowing a shaft of her light to enter.

"There's my Sunshine. I've missed her."

~

*I*f her connection with Colton was so wrong, how could it feel so incredibly right? It was wrong because he was leaving soon. It was wrong because he didn't want a relationship, commitments, or kids. Wrong because they were complete opposites in every way. Wrong because he had no misgivings about sleeping with several women at once. Yet, when they were together, they found endless topics to debate, from politics—which they agreed on—to morals—which they obviously didn't. Sometimes they laughed at their disagreements, but more often they got into a heated argument—him telling her she was a narrow-minded prude, and her calling him an arrogant, city-dwelling, pig.

Their dinners grew from once a week to almost every night. Afterward, they would sit on the porch and watch the sun dip below the mountains as Charlie played in the front yard with a friend. Sometimes he and Colton picked out songs on the guitar. Each day brought Alex closer to Colton and the knowledge that it would take a very long time for her heart to let him go. She knew Peyton was gone, never coming home. With Colton, there would always be the faint, impossible-not-to imagine, hope he might find his way back to her. She didn't want to cling to that tiny thread of hope, but knew she would.

~

*T*he next couple of weeks flew by quickly. Colton spent a lot of time on the river, fine-tuning his casting. He was determined this would be a pastime he'd take with him, providing he could find a place to fish. He took Charlie with him often. JT joined them, if he wasn't working, or Rowdy, when he could get away from his place of business. He was astonished by how much he enjoyed standing in a cold river, taking in the incredible beauty around him. Morning mists shrouded the mountaintops and towering pines. A wide variety of fern covered the forest floor. The river moving over the rocks, or swirling in the sunlight was entrancing. He'd never seen wildlife in their natural habitat. Two separate times JT pointed out a bull moose standing at the water's edge with its huge rack of antlers. Anytime of day, the view was stunning.

While Alex was in the flower shop or the mayor's office, he took Charlie and Tyson to the community pool after Recreation. They spent guys-only time romping and splashing through the heat of the day, and always ended the afternoon with ice cream cones, Popsicles, or juicy slices of watermelon.

He looked forward to running the trail with JT. Mornings had become a time of quiet reflection. Since arriving, his senses had become heightened to the sound of rain on the roof or splattering through the leaves of trees. His moments on the porch with its spectacular view of the mountains were committed to memory. Alex had him identifying Shasta Daisies from Blanket flowers, and Orange butterflies from Buckeyes. Erick Kerns showed him how to mow, just so he could enjoy the scent of freshly cut grass. His manuscript was on its way to his editor, and still he stayed. L.A. was calling his name, but he couldn't bring himself to pack his bags.

Saying goodbye to this place would probably be the hardest thing he'd ever do. And he knew he'd miss the people of Eden Falls for a long time into the future.

*H*is last Friday night in town, Colton was supposed to meet JT for a last hurrah at

Rowdy's Bar and Grill. He walked through the door and was blown away when a room full of friends yelled "SUR-PRISE!" The people of this little town managed to crack his hard heart, yet again. In his thirty-four years, no one had ever thrown him a surprise party. He went around the room, shaking hands, patting backs, and receiving hugs.

Patsy gave him a "To Go" certificate, to pick out all of his favorite pastries before leaving. Rance gave him the ultimate fishing rod in exchange for a promised, signed-copy of his next book. He didn't have the heart to tell the guy it would be awhile before the rod got any use. Rita Reynolds squawked loudly before handing him a box of her famous brownies. The list went on and on. Every gift had special meaning. Misty gave him a hug, and a kiss that Beam should have hit him for. Instead, he received a sound pat on the back and a handshake that almost crippled him.

Alex hung back, and he saved her for last. When he reached her, he leaned her over his arm and kissed her with an energy burrowed deep. The room erupted in shouts and cheers. When their lips parted, he noticed the pink of her cheeks. And tears. His stomach dropped. She'd be embarrassed if anyone saw such raw emotions, so he pulled her upright into a hug that placed her back to the crowd to give her time to dry her eyes.

❧

*A*lex, mortified by her tears, had just enough time to dry them before some of the men pulled Colton away for a drink. When she turned, Misty was standing in front of her, blue eyes blazing.

"I knew there was something going on between the two of you."

"You're right. He asked me to marry him. The wedding is Saturday."

The wide-eyed, open-mouthed, steam-coming-out-of-her-ears expression Misty wore was worth the lie. Alex wished she were the kind of person to walk away, leaving her to believe it. She wasn't. "Misty, he was just trying to embarrass me in front of everyone."

"Well, he never kissed me like that."

"It was all show." Colton was trying to make light of the time they'd spent together. He didn't want her, or anyone in town, to get the wrong idea. She'd received the message loud and clear.

She laid the jigsaw puzzle Charlie had wrapped, on the growing pile of presents and left, knowing she wouldn't be missed.

When she got home, she paid her sitter then checked on Charlie. He'd kicked his sheet off and his Ninja Turtle pajamas were twisted. She straightened them and pulled the sheet up to his chin. His beautiful bronzed cheek had a pillow mark. She smoothed her finger along it.

He opened an eye. "Did you give Colton the puzzle I wrapped?"

She smiled. "I did."

"Are we ever going to see him again?"

"I'm sure he'll be over for dinner before he leaves, sweetheart."

"But, will he come back to Eden Falls?"

She was tempted to lie. She wanted to assure her son that his new best friend wouldn't completely forsake him, but she couldn't. "I don't think so, baby. He's going to be very busy, now that he's finished his book." She kissed his brow. "Go back to sleep."

How ironic life could be, she thought, as she left Charlie's room. How was it possible that Charlie had discovered the closest thing he'd ever known to a father-son relationship with a man who didn't want anything to do with children? They'd both fallen in love with someone who wasn't able to return the sentiment.

She walked out onto the front porch and glanced up at the sky. Funny how days and weeks and months were forever the same, and then suddenly, they weren't. She wasn't sure when everything had flipped, but now she was looking at the world through different eyes. Nothing, and yet everything, had changed. The grass seemed greener, the stars shone brighter, and the man she'd been stunned to even consider a friend, had unexpectedly become so much more.

She sank to the porch steps and allowed loneliness to envelope her. Familiar as an old friend, yet this time, instead of striking quickly and leaving her strangling for breath, it drifted over her like a fog with ghostly fingers, encircling her body and chilling her heart.

She'd scheduled a meeting with a group of environmentalists for Wednesday, the morning of Colton's flight. She wouldn't make a fool of herself by breaking down at the airstrip with Beam and, possibly, Misty watching. She chose to shed her tears in the privacy of her night-shrouded porch, with only the stars as witnesses.

～

*A*lex spent Saturday morning finishing flower arrangements for a small wedding. After she delivered the wedding bouquets and table toppers, she was meeting her friends for dinner and a movie. They hadn't been able to get together for a girls' night out for several weeks, and she desperately needed some fun.

The church was already draped in tulle, and pedestals were set up for the bouquets she'd designed. She delivered the bridal party's flowers, oohed and ahhed over the wedding dress, and met the groom. Then she drove to The Dew Drop Inn where she added centerpieces to each table, a large bouquet on the buffet table, and another on a smaller dessert table. When everything was just right, she exited through the back door and came to a stop. Colton, in a suit and tie, stood next to a limousine.

The sight was so out of place in Eden Falls, she laughed, and then sobered just as quickly. This was Colton McCreed's life, comfortable in an expensive suit, with a shiny limo at his beck and call. While her life was jeans, T-shirts, and pollen stained fingers. "What are you doing here?"

He slipped both hands into his front pants pockets. "Waiting for you."

"Why?"

"We're going on a date."

She pointed. "In that?"

"Yes."

She regretted she had to turn the invitation down. She'd never ridden in a limo before. "I already have—"

"Plans with your friends, but not really. Charlie is at a campout with his cousins tonight, and JT will pick him up for us in the morning."

He threw the word *us* around loosely. She wasn't sure how that made her feel.

He opened the door of the limo and pulled out a garment bag. "You'll need to change."

She eyed the bag suspiciously. "What's in there?"

"Just go change. Please."

In The Dew Drop Inn's bathroom, she unzipped the garment bag and stared at a stunning black lace over nude sheath dress. The design was low cut, form fitting and, without a doubt, Stella's handy work. The strappy black sandals were to die for. Besides her wedding dress, she'd never worn anything so elegant. Or expensive. Stella had stowed a small cosmetics bag under the shoes. After a quick touchup, Alex released her hair from its clip and studied the results in the mirror. A hand to her stomach didn't calm the flock of butterflies tickling her insides. She hadn't felt this nervous about a date in a long time. Ten years to be exact.

When she stepped outside, Colton's low whistle and gaze of appreciation made her cheeks heat. She dipped her head, but he lifted her chin with his index finger and kissed her lips. "You look gorgeous."

I'm so far from gorgeous its laughable, but still... She appreciated the compliment. "Thank you." She hoped her breathless reply wasn't as obvious to his ears as it was to hers. "You look very handsome."

"Thank you." He opened the door, and she slid into an opulence she'd never experienced. Shimmers of excitement filled her. "Where are we going?"

"It's a surprise, so sit back and relax, Sunshine." He climbed in beside her and intertwined their fingers. When he raised the back of her hand to his lips, his hot breath tickled over her skin. "We have a long ride."

A shot of panic rose. "A long ride? I can't just leave Charlie—"

He turned her hand over and kissed her palm tenderly. "Would you, just for once, let someone else take the reins? Adam and Jeno have Charlie tonight. JT will pick him up in the morning. He's in good hands. All you have to do is sit back and enjoy." He picked up a small plate and held it out to her. "Have some cheese and crackers. The strawberries are delicious."

When the limo left town, she guessed they were going to Seattle. She'd never done anything like this before—ever. She was too practical, and Peyton had been, too. They'd also never had the kind of money Colton had.

FINDING EDEN | 261

She decided to follow Colton's instructions and enjoy. The strawberries were sweet, and the cheese was many steps above the canned spray cheese Charlie liked so well. They carried on a comfortable conversation, talking of mayor things and writer things, as soft music floated from hidden speakers. Colton described some of the places he'd traveled and answered her millions of questions. When they came to a stop in front of an elegant Seattle restaurant, she was amazed two and a half hours had passed so quickly.

She didn't want to let herself believe this night meant something, but how was that possible when a man brought her all the way to Seattle for dinner? She repeated silently, *"This is just an extremely wonderful gesture"*.

After they were seated at a table overlooking the waters of Puget Sound, she glanced at Colton. His intense gray eyes watched her as he reached across the table and took her hand. "After our conversation a couple of weeks ago, you think very little of me, don't you?"

"This is...I can't find words to describe how wonderful this is, but if you think dinner in Seattle will get me in your bed, you think very little of me."

"You're wrong, Alex. I've never thought more highly of an individual in my life. I've also never appreciated getting to know anyone as much as you. You are the most resilient, loving, and decent woman I've ever met." He squeezed her hand lightly. "I brought you here because I wanted to thank you for all you've done to make my stay enjoyable. You deserve a special night."

Something warm unfurled at his words. He might not love her, but he did care. Maybe she and Charlie had dented his tough, pessimistic exterior. Maybe they'd softened his heart enough that he could, one day, love someone, and make a commitment.

She had no words to describe how wonderful dinner

tasted. Everything was princess magical, and she didn't want to step out of the glass slipper. She was sure this kind of night was normal for someone like Colton, but for her it was a once in a lifetime experience. The fact that he'd gone to this magnitude meant more to her than she could ever express.

After dinner, the limousine whisked them off to a towering hotel. The driver opened the car door, then removed two overnight bags from the trunk.

"How..."

"Stella packed for you."

She lifted her eyebrows. "You thought of everything."

He bowed like a prince.

"You've done this before." As soon as the words left her mouth, she wished she could pull them back.

"Yes." He lifted her chin so their eyes met. "I'm not going to lie to you."

The porter inserted a special key, and the elevator whisked them to the top floor presidential suite. When he unlocked the door, Alex entered in awe at the floor to ceiling windows that overlooked the Sound. The suite was larger than her whole three-bedroom house and opulently decorated. She wandered from room to room in amazement. The master bedroom opened up on the left of the living room, kitchen, and dining room. On the right was a smaller bedroom with a view of the Space Needle.

She walked to the window. "I'll take this room."

In the reflection of the glass, she saw Colton nod to the porter and pull a wad of bills from his pocket. The porter placed her bag on a luggage rack set in the corner. After he left the room, she turned to see what Stella had packed. She lifted out a sexy, black lace—completely see through—nightie. Where on earth had Stella gone shopping? There was also a pair of jeans, a blouse, a jacket, and underneath it all lay a teeny, tiny bikini. She held up the microscopic pieces of cloth.

Colton knocked on her open door wearing a pair of swim trunks, and showing off his impressive bare chest. "I see you found the swimsuit Stella packed. There's a hot tub on my bedroom balcony."

Alex laughed. "She didn't pack a swimsuit. She packed a couple of Band-Aids."

Colton came into the room and took the suit from her, rubbing the delicate fabric between his fingers seductively. "Can't wait to see you in these Band-Aids."

Her whole body warmed at the idea. Colton had seen her in a swimming suit at the river, but it had covered a lot more than this would. "I can't wear that."

"Yes, you can." He handed the pieces back and left the room.

It took her ten minutes to gather the courage to walk onto his balcony wrapped in a towel. She looked down at the bubbling water a moment before saying, "You have to close your eyes."

He did as she asked.

She splashed into the water and settled as far away from him as she could get. "Okay."

He opened his eyes. "You look like a trapped bunny hovering for cover." He stretched out his legs until they came into contact with hers. Instinctively, she pulled hers to her chest. His eyes dropped and he smiled.

"Don't look."

"Not going to happen, Sunshine." He moved closer.

She wrapped her arms around her knees. "Did you buy this suit?"

He was next to her now. "With Stella's help."

"Did the two of you pick out that little nightie, too?"

"I picked out a red one, but Stella thought the black was sexier."

She put a hand out to halt his advance. "I hope you kept the receipt, because I'm not wearing it."

"I won't complain if you wear nothing," he said as he circled an arm around her waist and lowered his lips to hers.

CHAPTER 18

After tucking Charlie into bed, Alex answered the knock on her door. Stella and Jillian stood on the other side. She'd been expecting this visit, at least from Stella, and had made a batch of brownies for the occasion. She needed something rich and sinful to replace the *someone* she couldn't have.

"So? Tell us everything." Stella demanded, before she'd closed the door.

She waved them to the living room. "I'm fine. Thanks for asking. Come in and have a seat. I made brownies for the inquisition." She glanced over her shoulder at Stella as she headed for the kitchen. "But, I won't leave you hanging. Nothing happened."

"Colton told me there would be a hot tub on the balcony overlooking the Sound, so I picked out the sexiest bikini I could find *in Harrisville*, and you say nothing happened."

Alex came back into the living room carrying a tray with a plate of brownies and two glasses of milk. She set it on the coffee table between her friends, who'd taken either end of the sofa. "What you picked out was not a bikini. It was tiny remnants of fabric."

Stella wiggled her eyebrows as she reached for a brownie. "It was sexy."

Alex glanced at Jillian. "It was non-existent."

"Tell us what you *did* do," Jillian said.

Alex sat in an armchair facing them. "He took me to a romantic restaurant overlooking the Sound. Dinner was delicious." She turned her gaze on Stella. "The word bikini used for the scraps of material you picked out is stretching it, but the dress was gorgeous, and the sandals—"

"I know, huh?" Stella grinned. "I want Len to take me somewhere romantic so I can borrow those sandals."

Alex leaned back and covered her eyes with a hand. "If I knew what that one night cost, I'd be sick to my stomach."

"Colton can afford it. What I wouldn't give for a night like that." Stella took a bite of brownie and groaned.

Alex wasn't sure if the groan was because of the brownie —Rita Reynolds' famous brownie recipe—or the thought of her and Len in Seattle for a romantic evening. She smiled at Jillian.

"What did you order?" Jillian asked.

"I had the poached salmon and—"

"Who cares what they ate," Stella said with brownie stuck to her front teeth. "Get to the good stuff. Please, tell me there was some good stuff."

The good stuff. "We went to an opulent hotel." Alex described the suite and the view in detail.

"Bor-ing." Stella patted her lips in a fake yawn.

"He slept in the master, and I slept in the second bedroom."

"Why?" Stella asked.

Alex's mind skipped over memories. Nothing had happened. But it could have. Almost had. Their kissing and exploring had escalated until Alex, hastily, climbed out of the hot tub and grabbed her towel. "I can't do this, Colton. Thank you for the wonderful evening. It was "—her voice cracked embarrassingly—"enchanting. I...I'll never forget it." When he started to rise from the water, she sprinted inside.

Once in her bedroom, she shut and locked the door. He stood on the other side tapping and coaxing for ten minutes before he gave up, and went to his own room.

"Tell us something good. We have to live vicariously through someone, don't we Jillian?" Stella asked.

They all laughed. The simple gesture felt good. Alex turned sideways in the chair, her legs dangling over the arm. "Colton is leaving in three days, and has no reason to ever come back."

"He has you," Jillian said. "And Charlie."

"He doesn't want a family. He has a home in L.A. He travels all over the world. You should hear some of the places he's been. Wearing a tux and riding in limos are common-place for him. And he has women *friends*"—she made quotation marks with the fingers of one hand—"that he sees regularly."

"What do you mean sees?" Stella asked with a frown. "As in...?"

Alex glanced at the brownies, all desire for the rich and sinful gone. "Yes, as in."

"He told you that?" Jillian asked, wide eyed.

Alex laughed, but the simple gesture she'd enjoyed just a moment ago was also gone. "Well, he didn't offer the information. He, reluctantly, told me when I asked. There are three of them."

Jillian's eyes grew wide. "Three?"

"Wow," Stella said.

"Yeah, wow."

"Do you love him?" Jillian whispered more to herself than aloud.

The concern on Jillian's face made the tears that had threatened all day seep to the surface. Alex blinked them back, but not before her friends noticed.

"I'm sorry. I shouldn't have asked." Jillian's expression changed from concern to hope. "People can change."

Alex glanced at the ceiling, hoping to see the answer to all of life's injustices written there. Ironically, there was only a crack that began in the corner and curled around in the shape of a question mark. She blew out a breath. "Colton Mc-Creed isn't going to change. He has no reason to."

~

*C*olton entered Pretty Posies Tuesday morning. The trip back into Eden Falls with Alex hadn't been nearly as comfortable as the drive into Seattle. Alex sat on her side of the limo—pensive—and he sat on his side, keeping his hands to himself. He'd come to the conclusion, over the long sleepless night, that his feelings had become too strong. He was afraid of what he might offer, which wouldn't be fair to Alex, because he knew he wouldn't keep any promises. He stayed busy with packing on Monday, but, by Tuesday morning, he'd stayed away from her for as long as he could.

As soon as he entered Pretty Posies and spotted Alex behind the counter, he knew what he was feeling was stronger than friendship. He flipped the bell over the door and she glanced around the customer she was helping.

The man turned. "Hey, you're that author."

Colton held out his hand. "Colton McCreed."

"Colton this is Doug Farley. He's one of two pharmacists in town."

"My wife reads your books," Doug said, shaking Colton's hand.

"You don't?" Colton asked with a grin.

"I don't read much fiction." Doug rubbed his jaw. "I wish I had a book for you to sign. That would really make Carla's day."

Alex reached under the counter and produced Colton's last book. "Why don't you sign this? Doug can add it, along with the flowers he's taking to the hospital. His wife just had a baby girl."

"Congratulations." Colton took the book Alex held out and added a message before his signature.

"Thanks." Doug glanced at Alex. "I owe you."

She waved her hand. "Tell Carla congratulations. I'll bring dinner by on Thursday."

After Doug left the shop, he and the mayor stared at each other for a long moment. He was going to miss looking into those beautiful green eyes. He smiled, and she did the same.

"I have a few errands to run today, but I'd like to come over later and say goodbye to Charlie. I have a gift for him, and I never got the chance to thank him for the puzzle."

"Dinner at six?"

He wouldn't take the time to analyze why his heart was pounding at the speed of a freight train, but felt a slight relief at her dinner invitation. "I'll see you then."

～

*C*harlie slipped on his new backpack and showed Colton his Ninja Turtles lunch box. Soon, his first-grade shopping list and all the supplies he and Alex had been dashing around for, were displayed on the kitchen table. The anxiousness her son showed made Alex's heart pinch. Charlie knew Colton was leaving in the morning, and was trying to fit a years worth of words into a few hours.

After dinner Colton glanced out the front window several times, and Alex wondered if he was expecting someone. Then an unfamiliar car pulled into the driveway. Colton turned to Charlie. "I have a going away present for you, but you have to stay in the house with your mom for a minute."

He went out front and met the pretty woman who stepped from the car. Alex endured a wave of jealousy when they embraced. Was this one of his women friends from L.A.? Had she driven up to take him home to California? They walked to the back of the Subaru she was driving and pulled out a very large crate. Together they carried it to the front porch. Inside the crate was a dog—A BIG DOG. *Colton would not be dense enough to give Charlie a dog without a parental consultation first. Especially not a dog that size!*

They set the crate down and, before Alex could stop him, Charlie was through the door and on his knees, sticking his fingers through the bars so the dog could lick them. Alex followed.

"Alex, Charlie, this is Alicia Stone. She rescues Labradors. And this," Colton said squatting down next to Charlie, "is Barney. Alicia found him in an abandoned house, and nursed him back to health."

He glanced at Alex. "He's gentle and well trained. I've set up an account in your name at the pet store in Harrisville. All expenses for his food and supplies will be sent directly to me. I've also set up an account with the town vet in advance. I'll pick up the bills for shots and any medical treatment needed." He smiled at Charlie. "He just needs a little boy to love him."

Obviously, he is that dense.

"He's for me?" Charlie looked up at Alex, his big dark eyes filled with pleading. "Can we keep him, Mom? Look! He likes me. Can we keep him?"

Alex couldn't believe Colton was putting her in this position, yet it was exactly something he would do without thinking. If she said yes—Colton was the hero. If she said no—she became the enemy. Either way, he would shine. She opened her jaw to release the tension that was giving her a sudden headache. Grinding her teeth tended to do that.

Colton sent a plea in Alicia's direction. She flipped the latch that opened the crate's door. Barney climbed out wagging his tail so hard his hind end wiggled from side to side.

"Barney, sit," Alicia said.

The dog sat, but his tail continued to keep time like a metronome on a piano.

Alicia clipped a leash onto the dog's collar and told him to heel. Barney followed her down the porch steps and onto the sidewalk. She brought the dog back onto the porch and said, "Charlie, tell Barney to sit."

Charlie stood and took his mother's hand. "Barney, sit," he said in a serious tone.

The dog sat at Charlie's feet, panting, his tongue hanging out.

Charlie looked at her, again, with a little boy's beseeching expression. "Please, Mama?"

Alex ran her fingers through her son's hair before turning a deadly glare on Colton.

"JT said he'd help Charlie with Barney," Colton said quickly, as if that would tie a pretty bow around the situation. He turned to Charlie. "If your mom lets you keep Barney, he'll be your responsibility. Do you know what that means?"

"It means I have to feed him and love him." Charlie pulled on her hand. "I promise I'll feed him every day, and I'll give him water, and I'll play with him. Please, Mom?"

Alex took a deep breath, reaching deep into her soul for patience. "Being responsible also means giving Barney baths, brushing him, taking him for walks, *and* cleaning up his poop in the backyard."

Charlie's glance bounced from her to the dog and back again.

"Okay," he replied without as much enthusiasm as before.

"I mean it, Charlie. That's all part of taking care of a dog. And Barney is a big dog, so he'll have big poops."

Charlie squatted down next to the dog and giggled when he received a wet tongue to the cheek. "I promise."

Alex glared at Colton once more, as if it would do any good. "Okay, you can keep him."

Charlie jumped up and threw his little arms around her waist, hugging her tight. "Thanks, Mom! I love you so much!"

"Hey, buddy, what about me? Don't I get a hug?"

Charlie launched himself at Colton, who scooped him up in a tight hug. "Thanks, Colton. This is the best present ever!"

Alex glanced at the dog that had just become a part of their small family, a part of her son's life. *Fantabulous*. In her mind, this was Colton's way of assuaging his guilty conscience for becoming so close to her son and then leaving. It wasn't that she didn't like dogs. She did. She just knew the main responsibility of Barney would fall on her shoulders, because her son was too young to understand all that went into caring for a dog.

Suddenly, Alex felt very tired.

A grinning Colton had gotten what he'd come for tonight —even though he was leaving, he was still the shining hero.

After Alicia unloaded a pile of paraphernalia and left, she and Colton sat on the front steps to watch Charlie frolic in the yard with Barney. Her son was in heaven, his smile as big as she'd ever seen.

"Are you mad?"

She rested her folded arms on her knees without glancing

his way. "I'm saving mad for later. I'm starting out with furious."

Colton scooted close enough his arm touched her shoulder. "Come on, Mayor. Every kid needs a dog."

She turned to look at him. "Did you have one?"

"No, but I grew up in the city. Our yard had no place for a dog."

"You grew up in a mansion, and had a gardener." She shook her head. "You had someone who would have cleaned up the poop. Not *every* kid needs a dog."

"Don't you like Barney?"

His eyes were filled with as much pleading as Charlie's had been earlier. Suddenly, she realized Colton had always wanted a dog and had never been allowed. Did that make her feel sympathetic or more furious? She decided on the latter. "Don't you dare try to make me feel guilty, McCreed. I have nothing against Barney, but I am a mother first, then a mayor, and to top it off, I run a business. There's only so much of me to go around, and now you've managed to pile on one more responsibility."

"Charlie said he'd take care of—"

"And who's going to show Charlie how to take care of Barney? Me, that's who."

"Why didn't you say all of this while Alicia was here? She would have taken Barney back home with her."

She saw red. There was no one on this planet, besides Misty, who could make her this angry. "And then I become the villain."

"Don't you think you're being a little dramatic? Charlie wouldn't think of you as a villain."

"That's right. You'd know, because you're an expert with children."

He threw his hands in the air. "So Barney is one more thing you'll hold against me."

She looked back at Charlie, having the best time of his whole summer. Colton had just given him something that would change his life forever—in a good way—and all she could focus on was the negative. She just knew the upkeep would fall to her, and she was tired of all the maintenance she dealt with on a daily basis. "Barney will be the only thing I hold against you."

He tried to turn her face to his, but she stood. "You need to say goodbye to Charlie. I'm sure it's going to take me a while to settle him, and our new family member, down for the night."

Colton pushed to his feet. "You ran away in Seattle and now you're running away again. Is that how you handle difficult situations when they come your way?"

Her breath caught in a chest that was incapable of expanding further as fury coursed through her body. He actually had the audacity to say she ran away when things got difficult, as if her life was a walk in the park. She'd never run from anything in her life—but him—and who wouldn't? In three short months, he'd turned her and Charlie's world upside down.

And wasn't he, actually, the one running away?

She drew in a ragged breath as two spots on her cheeks burned. There was nothing she'd enjoy more than to double up her fist and punch him right in his perfect nose. If Charlie wasn't nearby…

As calmly as possible, she turned from the temptation. "Charlie, it's time to go in."

"Okay, Mayor, you win." Colton stepped onto the lawn. "Charlie, I need a huge hug. I'm leaving tomorrow."

"But you'll be back to see me and Mom and Barney, huh, Colton?"

"As soon as I get back to L.A., I have to fly to New York for a television interview."

"You're going to be on TV?" Charlie turned to Alex. "Mom can we watch?"

"I'll text your mom the details."

Nice and impersonal, cutting the strings as neat and tidy as possible. "Tell Colton goodbye, so we can go in and make a bed for Barney."

Colton picked Charlie up.

"I wish you weren't going away," Charlie said.

"Tell him thank you, again, for Barney."

"Thanks for Barney. He's the best present I ever got."

"I'm glad you like him. You take special care of him, okay?"

"Okay." Charlie wrapped his arms tight around Colton's neck. "I love you."

～

$\mathcal{C}$olton couldn't remember the last time he'd cried, but this pint-sized peanut, smelling of dirt and sweat and now, truly, wet puppy dog, choked his throat with tears. He swallowed hard. "I'm going to miss you, Charlie. You be extra good for your mom."

"I will."

Colton set Charlie on his feet and watched him bound inside with Barney on his heels. He grinned at Alex, hoping she'd smile back. She didn't. "I guess we can say goodbye tomorrow at the airstrip."

"I have a meeting in the morning, so JT will take you."

Colton snorted as he came toward her. "You planned that on purpose, didn't you?"

She didn't answer.

He looked down at the hand she held out, then up into her mossy green eyes. "No kiss?"

"It was nice to meet you, Mr. McCreed."

He took her hand and tugged her down a step. "It was nice meeting you, too, Mayor. Thanks for the use of your home and car. I hope you were compensated adequately."

"Just call me Jorgie was more than generous with your money."

He smiled at her stab at humor before pulling her down another step and wrapping his arms around her. He didn't want to stop and examine the odd sensation in his chest. The feeling he thought might suspiciously be love. His parents had stripped him of that emotion. They'd left a huge hollow space where his heart was supposed to be. He'd gotten used to that emptiness, and no mayor and her kid were going to change that. "You take good care of yourself, Sunshine. Don't work too hard." He ran a finger under her chin. "Eat more pastries."

Her mouth tipped up at the corners. "I think you ate enough pastries for both me and Charlie put together. Patsy will suffer financially after you leave."

"I'll have her ship a big box my way." He stared into the eyes that would haunt him for a long time, before leaning forward to kiss the lips he couldn't seem to get enough of. She didn't pull away, but she also didn't kiss him in return. "Thank you for all the dinners. This would have been a very lonely summer without you and Charlie."

Her gaze darted away as she gave a slight nod.

"I'm going to miss you. I don't like admitting that, but I'm going to miss you both. A lot."

"We'll miss you too. Take care of yourself."

He stepped back wanting more from her but unsure what. Tears? Desire? Regret? Something more than the indifference she was showing. Her detached response carried him back to his childhood, and the lacking that had haunted him for years. Irrationally, he struck. "Give me a call when you stop taking sex so seriously."

The hint of smile on her lips vanished. "You won't hear from me."

"No, I don't imagine I will, which is too bad. I think we could have had a good time together. I believe you have a lot of passion bottled up, just waiting for the right man to come along with a bottle opener." He let his gaze wander suggestively over her body. "I think we could have shown each other a real good time."

A hint of hurt crossed her face before she turned and followed Charlie inside.

He didn't want to miss her, or even think about her. He wanted to forget about this whole summer, as much as he wanted to remember every minute. He wanted Alex to show that she cared one iota that he was leaving, and she hadn't. He wanted...he wanted Alex more at this moment than he'd ever wanted any other woman in his life, which wasn't possible. This place had turned him upside down, and he wasn't thinking rationally.

At the moment, Alex hated him. That was for the best. She deserved more than he was willing to give. She was meant to have a house full of kids, a big noisy family, and a man who loved her with all his heart—a man who had a heart.

He stood on the sidewalk for a long time, staring at her front door, before saying to no one but the moon, "Find yourself a nice husband, and make lots of babies, Mayor."

Then he turned and set off down the streets of Eden Falls for the last time.

CHAPTER 19

Alex hadn't been herself since Colton left a week earlier, and she didn't like the person taking her place. She ran out to a delivery driver's van to apologize after she snapped at him. She forgot about girls' night out, until Stella called, demanding, "Where are you?" When Charlie came home from JT's house covered in mud, she barked at both of them. She was wise enough to know it boiled down to her feelings for Colton. She had to accept the fact that he was gone, and move forward with a semblance of decorum. She was embarrassed that her young son was more accepting than she was; but he'd been lucky enough to receive a consolation prize.

As hard as it was to admit, Colton had done a perfect job of picking out that prize. Barney was the sweetest, most adorable dog, with the added bonus of being potty trained. He was already devoted to her son, and Charlie was crazy about him. The dog slept next to Charlie's bed at night, lay at his feet while he ate, and they looked darling as they disappeared around the corner for their evening walk.

Alex took Barney to the flower shop with her each morning. He greeted her customers with a friendly doggy smile and a wag of his tail, as he kept vigil while Charlie attended his last week of Recreation. When Barney spotted Charlie coming through the door, he'd leap up and yap in joy, until commanded to stop. Then he'd sit at Charlie's feet until his tail was in danger of wagging right off his body.

At the mayor's office, Alex was caught in the middle of environmentalists waging war with the forest service over a new fire lookout tower being built. She struggled as the peacekeeper—though it didn't fall under her jurisdiction—when what she wanted to do was tell them all to take a flying leap.

In Pretty Posies, the bride of a huge fall wedding was demanding an exotic bloom that some blasted bug had destroyed. Alex had been in touch with several distributors, but was having no luck finding the rare beauty. Nothing she suggested to take its place was good enough for the bride.

To top off her frustration, tomorrow was the first day of school, and Charlie's excitement threatened her sanity.

Even though only one week had passed since Colton's departure, she felt as if it had been months. She hadn't realized what a sounding board he'd become for her. She'd come to depend upon his wise cracks, his dry humor, and, yes, even his cynicism. She missed his gray stormy eyes, his grin, and, most of all, his kisses.

She and Charlie snuggled on the sofa the night of Colton's interview. She had mixed feelings about seeing him, even if it was only on the television. One part of her was jittery with anticipation, the other part was stomping that anticipation down with the stiletto heel of the sandals she'd worn in Seattle.

How had she fallen in love with a man she really didn't know? Truly, she knew nothing about the Los Angeles Colton McCreed. Yet, while he resided in her world, she felt she knew him better than he knew himself.

The interviewer was young and vibrant. She sat on the edge of her seat in a bright yellow dress, her long dark hair arranged to perfection. Her long legs were crossed at the ankle with strappy pink sandals. She wore a chunky necklace the same color as her shoes.

The camera panning to Colton sent Alex's pulse into overdrive. Dressed in jeans, a blue oxford shirt, and a gray blazer, he looked tanned and toned and relaxed. He'd settled back into the swing of fame, as if he'd never left. The interviewer opened with the book he'd just finished. They talked release dates and a few appearances he had scheduled.

She asked about his writing process. He said this was the first book he'd ever written away from home. He mentioned Eden Falls, Washington, and the fact that he'd spent the summer there, first researching, and then writing. He portrayed an idyllic town and friendly people. He spoke about how helpful the chief of police had been in answering questions. He mentioned Patsy's Pastries, The Fly Shop, and Pages Bookstore. Rowdy's Bar and Grill received a plug, and his plane ride into town got a laugh from the interviewer. He talked about going to baseball games to watch his new friend Charlie play. Then he expressed appreciation for the mayor, who provided a house, a car, and enjoyable hospitality. "It didn't hurt that she could cook, and was beautiful, too."

The interviewer lifted a remote, and the wall behind them lit up with a picture of Colton with his arm around an exotic woman. Alex didn't keep up with the world of fashion, but even she recognized the famous lingerie model.

"Is Talia Laroux aware you spent the summer with a beautiful woman?"

Colton turned his head and took in the floor to ceiling image. When he turned back, a close-up by the camera revealed a subtle hardness around his gray eyes. "Why would it matter?"

"There's talk of an engagement floating around L.A."

The camera stayed close and his jaw tightened. "Those rumors are false. Talia and I are just friends, and have been for a long time."

"You and Talia looked like more than just friends at a party in Beverly Hills two nights ago," the interviewer said, as she flashed another picture on the screen behind them. Colton and the woman were engaged in what Alex considered a more-than-just-friends kiss.

"Is that Colton's girlfriend?"

Alex felt as if a boa was strangling her. "I don't know, sweetheart."

"She has a sparkly dress."

"Yes." She had to turn her head from the image. "It is very sparkly."

Colton's voice filled their living room. "That's the paparazzi making more of a situation than it is. Talia and I hadn't seen each other in three months. We were just catching up with—"

"You look to be doing more than just catching up in this photo."

Another picture appeared on the screen, and Alex grabbed the remote and turned off the television.

"Mom!"

"Sorry, sweetheart. It's time for bed."

Charlie turned pleading eyes on her. "But Mom, it was Colton."

Yes, it was. She attempted a smile, knew it was feeble at best. "Tomorrow's the first day of school, and you need a good night's sleep. Go brush your teeth, handsome."

Charlie stood and moped down the hall with Barney at his heels. He stopped at the bathroom door. "Mama?"

"Yes, honey?"

"I miss Colton."

Her tight chest didn't allow much room for air. "I know you do, baby."

"I wish we could call him," he said, bending to scratch his calf. Barney mistook the gesture as an intention of affection and licked Charlie's hand. He patted the dog's head.

Alex would never call Colton. A week earlier, he'd been kissing her and now... "He's in New York, and that's a different time zone. Its much later there than here."

Charlie scrunched his nose. "What's a different time zone?"

"I'll explain time zones tomorrow when we can look at a map. Go brush your teeth, baby."

After Charlie disappeared from view, she stood and walked to the front window. The last of the sun was filtering through clouds, giving the small part of her world an ethereal glow. She leaned her forehead against the cool glass and allowed a few stinging tears to fall, angry with herself for allowing Charlie to watch the interview, and furious at Colton for the raunchy pictures that had been displayed.

"Mom, I'm done," Charlie called at the same time her cell phone chimed a text message.

"Put on your pajamas and I'll be right there." She wiped her face, picked up her cell from the arm of the sofa, and read the second text she'd gotten from Colton since he'd left Eden Falls. The first was the information about the interview two days earlier.

She sank into the cushions and put her head in her hands. Of all the men she could have fallen in love with... He'd taken her to Seattle one weekend, and then was captured kissing and groping another woman in public the next. The images burrowed deep into her mind, and would likely lodge there for weeks.

She took a fortifying breath. Enough. Colton McCreed was gone. He'd made her no promises. Anything she'd conjured between them was on her. She set her phone down without a response and went to tuck Charlie into bed.

～

*T*he media and their hype was one reason Colton very seldom granted interviews. Once he'd escaped the interviewer, he'd called his publicist and threatened to fire her. Had Charlie seen it? Of course he had. Alex sent a text saying they would both be watching, which meant Alex saw it, too. How many other people in Eden Falls had watched?

He climbed out of the Town Car when he arrived at the airport, and stalked past the few paparazzi waiting for him. The tabloids would have him married by tomorrow. Why did anyone care about his private life? He wasn't an actor or a politician—he wrote books.

Sixty minutes later, he was seated in first class for his flight to Los Angeles. He sat back and tried to put the interview out of his mind, but he kept picturing Alex and her expression upon seeing— *Wait! The interview is being broadcast live, and New York is Eastern Standard Time. It hasn't aired on the west coast yet.* He pulled out his cell phone to text and noticed the time—too late. The interview was probably airing this minute. The announcement to turn off all electronic devices echoed in his ears, as he texted the only word that came to mind. **Sorry**

～

*T*he sound of Alex's voice over the phone hit Colton like a punch to the chest. He'd tried to deny the emotions swirling through him, but they refused to be ignored any longer.

He missed that quaint little town and its friendly people, but the loss of Charlie and Alex left him hollow inside. There hadn't been many hours in the last three weeks when they weren't on his mind. He went for a casual "Hey, Sunshine".

She was silent for a beat. Then an unemotional "Hello" echoed in his ear.

Okaaay, here we go. "How's Eden Falls?"

"Fine."

"How is the mayor?"

"Busy."

"L.A.'s the same. Smoggy." *Thanks for asking.* "How's Charlie doing?"

"He's fine, enjoying first grade."

Finally, more than a one word answer. "Does he like his teacher?"

"Yes. I'm sorry he's not here. He'd love to talk to you."

He rubbed at the hollow sensation in his chest with the heel of his palm, hating their stilted words. "Where is he?"

"I have a city council meeting, so he's eating dinner with my parents."

"That's right. It's Thursday."

Again, she was silent, leaving him struggling to carry the conversation. "So…How are Misty and Beam doing?"

She laughed, and he wanted to capture the sound. He missed her rusty laugh, her sunshine smile, her plump lips. "You'd think Misty would be happy. She's out of Eden Falls and in a big city, but they've flown in almost every weekend. I guess the grass isn't greener in a big city."

A comment aimed at me no doubt.

He was beating around the bush. Not only had he called to hear her voice, but to address the obvious elephant straddling the miles between their conversation. "Listen, Alex…I called to apologize about the interview, especially if Charlie was watching."

"He was, but I turned the program off and scooted him out of the room."

"I had no idea—"

"I have to go. The meeting starts in a few minutes."

He could tell he wasn't forgiven by the frost in her tone. *Why did I even bother to call? Stupid decision on my part— one I won't make again.* "Will you tell Charlie I called?"

"Yes. Good to talk to you, Colton. Bye."

Frustration simmered just under the surface, making his skin sensitive, but why? So what if his and Talia's kiss had been caught and broadcast? They'd missed each other.

He hadn't seen her since.

Talia was angry about the interview, too. She was hounded by the paparazzi, which demanded word of their engagement. They'd decided it would be best if they weren't seen together in public for a while. In fact, he hadn't seen many of his friends—male or female—since coming back to L.A. He wasn't interested in the endless parties and events. Instead, he wandered around his big house restlessly, missing the cocooned comfort he'd become used to in that tiny cottage he'd rented for the summer. Truth be told, that place had become more like home in three months than this house had ever felt. And he'd lived here for ten years.

~

*C*olton leaned back against his deck railing and grinned when he heard Charlie's cheerful little voice. He hadn't talked to the kid in almost two months, but it felt more like a year.

"Hi, Charlie. It's Colton."

"Mom, it's Colton!" Charlie shouted without lowering the receiver. "I didn't think you were ever going to call. When are you coming back?"

Colton loved the enthusiasm in Charlie's voice. *Nice to know someone in this big, cold world still likes me.* Was he feeling just a little sorry for himself? Well, so what. If he didn't, who would?

"I'm not sure, buddy."

He considered it a character flaw to miss Alex and Charlie as much as he did. He hadn't allowed himself to get close enough to anyone to miss them since he'd left home at eighteen. The fact that he'd succumbed now suggested a weakness, but despising that weakness didn't lessen his desire to see them. After Alex's cold reception the last time, he'd fought the urge to call again, but gave in. He'd made a promise to Charlie, and a promise was a promise.

"How's school?"

"I like my teacher. She's really pretty," he said, whispering the last sentence.

Colton laughed. "She is, huh?"

"Yeah. Guess what I'm going to be for Halloween?"

"What?" Charlie's excitement filled him with nostalgia. Colton wanted to be in front of him, eye to eye. He wanted to catch the enthusiasm, hold on to it, and pull it back out at night when his big, empty house was too quiet.

"Superman."

"That's awesome. Have your mom take pictures with her phone, and send them to me."

"I don't think she knows your number. I wanted to call when you were on TV—We saw you kissing that lady in the sparkly dress. Is she your girlfriend? Tyson has a girlfriend, but I don't."

That interview will be the last. And Alex knows my number. "No, she's not my girlfriend. And I'm glad you don't have one. You're too young."

"That's what my mom said, too."

Colton wandered inside. "You have a smart Mom. How's Barney doing?"

"He's the best dog ever. My mom and Grandpa Blackwood says so. And Uncle JT says he's really smart. But I don't like cleaning up the poop."

"No, I don't imagine anyone likes that job," Colton said with a chuckle. He sat on the sofa and looked over the jigsaw puzzle Charlie gave him as a going away present. He'd started putting it together on the coffee table, but couldn't bring himself to finish it.

"Charlie?" Colton heard the mayor call from a distance. "Who are you talking to?"

"I told you. It's Colton."

"Well, you need to tell Mr. McCreed goodbye." The mayor's voice grew closer. "It's a school night, and you have two more spelling words to practice."

"Ah, Mom." Charlie sighed into the phone.

I'm back to Mr. McCreed. "Charlie, you do as your mom says, and work hard in school."

"Okaaay."

He walked into the kitchen and pulled a bottle of juice from the fridge. "I'm glad I got to talk to you, hotrod. I'm sorry I won't see your Halloween costume in person."

"But you could come see it."

"Charlie," Alex said in a warning tone from very close.

"Well, he could."

"Mr. McCreed is a busy man."

"Let me talk to your mom before you hang up, okay Charlie?"

"Okay. I miss you, Colton. He wants to talk to you," Charlie said before he could tell the boy how much he missed him back.

He heard the phone change hands.

"Let Barney out one more time, and go start those words.

I'll check them in a minute." There was a pause and then, "Hello."

"Hey, Sunshine."

"I'm glad you called."

His heartbeat kicked his ribcage hard. "You are?"

"I wanted to thank you for the books you sent for the book drive. It was very thoughtful."

Disappointment settled his pulse back to normal. "It was nothing. I received a nice thank you note from the library."

"Okay, well—"

"It sounds like Charlie is doing well," he said quickly to stop her from saying she had to go. He twisted the cap off the bottle but didn't drink.

"He is."

Colton could hear the warmth in her voice. Her son had the ability to put that warmth there. He moved to a window overlooking the city, but found the view lacking. "How are you?"

"Busy as ever."

"Are you dating?" He knew the answer. He'd talked to her brother last week, bugged JT until he admitted she was. Then Colton had been sorry he'd asked.

"Occasionally." The ice was back, solid as a brick.

He hated that the news of her seeing someone bothered him, but it did. JT refused to tell him more. "Anyone I know?"

"None of your business."

"So, it is someone I know." *Brandt Smith is wrong for you, Sunshine.*

"My love life is not up for discussion."

Love life? He hadn't been gone two months, and she was referring to a love life. "It's already serious?"

"I'm not discussing this with you."

He suddenly felt—he wasn't sure what he felt—crazy

jealous? He had no right. He was the one to leave Alex and Charlie behind. So why did the thought of Alex dating—and possibly getting serious—make his stomach knot? She'd been alone for a long time, and deserved someone in her life. And he had to let go.

The problem was, he couldn't. He thought about Alex and Charlie all the time, and the longer the separation, the worse it got.

He heard Charlie calling in the background.

"I have to go, Colton. We have homework to finish, and then it's story time."

"Tell Charlie a story for me."

"For you?"

He set the bottle of juice on the windowsill and scrubbed his face with a hand. "Tell him a story I'd tell him, rather than a mom story."

She laughed. "So one wrought with intrigue and irony... and women?"

He smiled at the sound of her laugh. She sounded so good, it actually made his heart hurt. "No women. He's too young. Intrigue is okay, maybe a little irony. Throw in some baseball. There could be a cute little six-year-old girl who comes to watch Charlie save the day with the winning homer —but no kissing—well, maybe one kiss. On the cheek."

Alex was laughing outright by the time he finished. "I see you haven't changed a bit, McCreed."

"Nor have you, Mayor, but please don't. You're perfect the way you are—all sunshine and hope. There are very few people like you."

"Hope?"

"Yeah, I hear the hope in your voice that maybe, just maybe, I will change one day."

"No." A sad note replaced her happy. "Charlie likes you just the way you are."

"What about you, Mayor? Do you like me just the way I am?"

A weighty pause made him sorry he'd asked.

"If you changed, you wouldn't be you."

"That's not what I asked."

"I know what you're asking. You want your ego stroked. You want one more woman to say you're wonderful. Okay, McCreed, I'll play along. I like you just the way you are. You're handsome, talented, funny, and you definitely know how to show a woman a good time. I'll even go so far as to say you're a fantastic kisser." Her voice had softened, leaving him with a picture of hurt on her face. "You said I was dead inside, and maybe I was. You brought that part of me back to life. Thank you. Bye, Colton."

The dial tone sounded as dismal and empty as he felt. In a city of almost four million people, he'd never felt more shut off than he did at that moment. He was a dog and deserved everything she just gave him, and more.

He threw the bottle of juice into the kitchen sink. It exploded in a geyser of orange-mango mess. He spent the next thirty minutes cleaning, so Consuela wouldn't come in and find it in the morning.

When he finished, he went into his bedroom and sat heavily on the bed. For some reason, the memory of the first time Charlie hugged him, the little boy smell—grass, dirt, and a lingering of the fabric softener Alex used—washed over him. He remembered his embarrassment at the affection of a little boy. Now, this very minute, what he wanted more than anything was that little boy's hug, and a sunshine smile from his mother.

~

*C*olton hadn't called since October. He knew he had to have no contact if he was going to forget the mayor and her son. He'd received the picture of Charlie dressed as Superman and saved it, but there had been no message or further contact from Alex. Six weeks had gone by since their last conversation, and he couldn't get her—them—the whole stupid, pin-dot-on-a-map town off his mind.

The phone rang three times before Alex's voice came over the line. Her "Hello" was breathless, as if she'd run to pick up.

"Hi, Mayor."

The pregnant pause he'd come to expect followed. "Hi."

In his entire life, he'd never missed a woman the way he missed Alex. And they hadn't even slept together. Without her, the sun had stopped shining. His life had stopped making sense. He felt at odds all the time. JT kept him up to date on how most of the town folks were doing. However, when it came to Alex, he was tightlipped. Did JT mention their conversations to Alex? Did she know they talked every couple of weeks, that he pumped JT for information?

"Have you started your next novel?"

"Halfway through." He lied. He hadn't written anything worth keeping since leaving Eden Falls thirteen weeks, four days, and seven—no eight hours earlier. *Yep, I'm one sick puppy.* "How's Eden Falls running?"

"Smooth as silk. Santa rides through town this weekend, followed by the tree lighting in the square."

"Another parade? Does the mayor make an appearance in this one?"

"No, but I do throw the light switch on the big Christmas tree in the square that's being decorated at this very moment."

"Very exciting." He walked outside and looked over the lights of the city. "Do you have a big Christmas planned?"

"Of course. There are always parties around town, lots of family and friends and food."

Was she still dating someone? When he broached the subject with JT, he'd smoothly skimmed over it. "Whose parties?"

"The Blackwood's have a big family party. Stella's parents always have an open house, and Mom and Dad have a traditional Christmas Eve party."

"I bet Charlie's excited."

"I'm sure he'd like to talk to you. Hold on."

He wasn't ready to end their conversation, no matter how stiff it was, but she put her hand over the mouthpiece, and he heard a muffled, "Charlie? Colton is on the phone."

A second later, there was a grappling before the receiver hit the floor with a bang. "Hi, Colton! I've been waiting and waiting for you to call."

"Hey, hotrod. How's it going?"

"I got a hundred percent on my math test today."

"That's great. I'm proud of you."

"I have a new friend. His name is Zeke, and he has a dog named Digger."

Colton rested both elbows on the deck railing. The night was cool, but the air felt refreshing against his skin. "Digger, huh?"

"Yep. Zeke's dad named him that because he digs in the garden, and it makes his mom mad."

"How's Barney doing?"

"He poops a lot, but Mom helps me clean it up."

Colton laughed. It had been a while since he'd laughed. The action felt good. "You have a great mom."

"I know. Oh, and guess what else?"

"What?" His cheeks were getting a grin workout, which was good for the face muscles.

"I'm asking Santa for a guitar just like yours, so we can play together."

"Just like mine, huh?"

"Yeah! When can you come to visit?"

"Oh, buddy, I'm not sure. I have a lot going on right now." *Lie*.

"Could we come to visit you?"

In a split second, that suggestion took hold. Charlie and Alex could come to L.A. for a visit. He had plenty of room. Consuela and Charlie could make Christmas cookies. He straightened. "Yes, you could."

"Mom! Colton said we could visit him. Can we go tomorrow?" Charlie yelled.

He heard Alex's voice in the background. "...school tomorrow, and the Christmas parade and tree lighting are this weekend."

"Oh, yeah, but could we go after that? Colton said we could come."

"You have school, sweetie. We can't go see Colton." Her voice was closer.

"But he can't come to see us, and I want to play guitar with him."

"You don't have a guitar, yet. You have to ask Santa first, and then you have to learn to play it."

This was the dog situation all over again. He should have talked to Alex before making the suggestion.

"We can't come, Colton."

The gloom in Charlie's voice cut deep into Colton's heart. He walked over to a chaise lounge and sank back into the cushions. "I'm sorry, buddy. I forgot about school and Christmas parades. But, I want you to know something."

"What?"

"Even though I'm not there, I'm thinking of you. I think about you and your mom all the time."

"Me and Barney think about you, too. When I tell him I miss you, his tail wags."

Colton felt his throat constrict and swallowed hard. How had this kid wormed his way through the barricade he'd so carefully built over the years? "I hope you have a wonderful Christmas, filled with everything fun you can imagine."

"You, too."

"Can I talk to your mom, again?"

"Yeah. I love you, Colton."

At that moment, Colton figured out the sweet, heart-clutching sensation in his chest was pure, unadulterated joy. The feeling had plagued him since he'd met Alex and Charlie.

"I love you too, Charlie." And he meant it. He could finally admit to himself, and to this small child, that he loved him.

He loved Alex, too.

"I hope you didn't make him promises you can't keep," Alex said in the tone of a mother grizzly protecting her cub.

He dropped both feet to the deck and sat forward. "Give me *some* credit, Alex. I wouldn't do that to him." He ignored her humph. "I'd like to buy Charlie a guitar for Christmas. You can tell him it's from Santa, but I'd—"

"You don't need to buy—"

"I didn't mean to insinuate that you couldn't afford it. I'd just like to do this for Charlie."

"You didn't let me finish. I was going to say, you don't need to buy his love, Colton. You already have it."

Colton's body tensed. "I'm not trying to buy his love, Alex."

"Mom, Jeremy's here," Charlie called out.

"Okay, honey. Invite him inside."

Colton could tell Alex had tried to block her words with a

hand over the receiver, but he heard. His stomach tensed. "Who's Jeremy?"

"A friend."

"A friend of Charlie's?" He hated that his voice sounded so pathetically hopeful.

"No, a friend of mine. We're going to a movie."

His tense stomach suddenly burned with jealousy, an emotion he had no right to feel. An emotion he hadn't dealt with since he was a child vying for his parents' attention. He'd vowed he'd never allow himself to feel this way again. Yet, it had been knocking at the door ever since he'd watched Alex dance with Brandt at Misty and Beam's wedding. "He's taking both you and Charlie to a movie?"

"Yes."

"Where did you meet him?"

"I'm not discussing this with you, Colton. I have to go."

The range of emotions that raged through him came fast. Panic, regret, desperation. "Wait! Don't hang up, Alex." He stood and began to pace. "I think you and Charlie should come to L.A. for a visit. Next weekend. I'll have tickets waiting for you at the Seattle airport. We'll take Charlie to—"

"That's not a good idea. Your leaving was hard on Charlie. If he saw you again, it would only confuse him."

"What about you, Alex? Was my leaving hard on you?"

"Why are you doing this?"

He could hear the anger in her voice, but he had to know if she had any feelings left for him. He had to know before he made a fool of himself. "Answer my question, Alex. Has my leaving been hard on you?"

"No!" They were both silent for a heavy moment. "That's a lie," she said softly. "Yes, your leaving was very hard, and every time I talk to you makes it harder. If you want to call and talk to Charlie, I won't stop you, but we can't talk anymore."

"Don't do something stupid, because you're angry at me, Alex." He heard her soft breath over the miles. "Alex? Do you hear me?"

"I have to go. Have a happy holiday." She hung up on him. Again.

He stalked around the deck and then moved inside, where he paced back and forth until his heartbeat returned to normal. He stopped in front of the window and looked out at the sea of lights while replaying his three months in Washington. They started out with can't-wait-to-forget-this-place to sweet memories he relived over and over.

The next day, he shipped the best guitar available to Pretty Posies. The size would be perfect for Charlie.

~

The idea of Alex dating someone new, someone Colton didn't know, someone named *Jeremy*, festered for a week. When he couldn't stand it any longer, he picked up the phone and called JT. "Hey, Chief. How's life in that small town?"

"Life is great. How is the big city?"

Colton released a half laugh. "Making me wish I was in a small town."

"Come back. You know you'll always be welcome. Oh, Alex got the guitar you sent. Charlie is going to be ecstatic."

Colton had felt like a heel ever since his conversation with Alex. Sending a guitar hadn't made him feel any better. "I just wanted to do something special for the kid. Alex can tell him it's from Santa."

"She'll want Charlie to know it's from you. Hey, you should come back for some of the Christmas festivities. There's a party or two every weekend."

"My schedule is packed. Who's Jeremy?"

"Aha." JT chuckled. "The real reason for your call."

"I was talking to Alex and Charlie last week when the guy showed up to take them to a movie. I just want to make sure he's...a good guy."

"Jeremy Stevens is great. He's an insurance agent in Harrisville whose wife died a couple of years ago. He has two kids, a five-year-old daughter, and a son who's seven. Patsy introduced them. He's her insurance agent." JT rattled the information off like he was reading a script.

"So, I have Patsy to thank."

"No, Colton. You have yourself to thank. You left."

"My life is in Los Angeles."

"I read a quote by Dr. Seuss recently. 'You have brains in your head. You have feet in your shoes. You can steer yourself in any direction you choose.' You can write from anywhere, Colton. You proved that this summer. You choose to have your life in L.A. It's not fair to expect Alex to put hers on hold while you try to figure out if you can live without her and Charlie in yours."

"Listen to you rattling on like you know what you're talking about."

JT's full-bodied laughter irritated him. In Colton's opinion, JT was taking the fact that Jeremy could become Charlie's stepfather too lightly.

"Sorry. My mistake. Look, there's nothing to worry about. Jeremy is a good guy. He treats Alex like a queen and Charlie like a son. Charlie likes Jeremy, and he has a blast with Jeremy's kids."

None of JT's words made Colton feel any better.

"Both Jeremy and Alex want more kids."

Colton's mind yelled, *"Stop!"*

"They'll make a nice family," JT added as a final punch to the gut.

~

*C*olton overlooked a room packed with people, and felt more alone than he'd ever felt before. Jorge's annual Christmas Eve party for clients was an event he'd attended since Jorge became his business manager. An over-heated room where perfume and hors d'oeuvres warred for dominance on his sense of smell was the last place he wanted to be tonight.

His phone vibrated, and he pulled it from his pocket. A message from JT contained a video. He moved to a corner and hit play. Charlie and his cousins, wearing fake antlers and red foam noses, were singing "Jingle Bells". JT did a close up. Charlie's grin showed a black hole where his two bottom front teeth used to be. In that instant, Colton learned regret was a powerful emotion. Charlie had lost his first two teeth, and he'd missed it.

He went down a grand staircase and out onto Jorge's back deck with its spectacular view of the ocean. The moon lit a pathway from the shore to the horizon, but his only interest was to view the video again. Halfway through, his phone beeped with another incoming video. He pushed play and watched Alex and Rowdy acting out a skit where Rowdy was in a Santa suit and Alex in a bathrobe and curlers. He couldn't hear the words because their audience was laughing so loudly in the background.

He could be there, right now, watching in person. He could be there, but the idiot in him had chosen here.

JT panned his cell phone around the room, stopping on the familiar faces of Denny and Alice Garrett, Dawson and Glenda Garrett, Rita Reynolds and her blinking light earrings, Rance and Lily Johnson. The camera caught Misty, now prominently showing. Beam stood behind her looking content, his hands resting on his wife's belly.

Colton leaned against the deck railing and started the video over again. Was *Jeremy* there watching Alex? Was he laughing at her antics? How close were they getting? Was she in love?

Colton cared more than he ever thought he could about another human being—two human beings. He was in love for the first time in his life. The feeling so overwhelming, the realization so powerful, it filled his chest, and expanded to every molecule in his body. Now that he'd fully acknowledged the emotion, he couldn't ignore it, but wasn't sure how to proceed either.

"What are you doing out here? The party's inside."

Colton pulled up the video of Charlie and held his phone out to Jorge. "Eden Falls Police Chief sent me videos from his parents' Christmas party. The one on the far left is Alex's son, Charlie."

Jorge leaned against the railing next to Colton and watched. "Cute kid."

Colton started the video of Rowdy and Alex.

"And there's Eve," Jorge said with a smile. He glanced at Colton. "You left your heart in Eden Falls."

Colton didn't respond.

"You're just too stubborn to admit it. Or too afraid. You met a woman who is so far from the type you usually date— and far better than you deserve."

Colton shook his head even though Jorge was completely right.

"Over the summer, you grew to respect and, even more importantly, to trust that woman."

Colton shook his head.

"You haven't been the same since you got back, and your writing is suffering because of it," Jorge continued as if Colton hadn't spoken. He handed Colton his phone and pushed away from the deck railing. "Don't lose a chance at happiness because your mom and dad screwed up, Colton. Don't throw away what could be the love of a lifetime, because that's how long you'll regret it."

"I didn't say I loved her."

Jorge patted his shoulder. "You didn't have to. It's written all over your face."

Jorge disappeared inside, swallowed by the nameless, faceless, crowd as Colton's phone beeped with another incoming video. Stella, Jillian, and Alex were singing "Silent Night" in three-part harmony.

Suddenly, what he had to do became clear.

CHAPTER 20

The storm clouds hovered low over the mountains. Snow was in the forecast, but it hadn't started falling, yet. Colton stood under the awning of Pretty Posies, peering into the cozy interior. Though it was mid-afternoon, Alex had lamps on, glowing against the dreary dark of the day. Every shadowy corner of the shop was lit.

Alex appeared from the backroom. She held a delicate flower in her hand. As she fiddled with something on the counter, she touched the blossom to her nose and smiled. Then she disappeared from sight.

A band tightened around Colton's chest with just that glimpse of her. He was a writer and knew how to use words, but he was at a loss to describe the emotions swirling through him.

He pushed the door open, and the bell above his head jangled brightly.

"I'll be right with you," her voice floated from the back.

He squatted to scratch Barney, who'd walked over to greet him. "Take your time."

He stood and grinned when her head popped around the

corner, her mouth open. She closed her pretty lips and stepped from the backroom. "You're a long way from home, aren't you, Mr. McCreed?" she said. Her voice shook slightly.

He didn't have any right to expect anything from her. Since JT had closed the subject to discussion, he didn't know if she was still seeing the insurance agent. He walked around the counter and stopped in front of her, attempting nonchalance—he was anything but. His heart was thundering to the tune of a jackhammer. "They say home is where your heart is, and I seem to have left mine here."

Something flickered across her face, and then disappeared, as her mossy green eyes searched his face. "Is that right? Eden Falls seems like a strange place to lose something so important."

"I agree, a *very* strange place indeed, but there's a mayor who grabbed hold of one of my heartstrings and hasn't let go since I left." He reached out and took her upper arms in his hands, coaxing her closer, but she stood firm as she thrust out her adorable little chin.

"I'm not one of your women *friends*, Colton. You can't just fly into town and think I'll be waiting for you. I have a son that—"

"Yeah, about him. He seems to have grabbed the other heartstring and yanked even harder than his mama. You aren't the only reason I came back to this remote place, Sunshine." This time when he tugged, she took a tentative step, but the hands she planted against his chest stopped him from pulling her into his arms.

"I told you I don't do one-night stands or two-month stands or anything else. You need to go home, McCreed, back to your life in L.A. with *Talia*."

"Is that jealousy I hear? If so, you just stroked my ego, again." He grinned when her eyes narrowed dangerously. "I haven't seen Talia since the night those pictures were taken."

The admission didn't budge her, so he pulled out the big gun from an inside pocket of his wool coat. Her eyebrows rose at the sight of the smashed flower, her gasp almost imperceptible.

Her gaze slowly rose from the camellia blossom to his. "You wouldn't be holding that if you knew the meaning."

"I'm holding it because I *do* know the meaning. My destiny is in your hands." He tucked the camellia behind her ear. Then he reached into another inner pocket and extracted a velvet box. A handful of emotions raced over her lovely face. He opened the box and slid the diamond ring free, then lifted her left hand from his chest and slipped the ring down to her first knuckle. When he glanced back into her eyes, tears had replaced shock. Her lips trembled as she smiled.

"I've missed that beautiful, sunshine, smile. Is that a yes?"

"You haven't asked a question."

"You know the question."

Her eyebrows puckered together in the middle. "You still have to ask it."

"Do I have to get down on one knee?"

She lifted a shoulder. "Romantic but not necessary."

"Will you marry me, Alexis Blackwood?"

"I'm a package deal, McCreed."

He grinned. "Package deals are usually cheaper, and I'm a sucker for a bargain."

She fisted her free hand and punched his chest. "This isn't a joke."

"You're the one making it into a comical situation."

The line between her brows deepened. "Well, as the asker, you're supposed to be serious."

He blew out an exaggerated breath. He should have known she'd make this difficult. "Okay, seriously, will you marry me? I promise to be the best husband to you and the best father to Charlie. Though, I'll expect something in return. You'll have to promise to cook Brussels sprouts at least once a month, and Charlie will have to promise to be the best big brother to any little McCreeds that come along."

Her expression softened. "You want babies with me?"

"I can't think of anything more beautiful than you carrying my child."

Her throat convulsed. "What happened to no wife, no kids, no commitments?"

He ran his knuckles down the side of her face. "A mayor and her kid changed my mind."

Her frown reappeared. "What about all your traveling and promoting and book signings and flying off to Spain whenever you want?"

"We'll have to work it around the kids' school schedule."

He still had the ring poised at her first knuckle, as fresh tears filled her eyes and dribbled over the edge of her eyelids. He wiped one cheek with a thumb. "Of course this means you'll have to tell *Jeremy* to get lost."

She released a little hiccup of a laugh. "So that ego stroking goes both ways?"

"Yeah, it does. Jealousy does not look good on me."

"I haven't seen Jeremy since the Christmas tree lighting."

He started to pull the ring off her finger. "Oh, well, if Jeremy's out of the picture, there's no need for—"

She curled her fingers. "You can't take a proposal back."

He wiped a tear from her other cheek. "Well, I'm glad he's gone. He was all wrong for you."

"You didn't know him."

"I know his kind. Wait until the good-looking guy leaves town, then make your move."

She laughed before she fisted her free hand and punched him in the chest, again. "What took you so long to make your move?"

He lowered his forehead to hers. "I couldn't come to you and Charlie until I was completely sure I could leave my life behind. The funny thing is, it was Eden Falls that I left behind, not L.A. Once I got back there, I realized what an empty, unfulfilling, life I'd been living. Believe me, I tried very hard to get you and Charlie out of my head, but everything I did, everywhere I went, both of you were right there with me. I feel like I've come home. You are my Eve, and this quirky little town truly is Eden." He wiggled the ring. "I didn't think it would be so hard to get a yes out of you."

She leaned back from him. "Really? You thought I'd just fall down at your feet, so happy to see you back?"

"Something like that."

"You egotistical, city dwelling—"

He silenced her with his lips. Enjoying the sense of home, he took his time exploring the mouth he'd missed, and accepting the moment of sweet revelation that filled his chest. What he was doing was exactly the right thing. Any lingering anxiety fled on wings of surrender. He was hers and, if he could ever get her to say yes, she'd be his. He lifted his head. "Say you'll marry me, Sunshine. I'm not sure I can live with you, but I *know* I can't live without you."

"You are a romantic devil."

She really was punishing him. "I love you, Alex. With every particle of my being, I love you and Charlie, and I want us to be a family."

Her eyes filled again, so he lightened the mood. "How much longer are you going to make me wait? You know you'll say yes eventually."

"You really are arrogant."

He wiggled the ring. "You'll keep me in line."

"Well, I guess, since you went to all this trouble…"

"That's my girl." He slid the ring onto her finger and

kissed it. "Are you going to tell me you love me anytime soon?"

She glanced at the ring, then up at him with a feigned frown. "This isn't a ring you bought for some other woman and she turned you down, is it?"

"Ah, you're on to me as usual. The jeweler wouldn't take it back, so I thought to myself, what foolish woman out there would actually believe you bought the ring for her, and your face popped into my head."

She smiled. "I love you, McCreed. I have for a long time."

"I know, Sunshine."

ACKNOWLEDGMENTS

It takes a village…

On the home front, I wish to thank my husband, Rick. Without our travels, I wouldn't have come up with the fictional town of Eden Falls. Without your support, this book would still be a dream, the house would be falling down around my ears, and the fridge would be bare. I thank you from the bottom of my heart, babe. For every time I asked, "What can I do to help with dinner?" and you answered, "Just write", thank you. You are my sounding board, my rock, and my love.

To our children, Chris, Marnie, Carly, Sara, Kristen, Andrew, Richard, and Stefan, who've shown their support in different ways. I love each and every one of you for asking how things are going and encouraging me along the way. Don't think I don't know how many times you pretended to be interested as I babbled on about things unimportant to you. I appreciate your love and support.

Going further afield, I wish to thank my beta readers. My sister, Holly Hertzke, who, along with my mom, was my first reader, and dear friends, Jeanine Hopping, who helped with the synopsis (for which I owe her one of my children), Chris Almodovar (who always asks how things are going), and Amanda Pierce for all your comments and suggestions. I appreciate your willingness to set aside time to read my manuscripts. I'm so grateful for your time, support, and talents.

On the editor front, a big thank you goes to Lynnette Labelle (who completely turned this manuscript around and split it into a series without even suggesting such a thing), Joy Clintsman of Big Sister Edits, and proofreader, Amy Dix. *Finding Eden* is a better book because of your comments, suggestions and changes.

A huge thank you to Dar Albert of Wicked Smart Designs for the *Finding Eden* book cover. You emulated my vision perfectly. To The Blurb Queen, Cathryn Cade, thank you for relieving so much inner anxiety. I love to write the story, but synopsis, taglines, loglines, and blurbs give me hives. Thanks to Lori Corsentino of Harmony Creative Design for book-marks and business cards. They are beautiful.

Thank you to Richard of DivDev for my website, I appreciate your patience with someone who doesn't know.

I would be remiss to not mention the members of my critique group. Dawn Annis, Mary Hagen, and Sherri Valentine. Though they did not read *Finding Eden*, they encouraged and supported me through other writing endeavors. We laughed, told stories, and became very close over eggs, bacon, and pancakes. Hugs and kisses to you all.

I also want to thank friends and family members (you know who you are Suzanne, John, Bob, Louise to name a few), who always asked how things were going.

Lastly, I want to thank my local RWA chapter for freely answering so many of my questions and offering such great workshops. Colorado Romance Writers – Together We Can!

As you can see it took many to make up the village that contributed to *Finding Eden*. I am so grateful to each and every one of you. I hope you, dear readers, will enjoy our efforts.

Warmest regards,
    Tina Newcomb

ABOUT THE AUTHOR

Tina Newcomb writes clean, contemporary romance. Her heartwarming stories take place in quaint small towns, with quirky townsfolk, and friendships that last a lifetime.

She acquired her love of reading from her librarian mother, who always had a stack of books close at hand, and her father who visited the local bookstore every weekend.

Tina lives in colorful Colorado. When not lost in her writing, she can be found in the garden, traveling with her (amateur) chef husband, or spending time with family and friends.

She loves to hear from readers. You can find her at
tinanewcomb.com

ALSO BY TINA NEWCOMB

For a **free ebook,** sign up to receive my newsletter at
tinanewcomb.com

NOTE FROM AUTHOR

Thank you for reading my book, Finding Eden. If you enjoyed it, I hope you'll leave an honest review or consider telling a friend—the two very best ways a reader can support an author.

I'd like to share an excerpt from Beyond Eden, Book 2 in the Eden Falls Series. Enjoy!

Warmest Regards,
Tina Newcomb

P.S. - For a **free ebook,** sign up to receive my newsletter at tinanewcomb.com

You can follow me on:
https://www.facebook.com/TinaNewcombAuthor
https://www.bookbub.com/authors/tina-newcomb
https://www.instagram.com/tinanewcomb
https://www.goodreads.com/tinanewcomb
https://www.pinterest.com/tinanewcomb

EXCERPT FROM BEYOND EDEN

Book Two of the Eden Falls Series
by Tina Newcomb

Chapter 1

Misty Garrett grabbed her distended belly with both hands and hissed, air whistling through her clenched teeth. The rock hardness of her stomach sent a chill through her, even as perspiration wet her hairline and upper lip. The bone deep ache that had plagued the small of her back all morning crept around her sides and dug in with claws extended. She sucked in a ragged breath and exhaled on a groan.

Just as suddenly as it struck, the pain eased leaving her limp as wilted lettuce.

She eased back in her father's recliner and wiped the sheen of sweat from her forehead with the tail of her husband's flannel shirt.

Her due date was still two weeks away, so she couldn't be in labor.

At her last appointment, Dr. Jessica Thompson had assured Misty and her worrywart husband that everything was right on schedule.

"I've heard most first babies come late," Misty's husband said.

The doctor looked up from between Misty's knees and smiled at Beam. "Most first babies do come late, but every birth is different."

"So we should stay close to Seattle just in case."

"Well, don't feel like you can't go places, but I wouldn't recommend traveling very far."

Her doctor had yammered on and on about what they should do if... Make certain they had... She even mentioned something about false contractions. By that time, Misty's eyes had glazed over. Even the Energizer Bunny would be yawning after a few minutes of Dr. Thompson's monotone. If Beam were here, he'd repeat the doctor's monologue verbatim. Her husband's rapt attention, note taking, and quoting from pregnancy books was equivalent to living inside the Discovery Channel.

Misty rubbed two hands over her belly. All was still, so she picked up the carton of Ben & Jerry's Cherry Garcia she'd dropped on the side table. The ice cream was now soft enough to dig out the chocolate chunks and sweet pieces of cherry. She scooped a bite into her mouth and turned her attention back to the exciting drama unfolding on the *Real Housewives* of somewhere. The major mischief-maker was on the verge of being discovered and... "Awwhhh!"

Viselike tentacles of agony seized, doubling Misty forward, squeezing until she thought she might implode. She struggled for air, desperate to remember what to do, but her only clear thought was, *if Beam were a gloating man, this would be his moment to shine*. When she'd insisted on coming to Eden Falls, he'd argued she was too close to her due date, the weather in January was unpredictable, being two and a half hours away from Seattle and her doctor, who said to stay close to home, was irresponsible. She'd ignored his protests and come anyway.

When the pain eased, Misty heaved herself from the chair and waddled toward the kitchen where her cell phone was charging. She dropped the ice cream carton into the sink with one hand, and held her stomach up with the other. This baby was not coming out until Beam got her back to Seattle. He'd gotten her into this condition, and he would witness every throe of agony she was forced to suffer.

She gasped as warm liquid flooded down her legs. Bending over, she tried to see the puddle now soaking her socks. At least she'd made it to the tiled kitchen. *Sorry Dad*.

She grabbed her phone, and a new panic struck. Who could she call? Her dad's truck driver called in sick this morning, so he had to make a large lumber delivery himself. He'd be without cell coverage most of the day. Beam would take over an hour to get here in the Cessna, and that was only if he wasn't already chauffeuring a group of gawking tourists out to see Seattle from the air. Then the flight back would be another hour. She needed someone now. Stella was in a classroom surrounded by screaming second-graders, and Jillian would be at the gym, which left only one option.

She gripped the countertop for support when another pain ripped through her middle. More of Beam's words ran through her head, *"We've got to attend prenatal classes, Misty. We need to know what to expect."*

"What's the point?" she'd argued. "The doctor promised drugs, and I intend to get them, so there's no reason to sit on the floor of the clinic learning to breathe with a bunch of strangers."

Except now there is.

How did the women in movies do it? In through the mouth and out through the nose or was it short quick breaths? The pain slowly subsided before she could decide which method to try. Next contraction, she'd use them all.

She scrolled through her contact list until she reached the name of her go-to friend of twenty-two years, the one she'd refused to talk to since New Year's Eve. She hit the call button and put the phone to her ear.

After an eternity, she heard, "Good morning. Pretty Posies."

The happy voice made her eyelid twitch. "Put Alex on the phone."

"Misty?"

"Tatum. Get Alex!"

"Okaaay."

Misty wondered, for at least the zillionth time, why Alex had hired someone as incompetent as Tatum Ellis. After waiting an eternity, she decided to hang up and call back. Just as she pulled the phone from her ear, she heard, "Hello, Misty."

"I'm in labor and Beam's not here. You have to drive me to Seattle."

"Where are you?" The cautious tone Alex answered the phone with had been replaced by her no-nonsense business one.

"My dad's."

"How far apart are your contractions?"

"I don't know." Misty glanced at the puddle on the floor. "My water just broke."

"I'll be right there."

Misty disconnected the call and wrapped both hands under her stomach, which felt like it had dropped to her knees. She hated when her husband was right. She should have listened to him—not that she'd admit that aloud.

Walking up the stairs was a slow process, but she finally made it to her childhood bedroom. Longing tugged at her heart. Childbirth was a mother-daughter moment she wouldn't get to share with the woman who'd walked away over twenty years earlier.

Frills and girly ruffles still adorned the bedroom her mom decorated when Misty was five. A nearly threadbare pink and white gingham comforter covered the white canopy bed. The doll her mother bought for Misty's sixth birthday held a place of honor near the headboard, propped into a sitting position by delicate eyelet pillows. Misty's pink ballerina jewelry box and a photo of her mom at the base of Eden Falls, her happy smile forever frozen in black and white, were side-by-side on the matching white dresser.

Misty hadn't changed a thing. One day her mother would return and be thrilled Misty had kept everything exactly the same.

She felt another pain building, and stumbled to the edge of the bed, gasping for breath from her already oxygen deprived lungs. One moment, she was afraid she might pass out, and the next, she wished she would. The last nine months, from peeing on a stick until now, had been a nightmare. One she couldn't awake from no matter how hard she pinched herself.

When the pain released its clenching grip, she pulled off her wet things and wiggled into dry panties and a pair of warm but extremely tight leggings. She had eaten her way through pregnancy. Each day introduced new cravings. She discovered unique and quite ingenious ways to add chocolate or maple syrup to almost anything. This baby had kicked, elbowed, and stretched her body into a blimp. Once she gave birth, a few visits to her in-laws' gym for some much-needed toning would get her back to her original size four. These excruciating pains marked the countdown. She *would* be back in a bikini by June, less than six months away.

She discarded the thought of calling Beam's parents as soon as it popped into her mind. Dawson and Glenda Garrett's enthusiasm about first-time grandparenthood was over the top when she *wasn't* in labor. Being happy all the time should be against the law, but happy ran through the Garrett clan like blood through veins. And she'd married smack into the middle of them.

Stepping into the adjoining bathroom, she made the mistake of glancing in the mirror. Her unwashed hair pulled into a high ponytail highlighted her blotched, puffy face, which looked even worse than usual. She hadn't worn makeup in a week, trying to clear up a pimple outbreak on her forehead. Her black eyebrows had almost grown together in the middle since her last waxing, and the mole near her chin —which she'd always believed to be alluring—had a coarse black hair sprouting from the middle. She pulled open a drawer, but before she could grab tweezers to perform a quick extraction, another contraction shot through her middle, paralyzing her.

The doorbell chimed, yet she was helpless to do anything but grimace through a pain too intense to yell.

Please, please, let the door be unlocked.

She released a sigh of relief when she heard a male voice echo up the stairs. *Beam! But he wouldn't ring the bell. He has a key.*

"Misty?"

She released a groan and not from pain. JT Garrett. What was he doing here?

She sank to the toilet seat as his heavy footsteps hit the kitchen tile. "What the...?"

Great. He found the puddle I left.

Suddenly, the footsteps thudded up the stairs. "Misty? Where are you?"

He appeared, filling the bathroom doorway, taking up too much space, a talent the Garrett family seemed to possess. His dark hair and the shoulders of his police chief overcoat were covered in snow. "I hear my first cousin once removed is ready to make her appearance." His expression turned thoughtful. "Or is she my second—"

"Shut up."

"You okay?"

Misty wanted to smack the smile he was fighting from his face. "No, I'm not okay. I'm having a contraction."

He leaned against the doorframe and lifted a booted foot. "Yeah, I think I just stepped in one of those contractions."

She glared, trying her best to look fierce.

Losing the fight, he grinned. "It's good to see labor hasn't clouded your sunny disposition."

She was in too much pain for a witty comeback. "Where's Alex?"

"She's right behind me. She thought my SUV would be a more comfortable ride to Harrisville Regional than her dilapidated Jeep. Can you stand?"

"I'm not going to Harrisville Regional. My doctor is in Seattle."

He flashed an indulge-the-female glance as he slid his arm around her waist and helped her to her feet.

"Don't look at me like that. You're a cop. Turn on your lights and sirens, and get me to Seattle."

"How far apart are your contractions?"

She wrapped a hand under her belly and inhaled as deeply as possible. "I don't know."

The front door opened and slammed shut. "Misty?"

"We're upstairs," JT shouted.

Another set of footsteps pounded up the stairs and Alexis Blackwood careened around the corner, narrowly missing them in a head-on collision.

JT put his hand out to protect Misty's stomach. "Whoa."

"How we doing?" Alex asked breathlessly.

"Peachy keen. What took you so long?" Misty mumbled.

She and Alex had been best friends since kindergarten, but that had changed on New Year's Eve when Alex announced her engagement to bestselling author Colton McCreed.

"Aww, there's my sweet natured friend. I've missed you."

Misty scowled at the traitor.

Alex winked and ducked under her other arm. The brother-sister team got her halfway down the stairs before she sank to a riser, another contraction ripping through her. Alex rubbed her back and babbled instructions. JT gave her a hand to squeeze. After endless minutes, they finally reached the living room sofa.

"Where are your boots? It's snowing," Alex asked.

"In the bedroom."

Alex ran up the stairs. "Not your five-inch stilettos, Misty. Your sensible snow boots," she yelled, running back down. "Did you bring sensible boots with you?"

"Here they are," JT said carrying a pair into the living room along with Misty's coat.

Alex knelt in front of her and held out a boot. "Where are your socks?"

"I got them wet when my water broke."

"Oh, that reminds me." JT went into the kitchen.

Misty heard paper towels pulled from the roll and assumed Dudley Do Right was cleaning up the puddle she'd left. Alex made a third trip up the stairs. She ran down with clean socks in hand. "Is Beam on his way?"

"I haven't called him."

Alex performed her legendary—pursed-lip, squinted-eye —judgmental expression.

"When exactly would I have had time?"

"JT call Beam," Alex called to her brother.

JT returned to the living room, cell phone in hand. "I already did. He's on his way, but with the storm, he'll have to drive. Glenda and Dawson will meet us at the hospital."

"Call Beam back and tell him not to come here. I'm having the baby in Sea—" Misty released a low moan and grabbed her stomach when the next contraction took her body hostage.

JT offered his hand again, and Alex massaged her lower back. "Keep your breathing rhythmical, Misty. Your in-breath should match your out-breath. I know it hurts, but try to relax. As soon as this one is over, we'll get you in the car."

"I'm not going to a backwoods hospital to have some country bumpkin deliver this baby," Misty hissed on an out breath. She glared at JT. "You have to get me to Seattle."

"You're going to deliver this baby on your dad's living room sofa if we don't get going," JT said. "Your contractions are less than five minutes apart."

Misty swung a fist that connected with JT's chest. "I don't care if the baby is half out of my body. I'm not going to Harrisville."

JT and Alex ignored her as they helped her down the front steps to the SUV. She hefted her rear end into the backseat, and Alex followed. JT shut their door and ran around to the driver's side.

Misty massaged her belly and tried to relax the tight muscles. No one had warned her how bad this would hurt. She knew it wasn't going to be a walk in the park, but there were supposed to be drugs involved. She'd been promised drugs.

She glanced through the front windshield when JT turned left instead of right as they exited her dad's neighborhood. "This isn't the way to Seattle, JT."

"Misty, it takes two and a half hours to get to Seattle on a good day. It's snowing, the roads are slippery, and your contractions are less than five minutes apart. I'm taking you to Harrisville, which is only fifteen minutes away. You can argue with the hospital staff about an ambulance ride to Seattle."

"I hate you."

He caught her eye in the rearview mirror. "You'd hate me

even more if we had to deliver this baby on the side of the road."

She imagined JT pulling over and her baring her assets for the passing cars with Tweedledee and Tweedledumb as her delivery team. She turned her glare on Alex who winked. "I hate you, too."

"It's wonderful to see my good natured friend back to her old self. I was afraid labor might dampen your happy spirits." Alex echoed her brother's earlier sentiments, sealing it with the same Garrett grin.

The whole situation enraged Misty even as an unladylike snort of hysteria escaped. She was in labor, her ex-boyfriend was driving her through a snowstorm to a hospital in the sticks, while her ex-best friend sat beside her, and the baby's father was stuck in Seattle. This was the perfect setup for a comedy.

Or a horror flick.